OUR BEST INTENTIONS

OUR BEST INTENTIONS

A Novel

VIBHUTI JAIN

WILLIAM MORROW

An Imprint of HarperCollins*Publishers*

HarperCollins books may be purchased for educational, business, or sales promotional use. For information, please email the Special Markets Department at SPsales@harpercollins.com.

FIRST EDITION

Library of Congress Cataloging-in-Publication Data

Names: Jain, Vibhuti, author.
Title: Our best intentions: a novel / Vibhuti Jain.
Description: First edition. | New York: William Morrow, an imprint of HarperCollins Publishers, [2023]
Identifiers: LCCN 2022031107 | ISBN 9780063278783 (hardcover) | ISBN 9780063278776 (ebook)
Subjects: LCGFT: Novels.
Classification: LCC PS3610.A3835 O87 2023 | DDC 813/.6—dc23/eng/20220809
LC record available at https://lccn.loc.gov/2022031107

ISBN 978-0-06-327878-3

23 24 25 26 27 LBC 5 4 3 2 1

To my mother and father

OUR BEST INTENTIONS

FRIDAY, JANUARY 1, 2010

PROLOGUE

Babur Singh sits on Neha and Manan's blue velour couch and looks straight ahead at images of half-frozen, euphoric crowds whooping, jumping, and kissing one another amid a shower of confetti and cacophony of noisemakers. He stares hard at his friends' television, so hard that eventually, he is looking at nothing at all.

It's been six days since Purnima left him. Left them.

His daughter, Anjali, age six and a half, lies asleep on a reclining La-Z-Boy adjacent to the couch, her mouth half open and body curled in the fetal position. Her abdomen expands and contracts in steady intervals.

"This year, I'm going to cook more." His voice is flat, but it is Babur's feeble attempt at humor.

Neha gives Babur a sympathetic but encouraging smile. Manan walks to the kitchen, returning with three regular glasses and a bottle of store-brand sparkling wine. "To 2010! To health, wealth, and happiness!" he says, filling each glass to a frothy brim.

Neha shushes him, motioning toward the child.

"Sorry," Manan mouths to Babur.

Babur shrugs at his friend, indicating no harm done. Anjali slumbers on, oblivious to the new decade. The adults clink their drinks.

Babur knocks his glass back, uncharacteristically, intending to gulp it in one go. He stops midway, coughing from the carbonation.

"Whoa, boss," Manan cautions. "Take it easy."

Yet that is exactly what Babur is prepared *not* to do. This year, with this responsibility of raising another human by himself, he needs to get things right.

Purnima's departure is both expected, in that Babur was aware she wasn't well and wasn't improving, and unexpected, in that he didn't believe she would or could actually leave. Through it all, his friends Neha and Manan have been nothing short of remarkable. Anjali's school is on winter break, and Neha, without any fuss or acknowledgment of impact on her dissertation-writing schedule, has been watching Anjali while Babur is at work, and Manan drops in each evening with groceries or pizza and open ears.

This level of reliance, however, cannot be permanent.

Earlier that day, the initial shock and panic of being left having intermittently subsided, Babur drove to Walgreen's. He purchased a black day planner, a calendar featuring US national parks, and a whiteboard.

The way to survive, he postulated, is to plan. He hasn't worked out every detail, but he wants to routinize their lives, his and Anjali's, diarize everything, and eliminate, to the greatest extent possible, the spontaneous.

Meals, for example, the kitchen being Purnima's former realm, in line with arguably anachronistic cultural norms, will be rotated. He will establish a set menu according to the day of the week, with Fridays reserved for pizza, and leftovers, their lunch. In this way, Babur has to learn to cook only a half dozen or so dishes and can standardize a weekly shopping list. After school is trickier. There is no way Babur can reach home in time for Anjali's 4:00 p.m. arrival. He either has to find a babysitter, which is expensive, or enroll her in day care, also expensive and with rigid pickup times that are impossible in traffic.

Babur drains the last of his glass, a bitter aftertaste lingering, and shares his vision of "high-efficiency living" with his friends.

"That's brilliant, bhai," Manan says of the meal rotation. "I hope you make enough for guests, because I'm dropping by if the food's any good!"

When Babur describes his childcare quandary, Neha says, "Did you check the community center? They have after-school activities and it's next to her elementary school. I hear it's cheap, too."

Babur makes a mental note that he later records in the "to-do" section of his planner.

"More?" Manan lifts up the half-full wine bottle.

"Oh, please no." Babur holds up a hand in mock protest. "This was truly horrible."

"Made in Yonkers," muses Manan. "And only six bucks."

Babur chuckles, appreciating Manan's inability to pass up a deal. It is a short but genuine laugh, his first all week.

A few days later, Babur stops at the Kitchewan Community Center. He discovers he is late to enroll Anjali in almost everything, like a popular karate class, taught by an actual Japanese master, he is told, who, incidentally, also owns a hibachi restaurant in town. Apparently, community center activities are a life hack already familiar to a number of working parents.

Through polite persistence and indifference to appearing pathetic, Babur manages to elicit from the disengaged woman behind the counter that there's an opening in a weekly swimming class.

"I'll take it," he says at once, ignoring his personal terror of water deeper than his calves. "I'll take it," he repeats.

"All right, what day?" says the woman behind the counter, not looking up from her computer screen. "I have Monday, Wednesday, and Friday afternoons."

Babur pauses for a moment, the image of his absent, disaffected wife looming in his mind like a taunt. "All of them. I'll sign up for all of them," he says.

The woman looks up from her computer at Babur. "Mister, you want to sign your kid up for the same exact class three times a week?"

"Yes. She won't mind."

"Does she really like swimming or something?"

"She will, I think. She hasn't tried before."

"Okay." The woman shrugs.

Babur slips her a handwritten enrollment form completed in careful block letters.

His daughter, he thinks, will be different than him.

MONDAY, AUGUST 20, 2018

ONE

Where on earth is Chiara? This is the question plaguing Desiree Mat-thews on Monday morning as her bus, the royal-blue Kitchewan Circulator, lurches up to the parking lot of Hudson Memorial. Desiree, or Didi to most who know her, is racking her brain for clues or answers—something to make sense of her cousin's disappearance—and nearly trips over her own shoelace while stepping off the bus. The almost-fall catapults her back to her physical here and now. "Shit," she blurts, louder than she means to, grabbing hold of the bus's royal-blue handrail.

"Watch your step, hon," the bus driver says in a raspy smoker's voice.

Didi forces a quick smile at the driver to confirm she's okay, but it ends up coming out as more of a grimace when she realizes that's the first word she's said out loud today.

Outside, in the hospital parking lot, it's warm but not hot, with the peak of summer already in decline. There's a freshness in the air. The sky is palette-perfect blue with wisps of clouds. Birds chirp. The grass around the perimeter of the parking lot is green and dewy. All evidence of the weekend's hammering of heavy rains and gusty winds from Tropical Storm Felicity looks erased. *The calm after the storm.* Everything is in order. Only nothing is.

Chiara's missing. Officially, she's been missing since last Wednesday. That's five days, and the whole situation—her disappearance, a stabbing, the police investigation, their questions and implied accusations, not to mention the panicked calls from Philly—keeps getting muddier, and the worry lines on Didi's forehead keep getting deeper. She didn't think things like this happened in Kitchewan.

When she was younger, even as recently as before she moved here two years ago, she never imagined she'd be living and working in a town like this. A manicured-to-the-hilt riverside suburb where electric-car-charging stations outnumber public transport options, where even the hospital cafeteria sells organic apples, where municipal offices are landscaped with imported Japanese trees, where the police are most commonly seen assisting with pedestrian crossings rather than in hot pursuit. *A white people's enclave.* She's less than a hundred miles from Philly, but in a different universe entirely. Student Nurse Matthews, with her relaxed black hair, ochre-brown skin, and hefty scholarship to nursing school, reporting for duty—meant to be here, but not really.

Didi crouches down in the parking lot and lifts up the leg of her periwinkle scrubs. She double-ties the stray laces and takes a deep breath. It doesn't feel right to be at the hospital today. Not with Chiara still missing.

Chiara Thompkins, known in the family as simply Kiki, is Didi's baby cousin, eight years her junior, and her Aunty Maureen's youngest. She'd been living, as far as Didi knew, in North Philadelphia, like most of the extended family. And then, last July, a little over a year ago, she showed up in Kitchewan with little warning or explanation. Just a text to Didi from an unfamiliar 610 number saying she needed "a short break" and was on a Greyhound arriving in White Plains in two and a half hours. She asked if she could crash with Didi for a few days, and Didi agreed on the spot, setting Kiki up with a makeshift bed on the lumpy beige couch in the condo she rented with a roommate named Lucinda, a pharmacology student whom she'd found on an online message board through school. Didi didn't bother to check with Lucinda before taking Chiara in, reasoning that Lucinda hadn't bothered to check with her before turning their garage into a marijuana nursery.

At the time, Didi assumed Chiara and her mother had gotten into an argument, the trivial but tempestuous kind she and her own mother would get into when she was in high school, and that it would soon blow over. She was also aware from her mother that Aunty Mo had been particularly testy ever since a diabetes flare-up and resulting knee problems put her on indefinite disability from work.

Besides, Didi has always had a soft spot for Chiara. She's the youngest among her cousins and she seemed to have been left to fend for herself, even as a child, her aunt more focused on catching and keeping a man than on raising her fifth-born. Didi remembers going over to her Aunty Mo's house in her youth and finding a younger Chiara, hair unkempt, clothes mismatched, playing some version of patty-cake against a yellowing living room wall, or balancing on a stool to heat a saucepan of canned beans on the stove. "She's fine like that," Tenesha, Chiara's older sister and Didi's cousin and age mate, would say, noticing Didi's concern. "She doesn't need babying."

In fact, when Didi initially called her aunty to let her know Chiara was with her, that she was safe, that she could stay with her for a while if her aunt didn't mind, her aunt's response was surprisingly cool. "Go ahead," she'd said, "if you can manage her. That girl's a handful these days. She acts out, talks back, and is real sour all the time. She knows I'm not myself with my knee and all those meds the doctors have me on. But still, she's not even trying to behave in front of your uncle

Roderick." Didi had wanted to interject that Roderick, Aunty Mo's most recent husband, was no relation to her. "Send her on home when you get tired"—a pause—"'cause you will get tired."

Only Didi didn't. She hadn't been aware of how lonely she'd felt before her cousin arrived. She kept long hours between her nursing-school classes and shifts at the hospital; she hadn't made an effort to make friends in New York, keeping to herself at school and on shift; and her dating life was nonexistent. It was nice coming home to Chiara: making one-pot dinners from recipes that her cousin would clip from months-old housekeeping magazines Didi brought home from hospital waiting rooms, or sprawling on the couch, Chiara's makeshift bed, and watching cringe-worthy but binge-worthy episodes of something pretending to be reality on Bravo. They argued, to be sure, but over inconsequential things, like how Chiara didn't wash her dirty dishes; or how she didn't ask Didi before borrowing her favorite sweater; how she had a habit of falling asleep with the lights on and running up their electricity bill; and most often, how Chiara would accuse Didi of playing favorites when Didi would try to mediate spats between Chiara and Lucinda about who was eating whose groceries or who was hogging the TV remote. In the beginning, Didi asked about Philly fairly often, but she'd noticed her cousin's frame would tense up and her bottom lip would quiver, so she'd stopped. Besides, she liked having Chiara in Kitchewan, and Chiara seemed to like being there.

In fact, last August, a month into Chiara's stay, Didi had nonchalantly suggested that her cousin enroll in Kitchewan High, depositing paperwork she'd printed out from the school district website for her cousin to fill in. Didi's deliberate casualness was her way of telling her fiercely proud cousin that she could stay with her for as long as she liked without telling her. Chiara had responded in kind: shrugging in the moment but filling in the forms that very evening.

Things had been going well up until two and a half weeks ago, when Didi had come home from work to Lucinda screaming. When she'd walked in, Lucinda was calling Chiara a dirty, motherf'ing liar and a thief. "She's been swiping my dope," she'd told Didi. Before she could censor herself, Didi said, "Kiki, did you accidentally . . . borrow some of Lucinda's stuff?" Her words seemed to have stoked a bonfire within Lucinda. "It wasn't an accident, Desiree. She's a freeloader and a thief!" Didi had tried to intervene, but things escalated quickly. "She needs to get out of this house! I need her out of this damn house! Get out!" Lucinda had shrieked, then flung Kiki's backpack out the door. Kiki grabbed an armful of her belongings and ran out, snatching her backpack as she headed down the street. When Didi chased after her, she pushed Didi off, telling her to go away. Didi knew from Kiki's childhood that she needed space when she got upset, so she'd let her go, figuring she'd come back, then they'd talk and sort things out. But she didn't come back. And Didi had called what felt like a thousand times. She'd also sent volumes of texts to make sure she was okay. She'd gotten some delayed responses from Chiara as recently as a week ago. She confirmed she was fine but shared little else. Didi guessed the delay was her cousin's not-so-subtle way of letting her know she blamed Didi for not standing up for her with Lucinda, for possibly even siding with Lucinda, which Didi hadn't. But she could see how to Chiara, it might look that way.

When she'd first left, Didi hadn't worried. Not too much, anyway. Chiara had a habit of giving the silent treatment, and it hadn't been unusual for her to stay away from her mother's house for a few nights in a pointed sulk when she felt offended, or hurt, or embarrassed. In this case, Didi had no doubt she was all three. But when a couple of days turned into a week, and a week turned into two, she'd grown concerned. When this happened in Philly, Chiara had relatives (like Didi's parents) to stay with, and people in the neighborhood who would report back her whereabouts to Aunty Mo. Here, they don't have any family, apart from each other; Didi has yet to meet any of Chiara's friends from school, and she doesn't know her neighbors from a bar of soap. What's more, as of five days ago, Chiara's cell phone has been turned off, and the police are involved and talking about a stabbing.

Things seem different, serious. Chiara's never been caught up in anything serious before.

Didi walks across the parking lot toward the double glass doors at the
main entrance to the hospital. She pauses to scan her reflection before
opening the door. Looks have hardly been on her mind these past few
days. In fact, she got dressed in the dark this morning, since the power
on her street hasn't come back on after the storm, and although it was
after sunrise, her bedroom and the bathroom receive little natural
light. But she has to keep up appearances; she doesn't need people at
the hospital knowing her business. She smooths down her frizzing hair
and wipes at her shiny makeup-less cheek.

The hospital hallway is chilled and fluorescent. The smell of an-
tiseptic assaults Didi's nose and empty stomach like a sucker punch
and triggers the closed loop of questions that have been playing in her
head: Is this her fault? Could she have stopped Lucinda from throwing
Chiara out? Should she have quietly paid Lucinda for the weed she
claimed Chiara stole from her? Would she still be missing? Did Chiara
stab that white boy like the police are saying? How can they know until
they find her? When will they find her? Would this have happened if
she was still living with Didi and Lucinda? Is this her fault?

Didi walks to the elevator bank and presses the button. She waits,
stealing a glance at her watch. She's nearly half an hour late, which
would normally drive her into a frenzy. But today, she's too dazed.
Going through the motions but not there.

When the door to the center elevator opens, Didi walks straight
toward—and into—the chest of a rounded middle-aged white man in
brown slacks and a short-sleeved button-down shirt.

"I'm so sorry," Didi begins with a start. She's caught off guard by
the run-in and the hoarseness of her voice.

"Desiree Matthews?" the man says, startled. "What are—"

"Detective," she interrupts, "are you looking for me?" Her throat constricts and the knots in her stomach tighten. The detective is one of the two police officers checking in with Didi about Chiara. One is called Rhodes and the other Bridges. She remembers that when they told her their names, they paused, as if expecting a chuckle. Maybe she'd have played along under different circumstances.

The detective says, "I—uh—no. You, uh, work here, Miss Matthews? I thought you were a student." He squints, and Didi notices his skin is ruddy and there are beads of perspiration on his forehead, dotting his receding hairline. He swipes at them with the back of his hand.

She stiffens. She's tired of talking to the police. She's lost count of how many times they've called and showed up at her condo. Nothing they've been asking makes any sense—or is useful in helping to find Chiara. They also don't ask her anything straight, like they're hiding what they're after, and in return assume she's hiding something, too. Right now, for instance, the detective is looking at her with his eyes scrunched up as if he's catching her in a lie. She purses her lips into a tight smile and says, "I'm a nursing student at Milbank," referring to the local nursing school, and motioning to her scrubs. "I do my practical training here."

Rhodes and Bridges first appeared at her front door uninvited and unexpected five days ago. At that point, Didi hadn't seen Chiara since her argument with Lucinda over two weeks earlier, and heard from her only in sporadic texts. At the door, Lucinda had thrown Didi a glare like a dagger and muttered, "Don't let them in," her eyes darting to the weed nursery in the garage. Then, more loudly, for the apparent benefit of the police, Lucinda announced over her shoulder, "I told them she doesn't live here," and walked away.

The officers explained they were looking for a Chiara Thompkins, did she know where they could find her? Didi had tried her best to convey neutrality and conceal her distrust, answering that Chiara Thompkins was her cousin and she used to live there temporarily. "We need to get in touch with Chiara Thompkins," one of them said firmly. "Let's speak at the station."

At the station, during her voluntary-but-not-quite conversation with the police, Didi provided Chiara's cell and her aunty's landline in Philly. She added, only because she felt she had to, "It's been a while since I've seen Chiara . . ." She didn't tell them her aunty's phone is un-plugged more often than it's not. *Let them figure that out.* She reminded them they still hadn't told her what this was about. They answered by asking about Chiara's mental state and her "history of violence." "What exactly are you trying to ask?" she had responded with an edge in her voice. But they spoke in circles and half-formed thoughts, like they were sussing out how much—and in this case, how little—Didi knew. Eventually, they told her Chiara was a suspect in the stabbing of a high school student, a boy. A white boy, from what Didi gathered, and also assumed given it's Kitchewan. They rushed to explain that they came by because Didi's home address is the one on file as Chiara's address with the high school.

"Chiara didn't stab anybody. That's not possible," Didi had told them. Because it wasn't. Kiki has her flaws—moody in the mornings; messy even though being neat had been a condition of her staying on Didi and Lucinda's couch for the "few days" that bled into a year; in denial about being afraid of the dark; potentially dumb enough to swipe and sell crazy Lucinda's weed, even though Didi had warned her not to touch Lucinda's shit. But she's not violent.

"We have a statement from the boy who was stabbed, and there's another eyewitness," one of the policemen had countered.

"This is a mistake. Maybe"—she paused for a breath to calm herself before she continued—"you're confusing her with someone else."

"That's unlikely. We have a description." *If they're going to make me say it, I will.*

"Well, what's the description? That she's Black?" She hadn't raised her voice—much—but her eyes shone with anger.

"Miss Matthews, there's no need to get heated, or to imply things that"—a pause—"aren't there." *And that's how they do it. That's how they tell you you're the unreasonable one.*

That was last week on Wednesday.

Since then, the police had come to see her in person two more times and called her a handful of others, asking a series of random questions about when Chiara came to Kitchewan, when she enrolled in school, how she enrolled. To Didi, they were fishing.

In the doorframe of the elevator, the detective opens his mouth like he's starting to say something but then stops short.

Didi holds the door of the elevator open and asks, "Detective, what is it? Did you find Chiara?"

"The thing is, I can't reach the mother and the father," the detective says.

"Stepfather," Didi corrects.

"Right."

There's an elderly white couple waiting for the elevator, so Didi and the detective step away from it and into the hospital lobby.

"We have something I'd like to, uh, discuss about your cousin."

Impatience flashes across Didi's face. This sounds no different than when she'd spoken to the detective and his partner before. They ask to discuss something and then pepper her with indirect questions brimming with alternate meaning, providing only cryptic responses to any of her questions. Before she can edit herself, Didi crosses her arms and says, "Is it about the investigation? I saw the article in the newspaper the other day. It's not fair what they're saying about Chiara. She wasn't a menace. She didn't have behavioral problems at school. And why is everyone asking about how she got into Kitchewan High? It's a public school. Those two boys are making a fool of you, of everyone—"

"Miss Matthews, it's—it's not that."

Didi stares at the detective and feels a shiver course down her back, whether from the air-conditioning or the detective's uncharacteristically subdued tone. She lifts her eyebrows in anticipation.

The detective clears his throat and lowers his voice. "You see, Miss Matthews, I think we, uh, found her. Only thing is, we need some help . . ."

Didi's eyes widen and she scans the detective's face for more, but he deliberately avoids her gaze and doesn't complete his thought.

Before she can say anything, he says, "Can we?" and indicates the stairs.

Didi nods absently. She follows him, but as she moves, her insides contract as if in warning.

WEDNESDAY, AUGUST 15, 2018

FIVE DAYS EARLIER

TWO

It's late morning, and Angela Singh is on her usual route to Kitchewan High. She's headed to the school pool, where she's been swimming six days a week all summer. It's warm outside, and she's wearing a one-piece swimsuit underneath shorts and a baggy forest-green Kitchewan Indians tee with the profile of a sachem in a feathered headdress silk-screened across the front. Slung across one shoulder she has a faded navy duffel bag containing her goggles, swimming cap, and change of clothes. Her long brown-black hair that always smells faintly of chlorine, despite vigorous washing with strongly scented floral shampoo, is tied back in a high ponytail that bobs as she walks.

Her starting point, the Singhs' dandelion-colored town house in a complex of attached duplexes, Lakeview Terrace, has been her and her dad's home since Angie was in the third grade. The house is in northeast Kitchewan, closer to the town's lesser-known namesake river than to the banks of the glittering Hudson, which border the town's "ritzier" neighborhoods in the west. Fortunately for Angie, who's still a year away from getting her license and longer still from owning a car, Lakeview Terrace is walking distance to Kitchewan High. Only eight-tenths of a mile on foot if Angie does as she's doing today: cuts through the backyards of houses on Riding Road and Schoolside Way, and walks through a small patch of woods, over a narrow brook, across the football field, through the back door of the gymnasium, and into the girls' locker room, which connects to the pool.

The high school facilities aren't technically open during summer vacation—liability issues and all that. But the school, which boasts the only Olympic-length swimming pool in the county, and a beautiful pool at that, runs summer school and teachers' workshops for most of the summer, and is therefore unlocked. In fact, Coach Ford had told her with a wink, when she was worrying about where she would practice these past few months, that while he isn't encouraging her to use the school pool, he can't stop what he doesn't know about.

Kitchewan in the summertime is like a jungle. The roads throughout the town are rich with borders of dense greenery and seasonal vegetation, and on this particular August morning, after weeks of sticky, oppressive heat, it's unseasonably pleasant. The leaves of majestic maple and pin oak trees that dot the hilly residential roads flutter in the light summer breeze. Their freshness mixes with the smell of cut grass and sweet summer blossoms, tickling the air, tickling her nose.

Angela approaches the football field from the far end, behind a set of bleachers. The field is empty. No surprise. It's still another couple weeks before preseason practice begins. But as she moves closer, she notices the back of what looks like a person with short dark hair and brown skin. From a distance, she guesses it's Chiara Thompkins, a quiet girl and one of the only Black students at Kitchewan High. Angie knows her, sort of, from school. In fact, she's seen Chiara on the bleachers before at different times of the day, over the past couple weeks. She assumed Chiara was in summer school like her and waiting on a ride. But summer school recently ended, so she's not sure why she would be there today.

Angie frowns. Not specifically because of Chiara, who still has her back turned to her and appears oblivious to her approach, but because her entire walk over has been like this: She's been trying to visualize her workout—a mental trick she hears "the greats" use to train not just their body but their mind. Only her focus keeps getting interrupted, distracted. Like now, for instance, by Chiara. *What is wrong with me today?*

She shakes her head. She shouldn't have checked Instagram this morning. That's what started it. Rather than a flip turn, she's been stuck on this image of a group of girls: they're spread out on beach towels in matching striped bandeau bikinis at Croton Point Park, their eyes hidden behind oversized sunglasses, their mouths puckered in ridiculous kissy-face smiles, and in the center, her lips glistening in shiny pink gloss, is Samantha McCleary.

Samantha, or Sam, as everyone calls her, has been back from her fancy swim camp in Jacksonville for over a week. And nothing. No word. Even though Sam and Angie are technically "friends again"—which should technically make them best friends again—or so they'd agreed. Or so Angie thought. And even though Angie promised Sam, swore up and down, as embarrassed as she was at the time, that she had abolished all romantic thoughts of or interest in Sam's brother, Henry. Not that any ever existed, officially.

Henry McCleary. She sighs. She'll keep her promise to Sam. She will. But her stomach still somersaults—once, maybe twice—each time she thinks of Henry. His sand-colored hair that falls lightly across his piercing blue eyes, cerulean, if she had to describe them; his deep dimples that appear like creases of joy when he smiles, which he does often, lighting up his whole face and causing a small flutter in Angie's chest; the way his lips felt surprisingly soft and warm and his mouth tasted of wintergreen breath mints that time they were alone and he leaned in toward her, and by accident or gravitational pull, she leaned in, too . . .

But that's in the past, to the extent that it ever was. She hasn't seen Henry in ages, not since the beginning of summer. When he came into

Willoughby's, the local coffee shop where Angie's been working, and ordered a decaf mocha freeze, no whipped cream. He'd smiled at her, but they couldn't talk. Her boss was watching, and Henry was with his annoying friend, Chris Collins, a rising senior like Henry. Chris hadn't ordered anything but had been playing with sugar packets and made a mess on the counter that Angie had to clean up. Henry had shrugged, indicating he was sorry, and that was it.

It doesn't matter, though. She doesn't care. It's not like Henry McCleary is sitting around thinking about her. And Angie doesn't have time for boys. Not with swimming. Not if she wants to be great. And she does.

When Angie practices, it's for at least ninety minutes, although for the past couple weeks, it's been closer to two hours. And a few times a week, she practices twice a day, those particular days leaving her so exhausted she collapses into her pillow well before it's dark out. Training is a combination of laps and drills in the pool, a mix of speed and endurance, but with a small and growing dry-land portion, too—body-weight stuff like burpees, squats, push-ups, planks, and some shoulder mobility with these stretchy bands Coach lent her. Angie hates out-of-water exercise, but it's necessary. To get to the next level. This fall, Coach wants her and the other girls on the team to start weight lifting a few times a week. To transform her lean limbs into something thicker, more powerful—like the swimmers who get re-cruited by Division I college teams.

As a favor, Coach has been sending Angie suggested training plans all summer, and she's been following them like they're gospel. She doesn't tell him about the double workouts or that she sometimes doubles the number of repetitions he's written or increases the effort level in interval drills, because he'd warn her about "burning out." There's no point, she reasons, in worrying about that until there's at least flickering, and so far, she feels fine.

She doesn't know how to explain in words why swimming is so important to her. It's just that for as long as she can remember, it's been her thing. Who she is. In water, there are times she forgets it's her body she's maneuvering, like her limbs and joints are levers and cranks in a machine. And the amazing thing is, she can feel the machine getting better the more she trains. Quicker, more responsive, even just over this summer. Her ability to maintain her body in a plank from the tip of her outstretched arm down the back of her head, her torso, and her taut legs to augment her glide; the might with which she launches herself from the wall after a flip turn; the deliberate manner in which she maintains her elbows slightly elevated above her wrists and hands, drawing power from her shoulders and back—it's all improved.

The problem is, even as she's been getting better at swimming this summer, to be truly great, she needs to join a club. All serious swimmers are in a club. And not just during the summer, year-round. Everyone knows this, and it's been gnawing at her. All the good clubs near her are at country clubs and expensive, and the more reasonable municipal clubs are either not great or a thirty-minute drive. And her dad can't stop work to take her to practice. Even if he could, he'd need to take off pretty much every weekend for her meets, but weekends are "prime time" for his business.

Also, her dad doesn't quite get it. He's proud of her, to be sure. He tells anyone who'll listen, mostly the passengers he drives—his captive audience—that she's an "aquatic prodigy." He pins or polishes or displays every single swimming accolade she's ever earned, even participation certificates from elementary school, in their overcrowded bookshelf in the study, like each is a rare museum piece. But he doesn't understand why she needs to spend money on training. He believes people make it by grinding it out. No resources or professional coaching needed. Just grit. He probably thinks this way, she's decided, because he grew up in India. From her dad's stories, India is a semi-magical place full of poor village people who somehow, against all odds, and without any help, invent a number or discover a planet with just "scratch paper and their eyes." She's still waiting to hear if any are incredible swimmers, though.

Angie sighs. Her father's dutifully prepared "breakfast of champions" sits like a cinder block in her stomach. Each morning, before she wakes up and before her father leaves for whatever early driving gigs he booked, he makes her a ketchup-smothered boiled egg and sliced avocado on whole wheat toast and accompanying glass of lukewarm milk with a teaspoon of turmeric stirred in. There's no way she'll be able to train well so soon after eating all that. She frowns, irritated with herself.

Although it's not heavy, the strap of her duffel bag is digging into her right shoulder. Angie stops a few yards from the back of the bleachers to adjust the bag onto her other side. When she does, she pushes her shoulder blades, which have ridden up and hunched together, down and back. She hears them crack. The sound makes her self-conscious, but Chiara, the only other person around, remains facing the other way. No sign she's aware of Angie.

Nothing about today is going as she planned. She planned—a habit that must have rubbed off on her from her dad—to spend the morning finishing off the last of her summer-reading books for advanced sophomore English. The class will be a stretch for Angie academically, she knows, and a struggle because she's a slow reader and because *Jane Eyre* is, well, *Jane Eyre*. But if she'd dedicated the whole morning to it, she might have been able to finish the book. Then, in the afternoon, after properly digesting her breakfast, she'd swim. She'd do an extralong, extra-hard workout. The start of swim season is only two weeks away. She needs to—*she has to*—push herself.

Instead, she ended up on Instagram, staring at Sam's photos. She didn't care she wasn't invited to what looked like a trip to the beach. Not deeply. Because she might not have been able to make it, between summer school—Angie had taken geometry to lighten her workload during fall swimming season, math being her worst subject—and her summer job at Willoughby's. But it bothers her that the girls who Sam chose to go with, Sam doesn't even like that much—or she said she didn't, anyway. And it bothers her that she hasn't heard from Sam since she got back from Jacksonville. And it bothers her that the whole time Sam was out of town, she hadn't heard from any of her other friends, not even girls on the swim team—like they all forgot about her when Sam wasn't around. Normally—before everything with Henry—Angie and Sam spoke nearly every day, and Angie had a standing invite to hang out at Sam's house every weekend.

Angie misses going to the McClearys', and not just because her summer passed like molasses without her supposed best friend (and glimpses of Henry). She misses, strangely enough, being around all of them, Sam's whole family, even though she barely has anything to say to Sam's dad, an important finance person. When she was there, in their spacious, straight-out-of-a-magazine home, Angie could imagine an alternate life where she was a part of it. With no offense to her own family (her dad), the McClearys have a sheen, a sparkle, and it's hard not to be mesmerized: two attractive parents—a welcoming and put-together, yoga-lithe, philanthropist mother, a works-in-Manhattan father—still married, still in love, Angie is pretty sure, based on how Mr. and Mrs. McCleary exchange flirty smiles and find excuses to steal a kiss; one near-perfect (she blushes) honor-roll-student, varsity-athlete son; and one affable daughter, her best friend; living in a universe where money troubles or any serious trouble, as far as Angie can tell, are as foreign as the out-of-season blueberries used to garnish their salad.

Angie had felt a berry-size lump forming in her throat and pushed her phone to one side, determined not to care about Sam and all the places she wasn't invited, about Henry, about any of it. She'd spread out on the couch at home in the living room, book in her lap and green highlighter in hand. She took deep, deliberate breaths and told herself she wasn't upset. Half an hour later, however, she'd only managed to underline and re-underline the same paragraph, almost ripping the page from the weight of the green ink, so she gave up. She closed the book, threw on a swimsuit, quickly packed her duffel bag, and headed out the door. That was a little before 10:00 a.m.

Angie's cell phone buzzes from the side pocket of her duffel. She sucks in her breath, hopeful. But it's only her dad: "Ang—Spaghetti tonight—train well:-)!—Dad."

She rolls her eyes at first, but then feels a prick of guilt, as if in longing for the McClearys earlier she'd been disloyal to him.

His text to her is standard. He has an obsession with schedules and routine, especially this rotating meal system he invented, which, to be honest, Angie doesn't mind. In many ways, it makes her life easier, more predictable. And she knows her dad plans because he worries. About his driving business, about money, about nutrition, about Angie, about her mom not being around, about—she swallows away the metallic taste in her mouth that materializes every time she thinks of her phantom mother—everything. It wasn't until Angie was in middle school that she realized her dad is eccentric. That other families don't eat the same dinner the same day of the week, for instance. But by then, she'd grown so used to the meal plan, the calendaring, the minute-by-minute scheduling, that the unique strand of madness—or maybe genius—developed by her dad, Babur Singh, felt like home.

Angie resumes walking. She goes around the bleachers and looks up at Chiara. She is sitting on a high row, and Angie can see her more clearly now. She's in a white T-shirt and gray sweats. She's leaning forward with her elbows resting on her thighs and what looks like a backpack tucked into her lap. She holds a book, the title of which Angie can't make out.

They aren't friends, exactly. But as she passes Chiara, who doesn't look up, either intentionally or because she doesn't notice her, Angie wonders if she should wave.

Seeing Chiara with a book—the memory of Angie's abandoned Charlotte Brontë still fresh—alone, reading to herself, mouthing along, makes Angie feel, for a moment, connected to her. *She sees her.*

Sure, they don't *know* each other, but they do a little bit.

*   *   *

Angie and Chiara had been forced to spend some time together last school year. Angie had taught Chiara the basics of floating and the doggy paddle at her gym teacher's request. She hadn't especially wanted to, but it was last spring, the low point of her freshman year, when she and Sam weren't speaking at all, and Miss McGovern suggested that Coach Ford suggested that this would be a good idea, and at the time, Angie was worried that Coach Ford was worried about her emotional well-being, so she agreed.

According to Miss McGovern, Chiara was new to Kitchewan, had a tough life, was "a little rough around the edges," and was embarrassed to participate in gym during the swimming unit since she didn't know how. Passing the swim test is mandatory to graduate from the high school in Kitchewan. It's a local tradition with origins dating back to the seventeenth-century Battle of Kinoten Woods, where the town's indigenous inhabitants, the Kitchewan, ambushed the campgrounds of Dutch explorers by swimming across the Kitchewan River in the dead of night.

Angie hadn't spoken to or noticed Chiara until they'd begun the lessons. The first time Angie met her, she'd been struck by Chiara's disarmingly soft features, her round cheeks and wide, inquisitive brown eyes; they hinted at gentleness and innocence, suggesting there was more to Chiara than the solemn, close-lipped expression she wore like a uniform. Minutes before they got into the water, Chiara had announced: "I'm not getting my hair wet."

Angie had stopped contemplating Chiara's face and given her short, cropped hair a once-over. "Okay," she replied, unfazed and unimpressed. "What about your face?" Chiara shrugged. "I'm Angela, by the way. You can call me Angie."

"You look Indian."

"I am."

"Why's your name Angela, then? Shouldn't it be something . . . Indian?"

Angie's cheeks flushed in a flash of self-consciousness. It *was* something Indian, she could have said, but she and her dad had legally changed it after her mother left. To help Angie fit in, her dad had said. (To erase all signs of *her*, he'd left unsaid.) But why did Chiara need to know all that? Angie felt a familiar tightness in her throat and her eyes squinted in irritation. Chiara had broken into spirited laughter, taking satisfaction in Angie's reaction.

"Okay, Indian Angela. Don't get so serious on me."

After half a dozen lessons, with, to their mutual relief, minimal small talk and minimal hassle, Chiara was able to doggy-paddle the length of the pool. Angie had suggested she learn freestyle, pointing out that the optics of the doggy paddle were, well, ridiculous, but Chiara insisted it worked for her, since she could mostly keep her head out of the water. "I just gotta pass the swim test. I'm not looking for a medal or anything. I just need to graduate so I can get a job that pays well, like at a bank or someplace where you wear a suit, and get my own place." Angie couldn't argue with that.

Since then, they haven't really spoken. They didn't see each other except in the school hallways, and when they did, they exchanged a head nod at most.

Angie wonders again what Chiara is doing on the bleachers. She's pretty sure she lives on the opposite side of Kitchewan, near neither river, with relatives, an aunt and a cousin maybe. She's overheard other kids whispering about Chiara selling pot, but if she's here to sell something, there's no one around. Except Angie. And Chiara still hasn't looked at her.

By now, Angela assumes that's intentional. No book's *that* good. The impulse to wave at her has passed. She shrugs it off and strides across the empty football field toward the unlocked gym.

At least in water, things make sense.

THREE

Babur Singh's life is finally falling into place.

It's the third Wednesday in August, a mild seventy-eight degrees with a tepid breeze and mostly cloudless sky. The radio blares an infectious pop song about Havana that he can't help but hum and drum his fingers along to. His left forearm and elbow rest against the edge of the open window of his red Prius, and the dark hair on his arms flutters as he navigates midday traffic along the parkway.

The day feels ripe with promise and good fortune.

Babur, or Bobby, as most know him, is the sole proprietor and founder of Move with Bobby Transport LLC. The company, and consequently Babur, is having a record summer. Business is booming in spite of the surging popularity of various on-demand transportation applications, each seeking a non-negligible commission from drivers for use of their respective platforms.

In fact, Babur is en route from La Guardia, where he'd dropped off two of his regulars, the Burnett-Johnsons, a multiracial gay couple, both of whom "work in finance" and "in the city," to catch a flight up to Cape Cod for a long weekend. They had tipped with abandon— forty dollars on a one-hundred-dollar ride. *Some people have money to burn.* Babur couldn't help but feel judgmental, notwithstanding his pocketing the generous sum without complaint and with a toothy curb-side drop-off and farewell. He does not sacrifice quality customer service on account of others' fiscal irresponsibility.

He drives north on the parkway in the direction of the exit for Route 15 and smiles, genuinely this time, as he heads to his next destination, the Township of Kitchewan.

The Singhs moved to Kitchewan over a decade ago, back when Purnima was still around and Angela (then Anjali) had been in preschool. Babur remembers tripping over the peculiar town name, unversed at the time with the ubiquitous commemoration of the area's Native inhabitants (who were, so far as Babur could tell, no longer around to enjoy the honor). "Great schools, upscale people, and gorgeous river views. Kitchewan is where you want to be," their broker had told them, nodding with approval at the upwardly mobile young family: an earnest, clean-shaven husband, a company man—a Product Ambassador (aka salesman) for a biomedical-supply company; a formerly slim (but softer post-baby) wife, who nodded agreeably, if not bashfully, as she allowed her husband to do the talking; and an energetic young child with skin the color of burnt sugar and wispy curls of brown-black hair, as fine as bird feathers, weaving in and out of her parents' legs.

It turned out, ten-plus years later, after one intratown move and one Singh lighter, it was.

Babur hums a little louder to the music, decelerating as he approaches a sharp curve. He revels in a favorite pastime: running through his well-crafted daily itinerary in his head. Every task and appointment is already meticulously documented in his daily planner, but Babur relishes admiring the tidiness and order of it all, finding serenity and purpose in playing back from memory his choreographed life.

He plans to spend this afternoon in his home office, a modest but scrupulously maintained ground-floor study. He will station himself on his swivel chair before his desktop computer at his particulate-board desk (natural wood being out of budget—and who can tell the difference, really?), adjacent to a wood-composite bookshelf that doubles as a display case, mostly for his daughter's swimming accolades. Fortified by a toasted tomato sandwich and mug of milky black tea, he'll check his email and business Facebook page for passenger requests and then conduct a midafternoon status check on his other cars, or more accurately, his other drivers. There is, Babur has concluded, despite advice to the contrary from his voluminous collection of business-focused self-help books on the bookshelf next to him (*Entrepreneurship for Dummies, From Good to Great, Five Star Boss*), no management too micro when managing people who work for one's own business.

After that, Babur will tabulate his business accounts for the month to date, an exercise he does both midmonth and at month's end to keep a real-time pulse on performance. While it's been a bumper summer, he can't take his foot off the proverbial gas. Not now, with an almost college-bound daughter. And not in Kitchewan, where any success short of being a Fortune 500 executive or, say, a hedge-fund boss, like his daughter's friend's father, is considered modest.

Babur approaches the stretch of the parkway that runs parallel to the Hudson River. In his peripheral vision, he sees the surface of the water glittering in the afternoon light. He lets out a contented sigh, even as traffic congestion builds in front of him. Bodies of water remind him of Angie. She must be training now, he thinks, scanning his car clock and also his phone, which is affixed to his dashboard, to see if she texted him back in response to an earlier message he'd sent about dinner. She hasn't. She's probably in the pool.

Ever since she was in the first grade, when Babur enrolled her in swimming classes at the community center as a substitute for after-school care, Angie has swum more days than not. She has "trained" for the better part of the year, every year, since middle school. But this summer, she's dedicated herself with such focus that even Babur, who believes he knows his child better than anyone else in the world, is taken aback by the singular drive of his outwardly understated offspring. Seeing her grit, he agonizes, mostly in the middle of the night, when he has trouble sleeping because his mind seems to never turn off, over whether there is in fact a way to enroll Angie in one of the notable year-round swim clubs she has her heart set on joining. Can he cut back his weekend hours and adjust his weekday hours so he can drive her to meets and back and forth from early-morning and evening practices? But try as he might, boom summer or not, they cannot afford it. He tries not to panic about it in front of her, assuring her that using the school pool and emailing with the high school coach is as good as a club. But he knows it isn't, and Angie will eventually need better to reach the true heights of her potential.

Babur's phone buzzes and the car in front of him brakes in the same instant. As his eyes flash to his phone screen (a text from a client confirming a pickup at White Plains airport tonight), he delays applying his brakes and ends up sharply jolting to a halt. A paperback copy of Ralph Ellison's *Invisible Man* that had been resting on the passenger seat falls to the floor of the car. Babur winces. It's a bad omen for a book to touch the floor.

He's been reading Angie's summer books for her advanced English class along with her, to help her edit the reaction essays she has to write. He's not quite sure how helpful he's been; her school is a stark contrast to the open-air government school of his childhood in Hoshiarpur, where English literature study consisted of perfunctory ensemble chants of "Fire burn and cauldron bubble," and "Juliet is the sun" in response to the school ma'am's expectant "Double, double, toil and trouble . . ." and "It is the east, and . . ." But he enjoys the idea of his otherwise independent daughter needing him and his glimpse of an American education.

The traffic is at a standstill, so Babur unbuckles his seat belt and reaches for the misleadingly titled book (not a tale of optical illusion and superheroics), placing it back on the seat after touching it to his forehead. He rebuckles and hopes the karmic equivalent of the five-second rule applies.

Traffic recommences and he turns up the radio, nodding his head to a slightly crude pop song purporting to share "rules" for communicating with one's ex-lover. He hopes Angie doesn't start dating until after she leaves for college, and that she is able to solicit the guidance she may need in this arena from her professors. He's not equipped to parent his daughter through interactions with the opposite sex, his own experience limited to his tumultuous time with Purnima. Also, unlike other topics that he's uncomfortable navigating, like menstruation and bra shopping, he isn't sure that he can outsource this one to their sympathetic neighbor, Colleen Sullivan, one of several "women advisers" whom Babur has enlisted over the years to help fill the void of Purnima's abandoned duties. For example, when Angie was eleven, Colleen took her to buy her first training bra, using this occasion, per Babur's insistence, to speak woman to woman-to-be about Angela's changing body—a great relief to Babur, even if his daughter seemed less than pleased. (Better to learn of such things from another female than from Babur paraphrasing excerpts from *Our Bodies, Ourselves*.) But after Colleen's Fourth of July barbeque last month and her not-so-subtle invitations in the event "Bobby gets lonely," he's too embarrassed and frightened to reenlist her to chat with Angie about dating.

Fortunately for Babur, the subject doesn't yet appear to be on Angie's mind. The closest he and his daughter have come to speaking about relationships was a surprising recent ultimatum that Angie issued when he was researching university swimming programs. As a condition to her leaving home for college, Angie has made her father promise he will find "someone or something outside of work" so he won't be "all alone." Children these days are so emotionally complex, Babur remembers thinking, feeling guilty that Angie worries about him. He is also caught off guard by her pointed emphasis on "someone."

The idea of *someone* after eight and a half years of no one other than himself and Angie burns Babur's ears. It is out of the question—not a chance that he is ready or has time, or even with time, interest. He has Angie to take care of. He is both father and mother to the girl, and it's his obligation, his sacrosanct duty, to ensure she reaches every pinnacle of success. First back to regionals, then to state, then all-American, and then— He inhales sharply, stopping himself. No use in tempting fate. No, he thinks, he does not have time for barbeques and picnics and whatever else—he blushes—Colleen Sullivan had in mind. Besides, under the laws of the State of New York he and Purnima are still legally married. And although he owes Purnima nothing, not even, he thinks, clenching the steering wheel, a response to her latest audacious email, he can't, he won't, he shouldn't, for his own sake—and Angie's—introduce unpredictability into their diarized lives. Especially when he's dedicated the last eight and a half years to eliminating just that. Especially when things are going well.

He'll tell Angie that he'll take up an activity at the community center. A photography class, maybe, he thinks, as his eyes flicker back to the shimmering river on his right.

Babur's thoughts are interrupted by his phone, ringing through his car's Bluetooth.

He adjusts his headset and sits more upright, removing his arm from the window ledge, before he answers, "Hello, Move with Bobby. This is Bobby speaking." His standard greeting. Technically speaking, there is a "Transport" at the end of the business's name to avoid, upon the advice of counsel, confusion with a personal-training company in Fairfield, but colloquially it's "Move with Bobby," and around the house or in Babur's day planner, just "Move."

"Hi. Mr. *Bah-bar*, please."

Babur cringes at the butchering of his first name. It is a woman's voice. Not someone he immediately recognizes. "This is he. I go by Bobby."

"Mister—um, Bobby—this is Mabel Burrowes, Principal Burrowes of Kitchewan High School."

"Principal Burrowes? Is everything okay?"

"I'm so sorry to bother you, Mr.—uh—Bobby, but— Are you driving, Mr.—Mr. Singh?"

"I am. Yes. But it's no problem, Madam Principal. The school year hasn't even begun and I see they've already got you on the clock." He lets out an artificial chuckle.

The principal doesn't reciprocate.

"Mr. Singh, I'm calling about Angela."

Babur's heart stops.

"She's fine, let me say that up front."

His heartbeat resumes, but with gusto.

"But there's been an, um, incident at the high school."

"What kind of incident? Is she hurt?"

"No, nothing like that. She's not hurt and she's safe." She pauses. "I'd rather not say more on the phone. I think it will be best if you drive here. Can you make your way over to the high school?"

Babur checks his clock; it's 2:54 p.m. "Give me ten minutes."

"Great. I'll see you soon." She hangs up.

Babur immediately calls his daughter. After a few rings, the call goes to voice mail: "This is Angela. I can't talk right now, and I don't check my messages. If it's important, text me."

Babur ignores the instructions and leaves a voice mail. "Angela, this is Dad. I'm on my way." He hesitates, trying to decide if he should give her some advice, like stay safe or don't move, settling on "I'll see you soon," and hangs up.

He tucks *Invisible Man* farther away from the edge of the car seat, turns off the radio, pushes his shoulder blades back, sits at attention, leaning ever so slightly into the steering wheel, and drives.

FOUR

Angela's senses are warped. This can't be happening to her. This can't be real. She didn't really see Henry McCleary *like that*, just now. She shivers. *It's freezing in here.*

She sits in a chair in a white hall in Kitchewan High. Outside the principal's office. The hallway is bare except for a black-and-white print hanging directly across from where Angela is seated, a profile of the solemn Chief Kinoten. She stares at it. It's the same ever-present image seen on the Kitchewan High logo and statues across town. Angie remembers how she'd press her face against the glass display of an alabaster bust of the chief in the hallway of the community center when she was much younger and waiting for her dad to pick her up from swimming lessons. She'd study the stern image of the sachem and sometimes when she was bored, she'd pretend she and the chief were having a staring contest. She's briefly distracted by her memory, holding her eyes open until they water. But then someone walks by, steps directly in front of her, and her focus is broken. She blinks.

Several other adults brush by. They speak past her, to each other, at each other in hushed, urgent tones. They look at her but don't address her. She hears some of what they are saying, but the words come out distant and distorted. How things sound when she's underwater and someone is speaking above the surface.

In contrast to her muted surroundings, her insides are amplified. She feels the beat of her heart like the pounding of approaching footsteps. She's aware of the synchronized pulsing of her wrists and temples, and even what feels like the inside of her gut, all in time with her heart. Her legs feel cold and clammy, and they stick against the uncomfortable chair. Her long hair smells of swimming pool and feels like hay, coarse and brittle, matted against her head. She shivers again—or maybe it's a shudder, she's unsure. Goose bumps tingle down her bare legs, exposed from her shorts.

She wishes she knew the time. If it's been an hour, or multiple hours. If it's still daytime. She can't tell, and there are no windows in the hallway.

Thanks to her dad, she is used to always knowing the time, or at least being aware of it. She wonders if anyone has called him.

She looks down at her wrist and remembers that her watch is in her duffel bag—the duffel bag she used to prop up Henry when . . .

She short-circuits.

Angie tries to coherently replay the collision course of images assaulting her mind: She's exited the gym, hair wet and unbrushed. She's walking to the football field; her bag is slung across her body. She sees Henry McCleary. Vividly. He's on the field, in the grass. The sight of him evokes a psychosomatic flip-flop in her stomach that then nosedives into a plunge. Her eyes take him in.

He isn't himself. This isn't Henry, only it is. He's sallow, the color drained from his face, despite his summer tan. And hunched over, almost leaning forward, on his knees in the grass on the football field. He looks like he's constricted. His body quakes, jerks. He's looking down. Down at a cherry-red object. It's sticking out from his lower abdomen. It takes a split second, but then she gulps and shudders with realization. There is *something*—a stick, a rod, a knife, *something* with a red handle—stuck inside Henry, inside his gut. He's calling out, but

not to her specifically, just exclaiming, yelling, but not quite screaming. He's only a few feet in front of her but sounds far away. His voice
is warped, but even so she feels her skin tingle. His dusty-blond hair
covers part of his face, but she can still make out his blue eyes. They're
almost unrecognizable from the mesmerizing cerulean of her earlier
daydream. They bulge wildly—she worries they might fall out of his
head. He stares aghast down at the bloodred thing sticking out of him.
He looks over at her, motioning frantically with his hands, like he's
signaling for her to wrench the red thing out of him. "Help! Angie,
help!"

She feels frozen in place, struck by the sound of her name from his
lips, yet hot. Incredibly hot, like she's on the surface of the sun and
could melt. She feels pins and needles in her hands, in her feet. *I need
to stop blushing right now. Not while Henry is—whatever he is.* She scolds
herself. She needs to keep it together.

She says something. She can feel her mouth moving, but her ears
are waterlogged. She can't hear herself. She racks her brain for what
they learned in health class. Was it not to move a victim, or not to
leave a victim? She wishes she'd paid more attention. She doesn't think
she can remove the thing, the object, whatever it is—it looks lodged,
stuck, and she's afraid a cartoonlike spurt of red will come gushing and
drain all the life out of Henry if she does. She shakes her head, begging
off the request. *Please, I don't want to hurt you.*

Henry looks more desperate. His words begin to sound funny, like
he's gargling, but she knows he's asking her for help. She says something to him and takes off her duffel bag. She adjusts him on the ground
on his back, his knees still bent from when he was kneeling. He winces
and writhes at first, but he looks more comfortable like this. Maybe
the fount of blood she imagines pressurizing under the red thing will
stay inside him now. She debates if she should remove it now. He's
still pleading with her, shaking his hands, flapping them in short, rigid
movements indicating the red handle. His hands are sapped of color,
especially the palms. How hers look when she gets cold. She wants to

calm him, to warm his hands, to rub them in hers. She wants to help, but she can't pull the red thing. It could drain the life out of him. She grips one of his hands—it's cold, ghostly.

"Get it out," he gurgles, indicating with his pupils down to the knife. She shakes her head. "I can't. I'm calling for help."

"Get Chris," he says.

She looks around them and sees a boy—a lanky, familiar boy—running away from them, about three hundred yards away. Chris Collins. She holds Henry's hand, still cold, more tightly, almost possessively, tensing at the sight of Chris. She saw him earlier—she thinks—when she exited the gym and walked toward the football field, but as soon as she saw Henry she focused on him. Chris is yelling, she thinks, but she can't make out his words. He's too far away. *What is he doing? Is that— Is he chasing something, someone?* But she can't pay attention to that, to him, not right now.

She calls 911, keeping one hand in Henry's and both eyes fixed on his.

The call takes a long time, or at least it feels like it does. Henry's sweating and shivering and his pupils look unfocused. She's asked question after question, many about their location. She doesn't know how to describe it more clearly. "We're on the football field behind the high school. A boy—a student—has been stabbed." She wants to scream into the phone that this is an emergency. Henry McCleary is seriously hurt. But the voice she hears speaking into the phone, her own voice, is shaky but not raised. She holds Henry's cold hand throughout.

It takes the ambulance ages to get there, she remembers thinking. Internally, she is collapsing, falling apart, terrified, blood boiling with panic, but externally, she is saying things like "It'll be okay. Don't worry. I'm here. You'll be okay. Squeeze my hand really hard, okay?"

He squeezes but not hard. She feels nothing of the firmness, the purposefulness of how he'd drawn her into him, his hand on her upper back, when they kissed in his car that one time; nothing of the gentleness when his warm lips caressed hers.

At some point, Chris arrives. His square face is ruddy. He's out of breath and sweating. He gasps when he sees Henry, and his eyes dart between Angie and Henry. "Holy shit. Holy shit. This is bad, real bad. Is he okay?" He keeps repeating that and talks to Angie as if Henry can't hear him.

She doesn't know what she's supposed to say. She's surprised at how even at a time like this, her gut reaction is wishing Chris would go away. She says, "Yeah, the ambulance is coming. What happened?" But he doesn't answer. "Chris, what happened?" she tries again. He starts pacing, circling around Angie and Henry like a vulture around a carcass. His frantic energy starts a hammering in her head. Chris asks a thousand questions, makes a thousand disjointed statements.

"That bitch did this. I'll kill her. Did you see where she went? Did you see her? Is he okay? Is he gonna be okay? Oh my God, Henry . . ."

She can't keep up. She wants to tell him to shut up. Chris starts crying. He cries how she imagines a toddler who's fallen and gotten hurt does; his face balls up and his tears are fat and petulant. Henry seems more distressed. He's turning his head from side to side, whimpering. She doesn't recognize him. This isn't Henry, not *her* Henry—not that he's hers, she corrects herself, but the one she knows—the one she hasn't been thinking of, but who sometimes pops up in her head nonetheless, the one with the self-assured smile and fluid movements and even-toned voice. The one who looks at her in a way that makes something move in her chest, her stomach, her insides—she looks at the red thing, stopping herself. *Henry's insides.* "Stop it," she hisses at Chris. Chris looks at her and then stops pacing and sits down on the other side of Henry. He wipes at his runny nose and stops talking but continues to sniffle. He holds Henry's other hand.

The ambulance arrives. It feels like an entire SWAT team of paramedics gets out.

Angie lets go of Henry's hand only when the EMTs race up to them and separate him from her. They lift Henry away on a stretcher. The red handle is still lodged in him.

Chris is crying again and blurting things out rapid fire. "Is Henry okay? Aren't you gonna take that thing out of him? Is he gonna be okay? Can you find that girl? Can you get her? She did this! Is he gonna be okay?" An EMT, not occupied with the stretcher, is scanning Chris and asking him if he's hurt. Angie sees Chris shake his head and continue with his torrent of questions and comments. Another EMT has approached her and is asking her questions in an attempted soothing voice. He asks if she's okay, if she's hurt anywhere. She can't think, though. All she can hear is Chris, mumbling and fumbling and crying out in a loop.

"Can you shut up!" She doesn't mean to yell, but her voice carries. It startles the EMT who is attending to her and the one who is with Chris. It startles Chris. She's trembling.

Chris's tear-streaked, bloodshot eyes meet hers. He looks at her, bewildered, like a rabid animal caught in a trap. She stares at him without blinking. She doesn't mean to, but she feels her pupils shoot contempt.

Chris blinks rapidly and looks away.

She remembers the EMT writing something down and walking off, asking her to stay there. She's escorted by a number of adults and then seated. Chris is pulled aside, too.

"Sweetie," she hears someone say.

She opens her eyes. She's inside in the colorless hallway. There is a pair of brown eyes with faint crow's-feet around them peering at her. There's a petite brunette woman, bent down toward her wearing a small and what is likely intended to be comforting smile.

"Yes?" Her voice sounds amplified and scratchy, as if she has swallowed sandpaper.

"How about some water?" The woman hands her a plastic cup of cold water that Angie gulps down, having not realized how parched she is.

"I'll grab you some more." The woman takes the cup from Angie's hand and steps away. She returns, leans in again, and says, with the same intended-to-be-comforting smile, "Here you go, sweetie. Drink up."

Angie takes the cup but doesn't feel like drinking any more. She holds it in her hand, staring at it. She wishes the woman weren't standing so close to her. She smells like clean laundry and makes Angie self-conscious that she still smells like pool.

"We called your dad. He's on his way," the woman says.

Angie looks at her, even though she hadn't wanted to make eye contact, and nods into her expectant brown eyes.

The woman appears to take the nod as a sign to continue. "No one will ask you any questions until your dad gets here, okay? But the paramedics have come back and they would like to examine you one more time. Would that be okay?" Angie notices the woman's brow furrow into surprisingly deep-set lines as she speaks.

"Sweetie, is that okay?" the woman repeats.

Angie blinks and replies, "Yeah. Okay."

There are two paramedics this time, one man and one woman. They look young, like the close-talking brunette, and wear smiles of similarly forced warmth.

"Hey there," says the woman. "You are such a brave young lady."

When Angie says nothing she adds, "We wanted to check your heart rate and blood pressure again and make sure we didn't miss anything. Would that be okay?"

Angie nods, gripping her glass of water.

"Are you hurt anywhere? Anywhere at all?" the man asks.

Angie shakes her head.

"Can we hear you say that, please?" the woman asks.

"I'm fine. I'm not hurt."

They check her with a stethoscope and an electronic blood-pressure reader, and note down her measurements.

The woman seems satisfied and says, as if in an attempt to be reassuring, "You're okay. You're going to be okay." The man nods in agreement.

"But what about Henry? Is he going to be okay?" Angie blurts out.

The man and the woman exchange a look and then turn behind them to the brunette woman, who had stepped back to give them space but is still in the hallway.

The brunette chimes in, "He's in the hospital. Both the boys are in the hospital, sweetie."

"The one who was hurt, though—him—is he okay?" pleads Angie. She can hear a quiver in her voice as she speaks.

"The boys are getting excellent care. I'm not sure about the girl. That's all we know for now," replies the brunette.

"Girl? What girl? How many people are there?" Angie is agitated. She feels her throat tighten.

"You guys done here?" the brunette interrupts, speaking in a rushed voice to the paramedics, who nod and retreat. The brunette then steps toward Angie and says, "This is too much excitement, hon. Let's take a few deep breaths together, okay?"

Angie shakes her head. She doesn't want to breathe with this woman. She wants to know what's going on. She wants to know what happened. How Henry got hurt, why was Chris there, what girl?

Yet despite her intentions, she takes in a deep breath, holding it, letting it fill her entire abdominal cavity and heart and head. She imagines her lungs filling up like balloons. She continues to hold and then, slowly, she releases. It's calming, but she will not be manipulated into calming down. She won't.

But the oxygen and the pause feel good.

She closes her eyes this time, and repeats the deep breathing. *I'm not going to calm down.*

When Angie opens her eyes, she feels more lucid, more capable. The paramedics are gone, but the brunette woman is still there with her artificial smile. It doesn't bother her, though. It's amazing how different Angie feels just by changing her breathing, something she practices when swimming but rarely when on land. She closes her eyes again, relishing her ability to slow her pulse, to manipulate her tempo, to burst the bubbles of agitation knocking around in her head.

The brunette walks down the hall to check on something, telling her she'll be right back.

Angie doesn't care. She doesn't need a chaperone.

She sits, waiting in the empty hallway, studying the black-and-white chief anew, slowly sipping her glass of water, until she hears a door burst open. She looks over and sees her father.

FIVE

Exactly eight and a half minutes from the time his call with Principal Burrowes ended, Babur's Prius screeches into a faculty-only parking spot near the main entrance of Kitchewan High.

He doesn't come to the high school often, apart from attending the handful of Angie's swim meets that don't conflict with his Move schedule—and those times, he goes straight to the side doors to the gymnasium, not the front entrance. Today, when he runs through the double doors and into the school, he has no idea where to go.

Kitchewan High, formerly a sprawling, single-level encapsulation of 1970s architecture with halogen lighting illuminating its otherwise dark hallways, its rows of glossy blue-gray lockers and yards upon yards of laminate flooring, recently underwent a costly twenty-first-century makeover. Gone are the low ceilings and claustrophobic hallways. In their place are windows and skylights; motion-activated LED lighting; LEED-certification emblems; omnipresent Wi-Fi; granite flooring with stones sourced from the local quarry; and sleek, slate-colored lockers. The broad hallways spill into a central courtyard flanked with Scandinavian-style "café seating" and a coffee and juice bar branded as Willoughby's, a local favorite coffee shop at whose downtown outpost Angie had been working this summer.

Babur bounds down hallway after hallway, leaving behind a trail of illuminated motion-detector bulbs, but as the halls give rise to additional intersecting halls, he gets alarmed. Thankfully, as he races toward the café, after what feels like an eternity, but in reality has been only a little more than a minute, he hears the radio static and men's voices. He sprints over to where a pair of Kitchewan police officers stand like sentries in front of a closed frosted-glass door labeled ADMINISTRATIVE COMPLEX.

When the door to the administrative complex of Kitchewan High School opens, Babur's eyes beeline to Angie. She's down a long white hallway by herself, seated on a black metal chair in front of a closed office. She holds a clear plastic cup of what appears to be water. His daughter looks so vulnerable in her oversized T-shirt and jean shorts. And cold, or maybe scared. He swears he can see her hair standing on end even from a distance. If it weren't for the slow-moving police officer, the one who opened the door for him and now stands between him and the length of the hallway, Babur would gallop past the line of frosted-glass office doors and leap toward Angie.

But the officer is there, in no apparent hurry, so Babur scans Angie from afar: her limbs are intact, her head is on her shoulders, her digits, the ones he can see, anyway, appear to all be there, no wounds, no blood, and she isn't crying. He exhales with relief.

The sight of her reminds Babur of his and Angie's first few months as a family of two, in the wake of Purnima's leaving, when Angie developed night terrors. Babur had been distracted with perfecting his now fastidiously executed life regimen and attempting not to unravel at each whisper of forthcoming corporate layoffs at his then workplace and every unanswered, increasingly desperate call and email to Purnima.

Angie had never had trouble sleeping before, and these nightmares were not the typical bad dreams suffered by a first grader. She screamed, but in her sleep. She would produce a piercing wail, impossible for even the soundest of sleepers, as Babur had once been, to snore through. And like any parent, he would awaken and scramble bleary-eyed to Angela's—then still Anjali's—room, to find her with eyes closed but tossing fitfully, sometimes kicking and babbling, but all the while asleep. The first few times, he shook her awake in horror, fearing she might be possessed. "Beta, what is wrong?" he had asked.

Through half-closed eyes heavy with sleep, she had mumbled, "What? What's happening?"

"You cried out. Are you all right?"

"Yeah, Dad. I'm okay . . ."

Sometimes there would be multiple episodes in a single night; and sometimes none. But come morning, Angie would tell Babur she didn't remember anything at all.

In the slight tensing of her hands and flicker in her gaze, Babur would see flashes of Purnima, as if she had holographically imposed her likeness on his daughter. That was when it began—the illusions, the mind tricks that cut right into him. He was not a religious man, but in those glimpses he would pray silently to some higher power to let Angie be unplagued by the undefined terrors that gnawed at her mother. Let her be different. And then he would blink hard and fast until Purnima disappeared and he saw Angie once more.

He wasn't sure if he believed she didn't remember anything. She wouldn't hold eye contact, and she curled her lips together in a way that suggested she was holding back. Yet he didn't want to interrogate the child, his own emotional state then being fragile and further bruised by Angie's reticence.

He had sulked to his friends Neha and Manan, who were his steadfast support system in those early months. Manan was originally from Kapurthala, Neha from Jalandar, both proximate to Babur's childhood town, and they were therefore able to understand certain elemental fibers of Babur's being. Upon hearing Babur's confusion and hurt regarding Anjali, Manan had said, "Of course, yaar. She misses her mother. That's natural for a child, and you barely talk to her about your"—a pause—"whatever-it-is with Purnima." Babur had nodded, appreciating Manan's use of the present tense. It was true he had not adequately discussed Purnima's leaving with Anjali, but she was still a child, and he didn't know exactly how long Purnima would be gone. Besides, this was all uncharted territory that, when he thought about it too much, caused his thoughts to spiral into gibberish and echo in the hollows of his mind like a taunt, until his breath quickened, and his pulse raced, and his eyes teared, and his face flushed with heat, and then, suddenly, he didn't know what he was thinking or who he was, where he was, or how to explain anything anymore . . . So yes, he agreed, he had not really talked about his wife's departure.

"She's a child, Babur, but she senses things," Neha had said gently. "You know, the other day, when I picked her up from swim class, I heard her in the car telling that raggedy teddy bear she sometimes carries around not to be hysterical or else she'd send him away. She said that word, Babur—'hysterical.' And then she took the thing and practically suffocated it with a hug so tight. Babur, even if you and Purnima are having some . . . stresses, *you have got to talk to your daughter.*"

This had struck Babur as unfair. "But Purnima left; why must I clean up her mess?" He felt his cheeks grow warm. "I have barely got the basics together, Neha. When do I talk to her? How do I talk to her?" Moreover, he'd thought glumly, what could he say?

"Take her to a shrink then, Babur."

"A psychologist?"

"Yes, someone professional. A counselor, maybe. She needs to talk. These things, they firm up over time and cause real damage."

"Yeah," Manan interjected, "I'm still recovering from my mother calling me a son of an owl and pelting her chappals at me for breaking some crystal statue she got from Vienna. To this day, I don't let Neha buy crystal."

"Or shoes." Neha jousted Manan lightly with her elbow. Babur chuckled.

"No, seriously, man," Manan persisted, "I'm scarred. Just like your daughter might be."

Babur had, for the record, every intention of taking Angie to a psychologist. But, as if a cruel joke from fate, he received a pink slip from his job at the biomedical-supply company the next week and had to sort out more immediate concerns. Like what a Product Ambassador does when he's *let go*, a confusing phrase that better conjured a dandelion shedding dander than the heartless axing it was. There was also the matter of their rental, a colonial-style home, two stories, three bedrooms, a bit dated, with a problematic roof, not far from the Hudson. Their "starter home." There was no way they could afford it without his corporate salary. Babur needed to right-size their life, but didn't know what size was right.

And, as if it was a punch line, as Babur struggled to address these additional curveballs, whose sole purpose seemed to be to subvert his designs for routine and order—and all the while, Purnima still not returning his pleading calls and messages—the screaming stopped. He wasn't sleeping well those days, the darkening half-moons under his eyes a testament; so, for the first few weeks, the change passed undetected. By the time he noticed, and was pondering what could have been the catalyst, six-year-old Angie asked him, "Dad, can I go to my friend's house tomorrow after swimming class?"

"Friend?" He didn't mean to sound taken aback, but Angie hadn't historically initiated many playdates. In fact, she seemed to prefer the company of adults to other children, complaining of her peers' "sticky hands" and how "their noses are always running," observations difficult to contradict. "Yeah, Samantha, but she goes by Sam. Like a boy." She paused here to giggle. "She has a real big house, Dad," indicating gargantuan proportions with her modest wingspan, her exuberance eliciting a pang of self-consciousness in Babur about the uncertainties around their own living situation. "And she's in my Monday swim class." She broke into a smile and told him, "She likes to do 'monkey-bird-soldier' like I do," referring to the childhood swimming stroke.

"That sounds nice, beta, but Neha Aunty was going to pick you up tomorrow."

"Sam's mom can pick me and Sam up."

"I see. I suppose that could be possible, but I need to speak to this Sam's parents first and make sure this is all right with them." Angie raced to grab the cordless phone from the kitchen counter, climbing on a chair to reach. She deposited the phone, antenna extended, in her father's hand. As weighed down as he was by everything in his life that wasn't going his way, their way, he laughed at Angie's enthusiasm. Her eagerness to go to Sam's house is his lasting memory, coincidence or cause it was never certain, of when Angie resumed sleeping soundly and silently.

He sees Angie give him the smallest of smiles from down the hall. The police officer finally moves to one side, and Babur bounds to his daughter, leaving the cop behind. Water spills on Babur as he rushes to embrace her. Angie remains seated and unmoved as he kneels down, cradling her head to his chest and inhaling deeply, taking in the smell of her still-damp hair, a mix of sweet-smelling shampoo and pool chemicals—the smell he associates with Angie.

"Ang, are you okay?" he asks, still holding her tight.

"Yeah, Dad, I'm okay." Her voice cracks as she says "Dad," and she swipes the back of her hand across her cheeks with force, wiping away invisible tears, as if warning real ones not to form.

"Dad? Can you let go?" she whispers. "I can't breathe." Her eyes cut sideways at the young police officer, now a few feet away, observing them.

Babur drops his arms to his sides, releasing his daughter. He squints at the officer, trying to read his face. Babur sits in an empty chair next to Angie and whispers, continuing to eye the police officer, who eyes him back, "Angie, what happened?" He switches to Hindi, a language in which Angela is not conversant, but she can comprehend the basics. "What is all this? Are you in trouble?"

Angie replies in English, "A boy got hurt on the football field. I was walking home—"

"Hurt?" Babur jumps up, hushed tone forgotten. "Are you hurt?" He begins scanning her all over again for signs of harm. Her limbs look unharmed, no bruises are apparent . . . *head, shoulders, knees, and toes . . . her hands! Let me not forget to count her fingers.*

"Dad. I'm fine." Angie's eyes continue to dart between Babur and the officer a few feet away. "Henry—Sam's brother—he had—he was hurt."

"Henry. Who's Henry? Why are *you* here?"

Before Angie can answer, the frosted-glass door labeled PRINCIPAL'S OFFICE, which Babur had heretofore overlooked, opens. A middle-aged African American woman of medium build whom Babur does not recognize peers out. Upon noticing Angela, seated, and Babur hovering over her, she says, "Oh, good. You must be Mr. Singh." Her voice is deep and warm but still official. She looks at the police officer and gives him a nod. He nods back. The woman steps out of the office, closing the door as she does, so that Babur cannot make out its interior. He notices when she steps out that she is wearing a black pantsuit with gleaming white tennis shoes. His eyebrows rise involuntarily. "I'm Principal Burrowes, Mabel Burrowes."

She extends her hand toward him. Babur accepts. Her grip is firm, he notes.

"Bobby Singh, Madam Principal. What exactly is going on here?"

He observes Principal Burrowes and the officer in the hallway—the interloper on Babur and Angie's conversation—exchanging a look.

The principal shifts her weight and says, "I think you should sit, Mr. Singh. It's"—she pauses—"complicated."

Babur maintains eye contact, not breaking his gaze from Principal Burrowes as he takes the seat next to Angie. His bottom almost misses the chair, and he fumbles. His eyes tear up as he tries not to blink, determined to exhibit composure.

"Bobby is fine," he says and rests one hand protectively over Angie's.

SIX

"I could go in the ambulance," Chris Collins hears himself offer in a voice he hopes sounds weaker than he feels.

The cop who'd been standing next to him nods, and the couple of EMTs who were getting ready to drive back look at each other and shrug, nodding also. He doesn't look at her, but Chris can feel his mother staring at him.

They're all standing on the football field, off to one side by the bleachers. The first ambulance, the one with Henry in it, left what feels like ages ago in a blur. Chris isn't sure how much time has passed since everyone got there, but things feel calmer now. Slower.

Chris doesn't think he needs an ambulance. In fact, he feels fine to go home and probably doesn't need to be checked out by a doctor. He's not hurt or bleeding. He's a little jumpy is all, but he just saw his friend get stabbed. Who wouldn't be jumpy?

It sounds, though, like the cops or school, or someone, wants him to get checked out, just in case—standard procedure or something, he's not too sure. Maybe it's because he was a little worked up when the police arrived (because his friend got stabbed), and maybe it's because he's been nursing an ice pack against his head—because he feels warm (again, from the nerves of seeing his friend get stabbed)—a little too convincingly.

Whatever it is, if he has to go to the hospital, he'll go in an ambulance. It's not like it's skin off anyone's back to take him in emergency transport. He overheard one of the EMTs, the older guy, tell the police officer they have a spare vehicle. Besides, it'll be his first-ever ambulance ride, which could be cool. Siren blaring, speeding through red lights, maybe even sitting next to the cute EMT—the brunette girl with perky boobs who'd given him the ice pack. The ice is half melted now and droplets are dribbling down his face. Annoying. (How long does he have to keep this thing pressed against his head for, anyway?)

Most important, Chris is ready to do anything that involves not being alone with his mother. A ten-minute car ride alone with *her* would be torture. He can just tell by the way she'd been glaring at him while he was, quite respectfully, he thought, answering this mouth-breathing cop's tiring and repetitive questions. (How many times did he need to spell the facts out for the guy?) The cop was either slow or he didn't believe Chris, but whatever it was, all Chris could focus on as he was speaking was how his mom's eyes were cutting into him. She was like a fly buzzing in his ear, only he couldn't swat her away. She doesn't even know all the facts. He isn't the one who stabbed anyone, for crying out loud. But of course, he couldn't say any of that, because the cop was standing right there.

Point is, Chris Collins is not giving Roberta Collins the satisfaction of grilling him on the drive to the hospital. No way. He is not signing up to be alone with that woman in her crappy car that she wouldn't lend him and that started this whole thing anyway.

"I'm good." Chris waves off the EMT who offers him support as they walk to the front of the school, where the ambulance is parked.

He can see his mom out of the side of his eye. She's walking alongside him but speaking to some mousy-looking woman who's with the school district. He knows she's watching him as she's talking. She's speaking in her "professional voice," telling the woman she just came from the same hospital the ambulance is taking Chris to. She works there, she adds. Is that right? he hears the lady from the school ask. Will you go with your son in the ambulance, then? Chris holds his breath. He hadn't thought about that. No, I'll drive there so we aren't stuck afterward, he hears his mom reply. He exhales.

"Watch your step there, kiddo," the EMT says as they approach a curb. "Don't want you to trip."

Chris looks down at the uneven ground ahead of him, but doesn't bother to acknowledge the guy. It feels like everyone is watching him. Waiting for him to mess up.

Chris climbs into the ambulance with little fuss and no assistance, even though the overly eager EMT offers a hand, like he's some hero for helping Chris take a step.

Chris is seated and seat-belted, facing the open back door, ready to go. He waits for the EMTs, who are talking to the police officer. In the afternoon light of the not-too-sunny day, Chris takes a moment to finally look directly at his mother. Her under-eye circles look reddish purple, like eggplant-colored bruises, and her face is thin and tired. She looks old. Even the freckles on her cheeks don't help. Chris feels a flash of pity for her. But then, her gray eyes shoot daggers in Chris's direction, and all his warm feelings evaporate. She's giving him, or attempting to if he'd maintain eye contact, her "we need to talk" look.

And they do. Because this entire afternoon, the entire day in fact, is her fault. Well, hers and Chiara's.

The thought of Chiara makes Chris's pulse speed up and his face get hot. Did that local cop even listen to what Chris said? He'd told the police officer and all the other adults in earshot that they should be looking for Chiara Thompkins. "She's Black, and she's dangerous," he'd repeated a few times, before he stopped, realizing that his description, while accurate, might not sound right to some people. That he might get judged for it. Kitchewan's that type of place. Annoying, he remembers thinking. He hopes the cop wrote it down, though. Chris wants it on the record from the get-go that Chiara stabbed Henry. In case things get confused later on.

Chris had also explained to the same sleepy-eyed cop that when Henry was stabbed, he chased after Chiara. It was a knee-jerk reaction, he'd admitted, and based on the way the school people and the police officer looked at him, he figured adults would've liked it better if Chris had stuck around with Henry. But when someone stabs your friend—possibly your *best friend*—in broad daylight and then runs off, someone has to stop them. He wishes they'd all stop pretending they wouldn't be celebrating right now if Chris had caught her. He didn't say that, though. Besides, no-fun Angela Singh had been walking through the football field, and she called 911.

Chris jolts in surprise. The back door of the ambulance slams shut. He sees the cute brunette EMT, the one he noticed earlier, putting on her seat belt in the seat across from him. No sign of the annoying guy EMT, Chris notes, pleased.

Through the small window on the rear ambulance door he can see his mother standing with the lady from the school and the cop. They get smaller as the ambulance pulls away from the curb, but Chris can see that his mom is still looking at him with her eagle eyes.

The ambulance ride isn't as glamorous as he thought it would be. For one thing, it's bumpy. It reminds Chris, down to the canvas belt, of being strapped into a cheap carnival ride. He gets jostled around as the van turns and speeds. He's not one to get carsick, but the starts and stops make him feel queasy. He grips the side of the van and looks over at the cute EMT. Annoyingly, even though they're alone, she doesn't seem interested in him. She's looking at her phone with an amused expression. She's probably texting her boyfriend, he thinks, jealous, but not quite sure why. She seems to have noticed Chris looking at her, because she looks up and puts her phone away quickly. She gives Chris a small, embarrassed smile. He smiles back, but in the second it takes him to reciprocate, he sees her lips are back in a neutral position, and she's looking out the window.

Her disinterest is offensive. She's there to watch him, he thinks, irritated. For an instant, he wants to unfasten his crappy seat belt and reach toward her and grab her pale, thin wrists, lean in toward her too-perfect rounded breasts, let her feel his breath on her bare neck, and make her look at him. *Really look at him.* Into his eyes, and pay attention to him as he tells her his side of things. He doesn't. But the impulse to explain what happened reminds him, as he'd momentarily forgotten, that he's still mad at his mother.

Chris had today all planned out. It didn't involve the high school, or even being in Kitchewan. He'd finished summer-school classes—geometry and physical science, repeats for him since he didn't pass during the school year—a week ago. He isn't sure how he did on the finals this time around, but he has another shot to take both again during the school year, so he isn't worried. "It's not like I'm going to be a rocket scientist or surgeon or anything," he'd told his mother when she was hassling him about whether he'd studied enough. "I'm not even sure I want to go to college. At least not right away . . ." And so began their most recent blowout fight.

At the mention of college, all the blood rushed to his mom's freckled face and her veins bulged like vines. It looked like her head might actually explode. "Christopher Collins. Don't you dare! You think I work like a dog cleaning up grown people's diapers and vomit and open sores so my son can grow up to live on the street? Or so you can flip burgers or wash windows for the rest of your life? You think that's what I want for you? You think you can just throw away everything I have given you, like a piece of trash—like your life is trash? If you don't go to college, then the day you turn eighteen, *that day*, you are getting out of *my* house," she had yelled.

There was more yelling, more accusations thrown, more threats made. Eventually, it ended as things between them had been ending lately. Chris stomped up to his room, slammed the door, and marched around, kicking at the dirty clothes on the floor. He felt fidgety and ached for a joint. But—again, thanks to *her*—he'd purged his room of all his marijuana and even his cigarettes since his mother had taken to going through his stuff. He kicked hard at a crumpled navy-blue T-shirt lying on the floor near his bed and accidentally stubbed his toe against the leg of the bed. "Ow!" he cried out. He hoped she could hear him from wherever she was. She was probably still downstairs at the kitchen counter where he'd left her. He couldn't hear crying, but he hoped she had her hands buried in her reddish-brown hair and was crying fat, ugly tears. *Let her be unhappy, too,* he'd thought.

Chris doesn't realize it's happening, but his face must have tightened at the memory of his argument with his mother. The brunette EMT notices and reaches over, tapping his knee lightly with her hand. "You okay?" she asks.

Startled, he feels his leg tingle at her touch. His jaw unclenches. "Yeah." He nods hurriedly. "I'm fine."

She gives him a small smile again; this time, it lingers and is slightly crooked, with one side of her mouth curved more than the other. Chris can make out the trace of a dimple.

She doesn't say anything, but feeling encouraged by what feels like flirting, Chris fills the silence. He says, "I wasn't even supposed to be there today. That's the weird thing. I mean"—he pauses—"I had plans to be, like, out of town. It's just, well, my mom. She's kind of tough on me."

The EMT's eyebrows rise and her forehead wrinkles. After a pause she says, "We'll be at the hospital soon. Hang in there," then looks back at the window.

He sighs, bothered by her non-response.

But once he's expressed out loud the link between the incident on the football field and his mother, his mind gets stuck on it. Because it's true, he tells himself. In some way, in some alternate universe, none of this would have happened because in that other reality his mother wouldn't have stopped Chris from going to the beach in Connecticut with Henry. *She wouldn't have been such a stone-cold bitch.*

In this universe, however, things are different.

Chris's mom had left for work early that morning, as usual, and before Chris had even woken up. Sleeping in felt like a luxury. Up until a week ago, Chris had to be at the high school by 9:00 a.m. on weekdays for summer school—extra annoying since Chris and his mom had only one car between them, which meant the otherwise twelve-minute drive to Kitchewan High took Chris about thirty-five minutes on the Circulator, Kitchewan's local bus.

Chris had been rolling in and out of sleep until late morning. A little before 11:00 a.m., he'd reached for his cell phone on the edge of his bedside table. He noticed, eyes still half-closed, that he'd missed a few calls from Henry McCleary. It was unlike Henry to call instead of text, so, half-awake, Chris called him back.

Henry wanted to know if Chris wanted to go to his parents' beach house by Hammonasset Beach in Connecticut, about ninety minutes away. The McClearys had a lot of houses, Chris remembered thinking, aware of at least one ski house in Vermont and a time-share in Florida. "Yeah, sounds great," he'd replied almost automatically.

They could drive back the same day, but, as Henry explained, then they wouldn't be able to drink, and he had a few six-packs and half a handle of vodka stashed away. Plus, according to Henry, there were a lot of girls, and pretty ones, too, who went to the beach around there. All of this sounded great to Chris. "The thing is"—Henry had paused, and Chris could hear him sucking in some air before continuing—"I can't take my car. Sam will have a meltdown if I take the car overnight and don't bring her." Henry and his younger sister—who only had a learner's permit—shared their Acura. It was like the McClearys' version of setting limits, making their children share a car. But the way it worked out, at least from what Chris saw, Sam made out like a bandit. Henry either chauffeured her and her friends around or invited her to tag along wherever he was going. "And, bro," added Henry before Chris could react, "we can't bring her."

He didn't need to say that last part. Chris found Sam incredibly annoying. There was nothing wrong with her, exactly. Except she was a tagalong and Henry seemed to indulge her. Also, she was constantly demanding attention, unlike Henry, who didn't demand so much as command. Sam would force herself into the center of things even when no one wanted her there. Also, she had this awkward way of looking at people—at guys mostly—where she'd blink really fast, like she had a spider in her eye, and sort of lean in, like she was expecting something. She probably thought she was being flirty, but to Chris, she looked unstable. He hadn't said any of this to Henry, of course. He didn't even verbally agree on the phone, but he nodded his head on his side of the phone call in silent consent. *No, we cannot bring Sam.*

"So . . ." Henry had left the sentence hanging in the air.

Eventually Chris picked it up and had said slowly, "I guess I can ask my mom about picking up the Honda from the hospital. She's at work right now, but maybe she'd let me borrow it . . ."

"Oh, yeah?" Henry's voice had brightened.

"Uh, yeah. Lemme ask."

Chris knew before he even called that his mom wouldn't agree. She didn't like getting non-urgent calls at work; and she wasn't likely to let Chris take their silver Honda Civic hatchback overnight, especially given how much they'd been arguing lately. Also, the name "Henry McCleary" was like bug repellent to her.

And sure enough, after a tense exchange that they cut off just before either of them raised their voice, his mother said no.

"There's a public bus, you know. I took the Circulator every day this summer," he'd grumbled, when she said she wouldn't have a way of getting home if he took the car. He knew, though, even as he was saying it, that there was no changing her mind.

Chris's mother, Chris has noticed, seems to have some sort of prejudice about Henry because his family's rich. He'd told her this a few times, that morning being one of them. Incredibly, she hadn't even denied it. She said something like "I've been around longer than you have, and I don't get a good feeling from that family, the McClearys." *Like that was an answer. If they weren't white, that would be racist.*

"You know, Chris, maybe this afternoon you could spend a little time preparing for your SATs. That test is really important for your future." That was the last thing he remembered her saying before he'd said, "Mom, give it a rest already," and hung up. It was too much, all of it. If it wasn't his grades then it was college and "his future." He'd already agreed to retake his SATs this fall, as a favor—to *her*—and it would have been nice to have a single week go by, one of his last of the summer, the summer before his senior year at that, without his mother nagging him about "his future."

Chris had punched the wall next to his bed after he hung up, striking it a little too hard and hurting his knuckles. Which annoyed him even more. In his ambulance seat, Chris runs his fingers over the hand that had slammed into the wall. The skin is still tender.

Chris had waited about forty-five minutes before he'd grudgingly texted Henry the bad news: "No go."

The thing about Henry McCleary was that he had a lot of friends, and he was used to getting his way—not like a dictator exactly, but more like when he suggested something, it just sort of happened. So while Henry and Chris were—according to Chris at least—good friends, Chris didn't sense higher loyalty to their friendship from Henry. If it weren't Chris, it would be someone else. For this reason, Chris worried that when he couldn't do something, like get a car for an overnight trip, or go somewhere, or make a plan happen, Henry would just shrug and in a perfectly good-humored way find someone else who could and would. It was silly to fear this type of rejection, Chris knew, and it's not like he didn't have other friends, because he did. That wasn't the point. It's just, Chris didn't want to be cast aside by Henry, especially not because of his lame mom.

To Chris's relief, minutes after he texted, Henry wrote back. He suggested they go to the nature reserve by the Kitchewan River to chill with a joint and a beer or two: "Bummer. Hit up the reserve with some others? 🍺 🌲 🔥"

The Kitchewan Nature Reserve is a forty-acre park that runs along the Kitchewan River to its mouth, where it empties into the Hudson. The reserve is across town from the high school, closer to where the McClearys and other rich people live and almost the farthest possible point within Kitchewan township limits from the small two-bedroom home on Dogwood Lane where Chris and his mom live. It's an open secret Kitchewan High students go there and get up to no good, but the park rangers don't seem interested in patrolling areas not directly next to the picnic benches.

Whenever anyone mentions the reserve to Chris, he always needs a second or two to catch himself, to squash the prick of guilt he feels making plans to get wasted there. The truth is, the reserve reminds Chris of his dad. His most vivid memories of his father—the few happy ones he has—involve the reserve. They used to go there on weekends and catch bugs and skip stones; they'd climb on moss-covered rocks with twin backpacks of "provisions"—smushed PBJ sandwiches wrapped in layers of cellophane, and boxes of apple juice—ending their adventures by stripping down to their shorts and going for a swim in the river.

But Chris is used to pushing those thoughts out of his head. And that's what he did earlier that day. He caught his breath for a second and then texted: "I'm down, but out," reminding Henry he didn't have weed on him on account of his mom's snooping.

"Can you get some . . . ?" Henry had replied.

"Maybe. Or we just drink? 🍻"

In reply, Henry called him. He opened with "Come on. It'll be fun. It's the last real week I can party. Next week's preseason."

Chris had felt a flash of annoyance. Henry could be contradictory. He was on multiple sports teams and did a hundred other activities that made him "competitive" for college, and he'd complain to Chris about it all the time like it was a burden and he was being forced. But from what Chris had seen, no one was forcing Henry to do anything. He desperately wanted to be a carbon copy of his dad. In fact, Henry had once told Chris, while drunk and high on an earlier trip to the nature reserve, that his dad went to Harvard and was a three-time varsity athlete in high school, and so to "live up to him, to be good enough," Henry had to do the same.

"Chris," Henry continued, "how about you get some stuff, I'll invite a few people, and we'll meet at the reserve? I'll pay you back for whatever you buy."

Normally Chris would have agreed and that would have been the end of it. But that day, for some reason, the mention of money irked Chris. He could hear echoes of his mother's accusations that he treated his life like it was trash. He was always the one getting the weed, Henry McCleary's weed. What did that say about him? he wondered.

He must have been silent for a while because Henry said, "You still there?"

Chris remembered a girl one of the students in his geometry class had pointed out to him. He'd claimed she sold good-quality stuff that was cheap. "I can ask this girl I know if she's got anything," Chris finally said, quickly adding, "but why don't you come with me?"

"Or we can meet up when you're done?"

"Just come with. It'll be quick."

"Fine." Henry sighed like he was doing Chris a favor. "Text her first though? To make sure she's got."

Chris had the girl's number from the kid in summer school but hadn't actually spoken to her before. To Henry, though, he just said, "Yeah, okay."

A few minutes later Chris texted Chiara Thompkins and waited. At the time, which was in fact earlier that day, Chiara seemed all right to him. She didn't smile much but was otherwise okay. Just a girl they went to high school with. A girl whose only defining characteristic in their mostly white town had been that she was not. According to his "reference," Chiara bragged about selling stuff grown by her cousin's roommate who studied pharmacology. Chris had shrugged when he heard this, as if to say, he didn't need to know the girl's life story.

Ten minutes later, Chiara texted back, "How much are you offering?"

Chris had started to type, "Depends on what you got," but then erased it and wrote, "Whatever you're asking," figuring it was all the same to Henry.

Chris could see three dots blinking on his phone for a few minutes indicating she was typing. "Can't today," she finally responded.

"Seriously?"

More dots; Chiara was typing. Then the dots stopped, and there was no message.

Chris jiggled his leg, as he often did when he felt agitated or restless. Who was this chick, wasting his time?

Minutes later, she texted, "If you come by the football bleachers and give me money, I can get for you later."

It wasn't an ideal reply. In fact, it was obnoxious. She expected him—well, Henry—to just front her money? What the hell? But before he could respond to Chiara, Henry had called again and sounded impatient so Chris had said, "She sells by the football bleachers at KHS. Let's go there and figure it out," neglecting to mention Chiara might not have anything.

Chris hadn't mentioned to the police texting Chiara or the part about buying weed. Aside from repeating that Chiara stabbed Henry and telling them she ran away, he hadn't told the police much. They needed to wait for Chris's mom before taking a statement, and by the time his mom got there, all these other people from the school had showed up, too, and the cop Chris had been talking to got distracted. Now they won't take Chris's statement until after he's done at the hospital.

He hasn't thought about it clearly, because he was kind of jumpy and jumbled when everyone got there, but he doesn't know what to say to the police. He shouldn't be nervous, he knows. He has no reason to be nervous, he tells himself. Because *he didn't do anything*. They didn't end up buying any weed. And they didn't do anything else, even if maybe things looked a little funny for a while—not that anyone else knew that. Chiara, on the other hand, stabbed Henry. She *did* something.

The ambulance brakes sharply, and Chris jerks in his seat. He looks over at the brunette EMT and notices she's back on her phone. He clears his throat, and she turns to him. "We're just pulling up to the entrance."

Chris nods and says, "Do you know if my friend's okay?"

"That other boy, you mean?"

He nods. He wants Henry to be okay. It would also be good to talk to him.

"It was a nasty wound, but chances are, he'll be fine," the EMT says. She pauses and then adds, "You're lucky that girl came by when she did and called 911."

Yeah, Chris thinks to himself, luck's really been on his side today.

SEVEN

Principal Mabel Burrowes had received an urgent phone call about the incident while she was at a leadership picnic, a meet and greet for fellow principals in Westchester County. When her phone rang, Mabel's split-second—not to be shared, never to be admitted—gut reaction to the call had been relief. Relief that the number flashing across her phone screen wasn't her home number.

The past few weeks, and most of the summer, had been what Mabel referred to as a doozy. On one hand, there was work. Endless work. Contrary to what many think, being principal is a twelve-months-a-year job, and this year, it has felt more like fourteen months a year. In addition to her litany of usual administrative tasks—managing teacher hiring, conducting curriculum reviews, resolving facilities and maintenance issues, and keeping up with various certifications—she has a number of new duties now that Kitchewan High, under her leadership, has entered an elite band of "smart schools." The only one so far in the state of New York. Moreover, in well-paying school districts like Kitchewan, there are endless year-round meetings and consultations with the ever-diligent school board, the most recent ones focused on how to track and interpret data on how KHS students stack up against peer groups in the less-"smart" schools in Rye, New Rochelle, and Scarsdale.

Then, beyond that, there's her home life. Mabel and her husband, Robert, are on a trial separation this summer, emphasis on the trial. His idea, not hers, never hers. While she agreed they'd grown apart, that the spark—if ever there was one, she can't quite remember anymore—had dimmed, she didn't understand the need to break from their status quo absent a crisis. But normally mild-mannered Robert had been adamant. He felt "stifled" and "needed space" and made a rather caustic reference to Mabel's devotion to her work, as if this was somehow a shortcoming. What a cliché, she'd wanted to sputter, if only she'd had her wits about her in the moment.

With Robert in a rental in Brooklyn for the summer, living out a middle-aged fantasy of bachelordom, no doubt, he left Mabel a cliché for the summer. A single mother to their two boys, who are at the unstraightforward age of not having outgrown being rambunctious but all the while seamlessly transitioning into smart alecks. She enrolled them in a day camp over the summer, but it's ended. So for the past few weeks, her mother has come up from Kingston, interrupting her "very busy" life of afternoon tea with coconut custard and rounds of gin rummy with senior gal pals, to watch her grandsons and provide unsolicited (and unwelcome) housekeeping and marital advice to her adult daughter.

Needless to say, when Mabel's phone rang in the middle of a round robin on individual leadership styles and Mabel climbed off a picnic table bench to answer it, she couldn't help but exhale with relief upon noting it wasn't a call from home.

Her relief, of course, was short lived, succeeded by a gasp of horror and a hasty departure for the high school.

Mabel hadn't known what to expect at the school. She didn't receive much detail over the phone. Just that a boy, a student at Kitchewan

High, had been stabbed and there were at least two other students on school grounds with him. No details about who did it or the other students present, not even any of their names. "Best if you get here," she'd been told by a police officer who introduced himself as Detective Bridges.

She'd arrived to find her pristine office unlocked and two detectives plus a handful of police officers and school district officials, including a lawyer, crowded into it. They'd dragged in stray chairs and were presiding over her immaculately organized desk like it was a communal workstation. Some of them had looked up when she walked in, and one—or maybe both—of the detectives had acknowledged her with a nod. She received a cursory briefing from one of the detectives. A run-on sentence that went something like: a student, Henry McCleary, has been stabbed, he's in the hospital, in the ER, his family is with him, they're upset, their lawyer's here, two bystanders were on-site, both students, we have them, a friend of his and a girl, who called 911, there's a third student, an African American girl, she's the stabber, we believe—here Mabel could swear the detective had paused, just for a second, to scan Mabel's practiced poker face (her jaw clenched, but she knew how to wear impassivity) before continuing—she appears to have run off and is presumed dangerous. There was no opportunity for questions (of which she had many). It concluded with "Good that you're here. It's an active situation. We'll let you know what we need," followed by another nod, as if to say, "Run along."

What they needed, it turned out, was for Mabel to fetch people and papers and deal with the families. The McClearys had left by the time Mabel arrived. They'd gone to the hospital with their son. Naturally. In their stead, they left behind the family lawyer. Naturally also, Mabel supposed, although she couldn't fathom a reality in which it was natural to have an attorney on retainer, ready to be mobilized at the snap of a finger. The lawyer was a tall white man with a long European last name she didn't bother to commit to memory and a facial expression that rested somewhere between a sneer and a smirk. He peppered

Mabel and the school district's lawyer with dozens of questions about the school's insurance policies and whether Mabel might be able to arrange some "spare desk space" for him somewhere. Mabel had tried not to betray any personal distaste through a tight-lipped smile.

Additionally, Mabel had been tasked with speaking to the mother of the second boy, Christopher Collins. His mother had arrived shortly after Mabel had, and while it appeared her son was physically unharmed, he was shaken up, too shaken up to be questioned by Kitchewan PD at that time, and from what Mabel understood, he had caused quite the commotion among the EMTs attempting to examine him. The mother, in response, was understandably agitated and concerned and seeking answers, many of which were not available, and consequently, someone to blame. Mabel served as a convenient stand-in. And she'd taken it, the finger pointing, the raised voice, the distrustful glares. Cool as a cucumber. She accepted this as part of the terrain of being an educator, unwilling to entertain any other cause or contributor to the mother's reaction.

The detectives were preparing to interview the girl who called 911. Angela Singh. They believed she was an eyewitness, and unlike the Collins boy, she might be neutral and stable. During lulls in their discussion, Mabel had gingerly volunteered some insights on the disciplinary record of Chris Collins. "In case it's helpful," she'd couched it, sure that it would be, given the "active situation." In response, however, she had received withering, if not antagonistic, stares. And she started to feel more strongly a creeping discomfort that had been lingering ever since she arrived at the high school. Pinpricks in her insides, biting at her, asking, *Do the police know what they're doing?*

Of the various detectives and police officers, EMTs, and lawyers, Mabel is the only one, the only adult, who *knows* Kitchewan High School.

She knows the students, "the kids" as she calls them; not each and every one, to be sure, but she knows the student body, their currents and mores. She does, after all, walk the wide hallways with them between bells. Brushing shoulders with packs of jocks in forest-green varsity jackets, slapping each other's backs and fist-bumping. Navigating past gaggles of selfie-ready girls lingering in the atrium, eager to grow up too fast. Waiting in line at the school's recently requisitioned coffee bar, inadvertently overhearing the angst-laden commentary of the artistic crowd—the theater kids, who take themselves and their caffeine seriously, their attire and hair hue more colorful, literally, than those of their philistine peers. Looking on with curiosity at the budding couples exchanging meaningful glances, the intensity of these courtships, like friendships at this age, as easily forged as they are crumbled. Where's Waldo–ing the minorities, mostly Asian (South and East) and a handful of Black and Latino kids, sprinkled among various groups— something she officially takes pride in, but that in reality reflects their lack of critical mass more than a commitment to race-agnostic interaction.

Kitchewan High is an ocean of mostly decent, denim-clad children with tablets and backpacks—an arguable relic in their smart school, where the majority of textbooks are available electronically—moving in step with their respective cliques, keeping up and fitting in. She is the only one of all these adults who sees the students, these kids, who's with them, in this body of water every day, swimming.

But the police don't seem to care about that.

Mabel hears one of the detectives, as he shuffles through his notes preparing for the Singh girl, utter the name "Chiara Thompkins." He interchanges the name with "the perp," causing Mabel to stop short, just for a second, and audibly inhale through her nose. By now, Mabel has picked up that Chiara is suspected of stabbing Henry McCleary and that she appears to have run off. And in spite of herself, in spite of her cardinal rule not to play favorites, or anything that could be mistaken for it, especially when there are *optics involved*, hearing Chiara's name makes Mabel's heart descend. *Please don't let it be true.*

She knows Chiara. A transfer student. Quiet, serious, borderline solemn, with inquisitive eyes that appear almost too large for her face. Mabel had sensed some larger issues since the first time they met in her office last September, noting the girl's oddly incongruent appearance—a low-cut, ill-fitting magenta top, tomboyish black athletic pants and sneakers, and a faded gray backpack that she'd kept on her back even when seated, fidgeting with its straps between her fingers, like a child with a security blanket. She remembered how Chiara had come alone on her first day and bristled like a porcupine with its quills on end when Mabel asked about her parents.

She knew Chiara had some difficulty fitting in with her peers at Kitchewan High. Not entirely a surprise. Some months back, there had been a misunderstanding in the girl's gym class that had attracted an unusual amount of chatter among the students and even faculty, and Mabel had leaned in and worked with the gym teacher to sort it out. Because Mabel cared. Mabel cares. For all her students. (And, yes, fine. Not to be shared, never to be said aloud—she does, on occasion, find it a fraction of a margin of a hair easier to care for the students with the darker faces in the sea of otherwise light ones.)

She is lost in thought when one of the detectives, from behind Mabel's desk, clears his throat and says, looking directly at her, "Ms. Burrowes, did you hear me? We're ready for the girl now. Can you bring in the eyewitness and her parents for the interview, please?"

Mabel jerks back to attention. She has an impulse to correct him. She just looked up the Singh girl's file, and it is "parent" in the singular. But she doesn't.

She nods and stands up from a visitor's chair in her office, taking note, but trying not to, of the detective's balding head nestled against the back of her black leather executive swivel chair. She similarly only blinks in the direction of the McCleary family's lawyer, who has managed to secure permission to be present for this interview for reasons that elude her. He leans against her beautifully appointed cedarwood floor-to-ceiling bookshelf. His hand is grazing her antique mahogany mantel clock that reads twenty past three, and he's picking up and examining her carefully displayed framed photographs and various leadership commendations, replacing them in not quite the correct spots. She feels her pulse quicken. To the outside observer, however, she is unbothered; she is calm; she is cooperative. Mabel Burrowes is completely fine.

She opens her office door to retrieve Angela Singh and her guardian.

Mabel recognizes the girl. She does not recall ever conversing with her, but she has seen her before. She's on the swim team, Mabel is aware, having attended a few meets.

The father leaps to his feet upon seeing Mabel, and she notes his quick but critical scan of her tennis shoes, visible from underneath the pant legs of her black suit. *I didn't expect to be here*, she wishes to inform him. But then, she supposes, none of them did.

She reintroduces herself and launches into what she's been instructed to say: she requests Angela and her father's consent to a joint interview with the Kitchewan PD, herself, and a lawyer for the school district, as well as their permission to include the McCleary family's abrasive lawyer, who is now rifling through her display case. Mabel selects her words deliberately. She balances intentional warmth with practiced professionalism, a combination that has served her well in her work life in this sleepy riverside hamlet populated with very much awake, ambitious families.

The father's polite, formal air quickly gives way to irritation. "Is anyone going to tell me what this is all about?" he demands of Mabel, his eyes seeming even larger as he speaks.

Mabel has been told, or prematurely reprimanded, rather, by the detectives not to "influence witness statements," as they are still "fact-finding." Mindful of this, she replies with forced cheer, "I understand your frustration, Mr.—Bobby—I mean, Mr. Singh—I have a penchant for formality." She gives him a small smile, hoping to lighten the mood. When he doesn't react, she continues, "We would also like to understand what happened, and we are hoping Angela can help clear that up for all of us." She smiles at Angela this time, also unreciprocated.

"I don't understand. Is Angie in trouble? Why are there so many lawyers? Do we need a lawyer?"

"Oh, you're not in trouble, Mr. Singh, nor is your daughter; nothing of that nature. You see, Angela here called 911 and possibly saved a boy's life. We just want to ask her some questions."

"It's fine, Dad," she hears Angela whisper to her father. "Let's get this over with. I want to go home."

The father turns to Angela, putting his hands on her shoulders, and speaks in another language in a low volume.

Angela nods and replies in English, loudly enough for Mabel to hear, "Yeah, really, it's fine. Just say yes, Dad."

"Fine. Madam Principal, my daughter tells me this is acceptable." He pauses and adds, "But I will insist that the officers read us our rights before we begin."

Mabel is confused by the request but bites her tongue. She says, "Thank you, Angela and Mr. Singh. I'm sure we can work that out with the detectives."

Mabel motions that Angela and her father should follow her into her office, but she sees Angela freeze up as her hand reaches toward the door handle. "Angela," she says gently, "are you okay?"

Angela looks up at Mabel, who is not a terribly tall woman, but at five foot six and with a broader frame, Mabel feels like she is towering over the girl, who must barely break five feet. Angela's eyes are wide and glisten with what appear to be unformed tears; she asks Mabel in a serious almost-whisper, "Principal Burrowes, I am not too sure about some stuff, like some details. I have an idea, but I don't know. If I don't know something for sure, should I say it?"

Mabel's glance shifts between the girl and her father, who is standing directly behind Angela. Both look at Mabel, waiting for her guidance. She pities them. She doesn't have a clear idea of Angela's role in what happened, but she senses a fragility, a vulnerability in the Singhs. She wishes she could embrace the girl and tell her it will be okay, but she's not sure that it will be. Maybe the Singhs should have a lawyer. She sighs and says, "Well, dear, you should answer what you know as best you can."

Angela nods at this non-response.

Her father says something in a different language again to Angela. Angela turns around and nods at him, too.

"Are you ready?" Mabel asks Angela softly, motioning toward the office door.

Angela swallows and says, "Principal Burrowes, I don't want to do anything that would mess up the investigation—for Henry."

Mabel thinks of the McCleary family's lawyer, smugly shadowing these interviews, and she blurts, "Don't worry about Henry. He's going to be just fine." Why she says that last part, especially given the boy is in the ER, she doesn't know. She then adds, "You should focus on what you're being asked in there, okay?"

Mabel feels guilty, unsure of what she is leading the girl into, and the three of them, principal, eyewitness, and parent, walk in.

EIGHT

There are a number of people in the office already. Were it another occasion, Babur might have lingered appreciatively on the tastefully furnished and meticulously maintained office, with its thoughtfully arranged bookshelf display and inviting warm lighting. (Interior decor is not Babur's passion nor within his budget, but attention to detail in most contexts garners his admiration.) But this afternoon is not that occasion.

The office occupants stand when Angela, Babur, and the principal enter. There are two paunchy middle-aged men in khakis and button-down shirts seated next to each other behind the principal's desk, one balding, with an intense gaze, the other with dark, wavy hair and a more impassive but observant expression. There is a third man, tall and lean, with salt-and-pepper hair and a sunburned forehead, by the bookshelf; and a younger, bookish-looking woman, in her early to mid-thirties, seated in a chair off to the side of the room. She holds a tablet and adjusts her black-rimmed glasses.

One of the men behind the desk, the one with the intense gaze, introduces himself. He is Detective Bridges of the Kitchewan Police Department. Babur nods concertedly as the detective speaks. He wants to look engaged and cooperative. He hopes Angie is doing the same.

Detective Bridges establishes himself as the meeting chair. He does a round of rapid-fire introductions. He notes his partner, Rhodes, sitting next to him, who gives the Singhs a head nod in acknowledgment (witty commentary about the detectives' combination of last names left unspoken); he waves in the direction of the tanned man, Tom Ghirardelli ("No relation to the chocolate company," he manages to squeeze in with a flash of a grin), lawyer for the McCleary family—*Why do the McClearys have a lawyer here?* Babur starts to wonder before shifting focus to keep pace with Bridges; he points to the glasses-wearing young woman to the side of the room, and introduces her as Marilena something, lawyer for the Kitchewan school district.

Babur has not forgotten his request to be Mirandized, but he feels self-conscious about interrupting Detective Bridges, so he stays silent, waiting to be informed of what crisis could have possibly intersected with his Angie.

He has pieced together that someone is hurt. *Why didn't Purnima and I insist on teaching the girl how to speak in Hindi properly?* he scolds himself. Angie could have explained the whole situation out loud, in the open, in front of the suspicious police officers, even, with absolute privacy.

Before entering the office, he had offered, in the elementary Hindi Angie understands, that perhaps they go home for now and come back when she is feeling better, clearer. She declined. He also asked her if she's in trouble, which she did not quite address, triggering what felt like a minor cardiovascular event in his thoracic cavity. And finally, as a last resort, a Hail Mary, as they say, unsure of how else to parent in this situation, Babur reminded Angie to answer the officers politely so they realize she, his daughter, is a good child, and not criminal riffraff, or any associate thereof, who merits their pursuit or close scrutiny.

After all, the entire raison d'être of Babur's fastidious planning, plotting, scheduling, timing, and diarizing, for which he comes under the occasional light ribbing from Angela and even his employees—not having many friends since the California-bound departure of Neha and Manan almost six years ago—is not just to avoid but to eviscerate from the realm of the remotely possible situations like this one: police, lawyers, the school principal, a closed-door meeting of indeterminate length, "just a few questions," none of which he can anticipate or answer himself, his own asked and unanswered, and Angie inexplicably in the middle.

"Angela, Mr. Singh, thank you for making the time for us today," begins Detective Bridges. "We appreciate it." He pauses to look at Angela and his lips flicker into an upturn, an unnatural-seeming attempt at warmth. He says, "I know sitting in a room with so many adults can be scary, but we thought, Angela, if we did this all together we could get to the bottom of what happened this afternoon and save everyone—including you and your dad—some valuable time." He waits for a reaction.

Babur nods. Angie stays still, her hands clasped on her lap.

"Very well," says Detective Bridges.

Rhodes interrupts him. "Are we waiting on the mother?"

Babur sees the principal open her mouth to speak but then close it. He feels his throat constrict. Even after all these years, this question still strikes him as an accusation. He instinctively places a light hand on Angela's forearm. She has goose bumps. He says, "Uh, no. We can proceed with the two of us, Detective."

Rhodes peers at Babur, with what Babur believes is curiosity, but he says nothing.

Bridges appears to find this exchange unremarkable, and says, looking down at his notepad, as if reading from a script, "All right, let's start from the top. Angela, can you tell us what happened this afternoon—everything you remember?"

Angela looks at Babur before speaking. He nods, relieved by the eye contact.

She takes a breath and in a measured but soft voice answers, "I was heading toward the football field to cut across it on my way home. I heard some shouting; maybe it was arguing. I'm not too sure." She pauses here and looks around. Most of the adults, Babur and the principal aside, are taking notes and look up when she pauses, but no one says anything. She continues, "I sort of jogged toward the football field, and I saw Henry on the field." She stops again, and when she restarts there is a tremor in her voice. "He was kneeling and bent over and had something sticking out of him, out of his stomach, the lower part. It was something red. It looked like a red-colored rod or stick—I guess it was a knife, a pocketknife, maybe. I mean, I think that's what the ambulance people said. He looked pretty hurt and was asking for help. I wasn't sure— I didn't—I didn't know what to do. I didn't even know what it was. He wanted me to pull the thing, the thing that was stuck, out of his stomach, I think. I called 911."

Babur cannot hold on to a coherent thought. There are too many fragments, unfinished strands, running like an errant cassette-tape thread. He's getting mixed up. *Henry* . . . He doesn't remember a Henry. *And why are my daughter and I here?* He hopes this is routine. *Because surely they aren't accusing her, my Angie, of harming this boy. Surely this is not a trap like in that dated crime serial with the affable detective who stalks murderers until they confess. But wait*, he scolds himself. *Murder. No one said anything about murder. Besides, anyone can see that Angie would never—she could never—hurt anyone! Angie is a good girl. She called 911. She saved this boy—unless, that is, he's passed* . . .

He looks at Angie. She sits frozen, as if she's a statue, fingers interlaced on her lap. If he didn't know better, he would think she was praying, but neither Singh has much of a relationship with any higher being. He pats her lightly on the shoulder to convey she's doing well. *Is she doing well?* He tries to gauge the detectives' reactions. They scribble on their notepads and speak to each other too softly for Babur to make out what they're saying. He strains his eyes and tries to read their lips, but neither Bridges nor Rhodes moves his mouth much.

Bridges finally looks up at Angie and says, "That was brave of you, Angela. Henry is lucky you arrived when you did."

Angela sits up in her seat. "So he's okay? Henry's okay?"

Babur holds his breath. *Let him be okay.* He doesn't care about this Henry but *let him be okay.*

Bridges wrinkles his nose quickly before he replies, "We hope so. He's in the hospital is all we know for now."

Babur releases his breath and gives Angie's shoulder another light pat. It's not quite an answer, but it doesn't sound like murder to him.

The detective's partner whispers something into Bridges's ear, and Bridges furrows his brow for a moment and says, "Angela, why were you cutting through the football field?"

"I was swimming. In the gym pool."

"Is this part of a formal program or class of some sort?" Bridges asks.

Angela shakes her head. "I was just doing laps on my own."

"And how did you get in—to the pool?" the tanned lawyer for the McClearys interjects.

Bridges glares at the lawyer.

But Angela has already turned to face him. She replies, "It's unlocked, so sometimes I practice there"—she pauses—"on my own."

The lawyer continues, apparently oblivious to Bridges's nonverbal warning. He turns to the principal and asks, "Is there a lifeguard or someone on duty monitoring the school swimming pool, Principal Burrowes?"

Babur feels he is best positioned to clarify this point. He addresses the room. "Angela is a very good swimmer, one of the best in the high school. Please be assured that my daughter does not require a lifeguard."

Bridges cuts in, "Thank you, Mr. Singh. Mr. Ghirardelli, we'll ask the questions for now. If there's time at the end, we can see about your questions and your, uh, input." Rhodes motions with his head at Bridges, and Bridges adds, "But you can go ahead and clarify, Principal Burrowes. Is there a lifeguard or chaperone?"

The principal cuts her pupils from one side of the room to the other and says, "Well, we keep the school grounds unlocked for summer school and that includes the, uh, gymnasium."

Babur sees the McCleary lawyer's mouth open, but Bridges, apparently satisfied with the principal's incomplete response, says before anyone can speak, "Noted. Let's get back to where we left off." He asks, "Angela, you heard shouting—who was shouting? What were they saying?"

Angie looks down at her hands and then over at Babur. "I—I'm not sure. I don't remember if they were saying anything. I think they were just yelling."

"They were . . . just yelling . . ." Bridges repeats back as he notates.

"Well, that sounds a bit barbaric," the McCleary lawyer comments from the side of the room. This time, in response to Bridges's look, he mouths "Sorry" and closes his mouth.

Bridges asks, "Was it more than one person? A boy's voice, a girl's, both?"

"I'm not sure." Angie is looking down and wringing her hands now. Babur wishes he could answer for her.

"Not sure," Bridges repeats slowly. "When you got on the field, you only saw Henry McCleary?"

Angela nods, and then clarifies, "I saw a couple of people in the distance, but I just—I—I panicked when I saw Henry. He was stabbed. I've never seen anyone stabbed before. There was blood. It wasn't gushing or anything, but it was around the—the thing, the knife."

"The people in the distance, how many of them were there?" Bridges asks.

"Um, I don't know." She pauses to think. "Two, maybe? I think. I—I guess Chris Collins was one of them."

Babur's ears perk at the mention of this second new, unfamiliar name.

"You guess?" Bridges raises his eyebrows.

"I, um, I can't remember that part too well. But he was there on the field, where Henry and I were before the, um, ambulance—" Angie looks agitated and says quickly, "I don't know if this is what I was supposed to do, but he was in a lot of pain and so I moved him. I moved Henry onto his back. I put a duffel bag under him for comfort, like a pillow. I thought he should be lying down. And before he was hunched over and it seemed worse. I was trying to help. Did I . . ." A handful of fat teardrops slide down Angie's cheeks.

Now this is too much, thinks Babur. He gives Angie's forearm a squeeze and speaks up. "Detectives, surely you can tell she didn't do anything wrong. She was only trying to help." He turns to look over at the principal and the bookish woman who he'd largely forgotten about, seeking allies in reasonableness and compassion. Both women return his look with short half smiles but remain silent.

The detectives look at each other, and Bridges sighs and says with slight hesitation, "You called for help, Angela. That's the important thing. We don't have any more information on Henry." He pauses and gives Babur a nod. "Let's take a step back. You saw Henry McCleary. Do you know this person?"

Angie nods. "Yeah. We're on swim team together. The boys' and the girls' teams, we have different seasons. Henry's going to be a senior. I'm going to be a sophomore like his sister. I'm friends with her."

Babur is trying to recall if he's ever met this Henry. He knows Samantha and her parents. But he can't remember if he's met the brother.

"And you and Henry, are you friends?"

Babur detects a flush in Angie's cheeks, or maybe he's imagining things. She looks down at her hands again and says, "Kind of. We're friendly, but it's mostly through Sam, his sister."

Babur nods. This makes sense to him.

Bridges nods, too. He is still looking down at his notepad, writing, when he follows up, "And he asked you for help when you saw him?"

"Yeah, I mean, he was in pain. He was calling out for help, and I didn't—I didn't know exactly what to do, but—"

The detective cuts her off as her speaking becomes more rapid, more frantic. "And what was Christopher Collins doing when you called 911?"

"I think he was running. I'm not too sure."

"He was running?"

"He just showed up and was out of breath like he'd been running. He was really upset. I—I don't know."

"So you didn't see him running?"

Angie squints and pinches her eyebrows together. "I did, I think. I just— I wasn't paying attention to him."

"And he was . . . 'really upset'?"

She nods.

"Did he tell you what happened? Why he was upset?"

"No. I don't— I'm not sure why, but maybe—maybe he was mad at someone? Or," Angie adds, "about Henry being hurt."

The McCleary lawyer clears his throat and raises a pointer finger in the air to get the attention of the room. He looks at the detectives, indicating he'd like to chime in. Bridges looks annoyed, but Babur catches Rhodes flicking his partner a look, and then Bridges raises his eyebrows at the lawyer as if to say he can proceed.

"Angela," the lawyer says in a voice adults reserve for young children, "did Christopher hurt Henry, you think?"

Angie looks perplexed and looks at Babur, whose eyebrows are arched, waiting for her reply. "Like, stab him? I don't think so, but, um, I don't—I don't know. They're friends . . ."

"All right," Bridges reasserts himself. "If you don't know, you don't know. But, Angela, did you see or get any indication about who might have hurt Henry McCleary?"

She shakes her head quickly, and the detectives look over at the McCleary lawyer, who puts up an open palm in their direction, indicating he will return to observing.

"Did Christopher tell you anything about what happened?" Bridges asks again.

"No."

"Do you have any idea why he was running? Why he was yelling?" As Bridges asks her, both detectives lean in toward the desk and look at Angela carefully, as if they are straining to hear her in the otherwise quiet room.

Babur mirrors them and sucks in his breath.

"I don't know. It looked like—I think—he was chasing someone."

"Did you see who?"

"Not really. It was someone fast, though, I guess."

"Fast?"

"Well, faster than Chris. Because he couldn't catch them."

The detectives discuss something among themselves at an inaudible volume. They appear to disagree on something. Angie turns to Babur. She looks flushed. He focuses on appearing unperturbed and supportive, but he is getting a bit irritated by all these questions and the length of this interview. It is as clear as anything to him that Angie just happened to be walking by and has nothing to do with this at all. He will speak up if there isn't a logical conclusion soon.

Detective Rhodes breaks from his huddle with his partner and asks, "Angela, do you know Chiara Thompkins?"

She nods. "She's in school with me."

"Did you see her today?"

She shakes her head and then corrects herself. "Yeah, I did. I saw her when I walked over to the pool earlier in the day. On the bleachers."

"Okay, so she was near the football field this morning," confirms Rhodes. "Did you talk to her?"

Angie shakes her head. "I don't know her that well."

"Was she there later on, when you were walking back from the pool?"

Babur notices that Angie's eyes look stricken. He shifts in his seat, trying to catch Angie's gaze.

"Well, um," Angie says slowly, looking at the detectives, "I didn't see her exactly, but I guess"—a pause—"I guess she could've been on the football field."

"All right, so she was on the field, you think?" Rhodes is leaning all the way forward in his seat.

"I just— I mean—she was on the bleachers before, so." She pauses and repeats slowly, "Maybe she was with Chris." She then blurts, "Like, maybe he was running after her?"

The detectives look at each other and nod their heads in unison. Babur can swear he sees a flicker of a smile on Bridges's mouth.

Rhodes, more impassive, continues, "Angela, did Christopher say anything about Chiara?"

"I don't think so. But I'm—I'm not sure. He was saying a lot of stuff. I couldn't really— I don't remember." She looks confused, like she is getting upset again.

"But you saw Christopher chasing Chiara?"

"I—um—I—" Her voice wobbles. "Is—is Chiara in trouble?"

"Angela, we believe that Chiara Thompkins may have hurt Henry McCleary. Do you know anything about that?"

Angie's eyes widen and turn glassy.

Babur holds his breath. He desperately wants to reach out and squeeze her hands, to envelop her in an embrace, to remind her not to be scared, to tell these detectives whatever they want to know, to not overthink, because this is not—thank the heavens—their misfortune over which to agonize. But he cannot do that or say that, not here. Instead he presses his lips together and clenches his hands.

Rhodes speaks slowly, carefully, when he asks, "Angela, did you see Chiara Thompkins hurt Henry McCleary?"

Angie shakes her head, and Babur sees her bottom lip trembling.

The detectives seem oblivious to this. "Okay," Rhodes says. "And do you have any idea what Henry and Christopher were doing on the football field?"

She shakes her head again, looking at the desk and not making eye contact.

The detectives begin whispering to each other, and Babur can see color draining from Angie's face. He's ready to interrupt now, to ask how much longer and if they can wrap up, when Bridges looks at Babur and Angie and says, "Angela, Mr. Singh, thank you. I think we have what we need for now."

Babur can hear himself exhale. Finally. He is ready to take Angie and bolt out of there. Bridges starts explaining they may need to call them back to ask more questions and confirms how to reach Babur. The school-district lawyer, silent up until now, asks if Babur and Angie wouldn't mind answering some more questions for the school, should they arise, in the coming days. *Yes, we would mind*, thinks Babur, but he nods nonetheless.

The McClearys' lawyer says, "Mr. Singh, Angela, it's been a long afternoon, I know. But while we're all together"—he pauses, but not for long—"Angela, how well do you know Chiara Thompkins?"

Angie sniffles and replies, "Um, she goes to school with me." Her eyebrows are pinched together in concern, or maybe confusion.

"So how would you describe your relationship?" continues the lawyer.

"Relationship?" Babur answers before Angie can say anything. "She said there is no relationship. And the detectives said they have what they need."

"Mr. Singh—" the lawyer starts.

Babur feels bold and cuts him off. "It has been a long afternoon."

He stands and motions for Angie to follow.

It is time—well past time, in fact—for Babur and Angie to return home.

NINE

As Angela and her dad race out of Kitchewan High, she tries to swallow away a stubborn lump that's formed in her throat.

The interview by the police had been brutal.

She couldn't think. There were too many people in the room. Too many unsynchronized breaths, too much scribbling on notepads, too many throats being cleared in anticipation. Each sound had echoed in Angie's ear canal, derailing her train of thought. There were also the stares. Everyone in the room had looked at her with wide eyes, with concern, or pity, or maybe fear on their faces. Like she was a live wire that could spark at any time and set the whole place on fire, or worse, a caged wild animal, erratic and unpredictable. She could feel the weight of their looks pressing on her, constricting her.

She had tried to sit perfectly still, upright, her hands folded together in her lap, and to stare straight ahead at Principal Burrowes's oversized desk, at the silver engraved nameplate that read PRINCIPAL MABEL ANNE BURROWES in a clinical, official font. She had stared at each curve, each bend in those carefully crafted letters, figuring if she did, she'd look and feel less nervous. She'd discovered this trick when she was younger, when she used to cry at school about her mom's abrupt departure. She'd learned that if every time she could feel her throat getting heavy and her eyes welling, she focused on a spot, like the blackboard, or the back of one of her classmates' heads, or a shiny spot on the floor, she could regain control. All she had to do was stare. Like the spot was all that mattered.

She does a version of this even now, at swim meets. To stay composed right before a race, when her stomach is in knots, she concentrates her entire attention on a single spot a few yards ahead of her, in the water, in her lane. She studies it, the ripples on the surface and reflections of light. She stares and stares, imagining herself there, moving, stroking, racing, breathing. Blazing through that exact spot.

Only it didn't work in the principal's office. Someone coughed, and her concentration was broken.

They approach her dad's car in the parking lot. Her dad hasn't said anything since they walked out of Principal Burrowes's office. It's unlike him to stay quiet for this long. Maybe, Angie thinks, her father understands how she feels. Maybe he can sense she doesn't want to talk. That she can't talk, not right now. Not when her thoughts, like the contents of her stomach, feel jumbled and inverted; not when the idea of straightening them out makes her head hurt, pound, in fact.

But then he speaks, and this illusion shatters. Before he puts the key in the ignition, he turns to her, and with a surge of panic mixed with overbearing love and nerves, he sputters, "Angie," putting a hand on her shoulder, "beta, tell me everything. What—" He pauses, his eyes wide and staring into hers, as if searching for words there. "What happened?" Another pause. "I need to know everything." He squeezes her shoulder, and she sees him swallow. "Everything."

The lump in her throat is an anvil now. She wants to throw it, smash it, explode it. Yet there is something about her father and the way he's looking at her, with his inquisitive brown eyes, filled with gentle concern and also something that borders on wonder, that makes her feel weak. Like she might drop it instead. *I will not cry*, she tells herself, looking away, blinking fast. *I will not cry.*

Angie deflects, taking what she knows is a cheap and mean shot. She looks out the window at the parking lot and raises her voice: "I don't want to talk about it, Dad. I don't. Not with you, definitely not with *you*." She swats away his hand from her shoulder and observes his recoil in her peripheral vision. "You won't get it. You never get it." She winces as she hears herself, knowing her words will pierce him. That she's treading dangerously close to telling him he's not enough, violating their unspoken pact. She feels bad, but she can't handle him right now. She'll apologize later, she tells herself.

Angie's words sting her dad enough to win temporary silence. He turns away from her and starts the car. She doesn't look, but she can hear hurt in his silence and feel it in his staccato movements.

She swallows. The anvil is still there.

She wishes someone would tell her what's going on, what's actually happening. But no one will. The police and all those other adults won't tell her anything. And she can't call Henry. Maybe she can speak to Sam, but her brother's in the hospital, so maybe it's too soon. Maybe, she turns over the thought in her mind with a frown on her face, Chris Collins might know something. Although, she thinks, her nose wrinkling, it's Chris.

When the detectives first asked Angie about Chris, she'd been thrown off. She'd forgotten she mentioned him, and in fact, she'd forgotten he was there. She'd looked down at her hands and cradled her sunken stomach, sharing what she knew, which wasn't much. Her voice had come out thick, still clogged with unfallen tears, and she'd focused on sounding neutral. On trying not to be obvious that she didn't want to talk about Chris. That they weren't friends. That she didn't like him. Doesn't like him. Nothing about him: his too-small, square-shaped head on his lanky body, his pointy elflike ears, and his mouth curled in a broad smirk filling up his small face.

Angie mostly knew Chris from the McClearys. She never understood

how Chris and Henry were friends, but they were. Chris would sometimes be in the front seat of Henry's car when Henry and Sam gave
Angie a lift home. He'd talk the whole ride, providing a running commentary on their "lame" teachers, and "lame" classmates, and "lame"
school. She wasn't sure if that's what he actually thought or if it was
his version of a comedy routine. While neither McCleary would join
in exactly, they'd chuckle and roll their eyes, encouraging him. Angie
never laughed.

Also, for a brief period last school year, Chris had started calling
Angie "Pocahontas." It happened only a few times before Henry told
him to cut it out. That it was rude. That it was racist. Which was when
Chris had held up his hands in mock surrender, turned back to look
at Angie from the front seat of Henry's Acura, and said, with a wink
that made her shudder, "It's a compliment. Pocahontas is hot. But fine,
whatever."

More recently, Angie and Chris were in summer-school geometry together. Angie took it to ease up her class load during swimming
season, a happy, unofficial arrangement between the athletics department and school faculty. Chris had failed sophomore math and needed
it to graduate. Rather than try to pass the class so his time in school
over summer vacation wasn't a waste, Chris seemed more interested
in making sure everyone knew he was too cool to be there. He rarely
showed up on time, and when he did, he spent most of class snickering
into his phone, ignoring the sighs of the teacher.

She didn't say any of this to the detectives, though. To them, she
only said, in as even keeled a tone as she could manage, that Chris
looked upset.

She didn't share the obscenities Chris unleashed in surprise when
he saw Henry lying on the ground, or his quick transition into cursing
out "that bitch."

She wasn't trying to protect Chris. It's just that all those details, the
answers to those questions, they weren't important. Henry had been

hurt and Chris wasn't around. So it didn't matter when he showed up, what he said when he showed up, or even that he showed up.

She'd only said that maybe Chris was chasing Chiara Thompkins after the detectives had asked about her. Chiara had been on the bleachers in the morning. Angie had *seen* her; she'd even thought about her. She confirmed the former for the detectives, and when she tried to replay in her mind Chris Collins in the distance running around, she saw him running, but the figure, the person, he was running after was a girl.

She second-guessed herself as soon as she spoke. But the detectives latched on to it.

She wished she hadn't said anything.

As she thinks it over now, Angie can't remember clearly. She saw Chiara on the bleachers before; she's sure of that. But she can't remember if she saw her again. It's blurry. Everything is unclear and happened so fast, and she was focused on Henry. She tries to remember if Chris mentioned Chiara by name. She racks her brain. She doesn't know. She isn't sure. But she's sure from how the detectives took it that she'd said too much.

She recalls with a cringe how after she spoke, the detectives had leaned forward in their seats from across the desk. There was something predatory, hungry about them.

The Singhs' car slows before the stop sign in front of the turnoff from Indian Meadow Road to Lakeview Terrace. Each curve, each bend, each pock in the road is familiar, but with the panic of the interview replaying in her head, uncomforting.

Her dad clears his throat. "Ang," he says in a soft voice, glancing over at her, "spaghetti tonight." And then, "Is that still all right?"

Angie lets out a breath she hadn't realized she'd been holding in. Annoyed that he's interrupted her. Annoyed by his gentleness, a contrast to her earlier, sharper tone. All she can manage is a terse "I'm not hungry."

"You should eat something." Her dad looks at her again and then at the road. "I can," he stammers, "I can make something else."

They pull up to their driveway. She thinks of her father abandoning his beloved script and frantically sifting through one-pot-meal recipes they have the ingredients for at home. A tragicomedy.

Angie scoffs. Against her judgment and before she can self-edit, she says, "No, Dad. Leave it. Someone may have died today, but let's make sure we have pasta on a Wednesday."

She flicks the "new car" air freshener hanging from the rearview mirror. She doesn't dare look at him, afraid something will break apart in her if she does.

She reaches around to the back seat, as she normally does, for her duffel bag. But it's not there. It's probably still on the football field. Or with the police. She turns back around and looks at her dad. His eyes are shiny and pupils dilated.

She can't.

She leans forward with her elbows on her knees, hands covering her face. As if the anvil dropped or a dam wall ruptured, her eyes flood with the tears she's been pushing back for hours. *No more*, she thinks, and for the first time all day, she lets go, and she cries.

TEN

Sam answers Angela's call on the first ring.

"Hey, Ang," she says in a subdued voice as if she's been expecting her, as if this weren't the first time they were speaking in weeks and weeks. Their last real conversation, in person, not over text or Instagram, had been days after the end of their freshman year, back in June.

Angie feels off balance. She's sitting in her room on the edge of her seashell-printed bedspread. "Hi," she says, pressing her feet more firmly into the thick beige carpeting of her bedroom floor.

"What's up?" Sam asks.

It's strange hearing Sam's voice. Unsettling. Angie doesn't have too many friends apart from Sam, and of them, they're all better friends with Sam than her, interacting with Angie mostly in groups—groups that include Sam or involve the swim team. Angie credits her lack of popularity to being "quiet," keeping most of the vibrant commentary that runs through her head to herself, and not giggling as much or as readily as other girls her age. With Sam, however, it's always been different. Angie says more out loud. She still doesn't giggle, but she laughs. This phone call, in just a few seconds, brings up a feeling Angie's been trying to ignore, to bury under the routine of her intense swimming schedule, shifts at Willoughby's, and mealtimes with her dad, who's taken to reading her English books alongside her and alternates between wanting to discuss literary themes and her future eligibility for Olympics trials. But here it is now, coming up for air, quick and sharp like a sucker punch.

Angie blinks hard and fast and admits it to herself: she misses Sam.

"Ang, you there?" Sam says after what must have been an unexpected silence.

"Yeah, sorry. Hi, Sam," Angela replies quickly, looking down at her feet. "I was calling to"—she hesitates for a split second before completing her thought—"ask about Henry. Is he okay?"

Ever since their "misunderstanding," Angie is self-conscious about mentioning Henry in front of Sam. She's scared to show too much interest—or any, for that matter—in where he is, in what he says, in his sea-blue eyes and his confident but not overconfident smile. The accusations Sam hurled at her when she confronted Angie, like many things said in anger, still burn Angie's ears, and can't be unseared from her memory.

Sam doesn't answer right away. Angie hears muffled conversation in the background and Sam says into the phone, but apparently not to her, "It's Angela. Yeah, I know . . . Okay, fine." Sam then says, "One sec. Henry's sleeping, I'm going out into the hallway."

Angie nods and looks out her bedroom window, trying to slow down her rapidly beating heart. Her eyes adjust to the early-evening summer brightness, and she stares at the tidy, flowerless green patch that is the Singhs' front lawn. It was months ago, but her cheeks still flush at the memory of when Sam confronted her.

Angela had wanted to defend herself. She wanted to tell Sam she was blowing things out of proportion and that it was one kiss, or maybe one instance of multiple kisses—nothing monumental; kids they went to school with, Henry likely included, Angie thought glumly, were having sex, after all. She had wanted to contradict Sam's rapid-fire and unexpected assault: that Angie was using her—*she wasn't, Sam is her best friend*—that she had planned this all along—*she hadn't; she didn't even ask for a ride home; Henry had offered, and he'd given her rides home without Sam before*—*not just her and him and not loads of times but maybe two or three times*—*but still; how could she know that he would make her laugh like he did and that he would lean in when he did and that she would lean in back*—and that it figured Angie would do this because she's always been obsessed with Sam's family—*Angie liked Sam and her family. She liked them a lot, in fact. But she wasn't obsessed. Sam couldn't honestly believe that. She didn't believe that.*

As it happened, however, as Sam lobbed accusations at her, Angie didn't say much. She couldn't. She felt frozen. Too stunned and hurt and also embarrassed, turning Sam's words over in her mind, wondering if there wasn't any truth to what she said: their friendship, hers and Sam's, *was* real—*is* real. She isn't using her, but at the same time, Angie was aware of her growing fascination with Henry McCleary; how her cheeks would warm and turn pink when Henry would look directly at her, or how when their eyes locked and they shared a smile, through the rearview mirror of his car or at their "boys plus one girl" swim practices (as everyone called them) when Coach Ford would deliver inspirational talks on "visualizing victory," her stomach would flutter. She wouldn't call it a crush, a word she associated with flighty and superficial airheads, girls who planned their mascaraed, glossy-lipped existences around boys; that wasn't her. She did look forward to seeing Sam a little more when she knew Henry would be around, but surely that didn't count as using her.

"All right, I'm in the hall now," Sam says into the phone.

Angela sits straighter and turns away from the window. "How's Henry?" she asks again. She sucks in her breath as she waits for a reply.

"He's okay. We think he's going to be okay, I mean. He'll be in the hospital for another day or two, but the doctors don't think there's permanent damage." Sam speaks clinically, matter-of-factly.

Angie exhales deeply. "That's amazing, Sam. That's so great."

Sam doesn't return Angie's warmth. "Yeah—um—the whole thing

is bizarre. My brother was stabbed today by some girl he barely knows."

"They know who did it?"

"Well, yeah. You were there, right? Chiara attacked Henry and then Chris chased her off."

Angela processes Sam's statements, and says, "Well, I came a few minutes—or maybe seconds—after it happened. I didn't see anything exactly."

"But you saw Chiara running away though, right?"

"Yeah, I did, I guess. But I didn't"—she pauses—"know what was happening." Angela feels self-conscious as she speaks, very aware of the still-present rift in their friendship. She adds, only to immediately regret it after speaking, "I was pretty focused on making sure Henry was okay."

Sam is quiet for a second and then says quickly, with an edge in her voice, "What were you doing there anyway? Were you meeting my brother somewhere?"

"I was practicing, Sam—doing laps in the school pool. Like I've been doing almost every day all summer."

They're both silent. Angie sits back on her bed, leaning her head against her lilac-colored bedroom wall. Talking to Sam feels tiresome. It's making her head feel heavy.

"I thought you were joining a club this summer," Sam says at last.

"I was going to, but . . ." She doesn't feel like explaining what she's been explaining to herself and what Sam very well already knows, why she couldn't join a club. "Coach Ford sent me workouts and stuff, and he even met me a couple times before he went up to Maine."

"Oh, yeah, that's cool," Sam says with unnatural brightness, but like she doesn't believe it, like she's trying to make Angie not feel bad.

Angie feels a surge of self-consciousness. Sam must pity her. She needs to change the subject, ask about Jacksonville maybe, to let Sam know she isn't upset about her going there without her, that she never was, and even if Sam thought she was, she definitely isn't anymore. "How was Florida?"

"It was fine." Angie can hear Sam shrugging into the phone. "I mean it was hard. Like, a lot of practice, you know." A pause. "So, what've you been up to? Have you seen Trish or Lainie or Diana?" she asks, referring to some of their mutual friends.

Not much, Angie thinks glumly. She doesn't want to tell Sam that she hasn't seen or heard from those girls since the end of the school year. She feels her cheeks getting warm as she hesitates to describe her uneventful summer.

"Ang," Sam says, "hang on a sec. My mom wants to say hi."

Mrs. McCleary is on the phone before Angie can respond.

"Angela, dear, how are you? I wanted to thank you," she begins, with a warmth and familiarity that makes Angie's stomach flutter.

Angie scrambles to sit up again. "Hi, Mrs. McCleary," she replies, upright on the edge of her bed. "I heard Henry's okay?"

"Yes, yes, he will be, we think. Thank goodness."

"That's terrific."

"Yes, it is. He got stitches earlier today and is sleeping right now." She pauses. "Fred and I can't tell you how grateful we are to you. We are so lucky you were there. Henry's so lucky. Thank you, Angela."

Angie blushes, and she's reminded of crayons in elementary school. Sam's mom had been Angie's stand-in whenever she drew a princess or fairy or any maternal figure: "yellow sunshine" with streaks of "goldenrod" for her hair, "apricot" for her skin, "salmon" for her lips and cheeks, and a piercing "cerulean" for her eyes. She hadn't consciously thought about drawing Mrs. McCleary, at least she didn't think she had. It was just that the image of her felt interchangeable with everything good.

"I'm glad Henry's okay," she says.

"We all are, dear." Mrs. McCleary pauses and then says, "Angela, are *you* okay?"

Angie feels like her heart might leap out of her chest at the sound of concern for her in Mrs. McCleary's voice.

Before she can answer, Mrs. McCleary continues, "Tom told us you were just walking by when it happened. You must be pretty shaken up—seeing all that blood and Henry with a knife in his abdomen . . . I can't imagine."

Angela swallows, feeling guilty for worrying Mrs. McCleary. She imagines her, glamorous even in a sterile hospital hallway, her eyes shining.

Angie looks around her room, searching for the right response. But everything she owns—from her childish white desk to the assortment of knickknacks on its hutch: an elephant-shaped piggy bank, a dolphin-shaped beanbag that she got for being the fastest freshman swimmer, a discolored teddy bear from her childhood that she should probably throw away, and a snow globe with a sea turtle inside that she got at the Monterey Bay Aquarium when she and her dad went to visit two of his friends, Neha Aunty and Manan Uncle, who once lived in Kitchewan but moved out west—all seems so silly, so ordinary. She feels silly and ordinary.

She finally says, "I'm—I'm okay."

"Did you see the girl who attacked Henry, Angela? The—the African American girl?"

Angie winces. She doesn't want to disappoint Mrs. McCleary, but she isn't sure what to say. She bites her bottom lip, though, and settles on "I didn't see her—well, I didn't see her do it. But I think she was running away when I got there."

"Sam says you know this girl?"

"Um, kind of. We all go to school together, and I was teaching her how to swim—so she could pass gym. A while back. I don't know her exactly," she adds quickly. "We're not friends."

"I see." The sound of her voice, even when she doesn't say much, is soothing.

There's silence.

Then Mrs. McCleary says slowly, "If you see her, the girl—the one who hurt Henry—I know you know this, Angela, but please make sure you tell someone."

Angie nods solemnly into the phone. *So they haven't found Chiara.*

"They are still looking for her—" Mrs. McCleary pauses, and Angie holds her breath. "It seems—well, it seems like she's a bit of trouble. She stabbed Henry and on top of that, she has some other issues, they think. They think—the police think—the girl was never supposed to have been a student at Kitchewan High."

Angie frowns and her eyebrows pinch together. "What do you mean?"

"Well, I shouldn't say too much, but then again, you girls aren't young children anymore. Kitchewan's a nice town, Angela, and people sometimes try to take advantage of the town—our things, the schools, the community facilities. They lie and they trespass and then . . ."

"And then?" Angie isn't following her train of thought.

"And then things like this happen." She sighs. "It's a bit complicated, and the police are still figuring it all out. I should get back to Henry. Thank you for calling, Angela."

"Mrs. McCleary?"

"Yes, dear?"

"Can I come by to visit tomorrow? At the hospital, I mean?"

"Oh, of course you can. Please do. Henry would love that, and we haven't seen you in a while, so that'll be nice for everyone."

They hang up and Angie places her phone on her bedside table. She lies on her back and looks up at the ceiling. She can hear a few knocks and scuffles from downstairs and tries to block them out. She cranes her neck to the side and studies the sky through her window. It's still light out, no sign of sunset yet, the sky a cloudless "cornflower." It's funny how speaking with Mrs. McCleary put crayon colors in her head.

She concentrates on the weight of her body against the bed and closes her eyes. She can still sense light through her closed eyelids, and she breathes slowly and deliberately, pretending she's a statue, or a corpse, even. Whispers of the phone conversation swirl in her head and grow fainter. The light seeping through her closed lids grows dimmer, then nothing. Only darkness and her breaths.

Like this, Angela wills herself asleep well before it's nighttime and before her father comes upstairs and she needs to explain herself or anything else.

ELEVEN

Whoosh. He's done it. With the click of a mouse, seated before his desktop monitor in his modest home office, Babur Singh has done it. In a matter of minutes, he sent the message he hadn't been ready to formulate, much less send, for the past eight-plus years. And in an email no less. Unproofread. Abruptly typed. Sent with the care with which a child tosses a paper airplane. He's thrown it out there as if he's reckless or bohemian, or, at minimum, someone who improvises.

Thanks to the harrowing events of the day and his resulting disorientation, that's exactly how Babur feels this evening. Devil-may-care. Act first, think later. Maybe this is who he is now, who he has been all along.

But then his sports watch beeps, and he gasps. His heart starts to pound like a battering ram. He can't stop breathing in short, shallow spurts. Sweat beads form on his forehead.

What has he done?

He rapid-fire presses the back arrow on his internet browser. Click, click, click, click, click, click. But it goes back as far as his inbox and then stops. He clicks again and again and it seems stuck. The cursor icon has turned into a wheel. Is it broken? It must be broken. He then double-clicks "sent mail." It's there. Subject line, "Re: Hello," recipient, purnima1234@yahoo.com. His pithy and punchy email to Purnima that he felt bold enough to catapult into cyberspace mere seconds earlier is staring him in the face. It's sent. He wonders if that's the same thing as delivered, if it can be retrieved for unsending. Surely there must be an undo button. His eyes dart wildly, looking for an undo button. He fans his forehead with one hand. *Why is it so hot in here? What have I done?* And, oh, God, the pasta!

The alarm on his watch is still beeping. He needs to get back to the stove. He hurriedly locks the computer back to its screen saver, his email inbox still open, and races, almost tripping over the carpet, to the kitchen.

Angie had gone straight upstairs to her room when they arrived home from the high school. She had beelined there, tears still streaming down her face and an open palm and arm extended toward her father as if to say "don't."

Babur didn't.

He had let her go, perplexed and wounded, and had begun puttering downstairs in the kitchen, starting on dinner, not knowing what else to do. Officially, he was making spaghetti, but unofficially, Babur had been longing for consolation in routine and for something to dampen the stinging in his ears from Angie's earlier outburst in the car. Her accusation that he didn't understand sounded to Babur like something Purnima would say. It was one of her stock laments, along with "It all feels like too much" and "I can't take it anymore." *Take what, exactly?* He'd wanted to understand, finding it difficult to empathize with a woman so fixated on being miserable, on passing entire days like a zombie, as if being present, caring, paying attention to her family was too onerous. A woman ever ready to point out problems and wallow in self-pity and little green and white capsules, but who could not, even when there was a child involved, accept responsibility for her own happiness, much less for his and Angie's. He tried to make sense of how Angie had started to echo a mother she barely knew.

She had begun to look like Purnima, and not just when his eyes and mind were playing tricks on him. He'd been ignoring it, or trying to, but there was no mistaking it. The same sharp, almost black eyes and the flicker in her pupils when in distress; the same slope of her nose and its pinpoint tip, and the way it looked even more pointed in disdain; the same curve of her mouth in a slight frown when she was concentrating; and the same way in which her entire face, entire body, in fact, would bunch up and quake with helpless emotion when she cried. Just like her mother.

In the kitchen, Babur had deliberately exaggerated the sounds of his movements: clangs as he retrieved a pot for boiling water and a colander for the spaghetti, a shuffle as he opened the cabinet door and took out the pasta and jar of store-brand marinara sauce, a gush from the kitchen sink as he turned on the tap more energetically than required, to fill the pot with water, and a clatter as he placed the pot on the burner to boil. He'd used the din hopefully, to beckon to Angie to come downstairs, please. But she didn't, leaving Babur with nothing to do but continue to half-heartedly make Wednesday-night dinner.

When he'd measured out the spaghetti and removed prerolled grocery-store turkey meatballs and fresh basil from the fridge, his secrets for enhancing the otherwise bland but economical, ready-made pasta sauce, he asked himself if he'd failed somehow. How else could he explain the creeping presence of Purnima in his beloved Angie? As he washed and diced the basil, he wondered if perhaps his focus on Move and materially providing for Angela had come at the detriment of being there for her emotionally. Which reminded him: he needed to call one of the "boys," the grown men in his small fleet of drivers, to cover for him on his scheduled trips for that evening. Even if Angie stayed holed up in her room all night, Babur didn't want to leave her home alone this evening.

Therefore, once the water in the pot had bubbled to a boil and Babur had added the spaghetti noodles, turning the heat on low and setting the timer on his sports watch for six and a half minutes, the perfect al dente, he'd gone to his home office. He intended to take care of business, by which he meant Move business, and nothing to do with Purnima.

But technology and impulse had other plans.

He'd unlocked the computer's screen saver, the monitor opening straight to his email inbox, and had scrolled through the left-hand sidebar of the various email folders and subfolders he'd created. He'd searched for MOVE—AUGUST 2018, but by fluke or fate, his pointer hovered over and seemed to get stuck on the blandly labeled folder CORRESPONDENCE. Babur's heartbeat had hopscotched. He'd paused and taken a second to listen for sounds of Angie approaching. Nothing. So against his better judgment, or any judgment, for that matter, he double-clicked.

Correspondence. Aka his Purnima folder, the nondescript label deliberate to discourage snoopers, even though Angie was the only other person who had access to this computer, and she barely used it, preferring her phone or laptop instead.

From there, rather than arrange for substitute drivers, Babur found himself drafting and sending the feckless and reckless email over which he is currently hyperventilating as he stirs sauce into overcooked spaghetti.

Babur can't explain to himself, let alone to anyone else, why he has kept the existence of his correspondence with Purnima a secret from Angie. He reasons that it's not that he's concealing the exchanges so much as he is not mentioning them to his daughter.

The emails with Purnima started about five years ago, when Angie was ten, and since, Babur has dutifully filed each inbound and outbound message in CORRESPONDENCE. Although if the entire truth were to be told, he's read and reread most of said correspondence so many times that he has committed the deliberately polite and civil exchanges to memory.

Babur hadn't been emailing in the hopes of reaching amiable terms with Purnima. And nothing in the emails, infrequent and formal, held such promise. There was a distance in the messages, more left unsaid than not, each cautious of transgressing boundaries of familiarity that could quickly give way to resurrected accusations from their former selves. At least that's how Babur thinks of it: his former self.

Purnima left. She left eight and a half years ago, choosing herself over Babur and Angie—then Anjali—and she left on account of some confounding and physically indiscernible unwellness, the kind of unwellness that made her sit in dark rooms by herself and cry while baby Angie gurgled to herself in her equally dark nursery; that made her push away not only her young daughter, but her husband, who slept on the couch and ate meals in silence as many nights as not; that made her burst into heaving sobs over the slightest, most inconsequential trigger; and that in quick succession made her exuberant and spirited, gallivanting about the house, humming *filmi* songs from her childhood and dipping Angie cradled in her arms like they were a pair of Bollywood ballroom dancers, cooing at her as if what came to pass before had never even happened.

Purnima had insisted on taking medications prescribed by indulgent physicians who inflated her unfounded belief that there was something medically wrong with her. Babur had warned her that pills would not fix the problem. And they didn't. She'd gone on them for a while, the first time, some months after the birth of Angie, a thinly veiled excuse, Babur suspected, to abscond from her maternal duty to nurse their child for at least twelve full months. What's more, they dulled her. They made her forgetful and detached, and irritable and irrationally emotional when asked even the most innocuous of questions, like what did you feed our daughter for dinner today, why is she wearing the same clothes as yesterday, why is the oven turned on? The types of questions to be expected from a husband when he comes home in the evening after toiling all day to support his family. The pills also seemed to knock Purnima into heavy sleep for hours on end, erratically, even in the middle of the day, even once, Babur recalls with a flash of fury, in the bathroom while their four-year-old daughter had been splashing in bubble bath and the tub had overflowed. Purnima's own clothes were wet, soaked, and the girl was playing, singing to herself as if her mother's lack of consciousness were entirely normal. Angie could have— He stops before he becomes breathless, reminding himself he'd come home just in time, he'd extracted Angie just in time, saved her, turned off the taps, shaken awake his slumbering, oblivious wife.

No, pills did not work.

Yet, in spite of all this, despite all he put up with, Babur would never have told Purnima to leave. He was convinced that all she needed to do was will herself to be happy, that her so-called unwellness was a figment of the imagination, made up, self-wrought, an indulgence or excuse, the kind that afflicts Americans, maybe, but not people like them. Moreover, it was natural, instinctual for a woman to find joy in having a child, being a mother, building a family and a home, being a wife. In the first two years of their marriage, before Angie, while they were never quite blissful, they were all right. Perhaps they were even in the early stages of what his parents called "growing to love one another." Besides, everyone knows children need their mother; and husbands and wives, even those who are betrothed as strangers by their parents, per the mores of his and Purnima's culture, do not separate. Were it not for Angie, Babur would have fought harder to uphold these sacrosanct understandings. Ironically, because of Angie, he did not.

No, he would never have told her to leave. But he had forbidden her from taking any more pills or medicines, seeing any more doctors, wasting any more time treating a phantom illness. He wasn't particularly proud to take such a stance, but he needed to. And a couple of weeks after, she left.

In the days before, there had been no single breaking point or particularly horrific argument. Rather, there was mounting tension, increasing strain on the tightrope of their marriage. He could feel how Purnima resented him, avoided him, maintained physical and emotional distance from him; how she took out this resentment on their innocent child by, for example, forgetting to make a cake for her sixth birthday, embarrassing him and herself in front of a roomful of expectant party guests, or parking Anjali in front of the television all afternoon and feeding her microwaved hunks of breaded chicken, brooding or sleeping rather than bothering to prepare a proper meal for her child. In the immediate aftermath, even though he thought what she did was selfish and unforgivable, he did communicate via Purnima's cousin in Toronto that she could come back right away and he'd forget about it, tell Anjali she had gone on a short trip. A concession he'd extended not out of a willingness to forgive but out of a secret hope that he could avoid explaining to his family back in Punjab that he, the son who made it in America, couldn't keep his wife. Not that any of that mattered. Purnima refused. She wouldn't even speak to him. It was as if the woman had no sense of duty. And for this, he could never trust her. This black-and-white, hard-and-fast, unretractable line in the concrete was not for him, or so Babur told himself. It was for Angie. He could not subject his child to the whims of an unstable woman, one who he suspected was in fact medically fine, even if that woman was her biological mother.

And, yes, he supposed, if he was absolutely, soul-baringly, wake-up-in-the-middle-of-the-night-and-the-first-thing-you-spit-out honest, yes, there was a millimeter, a hair, perhaps, of thickness in the proverbial line that was for him, too.

Their emails touched upon none of this.

Email had become Babur's preferred medium with Purnima. In real-time conversation, it was difficult to navigate the delicate dance of not treading into minefields; it also required moderating one's tone to strip it of coded insults that masked latent hurt and sat on the precipice of biting anger. With email, Babur could think before he reacted. He could practice, writing a draft, editing it and even reediting it, considering and then reconsidering if a reply was merited at all. He could hit send only when *he* was ready. It also allowed Babur to easily enclose a photo or two of Angie, one of Purnima's recurrent requests.

Officially, he told himself, he was playing nice. He was avoiding an-
gering Purnima, who even after all these years might try to steal away
his daughter—Babur being well aware that American courts favor the
mother, even an unreliable, absentee one. Unofficially, buried beneath
his calcified resentment, his disappointment, his hurt, was a lingering
question mark, a stifled curiosity, a muzzled yet flickering hope that
their sterile correspondence could once and for all reveal a logic about
the woman he married.

That it would help him make sense of her.

Purnima's latest email to Babur arrived a month ago. It was brief, as
were all their messages. She inquired how Anjali was doing. (Babur
has given up correcting her on Angie's name change; at this point, the
error is intentional.) She told him she's been looking at the photo Babur
sent of her at a freshman-year swim meet. She can't believe how grown
up she looks. (Babur surmised that she noticed how Angie looks increasingly like her.) She can't believe that her child is a swimmer. She
herself does not even know how to float. She asked if Babur would
consider what she mentioned a few months ago. (She'd like them to
legally divorce. She doesn't want to push him but has mailed him some
legal papers to look over and think about.) There have been changes in
her life, she added, and it would make things more orderly.

When Babur originally read this message, he'd been relieved that
Purnima had not mentioned wanting to visit. On their final phone call,
around the time of Angie's tenth birthday, Purnima had brought up
seeing Angie with vigorous persistence, like a quasi-demand, and Babur
had really let loose. Rather than his milder past replies of "Let's think
about it. I worry that a visit might throw things off . . . ," he had spit
into the phone receiver, telling her with a turbulent rage what a terrible, horrible, catastrophic idea that was. When Angie had asked about
Purnima incessantly, when she asked if she did something wrong that
"made Mom leave," when she would fret that Purnima wouldn't be

able to find them at their new address in Lakeview Terrace, when she had night terrors, when she came home from school each May crying about not having a mother to make a Mother's Day card for, where was Purnima then? Now that he'd managed, in no small part due to his disciplined adherence to a schedule and plans, to raise a functional human, Purnima would like to pop in for a visit—*a single visit?* Absurd, he had sputtered. She was absurd, and she was selfish. She made no mention of the long term, no commitment, no future visits. No, she had spoken as if she could merely flutter in and flutter out without mucking everything up. Everything he had built. On his own. Then, as if performing a final flourish of his sword, he reminded her he could never forget how she'd almost drowned their daughter—*almost killed their daughter*—and that if pushed, he would make sure Angie wouldn't forget, either.

She had taken the verbal assault quietly. Perhaps she cried on the other end; Babur couldn't tell and didn't care. She likely hadn't expected this torrent from him, and after that, the semiregular, albeit not too frequent, check-ins switched to email and the requests to see Angie, while still present, were more timorous.

Three days after he'd received Purnima's email, a packet of what he could only presume were divorce papers had arrived by certified mail with a return address to a law firm in Topeka, Kansas. Babur had filed the manila envelope, unopened, in a Redweld folder in his desk drawer labeled MISCELLANEOUS. Which is where it has sat for the past few weeks, untouched.

He has been hesitant, for reasons he himself does not quite understand, to commit to signing papers officially terminating his marital union to a woman with whom he has no intention of salvaging a future.

While the forgotten pasta was beginning to overboil, Babur had removed the manila envelope from the Redweld and torn it open. He'd scanned, without reading, the contents: irretrievable breakdown in the relationship (you can say that again) . . . abandonment (yes, by Purnima) . . . cruel and inhumane treatment including caustic indifference to spouse's well-being and spousal neglect (ha!). He'd skimmed ahead, undeterred by the ludicrous allegations, and stopped short, almost gasping, at the first instance of Purnima's signature. He hadn't seen her written hand in a long time, and it had caught him off guard. Her penmanship was like the school ma'am's cursive from grade school in Hoshiarpur, foreign to an American eye, but at once reminiscent for Babur of schoolyard games of blindman's buff, after-school visits to the *jalebi*-wallah's cart for a fried sugary confection, and filling in dozens of composition books with repetitive penmanship exercises in an attempt to emulate ma'am's elegant cursive. It was not often Babur thought longingly of back home. He hadn't been to India since before Angie was born. Initially, it was on account of waiting for his and Purnima's green cards, but as the years passed, it was more about his dread of facing his family as well as a revolving door of gossipy acquaintances who would inevitably come by for an unscheduled chai with a side of *gupshup*. He could only imagine their know-it-all eyes collectively narrowing as they probed and pityingly clucked their tongues about Babur's failed marriage, his service-class job in America as a driver, and his daughter who could not hold a conversation in Hindi, much less say any Hindu prayer.

He'd set the paper back down and stared at a faded four-by-six framed photo next to his computer, a favorite of his.

It was a landscape print of Babur and seven-year-old Angie from an early-spring day at the beach in Westport. The skyscape behind them is a foreboding gray, and their hair whips across their faces from the wind. Father and daughter wear matching royal-blue windbreakers, and Angie holds what must have been a pail of sand or seashells, or both. She looks out to the left of the photo, her mouth open, as if she wants to say something. Babur is kneeling to her height, one arm on her shoulder, pointing at the camera, attempting to divert the direction of her gaze.

The image didn't capture a particularly remarkable moment or outing; in fact, it had been a decidedly unsuitable day for the beach. Moreover, Babur had been squinting on account of the wind, and Angie wasn't even looking at the camera. Nonetheless, it was the first photo, his first evidence, of Babur and Angie as a family of two. Looking at it, Babur could still taste crisp, salty air hitting the back of his throat. He could still feel a heady rush from the sea-drenched oxygen. He'd shivered and felt struck by an urge to do something.

Then, with a cursory rub of his eye, to erase the whisper of a nascent single tear (no, he had not been crying!), he'd picked up a pen and autographed the half dozen or so places in the packet of papers marked with "Sign here" tabs. He'd then slipped the signed paperwork into a provided return manila envelope already postage-stamped and prefilled with the recipient address of the law firm in Topeka and even with his own address in the return lines. Without so much as making a copy for his records, reasoning that if the envelope were to get lost in the mail, it was no skin off his back, he'd licked the envelope closed, planning to drop it in the mailbox after dinner.

With the bitter taste of glue lingering on his tongue, he had opened a blank reply message and typed:

Purnima,
Angie is fine. Even dead people can float. Order is important. Your
request is ok. The paperwork has been posted.
Babur

He had clicked send without a proofread, and then his watch timer had beeped, instigating an alarm within at his unnatural spontaneity.

In the kitchen, Babur stirs meatballs into the spaghetti pot, each gentle circle taking a few seconds. The stirring helps to calm his nerves.

Angie still hasn't ventured downstairs, and he's worried, grappling with when he should go upstairs to check on her: now, because dinner is ready, or later, to give her more time, even though the food will get cold.

Babur decides to wait and continues stirring, unnecessarily. He starts thinking again of the afternoon's events. Has he ever met the victim at the center of the tragedy, this Henry McCleary? He can't recall. He does, however, know the rest of the McCleary family, in particular, the daughter, Samantha, who bafflingly prefers to be called by a boy's name. He's met the mother, Claire, a number of times. He often sees her standing by the side of the pool at swim meets, cheering on Samantha, and she usually comes to the door and waves when Babur picks up Angie from Samantha's house. She seems like a nice enough woman but is not someone with whom Babur has engaged in conversation beyond pleasantries, and those mostly about what a nice girl Angie is, there being little apparent common ground between the slender, poshly dressed blond woman and himself. He has also met Fred McCleary, the father, but only a few times, and he's had a conversation that lasted more than a minute with Fred only once, at a parents' evening at Kitchewan High. Having heard from Angie that Fred McCleary works for a hedge fund in New York, Babur had expected to meet a sharp-witted man ready and willing to engage and spar about corporate insights, of which he, Babur, had many from his vigorous market research activities (e.g., reading the *Wall Street Journal* and listening to Bloomberg Radio). To his surprise, Fred had been a bit aloof, in a way that made Babur feel self-conscious. He had nodded politely at Babur's observations on companies that he "likes," finance slang for stock tickers Babur would like to purchase, if he had the funds, that is. Fred seemed distracted and quiet. "That's interesting, Bobby," he had murmured, indicating otherwise with his lack of eye contact and quick scan of his phone. Babur had walked away from the interaction wondering if the strange reception was because he's a driver. He wonders if Angie had properly clarified he is in fact a former Product Ambassador, a company man, and a current small-business owner, the engine of the US economy.

He doesn't have any memories of Henry, however.

From what was discussed this afternoon, it sounds like the atrocity his poor Angie quite literally walked in on was committed by a teenager, another high school student. He shakes his head and finally stops stirring. He covers the pot with a lid and turns the heat to low, then walks over to the sink to start on the dishes. According to the police, the student who committed the stabbing is Black. As he slathers the dish sponge with soap and turns the water faucet to a scalding temperature, ever wary of bacteria, he shakes his head and lightly clucks his tongue, unable to suppress judgment.

When they wrapped up the questioning this afternoon and Babur provided his contact details to the police and the others in the room, he assured them that he and Angie would do whatever was needed to help with the investigation.

One of the detectives patted him lightly on the shoulder, with a resigned look, and in a hushed voice said, "We appreciate that. It doesn't look like there's much to this one. Seems pretty open and shut. There's too much violence in our high schools, Mr. Singh." Noticing Babur's alarmed expression, he added, "Not in Kitchewan, thankfully. This is a new one for us."

"So you won't be needing my daughter?" Babur had asked tentatively.

The detective had sighed and said, "Well, we have to go through the formalities, so maybe. But, jeez, kids these days—they play these violent video games, they watch these horrible movies, and they go on the internet and chat with a bunch of crazies. God knows, this girl might even have learned some bad habits from home."

His partner shot him a look and added, "We'll be in touch if we need you, Mr. Singh."

Babur nodded but felt unsettled by the observations about violence.

The activities referenced didn't sound like anything of interest to Angie.

He's finished with the dishes and wiped down all the kitchen counters. He has even, although it is unnecessary, swept the kitchen floor. But still no sound or sign of Angie.

Babur walks up the stairs, stepping softly, hoping the carpet absorbs the sound of his footsteps. It's not that he's trying to sneak up on her, but he wants to know what she's doing. He approaches the door of her bedroom and gently turns the knob. He opens it a crack, unsure of what to expect, and then, when nothing happens, he opens it halfway.

He sees Angie, lying on top of her bedspread, the undrawn window shades letting in light from the still-bright evening sky. She is in her T-shirt and shorts from the day, and he hears the rhythmic sound of deep breathing, and sees a steady expansion and contraction of her abdomen. Babur tiptoes over to examine her.

"Dinnertime," he intends to say, wishing to say much more. But she is fast asleep.

THURSDAY, AUGUST 16, 2018

TWELVE

As they pull up to the main entrance of Hudson Memorial Hospital, Angela's dad turns to look at her and says, "I'll come back in forty-five minutes," even though she's already told him she could take the bus.

Angie shrugs, as if to say, suit yourself, and clutches the oversized bouquet of assorted flowers they'd picked up from Stop & Shop at her dad's insistence. It's hard to hold with one hand and too big to lay on her lap without it spilling onto the driver's side, so she's been awkwardly balancing the flowers upright against one of her shoulders. She looks out the car window at the glass doors leading into the hospital and starts to second-guess the visit. She didn't confirm a time to stop by with Sam or her mother. She hopes they're not busy—or operating. She shudders, wondering if they would in fact need to operate on Henry. If only she could turn around and go home, but now that she's here and semi-argued with her dad about the visit, she has to go in.

"Angie," her dad begins gently, "beta, should I join you?"

"No, I told you no," she snaps, annoyed that he may have sensed her hesitation. She rushes out of the car, closing the door harder than necessary.

Henry is on the third floor, in the pediatric ward, a receptionist on the ground floor tells her. Angie tries to hide her surprise. She's never thought of Henry as a child.

"You must be seeing someone real special," the receptionist continues, with what looks like an amused smile as she takes in the flowers precariously balanced in Angie's arms.

Angie's cheeks burn. She knows the bouquet is too much, but her dad, having lost their disagreement over her visiting Henry, had both insisted he drop her off and that they stop at the supermarket on the way over to pick up their gaudiest arrangement. She hopes Henry doesn't think the flowers were her idea, much less a declaration of her feelings.

The third-floor hallway is decorated with decals of vines and smiling jungle animals. There's an adult-size Lego statue of what appears to be a grinning elephant a few feet in front of her when she exits the elevator. She can't imagine Henry here. Nothing about this feels right, including her coming to visit like she's a member of the family or Henry's girlfriend—she blushes at the thought. There's still time, she thinks, to turn around, trash the bouquet, and Uber home.

But instead, she runs into a woman in scrubs with long curly hair and a friendly face. "Those look awfully nice," she comments on the flowers. "You looking for someone, hon?"

Angie can feel her heart pounding. She takes a deep breath, audibly exhaling, a habit that calms her before swimming races and school exams and says, "I'm here to see Henry McCleary." There's no backing out now that she's said it out loud. Her eyes cut to the side. She catches a glimpse of her reflection in a glass panel on a nearby door and frowns.

After Angela had insisted on visiting the hospital, she'd spent nearly an hour in the bathroom, leaning into the mirror, examining her skin as she would a cell sample under a microscope in biology class. Up until recently she's never thought much about her appearance and has never gotten into makeup like her peers. There's no point, she would tell herself, channeling Coach saying, "This is practice, not prom," whenever a girl's eyeliner would streak in the pool. Yet, over the summer, Angela's been, if not self-conscious, then hyperaware, at least, of how she looks, spending time in front of the mirror turning her head from side to side, wondering if she should start using the largely untouched "golden tan" powder foundation and bright pink lipstick she'd bought on a whim at CVS before spring formal—not that she even knows how to apply it. She doesn't feel ugly, exactly, but she feels uncomfortable. Dissatisfied as she spots blotches on her cheeks or stares at the yellowish undertones of her dull brown skin, peering back at her almond-shaped brown-black eyes, and catching increasingly hard-to-miss traces in her eyes, in her nose, in the point of her chin of the woman she tries her best to blot from her memory.

Angie feels her shoulders bunching up the way they do when she wishes she could shrink into herself. She pushes them back down and pushes away the thoughts of her mother.

The curly-haired woman is waving her in the direction of a hallway labeled PEDIATRIC CRITICAL CARE WING. Henry is in a private room, she tells Angela, adding, "He's got a corner suite, getting the real VIP treatment."

Angie pauses in front of the closed door to Henry's hospital room. The door has a narrow glass pane allowing her to look in before knocking. She can see Henry's parents sitting side by side in low-to-the-ground blue-gray fabric chairs, facing the door, their backs to a large window. Mr. McCleary is wearing a polo shirt and beige slacks and poring over the morning paper, discarded sections of which are at his feet. If Angie didn't know he was in his son's hospital room, she might have guessed he was dressed for a game of golf. Next to him, Mrs. McCleary sits with her lips pursed, engrossed in a book, her golden hair smoothed neatly to one side; she is wearing a cream-colored sleeveless blouse with a brooch or some type of jeweled embellishment pinned near her collarbone. She appears elegant and put together even under the circumstances. Angie can't see Sam from the doorway, but she spots a forearm protruding from an armchair by Henry's bedside with its back to the door. The armchair plus an IV drip block most of her view of Henry, but she can make out his profile. He is sitting up on his bed, resting against a pile of thick pillows, looking upward and across the room. She wishes she could see his face, assess how he's doing. The image of him lying on the football field with wide, desperate eyes and a bloodied stomach flashes in her mind, and she shivers.

She raises her hand to knock on the door but hesitates. The McClearys seem so peaceful. She wonders if she's intruding on a family moment. Angie thinks again of Henry, but this time as he normally is, smiling his confident, dimpled smile, his eyes shining; she blushes and gives her reflection a once-over in the door's metal doorknob, her image distorted like in a fun-house mirror. She re-rationalizes her casual clothing choices—a faded red T-shirt and some of her oldest jeans—reminding herself that she has to work a shift at Willoughby's afterward, where whatever she wears comes out reeking of coffee grinds and stained with steamed milk. There's also a risk that Gavin, a coworker and second-time senior at Kitchewan High—the same coworker who told her, after she'd turned down an invitation to watch an amateur wrestling match in White Plains with him, "You know, a lot of guys wouldn't ask out a Middle Eastern girl, but that's not the kind of guy I am"—would read too much into it if she dressed up.

Enough, she finally tells herself, and knocks.

The McClearys look up or turn, respectively, at the sound. Sam gives Angela a small wave and smile, without getting up, and Claire McCleary places a bookmark in her paperback and stands, motioning her inside.

Angie opens the door and Mrs. McCleary continues to wave at her and says, "Angela, dear, come in," over the sound of the television.

Angie hasn't been in a hospital room before. When she walks in, the first thing she notices is Henry's bed. It's clunky and machinelike, with lots of buttons and dials along the side. Stepping closer to Henry, she sees he's awake, but his eyes look tired, and even though he was stabbed in the stomach, his normally carefree, precisely structured face looks swollen and sallow.

Angie sees Mrs. McCleary give Henry a look, and Henry mutes the TV, which is playing a *Big Bang Theory* rerun.

"Hey, Henry." She's not sure what to do with the bouquet. She holds it with both hands and says, slightly embarrassed, holding it out farther in front of her, "From me and my dad."

Mrs. McCleary walks over to intercept the flowers. "Thank you, dear. They're beautiful. How nice of you both." She sets them down on the windowsill.

Angie says hello to Fred McCleary, who nods formally, and then to Sam, who, after Angie catches her mom shooting her daughter a look, stands and gives Angie a quick hug, then sits back in the armchair. "Good to see you, Ang," she says. She looks tanned and slimmer since Florida.

There isn't a free chair for Angela to sit, so she remains standing to one side of Sam's armchair. Mrs. McCleary also remains standing, on the other side of the bed.

Angela looks at Henry, whose eyes are on the muted TV, and asks, "How are you feeling? Are you in pain?"

He looks at her when he replies, "Comes and goes. They're giving me a lot of meds, though, so that helps." He attempts a cheerful tone, but he sounds drained of energy.

"He had emergency surgery to sew up his abdominal wall yesterday. Fortunately, the wound didn't puncture any organs or nick his intestines." Mr. McCleary stands up from his chair and walks toward the bed, standing next to his wife. He puts an arm around her waist and looks at his son as he speaks, apparently most at ease when he is providing information. He shakes his head and adds, looking at Angie, "What kind of sicko stabs someone like this?"

Angela isn't sure if that's a rhetorical question, but thankfully Mrs. McCleary chimes in almost immediately with "It's been horrible. They had to disinfect the wound first, you know, because there could be God-knows-what diseases on that weapon . . ." Her voice trails off, and she leans in toward Henry and strokes his sandy hair. "My baby," she murmurs.

"At least we got a nice room," says Mr. McCleary. "I had to make a few calls to a buddy of mine—the head of Orthopedics over here." He drops his arm from Mrs. McCleary's waist and shakes his head in agitation. "They wanted to put him in the adult ward, but lucky for us, Henry's not eighteen yet and can still be in Pediatrics. Not around gunshot victims and whatever other criminal elements turn up in here."

Mrs. McCleary pats her husband lightly on the shoulder, as if to calm him down.

Mr. McCleary looks at Angela again and says, "If you'd come by in the afternoon, you might've seen the clown they send around to the patient rooms, to cheer up the kids."

Angie smiles politely but doesn't know what to say. She never quite knows what to say to Mr. McCleary.

"They haven't been able to track her down, apparently," Sam announces, obviously for Angela's benefit, since the other McClearys must know this. "Chiara, I mean. She was living in one of those apartments by the old warehouses."

"That's the address she gave the school, Samantha," Mr. McCleary corrects his daughter, "but it doesn't look like she lived there. It's quite serious, you know, a crime, forging your way into another town's school." Turning to Angie, "Do you know this girl, Angela?" Mr. McCleary looks directly into Angela's eyes, the focus of his gaze unsettling. "Sam says you know her."

"Kind of. I was helping Chiara—"

"The gym teacher made Angie teach her how to swim, Dad. I didn't say Angie *knows* her. Angie doesn't *know* her. They weren't friends or anything, right, Ang?" Sam interrupts Angie, as at ease with being authoritative as her father. She looks at Angela expectantly.

"Uh, yeah. That's right," Angie confirms. Her hands are in her jeans pockets and her shoulders are inching upward.

Mr. McCleary looks at Angie curiously before abruptly pulling his phone from his pocket. "Ladies," he says, "how about we make a quick trip to that café thing downstairs and leave Angela to entertain Henry for a bit? I could stretch my legs and check my voice mail. Reception's pretty spotty up here."

"Always with the work, Dad." Sam rolls her eyes. She adds, "I'll stay. We were watching something on TV."

"A bite sounds good," says Mrs. McCleary, reaching for her handbag. "Henry needs to take it easy with the TV, Sam. Besides, weren't you just saying you're hungry?"

"The cafeteria doesn't have anything I want to eat." Sam shrugs.

Angie notices Mrs. McCleary give Sam a look.

"I'm really not hungry," Sam says.

Angie notices Mrs. McCleary's lips purse and she looks at Sam more sternly, as if displeased.

"Fine." A sigh. "I'll go. Whatever." Sam stands up again and reaches across Henry's lap for the remote, zapping off the TV.

Mrs. McCleary walks over to Angie and clasps Angie's hands in her own. Angie can feel her heart skipping. She catches a faint scent of gardenias from Mrs. McCleary's perfume. Mrs. McCleary looks at Angie with her mesmerizing blue eyes and says, "Thank you for coming, dear." She hugs her and Angie breathes her in, unexpectedly reminded of the woman she tries not to see when she looks at her reflection. She can't help thinking how much better it would be to see traces of Mrs. McCleary instead. Sam is so lucky.

"Angie, that red button next to his bed calls for help, if you need it," Mrs. McCleary says as she parts from Angie and joins her husband in the hallway.

Sam glances back at Angie as she walks out, closing the door behind her.

Angela and Henry are alone. Angie tugs at the edge of her T-shirt
with one hand, twirling its end around her index finger. She looks at
the foot of Henry's hospital bed rather than at him. She feels awkward.
And nervous. It's not lost on her that the McClearys wanted her to be
alone with Henry. She blushes.

Henry's playing with the dials on his bed. He increases the angle of
incline so he's almost sitting up, oblivious, it seems, to Angie's discomfort. He stops fidgeting with the bed and turns to look at her, attempting
a smile. His normally piercing blue eyes look muted and grayer.

When he says, "It's nice you came to see me," Angie nods, catching his gaze but then quickly looking away, afraid that if she doesn't,
her fluttering stomach might somersault out of her body and that her
cheeks, likely a deep shade of pink by now, might combust.

The last time they were alone, just the two of them, Henry had offered to drive Angie home from swim practice—boys' swim practice,
technically, but Coach would let her informally join the boys' practices
since the girls' season was over by then. It was the beginning of March,
nearing the end of winter, but still brisk by late afternoon. "I'm fine
walking," she'd said, and she was. "It's cold out today. Plus, I don't
mind," he'd replied. Her stomach had tumble-turned, and she'd nodded, hopefully not too eagerly.

That wasn't the first time Angie had gotten a lift from Henry without Sam. But the other times it wasn't just the two of them. Another
guy from swim team or Audrey Ryan, Henry's attractive but not particularly nice then girlfriend would be there, in the passenger seat, and
Angie in the back.

They'd been talking about an elective in digital literacy that they
were both taking, but at different times. It was a school-wide require-
ment, a class for Kitchewan's highly digitally literate students on how
to responsibly manage their social media, taught by an out-of-touch,
socially awkward young teacher, Mr. Bennett. Henry had been telling

Angie about how Mr. Bennett's Facebook inbox had popped up when he had his computer screen projected in front of the class and how everyone saw the teacher had been messaging the attractive, unmarried school librarian, Miss Young. Angie had burst out laughing at Henry's descriptions of how Mr. Bennett turned as red as a tomato and tripped over a wire in a race to un-project the computer screen. Henry had been laughing, too. She'd still been smiling from his story when he'd leaned in, without warning, at a red light on Indian Meadow Road, and kissed her.

She feels her lips curl up at the memory, only to realize she's standing goofily in front of Henry—in his hospital room. She shoves her hands in her pockets and feels her shoulders tense. "You look—you look pretty beat up," she says, immediately wishing she hadn't.

"Yeah, well, I feel beat up." Henry attempts another smile.

Her heart jumps. "How long are you in here?" There, that's better.

"I don't know. A few days." He shrugs, wincing a little as he does.

She's unsure of what to say next and wishes his parents and Sam were back in the room to break the silence, ease her embarrassment. She catches sight of the oversized bouquet resting on the windowsill. Her cheeks redden again, and she looks away from it, fixing her eyes on the foot of Henry's bed.

"I heard you called 911 for me," Henry says.

It's Angie's turn to shrug.

"What were you doing on the football field, anyway?" His eyebrows arc.

"I was walking home. After doing laps."

"Of course. No rest for Kitchewan's mightiest Indian." He half smiles, half scoffs.

Angie can't tell if he's amused or annoyed, but neither reaction feels fair.

Henry asks, "So are we going to be unofficial teammates again this winter?"

It sounds like he's trying to make a joke, but Angie doesn't feel like talking about what she's going to do this school year to train year-round. She shrugs and changes the topic. "You talk to Chris?"

"Not really. He called a bunch, but I don't get good reception in here and my parents said he's been kind of hysterical about the whole thing."

"He was pretty upset when I saw him," Angie agrees.

"Sometimes Chris just loses it . . ."

Angie figures this is as good an opportunity as any. "Henry, when I was walking over, walking home, I mean, yesterday, I couldn't really hear, but it sounded like maybe you, Chris, and Chiara were arguing?"

Henry opens his mouth to speak, says nothing, and then after some seconds of silence responds, "I'm a little fuzzy on the details, Ang. It's the meds, maybe."

Angie attempts to remain neutral but inadvertently frowns.

Henry adds, "You know that girl sells dope, right? I mean, I don't smoke too much, but you know Chris and his weed . . ."

"So you were arguing about—about"—she pauses, not quite sure what word to use—"marijuana?"

"I don't know, Angie. I don't remember." Henry sits more upright in his bed and continues, "Are you talking to the police? My parents told me they're investigating."

"Well, they have some questions—"

"I'd really appreciate it if you don't mention anything about weed or arguing or anything. It's great that you were there, and that you called 911 and stuff, but I don't want this to turn into some small-town-news caper. And I mean, you don't want to get caught up, either."

Angie can't help thinking how Henry's words, bizarrely, sound like her dad's. He'd been adamant this morning that Angie stay out of this, that she not make herself a target, that they cooperate with the police, but nothing more, including no visits to Henry. Angie wonders if Henry wishes she hadn't come to visit.

"Besides," Henry continues, "my parents would kill me. They're so obsessed with Harvard. It's all they care about. I don't need any . . . complications, you know?"

Angie swallows and nods, even though she doesn't mean to.

"If you can tell them you found me, bleeding or whatever, and that you didn't see or hear anything else, that'd mean a lot. To me." Henry looks at her, like he's trying to read her face. He adds, "We didn't buy anything, just so you know."

Angela chews on her lip before asking slowly, "But you guys were arguing about something?"

"Ang, don't take this the wrong way, but there's something up with that girl. She had these blankets and a bag and stuff under the bleachers. Like she lived there. Like some hobo."

"It's just"—she shrugs to downplay her disagreement—"are you sure? 'Cause I don't know. She seemed all right when I gave her swimming lessons and everything . . ."

Henry sighs and says, "Trust me, Ang. That girl is not all right. I mean, she attacked me." Color returns to Henry's cheeks, which flush pink as he says, "If I were you, I'd just stay out of it. There's no reason to make everything"—he pauses—"complicated."

"I'm not trying to create problems for you, Henry." She hears herself as she speaks and is annoyed her voice sounds more unsteady and unsure than it does in her head. She continues, "I just—it's just—the police asked me a lot of questions, and they might ask more. And I—I don't get it. What happened?"

Henry sighs again and turns his head away toward the wall with the window. Maybe she's imagining it, but he seems annoyed. "Ang," he says, "my head hurts. I'm supposed to take it easy. Do you mind stepping out?" He presses a button on the side of his bed, and it reclines to 180 degrees. He closes his eyes, not waiting for her to respond.

Angela stands at Henry's bedside for a few moments, unsure if she should say goodbye. He doesn't open his eyes, but she guesses from his shallow breathing that he's still awake.

Without saying anything, she turns and leaves. She closes the hospital room door softly but firmly behind her, and the brief thrill of the last time they were alone together feels as unrecognizable as if it happened to someone else.

When the elevator going back to the ground floor arrives, Angela sees a familiar tall, tanned, slender man. He almost runs into her, not noticing her from his height, and it takes her a few seconds to place him.

"Oh—I know you," he says, looking down, holding the elevator door open with one of his long arms.

Reading that Angela doesn't remember his name, he says, "I'm Tom Ghirardelli. We met at the interview yesterday. I work for Fred—Mr. McCleary, that is. I'm the family's investigator."

She nods slowly, recalling he was standing by the bookshelf.

"Angela Singh, right?"

"Uh, yeah."

"Did you just come from seeing Henry?" His teeth, she notices, are gleaming white, a sharp contrast to his deep tan.

She nods.

"How's our boy?"

"Um, good, I think. He's sleeping."

He shrugs and says, "Ah, I'll wait or catch up with his folks." With a wide smile, he indicates with a tilt of his head to the elevator door he's holding open, "Well, I didn't mean to hold you up, Angela Singh."

She steps into the elevator and the doors close as Tom Ghirardelli strides toward Henry's room. *Investigator? But didn't he say he was their lawyer?*

THIRTEEN

Babur Singh does not expect his last moments on this earth to be spent curled in the fetal position on a patch of muddy grass in a suburban hospital parking lot, panting, gasping, sweating, fumbling to unbutton the collar of his sky-blue polo and to unlace his New Balance sneakers; both his neck and his feet suddenly feel bound, trapped, pressurized, as if they might explode. But he is unable to complete either task. His hands are limp, lifeless, useless, devoid of fine motor skills, and as he writhes under a cloudless sky the same color as his shirt, the atmosphere taunts him. It plays tricks on his eyes, which vacillate in and out of focus. The blue above him distorts like an IMAX-theater demon or like waves that are crashing toward him, into him, and holding him down.

Here it is, he thinks, the end. And here he is, alone, unable to let out even the most meager of whimpers for help, his shiftless, shapeless mouth as mute as if someone hacked the cords in his voice box.

To die outside a hospital! What irony, he laments, because while Babur is not particularly focused on his heart, he is certain it has failed him and that he is dying. He is positive his heart has either stopped dead in its tracks—even in death, he can't help himself with the wordplay—or it's ticking with the frenetic energy of an amped-up wind-up toy that will eventually overheat, overtire, short-circuit, fall on its side, until boom, kaput, *khatham*, he is no more.

Oh, this isn't meant to be the end. It can't be. *What about Angie— how will she . . . what will she . . . what if Purnima . . . ?*

At the thought of Purnima, he musters the bodily control to wriggle onto his back, managing to splay himself like a human starfish. The ground is damp and smells of moisture from seasonal humidity and thundershowers earlier in the week. He continues to pant and looks up at the sky. *Am I still dying? Or worse yet, am I dead already? Why can't I get up?* The sky . . . He blinks rapidly. It's changing. The blue is no longer shape-shifting into ripples that crescendo toward him. There's something else, something brown and white, something tan. His eyes sharpen into momentary focus. It's a face, a woman's face, with two soft eyes and irises like umber pools, cheeks rounded with youth, skin a touch darker than his, and full rose-pink lips that move, that are moving. He hears a voice that sounds like sugar in chamomile tea say, "Are you all right?"

A woman is standing, peering down at him. She wears bright turquoise scrubs and has an ID badge clipped to her chest. Babur makes out the words DESIREE MATTHEWS, NURSE beneath a solemn thumbnail image of her. He then jerkily averts his gaze to the grass, for fear the woman might think he's staring at her chest. She's a pretty lady, but she's young, and he's not the type of man to unabashedly stare at a woman's bosom. He attempts to sit up, the blood rushing to his heavy head, and fumbles, sliding a bit as his heels dig into the mud-slick ground.

The woman crouches and offers him a hand. He hears the same soothing voice say, "Easy there. I got you."

With her help, he sits upright, smiling uneasily at the ground beyond the woman, still avoiding eye contact.

"Are you all right?" she repeats.

He manages to hoist himself onto his feet, without help this time. "I, uh . . . I—" He searches for an appropriate impersonal response, his eyes cast downward toward his muddy hands. "I'm visiting someone," he says quickly, tucking his dirty hands behind him. In response to the woman's quizzical eyes, he adds, "That's my car." Babur motions to his Prius, parked in a spot a few yards away, the door flung open, beeping, and keys still in the ignition, as if that explains everything.

The truth is, Babur *was* planning to visit someone, or more accurately, he'd been working up the courage to. This is his second trip to Hudson Memorial that day. Earlier, on his first, he'd driven Angie to see the McCleary boy, a visit he'd advised her against, counseling that she should stay out of things now that it was a police matter, but she'd insisted and also pointedly excluded Babur from joining.

It was while he was sitting in his parked car at the far end of the hospital's open-air lot, waiting for Angie, neurotically refreshing and re-refreshing the landing page of the *Westchester Gazette* and the KHS parents' Facebook group on his phone for any mention of yesterday's stabbing (none yet, but an awful lot about the forthcoming tropical storm), that he'd received the call that prompted this repeat trip to the hospital.

He'd answered the call from the private number on the first ring. "Hello. Move with Bobby, this is Bobby," he'd said with practiced cheer.

"Mr. Singh," a self-assured voice spoke into the phone. "This is Tom. Tom Ghirardelli. We met yesterday at the high school. I represent the McClearys."

Babur had nodded silently into the phone, remembering the tall, tanned man.

"Is this a good time for you to talk?" he'd asked.

It wasn't, Babur had wanted to say. He'd convinced himself the newspapers didn't have any coverage of the stabbing and that what he should be doing while waiting for Angie—who should be wrapping up soon in any event—was checking on his boys, the drivers who worked for Move. In particular, he wanted to check on Igor, a recent Belarusian transplant who moonlights for Move and was covering for Babur on his trips that morning, including a JFK pickup for a repeat client. He hoped Igor remembered to deliver service with a smile rather than his usual snarl. Perhaps it was a mistake to trust Igor with a loyal client. Maybe—

"Mr. Singh?"

Babur had cleared his throat. "Uh, yes, I—I can talk. Have you— uh, have the police found the culprit?" he'd asked, unable to fathom why else the well-heeled lawyer for the McCleary family would be calling him.

"No, not yet, I'm afraid. I was phoning to ask if you might be available to see Mr. and Mrs. McCleary later today. They'd like to"—he'd paused—"discuss the situation."

"You mean with the police?"

"Not quite. The McClearys want to meet with you—privately—to, uh, get on the same page about things. You understand, I'm sure."

Babur wasn't sure, and something in the man's smooth voice had caused the hair on his arms to stand on end. He'd replied slowly, "No, I don't." Under normal circumstances, Babur would have leapt at the chance to have a private session with a successful man like Fred McCleary, to pick his brain on business and investing, but not now. "The police are investigating, you see, Mr. Lawyer. In fact, there's a search for the stabber underway. If we have things to discuss, we should discuss with them, to—to cooperate, isn't it?"

"Oh, yes, of course. I didn't mean you shouldn't cooperate, Mr. Singh. You absolutely should." Babur heard the lawyer breathe heavily into the phone, as if already exhausted by the conversation, before he said, "It's just the police, you know, they . . . well, you know . . ."

"No, I—I don't, Mr., uh, Mr. Lawyer. And, if I must be honest, we would like to help, but my daughter was only walking by, you see. So I'm not sure how much help we can be. This seems to be a matter between the McClearys, the stabber, and the police."

"It's interesting you say that, Mr. Singh. Now, I couldn't agree with you more. But, well, off the record"—he'd paused as if about to divulge a great secret—"these Kitchewan police are not exactly NYPD. Sure, they're looking for the perpetrator, but they're overwhelmed and confused. We're not used to this kind of crime in this type of town." Babur had nodded in agreement. "And so, well, pardon my bluntness, but it seems they're questioning if the stabber had some help, you know." At this, Babur had felt a shiver course down his arm. The lawyer continued, "It's highly unusual for a teenage girl to escape on foot undetected for a full day, and in this case, well, Angela was at this deserted football field by herself, which is odd, and apparently she, uh, knew the girl. And so they're asking questions—"

The shiver then felt like a bee sting. Babur interrupted, "Who's asking?"

"Well, I can't say for sure, but the police, the school, maybe the newspapers once they get wind of it . . . There's a lot of people asking a lot of questions, Mr. Singh."

"But this is—but how—but Angela has nothing to do with this!"

"Yes, *you* know that, and *I* know that, and the *McClearys* know that, but the optics are, uh, fuzzy, Mr. Singh."

His heart was thumping. The police couldn't possibly think that Angie had something more than absolutely nothing to do with this. No one in their right mind would. "So what—what exactly do I do?" he'd burst out.

"Well, *we* get in front of it. The McClearys want to manage this and could talk to you about how to, uh, keep everyone on track." He added, "No one wants this to turn into a circus, after all."

Babur had continued nodding silently, staring ahead at his dashboard. The prior shiver and sting now felt like they had settled into his stomach, hitting him with a jolt of nausea. Multicolored spots appeared in his peripheral vision. He'd blinked hard and fast, hoping they'd go away.

The lawyer continued, "They're in the hospital all day, naturally. So perhaps you can come this afternoon to Hudson Memorial and meet them in the cafeteria, say three p.m."

Babur, still blinking fast, had nodded again, forgetting the lawyer couldn't see him. Darn these spots!

"Mr. Singh?"

At that moment, his phone buzzed with a text from Angie. "I'm done," it read, and Babur had hurriedly said into the phone, "Yes. Fine," committing himself to a second trip to the hospital. "The cafeteria, three p.m. I have to go." He hung up, exhaled deeply, turned on the car, and drove from the parking lot to the hospital door to collect his daughter from her visit to the McCleary boy.

In the intervening break before his 3:00 p.m. appointment at the hospital, he'd dropped a tight-lipped Angie off at Willoughby's, completed a brief shift on Uber (a supplement to his private trips), and connected with his Move drivers, including Igor, who was now on his way to drive one of Babur's regulars to the Hamptons and had insisted, in his characteristic manner of using what weren't quite idioms, that "All is sunshine and kittens, boss man," hanging up before Babur could ask him what exit he was near.

When he returned to Hudson Memorial he'd arrived fifteen minutes early for his meeting with the McClearys, enough time, he'd thought, to do a quick scan of his Move inbox—in retrospect a horrible idea. When he'd opened his email, there was a new message from Purnima at the top, just arrived. Babur knew better than to open a message from his soon-to-be ex before an important meeting, but his phone already showed a preview, so at that point, he needed to read the rest.

Purnima had written a response to the email he'd sent last night regarding the divorce papers. Despite last night's anxiety, Babur had placed them in his mailbox that morning, skittish still but determined, in the wake of his daughter's needing him to help her navigate the situation with the police, not to let the official termination of his already broken union or anything else relating to Purnima unravel him.

Babur,

Thank you! I worried that this might become a tedious affair, but I underestimated you. My lawyer will be in touch to discuss the details (maintenance, custody, etc.).

Yours in amity,
Purnima

Each clause was like a separate blow. What did she mean by tedious affair? What possessed her to underestimate him? Purnima has a lawyer? He knew this, he supposed, but he'd assumed the Topeka address was an administrative arrangement only, not actual legal representation. Maintenance, like he's Bill Gates? Had she lost her mind?—leading up to the final throat-slitting climax: her reference to CUSTODY! Custody of who? he'd wanted to scream, his fists balled into twin mallets. How could she, a two-faced, absentee un-mother, make any legitimate claim on his beloved Angela? She must have knowingly waited until Babur posted the divorce papers to toss this grenade. Maybe, he'd thought frantically, he could recover the signed papers from the post office. Surely they could trace the envelope, send it back to him, retract it. Because no one can split up him and Angie. No one. No, no, no!

Babur had felt the four corners of the Prius closing in on him and the expanse of the parking lot falling away. His fists wagged directionless as hot blood rushed to his face. He'd opened his mouth to yell, but it was as if all the air had been sucked out of him. He couldn't breathe. Where did all the oxygen go? His lungs felt like they were collapsing. His surroundings faded in and out like he was on a seesaw, like he was moving. Oh, God, he was getting dizzy. And the ground was moving!

Good God, he realized, *I'm dying.* He must be dying. And all because of *that woman!*

He'd managed to open the car door a crack for air to revitalize him, to stop his surroundings from resembling the surface of a disco ball, to stop his head from bursting open with outrage, and as soon as he did, it was as if his body became a weighted, gelatinous blob. He'd tumbled out of the car, nothing to break his momentum and no bodily control, and there in the mud, in a morass of confusion and blurriness, he'd started to die of a heart attack until the kind nurse found him and he'd stopped dying.

"Do you want to come inside for a checkup?" the woman asks slowly.

Babur can feel Nurse Desiree Matthews scanning him with her chestnut-colored eyes, and he feels himself sweating profusely under her concerned—or is it confused—gaze. He's still pointing to his car, he realizes, like a fool. He drops his hand, a bit too quickly for it to be casual, and blushes. He looks down at the muddy grass beside him and says, "No, Miss Desiree Matthews, I'll be fine," in what he hopes is a calm voice but sounds croakier than he would have liked.

Desiree's eyebrows rise. "How did you—"

"Your badge, madam." Babur blushes again, as Desiree touches her hospital ID.

"Oh, right. Are you sure you don't want to go in to get checked out?" She speaks slowly, as if she doesn't believe him.

He isn't sure, but doesn't know how to explain to this innocent woman that just moments ago, he'd been checking his email in his car and had sort of, well, fallen out in response to a heartless email from his soon-to-be ex-wife, and then tumbled around on the ground, in the mud, on the brink of cardiac arrest, and is now running late—oh, is he late!—to a very important but murky meeting with some powerful people who want to strategize to save him and his beloved Angie from entering the circus—not a literal circus, but the apparently inevitable head-spinning chaos triggered by events unrelated to the Singhs. More-over, there is the pesky issue of his high-deductible health-insurance plan. He hasn't budgeted for the luxury of an outpatient checkup this quarter.

"No," Babur says more assuredly, "I'll be fine. I was . . ." Babur looks down at his dirt-coated exterior, searching for words but failing to find them. Instead, as he looks at Desiree Matthews, the absurdity of the moment—of being in a hospital parking lot, tumbling to the ground outside his parked car, dying but now maybe not, this kindly young nurse finding him—ignites a sharp tickle, and as Babur's eyes meet Desiree's their mouths upturn and their faces spasm at exactly the same instant and something pulses through both of them: they burst into unexpected, uproarious, and unfettered laughter.

Babur feels like a snake shedding dead skin or a turtledove released from a magician's cage. In laughing, he forgets for a moment the ab-horrent, earth-shattering email he'd received from Purnima, the one that nearly sent him to his grave, a hyperbole Babur will forever refuse to recharacterize.

The laughter lifts Babur outside of himself. He could swear his head is floating above the rest of him, and as he blinks, the sky spar-kles in a ravishing azure, and the slate-gray asphalt of the parking lot twinkles like a crystal prism in the spots where sunbeams hit. He feels his arm hair kissed by a refreshing breeze that he hadn't noticed before and his nose tickled by the fragrance of late-summer magnolia blossoms, to which he'd previously been oblivious when down on the ground. The nice young nurse, with her gentle eyes and calm-ing voice, relieved him somehow of his prior agony. Purnima seems small and insignificant, manageable, and the request for a meeting by the McClearys frivolous. Everything is sunshine and kittens, to quote Igor.

But eventually, the trance passes. The hearty laughter dies down, and Babur is wafted and, in his final seconds, plunked back on earth.

Desiree Matthews, still smiling, says to Babur, "I needed to get out of my head for a bit. Thank you." She then stares solemnly into the parking lot and says almost to herself, "I'm having a day myself."

Babur is silent for a moment, the comedown from his prior headiness disorienting. The nagging thoughts of being late to meet the McClearys and Purnima's audacious email demands buzz like mosquitoes in his ears. He wants to swat them away, to recapture that feeling from seconds ago. But how? What can he say to this woman to recast a spell on himself? "What's wrong?" he finally settles on.

Desiree sighs in a way that allows Babur to feel the weight of her worry. "I can't unload my problems on you," and with a small smile, she adds, "You have your own stuff."

"No, please, Nurse Desiree, you saved my life. Unload, please."

Desiree lets out a short but smooth laugh. "I did nothing like that," she says.

Babur shrugs it off, pleased he's made this nice young woman laugh once more, wanting to laugh along with her again, but not quite feeling it. He says, "I thought I was dying, you found me, and now I'm not."

"Okay, I'll take it. It's Didi, by the way."

"All right then, Nurse Didi, tell me what's on your mind. I counsel a lot of people, you know."

"Are you a shrink or priest or something?"

"Oh, no," Babur says, reaching for a bent business card in his pocket and presenting it, with both hands, to the nurse. "I'm in the transportation business."

She accepts the card with raised eyebrows. "Move with Bobby," she reads.

"I'm Bobby. A lot of my clients like to discuss their problems with me while we're on the road."

Didi shakes her head. "It would take a really long trip to explain my problems."

Babur points to his red Prius, the driver-side door still flung open. The car has stopped beeping, but the internal lights remain on. He can feel that the moment has passed, that it is fading, becoming fainter and fainter. The mosquitoes are getting louder, more persistent, yet he continues to grasp hopefully.

He sees Didi bite her lip, as if she's considering it. "This is crazy, you know, but what the heck?" she finally says, and then, Babur hears Didi's phone go off. She takes it out from the pocket of her scrubs. Her body and face freeze. "Ah, shoot! I'm so late. I'm so late. I'm on shift. I totally lost track of time. I gotta go." She starts jog-walking away toward the main entrance and turns around. "Nice to meet you, Bobby," she says with a wave.

"If you ever need a ride—or a talk—you know how to reach me, nurse," Babur calls after her a bit more loudly than necessary. The mosquitoes are really buzzing now.

Didi recedes to the hospital entrance without turning around, leaving Babur with the reality of a drab parking lot on a humid afternoon, a missed appointment, a soon-to-be ex-wife, a daughter who won't confide in him, an unreliable heart, beating now but perhaps not for long, and unacceptably dirty clothes.

He stands in statuelike silence for seconds, minutes, hours, he's not sure, and for once he isn't keeping track.

FOURTEEN

The messages start during Angie's afternoon shift at Willoughby's. She's not supposed to look at her phone, but it's a slow afternoon and besides, everyone else who works there does. Including her coworker Gavin, who had been left in charge by the shop owner for the afternoon, and who, to Angie's dismay, had been noticeably mean to her ever since she turned down a date with him.

It begins as a trickle of texts that Angie reads surreptitiously, holding her phone low behind the counter on its dimmest setting. A few girls on the swim team who Angie's friendly but not quite friends with write things like: *Wow, Ang, I heard you saved Henry!* 😊 and *I can't believe Henry got stabbed!!* The hair follicles on the back of her neck tingle. It's jarring to see what happened referenced in typed-out words. It feels surreal but also like an invasion of privacy, as though the moment she shared with Henry on the football field, when Chris was God-knows-where and Henry had called out *to her* for help and she'd held his hand, has been projected on a screen for everyone to see.

She continues stealing glances at her phone throughout the afternoon, looking to each side for Gavin or an approaching customer before she does. She doesn't dare write back at work, but she rereads her messages until she's practically memorized them, each one taking her back to the football field, the raised voices, the bloody pocketknife with a bloodred handle, the blood, Chris yelling and running around like a lunatic, Henry lying there, her holding his hand—*poor Henry*. Her pulse quickens at the reminder of how helpless he'd looked.

She wonders how Henry feels about what people are saying. She also wonders if he's annoyed at her. He'd been so distant at the hospital. Maybe she shouldn't have asked so many questions or brought up the arguing she'd heard. What if he's mad at her?

Please don't let him be mad at me, she's thinking as Gavin sneaks up behind her, practically pouncing and hissing into her ear with his smoker's breath, "Quit looking at your phone, Angela Singh."

Angie's shoulders creep up to her neck and she stiffens like a thief caught in the act. She tucks her phone into her back pocket. "Sorry," she mumbles, later wishing she'd said something snappier, like reminding Gavin he's not her boss, and in the moment, wishing her shift would hurry up and end already.

Angie next checks her phone after they close Willoughby's for the day. She's outside by the curb, scuffing the tops of her Converse against the sidewalk, waiting for her dad to pick her up. He's almost fifteen minutes late, which is unlike him, but Angie is so engrossed in her texts that she barely notices.

She's received a number of new messages from classmates not on the swim team, guys and girls, some with numbers she doesn't have saved in her contacts. The texts are more or less the same. Well wishes, like: *Way to go, Angela Singh!* 👏 and *You saved Henry!* ☺. Questions about yesterday, like: *Did you see the stabbing?* and *What happened yesterday?* and then some non sequiturs: *OMG—a stabbing at Kitchewan!!* And one specifically calling Chiara "a drug dealer and a psycho."

After having mulled over and remulled over her interaction with Henry this morning, Angie is embarrassed about putting pressure on him. She'd been rude and pushy, she's convinced. To make it up to Henry, she starts responding to each text: *I called 911* and *Anyone would have done the same* and *Thanks, I didn't do that much. I just called 911.* She even replies when she's not quite sure who the message sender is, hoping this makes up for her behavior at the hospital: *I didn't see what happened. I just called 911* and *Yeah, I can't believe it either.*

Her replies prompt more replies, and Angie quickly finds herself reading through a crop of new texts. More questions. Asking for more details. She can't keep up. *Is Henry going to be okay?* and *Did you see the knife?* and *Was there a lot of blood?* 😮. She's typing so furiously she doesn't immediately notice her dad's fire-engine-red Prius pull up.

He rolls down the passenger-side window. "Sorry I'm late, beta," he says with a weak, almost goofy look on his face.

Angie squints at him. She senses something strange about his mood, something off balance in his manner.

He leans to open the passenger-side door from inside and she decides to shrug it off. She slips her phone into her back pocket and climbs in, grateful for a break from her texts.

"How was work, beta?" he asks in a tone that sounds like he's vibrating. Buzzing.

Something's definitely up with him, she thinks, but decides to ignore it.

Her dad has been the opposite of helpful these past twenty-four hours. Rather than comfort her, he's made her jumpier with his unpredictability. One minute he's hyperventilating outside the principal's office, checking she still has all of her limbs intact and hugging her so tightly she can hardly breathe; and the next, like this morning, he's skipping around the kitchen cooking and simultaneously cleaning, talking a mile a minute in a singsong voice about absolutely nothing, like Mary Poppins, making Angie an enormous breakfast that she tells him she's not hungry enough to eat; and then the next, like after her visit to Henry, he's silent and sullen. Sure, they'd argued about visiting Henry, but seeing him with his large, sad eyes, glistening with liquid on the brink of bunching up and falling, it was too much.

Angie looks straight ahead and says in a flat voice, "Fine. It was slow." She takes her phone out of her pocket. Even though she's muted it, she intuits the screen lighting up with new notifications.

"Are you working this weekend, beta?" her dad tries again.

"Yeah," she says after a pause. "Tomorrow, but I don't know about Saturday." Her phone keeps flashing. She can't help but look. "There's a storm coming this weekend," she says, her eyes glued to her phone, "so we might be closed."

"Oh, yes, the storm. It might get upgraded to a hurricane."

"Uh-huh," Angie replies, focused on her latest messages: *Why'd Kiara do it?* and *Did Chris get hurt?* She feels her forehead knotting as she types: *I didn't see anything. I came after; I didn't run after anyone. I called 911; I don't think so.*

". . . and did they say anything to you?" Her dad's looking at her with his irritatingly gentle eyes and an expectant smile.

"Huh?" Angie looks up from her phone.

"Samantha's parents," he says. "Did they"—he pauses, and in her peripheral vision she catches him twist his mouth in hesitation—"ask about me? To speak with me, I mean?"

Angie tries to temper the impatience in her voice, but it's hard when he so blatantly ignores that she doesn't want to talk. "No, Dad. I told you already. I didn't see Henry's mom and dad for long. And Henry was really tired from all the medicine and stuff."

"So they didn't mention anything about wanting to see me"—he pauses—"to discuss anything?"

Angie continues to get new messages. Some of them border on bizarre, like: *I heard Chris Collins chased Chiarra but then let her go to help you save Henry* and *Did Chiara really have a gun?* and *I always knew there was something wrong with Ciara. She never smiled at anyone* 💀 and finally, *Kierra's homeless?!* Angela can feel her shoulders hunch up and her eyes pinch together.

"Beta, after you went to the hospital, I—"

"Dad, stop!" Why is he making her raise her voice at him? She continues, "They didn't ask about you. They didn't ask for your number to personally thank you for the enormous bouquet of flowers. And they didn't ask how you're doing. Their son is in the hospital. He's just been stabbed, in case you forgot!" As she says this, her annoyance at her dad for forcing her to bring Henry those flowers resurfaces. She's indulged him enough with the bouquet and answering his questions about her visit to see Henry. She hadn't even complained about him waiting in the hospital parking lot the whole time she was visiting Henry—like a stalker or like he didn't trust her. He didn't acknowledge it at first, but she'd seen his firecracker-colored little car drive up from a spot in the parking lot to the hospital entrance to pick her up. "It was an odd-sized amount of time," he'd admitted, when Angie asked him. But there's a limit to her patience.

Angie looks back down at her phone again as her dad holds up his hands in surrender, dropping the topic of the McClearys. Some new texts have come in: *Did you know they can't find Chiarah? And they think she's homeless!* Angie rubs away the goose bumps that appear on her arms and adjusts the passenger-side air-conditioning vents away from her. The texts about Chiara make her crave fresh air. She cracks open her window an inch without turning off the AC and inhales deeply.

It's not that Angie doesn't believe Chiara stabbed Henry. Henry said she had, so she must have. But she can't make sense of it. It doesn't add up. Why would she do this? Why would Chiara hurt Henry? The lack of logic gnaws at her, giving her a cramp in the hollows of her stomach. She is having trouble believing Chiara did this for no reason, and even though she hasn't mentioned this to Sam, or Henry, or her dad, or the police, or anyone—nor will she, given how things are heating up—Angie feels sad when she thinks about Chiara. Bad for her. Not quite pity but something similar. Maybe, Angie thinks, this is how people felt about her in elementary school after her mom had left and— *Stop it!* she interrupts herself, pinching her arm and shifting back to Chiara.

It feels dirty and wrong how people are texting about Chiara like she's a monster and doesn't belong at Kitchewan High. The girl Angie was guilted into teaching to swim wasn't friendly, but she was also just a regular teenage girl, like her, at least as far as Angie could see. She presses her lips together in a cringe, remembering how Chiara had clung to her, fearfully, vulnerably, the first time they'd gone into the deep end, how her gentle brown eyes had appeared to tremble but then, noticing Angie looking at her, she'd blinked it away; or how when Chiara first made it across the length of the pool, she'd broken into this all-body grin that made her radiate, but that she bizarrely wiped off, like she was embarrassed when she remembered Angie was there.

Angie's eyes and throat get heavy. She opens her window another few inches, relishing the breeze against her cheeks and eyeballs. She bunches up her face in concentration, trying to remember when exactly she saw Chiara. She didn't see her hurt anyone, but she saw Chris running on the football field. She's pretty sure he was chasing after someone, because he was yelling the types of things someone like Chris would yell if he was chasing someone. So—Angie chews her bottom lip again—that someone could have been Chiara. Or it could have been someone else. Apart from when Chiara was sitting on the bleachers earlier, before everything, Angie doesn't recall seeing her. But wait. She did see her, though. She must have. Because that's what she told the police.

Angie opens her window all the way, hanging her elbow out of the car. She feels nauseated, and the fresh air is no longer helping. From the corner of her eye, she sees her father, without commenting that Angie knows better, turn off the AC and open his window, too.

"If I work tonight, will you be okay?" she hears him ask.

"Yeah. I'll be fine." Can't he see how painful it is for her to speak right now? How her insides might come exploding out of her, like, she thinks with a sharp swallow, Henry's had on the football field.

"Are you sure?"

"Seriously. Yes. You should work. You're always saying money is tight, so go ahead. I'll be fine."

"Yes, beta. I was . . ."

Angie tunes him out. Dazed. She stares at her most recent message commenting on Chiara being homeless. Yesterday, Mrs. McCleary had insinuated that Chiara did not live in Kitchewan, and Henry had also said something about Chiara being homeless. Angie had found these comments odd but hadn't bothered to correct either of them. She's pretty sure Chiara lives in town. But maybe, she thinks, she doesn't know the little about Chiara she thought she did. Because Mrs. McCleary wouldn't say something unless it was true. Angie chews on her lip again, even though the skin has broken and it's bleeding a little.

Her dad interrupts again. "Ang, are you feeling all right? You've been looking at your phone quite a bit. All okay, beta?"

"Yeah. I'm just figuring out what's going on with my work shift this weekend," she fibs without looking up.

Angie strains her memory. She can swear Chiara told her she'd borrowed a cousin's bathing suit for their swimming lessons. There wouldn't be a cousin if she's homeless. Angie feels her heartbeat picking up and can't slow down her tumbling thoughts: She wants to know where Chris Collins was when Henry was stabbed, and who the pocketknife belongs to, because it would be strange if Chiara carries a knife on her all the time. She wants to know if the police found the marijuana that Chiara sells; and also—she feels her breaths coming quick and shallow and her hands tighten around her phone—she'd like to know how Chiara's being homeless fits into any of this. A lone fat teardrop trickles down Angie's cheek. Rather than rub it away, she lets it fall, the corners of her mouth drooping down along with it.

"Angela, beta, listen to me." Her dad touches her shoulder lightly with his right hand, giving her a start, before replacing it on the steering wheel. "I know you're working hard to save up for a car, and I know I sometimes worry about money. But we'll be okay. Don't cry if you don't have a shift on Saturday. We'll figure it out. Really." He pats her on the shoulder again. "Don't worry."

Angie sniffles and nods at her dad. It's easier than correcting him. She slips her phone back into her pocket and stares out her open window.

That night, at home, Angie is absently turning pages of Charlotte Brontë and half watching a *Big Bang Theory* rerun. Her dad, as promised, has gone out to work, telling her not to wait up, that he'll be home after midnight, and reminding her that spaghetti from the day before is in the fridge for her to microwave. Her cell phone is facedown on the coffee table, on silent but taunting her with its presence.

She'd been determined not to look at it. There are too many messages to keep up with and everyone is asking the same gossipy questions that fill her with unease. But her book is boring, and the TV laugh track is irritating her, so she zaps off the television, puts her book down, and sucks in a breath, flipping over her phone.

She expects a dozen or so new messages asking how much blood she saw or how big the knife was or if it's true that Chris Collins heroically tackled Chiara. But instead: "What is this?" she murmurs slowly as she unlocks her phone screen. Sixty new text messages and dozens of Instagram notifications just in the past couple of hours.

This is going to take her ages to get through, not to mention she still has unanswered messages from earlier in the day. And if everyone keeps responding, beyond ages. Before she can second-guess herself, like it's second nature, she calls Sam.

"Hi." Sam sounds breathless when she answers after a few rings.

"Hi, it's me. Are you busy?"

Taking a second, Sam says, "Uh, no. Just ordered some Thai food for dinner for my dad and me."

"What about your mom?"

"She's not home. She refuses to leave Henry. She's driving him crazy. Poor Henry." More brightly, Sam says, "Good thing is, the doctors say he can come home sometime this weekend."

Sam sounds normal, like before all the weirdness between them, which makes Angie smile into the phone as she says, "Oh, yeah? That's great."

"Yeah. So . . . what's up?"

Angie pauses, thinking about how to bring up the messages without sounding insensitive.

"Ang, you okay? You seemed kind of funny at the hospital earlier. Henry said you were a little out of it."

Angie's face gets hot. They were talking about her, and Henry thought *she* was out of it. She wants to ask Sam exactly what he said. But she doesn't. *Serves me right*, she thinks, *for upsetting him when he's in the hospital.* In her best attempt at a carefree voice, she says, "I'm good. I was just wondering how you were all doing." And because it's nagging her, she adds as casually as she can manage, "I've been getting a lot of messages from people at school."

"Yeah, me, too." Sam sounds unfazed. "Everyone's worried about Henry."

"They have a lot of questions and stuff, you know."

Silence.

Angie continues, "It's kind of weird that all these people are asking me about what—what happened." She pauses. "Like, I don't even know some of them."

"Well, you were there, so it's not *that* weird."

"Kind of. I was *kind of* there," Angie corrects Sam. "I wasn't there when—when it happened."

"This is Kitchewan, not Baltimore. People are really freaked out and you were there."

"I know . . . It's just—the stuff they're asking me is weird."

Sam jumps in. "What weird stuff?"

There it is. An opening. Her chance. Angela takes a deep breath, ready to tell Sam it's strange people are saying these things about Chiara and fixating on details about where she lives, and how she doesn't know where they're even hearing this stuff. She could even maybe ask Sam if she knows *why* Chiara hurt Henry.

But before she can start, Sam adds, "Angie, my brother was violently attacked at our high school by another student. Like, someone we walked past in the halls and sat in math class with and who you had to teach how to swim. And she was carrying a murder weapon! And now the police can't find her. She's on the run or something. Of course people are freaking out."

It's chilling to hear Sam call the pocketknife a murder weapon and by extension, Chiara a murderer. It was terrifying to see that thing inside Henry, but the mention of murder when no one had, in fact, died elevates the situation and the knife. Although, Angie thinks, replaying what Sam said, if she hadn't shown up when she did or if the knife had landed in a different part of Henry . . . Thinking about things the way Sam had put them, the whole thing is serious, very serious.

"Ang," Sam repeats, "what are people saying that's weird?"

"Well," Angela says weakly, unsure if she should continue, but backed into doing so, "there are a lot of questions about Chiara, and some of them are"—she pauses to think of the right word—"mean. Like, people are saying she's homeless and they're saying all kinds of stuff about how she was crazy and violent."

"She tried to kill my brother. That is crazy and violent. And no one can find her. The police went to look for her at the address she gave the school. She doesn't even live there!"

Angie bites at her bottom lip again. She shouldn't have said anything, and she definitely can't ask Sam if she knows what happened that caused Chiara to stab Henry. She sounds insensitive. She needs to get over whatever it is that's bothering her because *Chiara could have killed Henry.*

Sam asks, "Hey, Ang, how come your dad stood my parents up this afternoon?"

"What? What are you talking about?"

"Your dad was supposed to see my parents and he flaked. How come?"

"Why was he—"

"Are we cool? Are you mad at me or something?"

Are *you* mad at *me*? Angela wants to ask in return, feeling a lump form in her throat and her eyes well up.

Sam continues, "Because while we're talking about being weird, you're acting pretty weird. And it's weird your dad blew off my parents. My parents are trying to help. They're working with the police and talking to the school. And that's a whole mess. Principal Burrowes," she scoffs, "doesn't know what she's doing. She let this dangerous person enroll in the high school when she doesn't even live here; and then she left the school unlocked all summer, and it's like no one has any idea how to find Chiara, and half the police department is looking for her." Sam paused. "I'm sorry you're getting a lot of texts and questions, but is that a big deal after my brother almost died? Seriously, Ang."

Angela's stomach turns. *I'm a jerk*, she thinks, and feels tears falling in quick succession down her cheeks and past her lips. Her bottom lip stings with salt from her tears. "No," Angie says, attempting to conceal any hint of her crying in her voice, "I'm not mad. I just got worried by all the questions." She sniffles, giving herself away. "But I want to help. And you're right. This is a really big deal and I've been"—she pauses—"I haven't been thinking clearly."

"Well, it's fine," Sam says. "We all freak out, I guess, and it was probably scary to find Henry like that." She pauses. "You might not like people asking you questions, but you were there. And do you think I like always being part of the Henry show? I mean, he's my brother and everything, and I love him, but— Hey, listen, I gotta go. My dad's waiting for me to eat." She yells away from the phone, "One minute, Dad! I ordered you the beef pad see ew." She says into the phone, "Bye, Ang," and hangs up.

Angela sniffs and wipes her face with the back of her hand, ashamed of herself. She's overreacting. Sam is right. This is a big deal, and whatever Angie saw or heard or didn't, she needs to be helpful. She *wants* to be helpful. Henry could have died, after all.

She trudges upstairs, phone in hand, curls on her side on top of her seashell-print bedspread, and starts going through, one by one, text by text, social media tag by tag, Facebook message by message, and replies to each as neutrally and graciously as she can, pushing her lingering questions about what happened yesterday to the recesses of her mind. Doing her part to help the McClearys and Kitchewan. She does this until her eyelids droop and her head becomes too heavy to hold up, at which point she sets it down on her bed, *just for a moment*, closes her eyes, *just a short break*, and, lights on, in her clothes from the day, falls into a thick, dreamless sleep.

Angie wakes up the next morning disoriented. She reaches for her phone and blinks into focus. There is a fresh avalanche of new messages. More than yesterday. She reminds herself this is nothing compared to what poor Henry, who's waking up in a hospital bed, with his gut freshly sewn closed, has to deal with. Angie hopes Sam didn't say anything to him or her parents about how she'd called her to complain last night.

She looks down at her phone screen again. She sits upright, cross-legged on her bed, and starts scanning the texts, Instagram posts and messages and friend requests: there are more questions about whether she saw Chiara stab Henry; someone asks if she tried to fight her off; more questions about the knife and how much blood there was; if she was scared; comments about how unbelievable this is!; comments about how dangerous Chiara is; observations about clues of Chiara's violent tendencies, like how she didn't smile at anyone and kept to herself and how she'd once told Miss McGovern, the gym teacher, that she was acting like a bitch. Apparently, now, two days later, the police still haven't found Chiara, and someone started #prayforHenry on Instagram and Twitter. A bunch of people tagged her in their messages of well wishes for Henry McCleary. Some seniors and juniors, including popular ones who'd never given her the time of day, sent her friend requests, and a few adults, too, like Miss McGovern and . . . wait—*hold on!*—she rubs her eyes—*no, wait, is this*—could this—*it's* . . . *Her.*

She holds her breath and stares at one friend request in particular buried among dozens of others. It's from a middle-aged woman with a tan complexion not unlike Angie's, but with fuller cheeks, with hints of acne scars and intense dark brown eyes. Her sharp chin and pointed nose have familiar curves (Angie grazes her own) and her eyebrows rise and arc in a manner she knows well (Angie traces one of hers with her pointer finger). The woman stands in front of a tall building that forms part of an unfamiliar and unimpressive skyline on an overcast day. She's doing that cheesy pose where she's trying to make it look like she's touching the top of the building with her outstretched arm, but the alignment is off so her hand juts in front of the top floors of the building. She wears a closed-mouth smile, like she's hiding her teeth, and her eyes focus directly at the camera. It feels like she's looking directly at Angie. Like she's waiting for something, expecting something.

She's dressed in straight-leg jeans that neither hide nor reveal much of her figure, and a maroon short-sleeved top with holes cut out at the shoulders, a style Angie dislikes. Angie sees evidence of a soft stomach. Nothing obscene, but the type of small paunch some middle-aged women have, like a mom— She stops herself, holding her breath for a second. The profile says the woman lives in Lawrence, Kansas. *Purnima C.* The "C" must be for her maiden name, Chauhan.

Angie stares at the woman. Stunned. Frozen. She exhales more breath than she thought possible to hold in her lungs, and her finger hovers over the "confirm friend" button. It then moves over the "ignore" button on her phone screen. She presses neither and instead locks her phone screen, clenching her jaw. She chucks her phone on her bed like it's radioactive and leaps to her feet.

Her face feels hot in patches. Her shirt is itching her; she extends one arm around her shoulder, trying to reach the center of her back. She scratches the sides of her shoulder blades a little too hard, okay with the possibility of drawing blood. She can't reach the spot that's troubling her, so she gives up. In a frenzy, she rushes to the bathroom and splashes cold water on her face. She ties back her hair in a bumpy ponytail and rushes back to her bedroom to slap on a one-piece and throw on a ratty T-shirt and cutoffs over it. She snatches a small backpack from under her bed (her duffel still in police custody), tosses in a change of mismatched clothing, swimming goggles, and a swimming cap, and runs down the stairs to chug her room-temperature turmeric milk (covered by a Post-it note that she doesn't bother to read from her dad, who's on the road already, working). She grabs a banana and her house keys and slides on her Toms, almost tripping as she dashes out of the house.

As she locks the front door, she realizes she left her phone in her room, but she doesn't care. She doesn't want it or need it right now. What she needs is to move quickly, deliberately, precisely, to focus on her next step, to make that next step quick, because if there's a gap, a space, a pause, anything, she's afraid she'll see that woman in that cheesy pose wearing that horrible crimson shirt with her half-there Mona Lisa smile and eyes that are looking directly at her.

Angie run-walks most of the way to the high school, sweating from the humidity and her adrenaline. She's oblivious to her surroundings, to the sticky summer air, to the foreboding thick clouds, to everything. She approaches the football field, her heart like a sledgehammer. There's no one on the bleachers today and the field is empty, silent. There's some yellow police tape around a circle of grass toward the middle of the field but no police officers around. She gives the yellow tape circle a wide berth, racing past it.

She beelines for the side door to the gym, breathless and ready to swim, ready to move, ready to move on.

She pulls on the metal door handle. But the door doesn't budge. She pulls again, with more force this time. Still nothing. She pulls at it wildly but in vain. It's locked.

She walks around to the main entrance to the gym, the double doors that open into the basketball courts, and tries pulling those, leaning back with her entire body weight. But no use. They're also locked.

In disbelief, she takes off her backpack and plants herself on the ground, her back against the main entrance to the gym. She closes her eyes, and all she can see is that woman with her nose and her chin and her way of looking right at her. And even though Angie never swears, not even in her head, she opens her eyes and blurts, "What the fuck?"

SATURDAY, AUGUST 18, 2018

FIFTEEN

"Chris, open the door," he hears his mom say. "Are you in there? Open the door." *Bang, bang.*

Chris removes his flannel comforter from his face, and his eyes squint open, adjusting to daylight bouncing off his navy-blue bedroom walls and the Yankees posters pinned on them. They're from when he was younger and used to watch games with his dad. He doesn't watch baseball much anymore and should probably take them down, he thinks.

Bang, bang. "Chris, wake up! We need to talk."

He groans softly to himself. He slept funny and has a crick in his neck. He continues lying on his back but turns his head to one side, toward the window. He hears his neck crack as he does. The window is open. He'd been smoking last night and didn't want his bedroom to smell like cigarettes. He eases himself into a sitting position, grunts slightly from the stiffness in his neck, and scans his room for stray butts, an ashtray, or any other evidence that might be mixed in with his discarded clothes strewn across the floor. He needs to hide his smoking, like so many other things, from his mom. But then, he thinks, what's the point; she's like a bloodhound about this stuff and whatever he thinks he's covered up, she finds anyway.

"Chris!"

"Give me a minute!" he yells back, his voice hoarse and still filled with sleep. *Can't she ever just chill out?*

"Chris, I have to go to work. Open the door!"

"Isn't it Saturday?" he replies instead of moving toward the door.

"Yes," she says. "I told you I'm working this weekend. We need the overtime."

He scoffs. He hates when she says "we" like that, like they're in it together. Like it's his job to help figure out adult stuff, like household expenses, even though his mom doesn't treat him like an adult. Things would be easier financially if his deadbeat of a dad pitched in, she always complains. But then when he asks her why she doesn't go after him for child support, she gets hyperdefensive. Last time, she said something like "You and I are doing just fine without *him*," like *he* was a contagious disease.

Bang, bang.

Fine, he thinks and gets out of bed. He throws on a pair of jeans that he finds crumpled on the floor and walks to the door. He turns the knob to unlock, but he doesn't open the door.

"Chris?"

"Yeah, it's open now."

His mom wastes no time. She practically dives into his bedroom. Her reddish-brown hair is tied back in a messy low ponytail and her usually pale cheeks are tinted red with excitement. She waves a newspaper at him, and before he even knows what's the matter, Chris feels a small pit, the size of a cherry stone, appear in his stomach. He feels sick.

Chris never should have told his mom as much as he had. It was a mistake. A colossal one. And he never would have. Not in his right mind. Except he was having a moment of not being in his right mind on Thursday. The day after it happened. He still hadn't heard from Henry and had called him multiple times and sent about a dozen text messages. He'd even tried calling Sam. It all seemed so stupid now, that he said anything to his mom, his high-strung-always-on-his-case-always-stressed-out mom. Even if Henry and Sam weren't answering, that was a mistake.

But at the time, all he could think about was why Henry wasn't calling him back. He was in the hospital, sure, but it wasn't like he was in a coma. And Chris needed to talk to him. To find out what he told the police. To talk about what happens when the police catch that girl, Chiara. Because what then? What then? WHAT THEN? He and Henry needed to discuss, or agree, or something on a version of what happened. That was the only way. Because with the two of them against her, everything would be fine. Totally fine. Especially if Henry was one of the two.

The thing was, the way things sounded if Chris described them was way worse than it actually was. That was the thing. That was what was making Chris freak out. Because if you'd been there, if you'd seen the way that girl had scowled at him. Looked at him with her eyes half-closed into little slits like she couldn't even be bothered to open them all the way. Like he wasn't worth her time and was beneath her, like an insect or pest, like he wasn't as good as her—like he wasn't as good as the girl with the boy haircut and the musty smell and a homeless-looking sweatsuit and no friends. If you'd seen it, well, then, maybe you'd get it.

Maybe it would make more sense why Chris got a little annoyed and threw that raggedy old book she was reading into the dirt under the bleachers. And maybe it'd be clearer that when Chris grabbed that ratty gray backpack and turned it upside down, shaking it a little, he was just checking she was telling the truth about not having any weed. Moreover, he was making a point—a funny point—that there wasn't any reason for her to look at him like that when they were coming around to give her money she clearly needed to buy some soap to take a shower.

He didn't know when stuff started falling out of her bag—with

Henry holding her back to keep her from lunging at Chris and say-ing, "Easy there," like she was an unbroken horse or something—that there wasn't going to be weed in there. That she'd be toting around a sad three-pack of drugstore panties, a frizzled toothbrush, a hair comb, a handful of humongous sanitary napkins—gross!—and a towel in-stead. And maybe she didn't have weed on her. But by that point, she was screeching and howling so loudly about Chris emptying out her stupid bag—which was a little mean, but it was also a joke, and it was funny; Henry was laughing, anyway, or at least he was part of the time—that the only thing Chris could do was lighten the mood and tease her about all the weird shit she carried around with her. And it wasn't so far-fetched, for someone who'd seen the inside of her back-pack, to say, just as a joke: "Are you homeless or something? You carry stuff around with you like a hobo!" To be fair, Chris couldn't have known that kind of playful and maybe a little mean teasing would make the girl, like, basically growl at him.

Yeah, at some point maybe Henry did let go of her and step away because she was acting all wild and making a lot of noise. And maybe he did say something like "Let's forget it. Let's just leave." But it's not like Henry insisted, and he definitely didn't say it loudly. That was the other thing: Chris could barely hear over all her yelling and going on about her stuff. And Henry was laughing for a while. Yeah, things got out of hand a little—no one's denying that—and maybe Chris shouldn't have joked the way he did or gone at her the way he had after Henry let go of her. But anyone could see that he was just trying to scare her a little as a joke . . .

If someone had been there, they'd have seen that it wasn't meant to be the way it ended up. That it wasn't how it sounded, even. It was a misunderstanding, a few jokes that went a little too far. And if Chiara hadn't been so crazed and if Henry had just held on to her a little more tightly and had quit egging Chris on by laughing like he was having the best time ever or if he'd at least watched where her hands were, this whole thing wouldn't have turned into anything.

Now the police wanted to interview him. Like, really interview him. They'd given him a pass on formal questions the day of on account of him needing to get checked out by the hospital. But the day after, they called bright and early asking for Chris and his mom to come in. His mom was holding them off, or trying to. She threatened to call their lawyer (they didn't have a lawyer), because that's what she told Chris rich people did to get other people to leave them alone. It was funny how his mom already knew something was up, like she had a sixth sense. In any case, Chris knew he'd have to talk to the police eventually, and he couldn't stop thinking about what he'd say.

They'd want to know what he and Henry were doing at the school. They'd probably also ask about whatever lies Chiara told them. And also—he made a face—there was also no-fun Angela Singh. He'd almost forgotten about her. She wasn't there, but she showed up pretty soon after. Maybe she saw or heard something, or thought she did. The good thing was Angela could be handled. She had this pathetic puppy-dog crush on Henry. At least Chris was pretty sure she did from the way she got all fidgety with her hands and her eyes and spoke faster and in a higher pitch when Henry was around. It was pathetic because Chris was pretty sure Henry hadn't noticed—although, personality aside, Angela wasn't half bad, kind of cute even, in a flat-chested, ethnic Disney princess kind of way. The point was, Henry could probably talk to Angela and figure that part out. But on the other stuff . . . *Henry needed to call him back already.*

Together, they could fix this. Clear it up. Get their stories to match up. Because even though things didn't sound good, they hadn't done anything. Chiara didn't have any weed, so they didn't buy anything. And yeah, Chris emptied out her backpack, but he'd shoved all the stuff he threw around back into the bag before the ambulance arrived . . . It was just a joke! And she stabbed Henry, so that erased everything they did, didn't it?

While he had been panicking about what to say to the police, Chris's mom had been acting really sweet, talking to him in this soft voice, like he was fragile and might break. Not like she usually spoke to him.

And he was feeling mixed up, freaked out, and definitely not thinking clearly when his mom asked, "Chris, honey, are you okay?"

He hadn't meant to start crying, but once the first couple of tears fell, it was like a flood. A calamity. Like that tropical storm that was supposed to hit the town this weekend that the local news has been going on about like it was the End of Days. He'd taken a deep breath to stop, to get a grip. But he couldn't.

He hadn't cried that hard since he can't remember—oh, wait, he can. Game 6 of the 2009 World Series, the last time the Yankees won. The night his dad told him he was moving out in between slurps of his Budweiser, during a commercial break. *Like that was something you casually mentioned during a commercial break.* Minutes later, Matsui hit his first homer of the night. While his dad jumped up and whooped like he won the lottery (which, to be fair, may not have been that far off—he used to sports-bet a lot back then), nine-year-old Chris had sat staring into his can of root beer, determined not to cry in front of his father. But the drops just started. And once they did, they wouldn't stop. Not until he was full-on weeping and his chest was heaving. It took his dad what felt like an eternity to finally turn, look at him, let out a soft belch, and say, "Chrissy, you catch that double over all that noise you're making?" Chris had wanted to reply, but the tears got heavier and faster. Like a downpour. He couldn't get his mouth to open, his lips to form words, his voice box to produce even a whisper. He remembers feeling a tingling along his mouth, along his lips. Pins and needles, pricking at him, urging him to answer. On the inside, he screamed: *Don't leave. I'll be better. I'll be good. I'll be anything. I promise. Don't go. Don't leave. Don't leave me, Dad! Please. Dad!* But on the outside, he could only cry.

Chris had also tried to stop himself from crying in front of his mom two days ago, but his eyes were like faucets and his nose, too. The more he tried, the harder and deeper the sobs came. First, his shoulders shook, and then his whole body. When his mom put her arms around his shoulders, him sitting at the table, she standing over him, smelling of clean laundry, and then stroked his hair, he felt a wave of peace wash over him. And he let go. He let it out.

"Mom," he said weakly, "we messed up. I messed up." His voice was shaky and muffled as he continued, "We went to the high school yesterday to buy weed from that girl. Henry and me." He sniffled. "That's why we were there. And now—and now the police want to interview me, and I don't know what I'm supposed to say." He paused to swallow a half-formed sob. "We didn't do anything. We didn't buy anything. We argued with that girl a little. But then—and then she stabbed Henry and we didn't—we didn't—I don't know what to do, Mom."

"Chrissy," she said, gently brushing away some of the tears on his cheek and calling him by the name she and his dad called him when he was a young child, "slow down." She patted him lightly on his back. "Take a deep breath. Tell me more slowly. What happened?"

Chris looked at her. Really looked at her. He couldn't spot any anger lines on her pale freckled face. There were no sharp points in her eyebrows. Her wide-open eyes, more gray than green at that moment, were inquisitive, concerned, but not looking to blame anyone. And her thin, pressed-together lips were set in neutral, rather than creased in disappointment or scrunched up, waiting to scold. All he could see written on her face was concern. And love.

He wrapped his arms around her tight. As tight as he could, and he felt her return embrace pass over him like warm water in the bath.

He released his grip and repeated himself. More slowly. Without tears. Just as she asked.

But now things are back to how they always were. His mom is worked up again, and the newspaper is flapping around inches from his face. She's shaking it so he can't read it.

"What, Mom?" he says, annoyed by her theatrics.

"Chris Collins. We need to speak about *this*." Her voice is back to the stern, testy tone he knows so well. She stops waving the paper and holds it out in front of his face with both of her hands. "Look."

It's today's *Westchester Gazette*. Saturday, August 18, 2018. Beneath a headline, "County Prepares for Worst as Tropical Storm Felicity Nears and Continues to Gather Strength," he sees another article, also on the front page, "Senseless Stabbing of High School Student at Kitchewan High." His breath stops.

"Where did they get all this from, Chris?" his mom demands.

What is she talking about? She's moving the paper again as she holds it out so he can't read it properly. He grabs the paper from her, making sure to huff for her benefit. His eyes race through the article, leaping from clause to clause, hungrily, frantically, getting stuck on some and repeating them: ". . . rising high school senior, twice-varsity athlete, and former student body president Henry McCleary was stabbed earlier this week in what appears to be a senseless and misfortunate chance encounter. . . . McCleary was accompanied by a classmate and friend Christopher Collins. . . . While McCleary was taken to the emergency ward of Hudson Memorial, Collins boasted of chasing away the attacker. . . . In text exchanges and social media posts reviewed by the *Gazette*—" He rereads that last part: *They're looking through my texts?* He continues: "Collins, unharmed, reportedly told classmates that Thompkins came at McCleary 'like a wild animal' and that he 'chased her off.' He warned her to 'keep running and never look back.' . . ." Chris recognizes the quotes but wishes he didn't. He sounds crude and dumb and maybe even racist. *But I know things don't sound good! That's why I need to explain the full picture, that's why I need to talk to Henry.* ". . . McCleary is believed to be in stable condition . . ." That's more than he knows about Henry's condition, he thinks bitterly. ". . . Chiara Thompkins, the African American runaway teen believed to have committed the assault, is still at large . . ." *So they haven't found her.* ". . . Sources close to the investigation have disclosed to the *Gazette* that Thompkins has no confirmed current residential address. She is estranged from her mother and stepfather, both longtime residents of Philadelphia, and has attended Kitchewan High School since the 2017–18 academic year. . . . Police found a backpack of feminine personal effects on the football field"—Chris feels his face get hot as he continues reading—"near the site of the assault as well as a garbage bag of girls' clothing in the high school library. . . . A representative for the McCleary family thanked town residents for their outpouring of support and said: 'We appreciate your thoughts and prayers for our Henry.' . . ."

He wants to scream. Instead, he looks at his mom. Her eyes are burning into him. He says, "Mom, I didn't speak to any reporters. I swear."

She doesn't say anything right away, so he adds, "I just— A few of my friends called and texted and stuff. They heard about the—the thing. And I wrote some of them back. But—but it was private, Mom, I swear. And I don't post on public pages. There's a closed group for KHS on Facebook, and people were tagging me . . . But it's not public, Mom. It's just for students. I didn't—I didn't—I didn't know." He feels that familiar lump take hold of his throat and his eyes grow heavy like storm clouds. *God, this is so unfair.* He can't believe the paper can print all this, that they read his private messages. How did they do that?

His mom is taking a step back and shaking her head. She's still not saying anything.

"Mom, I swear." She walks toward his bedroom door. "Mom, where are you going?" he calls after her.

"I'm calling the paper, that's what I'm doing," she snaps. "I'm reminding them you are a child. A naïve, immature, silly child! Don't they have any decency—printing something like this?" Her face is red hot. She continues, "And then I'm calling your father. Which you know I love doing." Her voice drips with bitterness. "He's been in enough hot water in his lifetime, God knows, so maybe he can help you figure out what to do. Because I sure as hell don't have a clue." She pauses to collect herself and says more slowly, "All this, after we talked about it—we talked about how you wouldn't say anything to anyone until you and I met with a lawyer. Until we spoke to your richy-rich friend and his snooty parents. But you couldn't wait! I hope you're happy, Chris. I hope you're happy." She shuts the door to his bedroom, and he can hear her footsteps retreat down the hall.

Mom, I'm sorry. I'm really sorry, he wants to call after her. *I didn't mean to mess up. I didn't know* . . . But when he opens his mouth, nothing comes out. Not even a whisper. Instead, a tingling sensation moves from his toes up his legs, from his torso to his neck, from his fingertips to the tops of his shoulders, and it lands, buzzing, whirling, in his head and around his mouth. Familiar but long forgotten: pins and needles on his open lips around his silent mouth. *Déjà vu.*

SIXTEEN

When Superintendent Bill Landrieu drops his latest bombshell—that she should skip the emergency town hall at Kitchewan High tomorrow evening—Mabel Burrowes's nostrils flare, her breath quickens, and her insides begin to bubble like a kettle reaching its boiling point. She stares at the floor of the superintendent's living room, at the Persian-style rug with its explosion of overdone colors and flourishes that Mabel suspects is not from Persia. She tightens her grip around the handle of her teacup, covered with images of roses and filled with lukewarm English breakfast tea.

When she's certain her voice won't waver or sharpen into a tone that could be labeled shrill, she begins to respond, looking directly into the nutmeg-colored eyes of the superintendent of Kitchewan Unified School District, her longtime supposed friend and mentor. "But, Bill, I—"

"Mabel, I know." The superintendent's long face nods vigorously and he holds up one of his large, thin hands. Mabel's eyes are drawn to his silver wedding band, glinting from his movement. "The thing is," he continues without specifying further what exactly he knows, "this is quite a pickle for the school district. Apparently, the McCleary boy's parents might sue the school dis—"

"But"—she puts one hand on the back of her neck and gives it a tight squeeze as she feels individual vertebrae tensing up—"sue for what?"

"There's concern about the school being kept unlocked all summer, some duty of care or negligence business." The superintendent swats the same hand in the air, light reflecting off his ring, gesticulating to indicate he's not certain of the specifics. "The boy's father, well, he's one of those New York banker types. And apparently he's got an army of Manhattan legal eagles looking into every single detail of this thing with a microscope, working out the different angles. Including ways to blame the district." He pauses here to bite into one of the butter cookies from a tray set before them on the coffee table.

Mabel takes the opportunity to jump in. "I don't understand what this has got to do with me not being there tomorrow evening."

The superintendent dusts crumbs from his face and lets out a protracted sigh. He puts down his teacup directly on the hardwood coffee table and not on a coaster decorated with scenes of a nondescript countryside.

Mabel tries not to cringe at either the overwrought décor or at Bill.

"Mabel," he says, "you and I have known each other for—what—over a decade," looking directly into her eyes, "and you know I personally vouched for you to come on board as principal here. Some would even say," sucking some air before continuing, "I stuck my neck out for you." He pauses to scan her face.

Mabel draws her head into a slow and steady nod, with her lips pressing together more tightly at that last part.

Bill breaks his gaze from Mabel and reaches for another cookie. "Now, I'm not looking for a medal or anything." More gesticulating, his thin fingers wrapped around the cookie. "That's not the point. I just want you to know I care about you and I'm looking out for you." He leans back and puts the cookie into his mouth in one bite.

Mabel gulps away a lump that is forming in her throat and winces as the crick in her neck sharpens. For how long does she "owe" Bill for recommending her for a job for which she was well qualified and has done damn well by any metric? she wonders, tasting a bitterness in her mouth. She notices Bill is chewing energetically and looking out a window at the overcast sky rather than at her. She's ready to tell Bill how much she appreciates his having her back when he turns back to her and says, "When I tell you this, Mabel, don't take it the wrong way . . ."

His eyes pinch together, and he shifts in his seat. "The, um, optics of this thing are tricky." He pauses, and it appears he's examining the pattern of flourishes on the faux-Persian rug. He then says, looking at her, as if he's grappling with himself, "Ah, the heck with it. Let me be straight with you, Mabel. As a friend."

Mabel swallows again.

"The boy's family lawyer has said you showed favoritism to that"—he pauses—"girl—the criminal—" Mabel blinks back any re-action but can feel her head throbbing. "That you knew about her, uh, situation. That you enrolled her in the school when you shouldn't have. That you put our kids in danger for *emotional reasons*."

Mabel's grip tightens around the teacup handle until she feels her nails digging into her palm. She sets the cup down on a coaster. Her hands ball up and her head grows hot at the accusation. Bill's words ring in her ears, as she replays when she'd enrolled Chiara in Kitchewan High last September: how Chiara had come alone to the school, and Mabel—intrigued (and excited) by a new Black student and also the prospect of meeting her parents—had asked if they should wait for anyone else, parents being optional at these meetings but recommended, that they could reschedule when her folks were free, only to be met with a firm, defensive "I can do this myself. I take care of myself." So she'd dropped it.

She recalls how she then accepted a crumpled report card from a high school in Pennsylvania that Chiara had produced after sifting through a motley assortment from a dirt-streaked backpack. Mabel could have asked why Chiara was carrying around things like a change of clothing, deodorant, and loose childhood photographs, but Chiara had appeared so self-conscious and eager to zip everything back in her bag that Mabel pretended not to notice. Officially, Mabel was to insist on a formal transcript, but unofficially, Chiara was there, she had her report card, and in Mabel's judgment as an educator, it would be best for all—pupil and teachers—if she started her school year at the same time as everyone else. Besides, Mabel could already predict the culture shock in store for this teenager when she met her better-groomed, well-heeled, lighter-skinned peers; there was no reason to complicate things further, she'd reasoned with a sigh.

Mabel sighs now.

Bill is still talking. "The thing about tomorrow is," he says, "well, the other parents might"—he pauses—"they might have questions. Uncomfortable questions." He pauses again and, looking her dead in the eyes, asks, "Mabel, did you know the girl was violent?"

Mabel feels her eyebrows compress and her forehead crease. "No," she says quickly, forcefully, more forcefully than she intends. "Of course not," she adds in a softer voice.

She notices for the first time that Bill is looking down at something, reading from a folded-up piece of paper on the table in front of him. She'd missed it before, but it looks like he has handwritten notes. She feels her eyebrows strain closer together. She thinks of how casually Bill had proposed they catch up this morning. Like it was an impromptu thing, a discussion between friends, colleagues. Not something deliberate, rehearsed.

Beads of sweat condense on Mabel's upper lip, and her insides pulse. She wants to know why Bill is asking her all this. Only she suspects she already knows. None of this would be happening if she and Chiara weren't both— She catches herself, jaw clenched. She didn't get this far through gut reactions, through volatility. What is it her therapist tells her to do at times like this, when she's getting heated? *Ah, that's right: Slow it down, she says. Take slow, deep breaths and count to ten, backward, since that requires more concentration.*

"The thing is, Mabel, I've been told there was an incident during the school year that some of the students are talking about on Facebook and Twitter and whatever else they use in place of face-to-face conversation," Bill says. "The girl swore at a gym teacher, in front of the whole class. Yelled, charged at her practically. And you—you spoke with her after."

Mabel's heart is pounding. Her words sound distant, like someone else is speaking. "It wasn't like that, Bill. Chiara didn't charge at anyone." She pauses to inhale, reminding herself to remain calm. "I spoke with the gym teacher, Bitsy McGovern. She—Chiara—got upset during the swimming unit of phys ed. She didn't swear at Bitsy." Mabel feels her professional smile, the one she wears when she's annoyed but needs to be cordial, spread across her face. "Or, well, she didn't mean to." A pause. "She was embarrassed, you see, because she didn't know how to swim, and Bitsy didn't know that and had come down hard on her." She shakes her head as she describes the misunderstanding. "It was wrong, it was, but teenagers sometimes talk back to teachers. It comes with the territory. Besides, I spoke with Chiara, Bill. I gave her detention." She sets down her teacup, feeling an urge to emphasize her words with her hands. "I explained we don't condone outbursts like that at Kitchewan High. I explained that. But we came up with a solution. Bitsy and I"—a gesture with both of her hands—"arranged for Chiara to learn how to swim in a private setting, from another student. It was sweet in a way, you know." Her lips curl and her head tilts. "Because in her old community, in a lot of communities, really, the children don't learn how to swim, they don't have access—" But when she looks over at Bill, she sees he's sitting with his hands clasped together, his face resting in patient disinterest, waiting for her to stop speaking. *He's not even listening.* She closes her mouth, clamps her jaw, and exhales forcefully. *Ten.*

"That's all well and good, Mabel. If the girl hadn't stabbed someone." Bill sighs as if pained and says, "The lawyer for the boy's family, he's saying the school should have known about the girl's living situation. That we *effectively* knew."

Mabel feels her cheeks get warm. It was true she'd noticed Chiara hanging around alone after school on a number of afternoons, by the outdoor bleachers or in empty classrooms. She'd even gently asked if everything was okay on one occasion. But she'd received a half shrug and something about how it's quieter here than at home. So Mabel, self-conscious about questioning a Black student when many of her white students spent time at the school after hours without being subject to questions by the principal, hadn't pressed any further. She imagines the smug, long-faced McCleary lawyer, with his copper-toned skin unnaturally absent of wrinkles, twisting and manipulating Mabel's appropriate show of concern for and reaction to Chiara Thompkins into a something else. She shakes her head. *Nine.*

Bill seems to take her gesture as a denial. "I'm not saying I agree, Mabel, but"—he pauses—"did you know the girl was apparently living in the school this summer? Like in that Tom Hanks movie where he lives in the airport . . ."

Of course she didn't know, she wants to protest. The nerve of Bill to ask her if she'd suggest the poor child, any child, live without a proper home. She swallows. *Eight.*

He continues. "And when we found out Chiara doesn't live in Kitchewan, well, the question became, how is she in the school in the first place?" Mabel grinds her teeth. *Seven.*

"I'm not saying you did anything wrong. But in these situations, the parents look for someone to point to as they look for answers. Not a scapegoat, but someone . . ."

Her heart beats like a hammer as she thinks about how she feels about being Bill and the school board's scapegoat. Instead of telling him, she outstretches her fingers, as if she can concentrate all of her angry energy in her individual digits, compartmentalize it. *Six.*

"With the swimming pool being unlocked, it all goes to this issue of if the school was taking good care . . ."

Mabel is tempted to chime in, to remind him the school has been unlocked for as long as she can remember. And how ludicrous this all is. But Bill doesn't pause.

". . . when we think about what parents are going to want to hear tomorrow night, well, maybe it's for the best if they hear from someone with more distance." Bill's voice sounds distant, obscured under the sound of her heavy exhale. *Five.*

"We'll obviously want to convey that our thoughts and prayers are with the boy's family as he recovers . . ."

Okay, this counting thing is working a little, kind of. She feels her pulse slowing, and she stops herself from interrupting to remind Bill that according to this morning's *Westchester Gazette*, Henry McCleary is doing just fine.

". . . not to mention the other children. The Singh girl and the other boy. They weren't physically injured, but there could be trauma or PTSD . . ."

Her hands clench up again and her shoulders rise. She remembers the look of confusion and worry in Angela Singh's large, fearful eyes when she walked into the police interview with her father. *Four.*

"Don't consider this a punishment, Mabel, because it's not. It's just that you're close to the situation, to the runaway girl. Not in fact, perhaps, but optically, you know . . ."

His constant repetition of her name was really starting to aggravate her. *Three.*

". . . and, Mabel, this goes without saying, but I stand by you one hundred percent."

Bill's wife walks into the sitting room with an empty tray. In a sweet voice that strikes Mabel as mock naive, she says, "I hope I'm not interrupting. You two have been holed up in here for a long time, and on a Saturday in the summer, no less." Turning to Bill, "Honey, you need to let Mabel get back home, especially with this bad weather we're supposed to get."

Mabel would normally take this as her not-so-subtle cue to excuse herself, but her face is hot and her blood boiling. She ignores Bill's wife with her artificial smile. She pretends she doesn't see her standing in wait to insincerely protest Mabel's departure. Still seated, staring straight at Bill, Mabel says, "Let me go to the town hall tomorrow, Bill."

Bill's eyes widen in surprise at the firmness in Mabel's voice and the confidence of her gaze. It's obvious he didn't expect her to challenge him. He throws a look of bewilderment over at his wife, who steps farther into the room, blocking Mabel's line of sight of Bill, like a physical barrier. She says, "Mabel, you're welcome to stay for lunch if you'd like . . ." The way her voice trills upward and trails off, Mabel understands she means just the opposite, that her time is up. Not that Mabel could stay. *Two.*

This time Mabel stands and collects her handbag. Solemnly, "I should get going. I promised the boys I'd pick up lunch." With a pursed smile, "Thanks for the tea, Nancy."

Bill stands up, too, visibly relieved. He walks Mabel to the front door. "I'm glad we had a chance to talk, Mabel. You know how much the school board and I appreciate you." He adds, "Send Robert and the boys our best."

The mention of her estranged husband's name causes Mabel's knees to wobble. A surge of unidentifiable emotion washes over her. She nods vigorously at Bill and his wife, who stands just behind him, and gives them both a forced grin, hoping they don't notice what's coursing within her. For good measure, but in a less than steady voice, she adds, "I understand, Bill. Thank you so much," only to immediately regret her words and accompanying shit-eating smile.

As Mabel walks to her sedan, she scolds herself for blurting the exact opposite of what she thinks. She feels resentment brewing, along with a creeping suspicion she normally doesn't allow herself to entertain:

that Bill's behavior, that his view of things, in spite of his knowing her work, knowing her family, knowing her, for fifteen years, in spite of them being not just colleagues but friends, was colored by—she hesitates to even think it—her color. *If this is how they treat us when they know us, what chance does Chiara Thompkins have?*

A rumble rolls through the air, accompanied by a gust of wind that causes the leaves on the oaks lining the Landrieus' driveway to rustle as if they're shivering. The sky darkens, and, seated in her car, Mabel shudders. She looks into her rearview mirror to reverse out of the Landrieus' long driveway. The corners of her mouth point downward in a thick scowl. Enrolling Chiara Thompkins in the high school had been the right decision, she tells her reflection; perhaps not technically, but it was the correct course of action, in the best interests of the child. And what followed on the football field—her jaw tightens—was not a direct consequence. There was more to it; something happened, something less convenient than pointing a finger at her. She exhales forcefully before declaring, out loud this time, "One. Fuck you, Bill, and your goddamn school board."

She peels away from the driveway, more quickly than is prudent, leaving behind the smell of burnt tires in the foreboding afternoon air.

SEVENTEEN

For as long as she can remember, Angie has had conversations with her mother in her sleep. Awake, conscious, she does everything she can to push the woman, the figment of a woman, really, from her head, from her heart, and from the top of her mind. Yet when dreaming, as much as she tells herself she doesn't want her, doesn't care about her, doesn't think about her, and certainly doesn't need her, she's there. Not every sleep, but she shows up every now and again. And confoundingly, without fail, Angie doesn't feel angry or ignore her like she imagines she will. Confoundingly, they get along just fine. Confoundingly, it feels natural.

It's always the same: They sit on the front steps of a house that Angie's never seen in her real life, the same dandelion color as the house on Lakeview Terrace. There's a wraparound porch and a porch swing with worn cushions in a seashell print—the same fabric as the one on Angie's bedspread.

They are surrounded by a sun-drenched field of tall grass that dances in light wind and shimmers with what appear to be flecks of gold. It's always sunny. Endless summer. And it's always just the two of them. No one else.

Her mother is braiding Angie's long hair, which looks more auburn than brown-black on account of the light. It slips in and out of her fingers and glides through the bristles of the hairbrush like it's made of satin. Never mind that Angie never wears her hair in a braid and that her actual hair is sharp and brittle like hay or dead grass, dried out from chlorine. Never mind that the braiding, which should only take a few minutes, is interminable.

On the steps, Angie does most of the speaking, when they're not sitting in silence, always with her back to her mother, facing the grass. The uneven tufts remind her of the surface of water, always in motion, always changing. She tells her mother that. She tells her other things, too. About a recent swim meet and how she was worried she might throw up from nerves before the race; how it feels to be in water, to move in water, to hear nothing clearly but the water itself—because in her dreams, her mother can't swim, a detail she may have assumed based on her father's fear of water deeper than calf level.

Sometimes Angie tells her mother about more personal topics: like how in a group, she forgets to speak up, to share what she's thinking. She forgets because she's so absorbed in listening and observing and there's never a natural break. Only it turns out that when she doesn't speak, people think she's stuck-up or not interested, or they forget she's even there. What can she do differently, she wonders, and will it always be like this? Her mother seems to understand, because she pats Angie's head, and when she does, it feels like she's lifted a weight. Unwrinkled a crease in Angie's brain.

Angie doesn't speak with her mother about her dad. She's afraid to mention him, worried that if she does, the steps, that sunny day, that gentle breeze, this woman so lovingly forever braiding her beautiful hair will disappear.

She avoids other topics, too—things that make her cheeks redden or voice wobble. Like how she's been thinking about Henry a lot recently or the fight she had with Sam a few months ago. Yet it's like her mother already knows what Angie doesn't say. She sprinkles in gentle but relevant comments, always framed as an observation or a question, like "You were happier when you weren't arguing with Samantha. Should you try harder to patch things up?" or "Sometimes when we think about someone so much, we invent in our minds who they are. It's good to get to know people who interest you in real life." Angie doesn't say anything in response, but her throat swells, and she gulps and nods, feeling both vulnerable and relieved to be understood.

The episodes always end the same way. When Angela turns to look into her mother's face, spots appear. Like blots when you stare directly into light. They grow larger, as if they're bleeding, until they're not blots but a red stain that washes over everything. Until she can't see anything. She can't feel anything. She can't smell anything. Her breath gets caught in her throat, and it's over. It's all gone.

Today, however, it's different. For the past twenty-four hours, in between everything else, Angie has been staring at "Purnima C." On her phone screen, on her laptop, on her tablet, and in her mind. Angie has an image. An actual photo. Of the face that she's been searching for and turning toward for years now, only to have it disappear every time.

Purnima C's profile is public but bare, as if she only recently joined Facebook. She has just two other friends and no personal information or photo albums. Angie hasn't decided what to do about the request. But she has been staring at the profile photo, tracing the woman's eyebrows, her soft jawline, her thin lips, and even the half-moons underneath her eyes. Never mind that the woman in the photo is standing in front of a dumpy city skyline on a not-sunny day. Never mind. *Because it's her. At last, it's her.*

And yet, something's changed. In seeing her, the real her, something feels off. Not as she expected. Not who she expected. Or at least that's what Angie thinks as she lies on the couch in the family room of her empty house and half watches a *Big Bang Theory* rerun, *Jane Eyre* facedown on her lap.

She feels her mouth stretch into a broad yawn, the kind that gives even her molars some air, and her eyelids grow heavy, like they're weighted. She yawns again.

Angie is back at the dandelion house, sitting on the lower step; wisps of her glossy, sun-drenched hair tickle her face. She squints from the brightness of the day. And the woman, her mother, sits behind, steps above her, brushing her hair, dividing it into sections, getting ready to braid it. She smells of ginger and lemon and a hint of perspiration.

It's the same, but something's different.

The brushing. The bristles of the hairbrush. They feel harder against her scalp. The pressure feels stronger. Not painful, but different.

"I've been getting a lot of questions about what happened on the football field," Angie begins. "I feel really bad about it . . . I have been trying to—"

"What do you feel bad about, Anjali?"

She shivers. Anjali. No one calls her that. She doesn't even recall her dream-mother calling her that before. Angie and her dad made a conscious decision to change her name to Angela when she changed elementary schools, when they moved from the house with the big garden and empty bedrooms to Lakeview Terrace. The name change was meant to help her fit in with the kids at school, officially, but Angie knew, even then, that there was more to it. After all, her dad has gone by Bobby for as long as she can remember, but he never changed his legal name. "I guess I feel bad that—that Henry got stabbed," she says.

"Mmm . . . that's the boy you've been thinking about, isn't it? Henry."

Angie blushes. She never told her that.

"What about the girl? The one who ran off. What happened to her?" her mother asks.

"I—I don't know. She stabbed him and ran away."

"Why did she do that?"

Her question seems innocent enough, and it's something Angie has been wondering herself but trying not to. Her scalp is tingling from the hairbrush bristles. "Because she's violent, I guess." Angie shrugs. "She's homeless and maybe that made her desperate and—and violent—ow!" Her mother is pulling her scalp too tightly.

Her mother drops Angie's hair from her hands and pats her head. "Sorry, beta. I didn't mean to hurt you." She undoes the braid and starts anew. "Keep going."

"Well . . . I don't know if she's violent. But I think she is, since she stabbed Henry. I don't—I don't know her like that." The words tumble out of her and she can't stop them. "I just taught her to swim. Because I had to. The teacher asked me to. She seemed fine, but—but"—a pause—"we aren't friends."

"Did you want to be friends?"

Angie shrugs again. What a strange thing to ask, she thinks, especially after all that happened. "I never thought about it, I guess."

"Are these boys, the ones who were there, on the field, are they your friends?"

Angie bites her lip and watches the grass swaying in the breeze. She swears she didn't tell her mother about any of this before, but she knows anyway. "Yeah, we're friends." Ouch. Her mom's pulling too tightly again.

"Hmm . . ."

"Well, not friends, maybe. I mean, I don't really like one of them, Chris. He's kind of mean and he's always saying not-nice things about people and to people. As a joke, I guess, but it's not funny. And Henry and I—well—I know him and he's nice to me . . ." Her voice trails off, and she thinks about how neither of them—neither Chris nor Henry—could in fact be described as a friend. She didn't like the things Chris said to her—not just the Pocahontas stuff, which was annoying, but he hadn't done that in a while. He'd also told her if she swam too much, she'd look like a flat-chested lesbian because, according to Chris, sports bras and sports clothing "compressed" you. "That's why you see lots of lesbians playing sports," he'd told her authoritatively, as if any of his statements made remote sense. Angie remembered avoiding eye contact with him when he'd said that and staring at the floor of Henry's car. She remembered feeling his creepy eyes lingering on her chest, and slouching deeper into her baggy sweatshirt. Henry had been there. He hadn't laughed or anything, but he also hadn't told him to stop it. It was Sam who told Chris to quit being ignorant. But, Angie reasons, none of that was Henry's fault. Henry is different. Not a friend, perhaps, but he gave her rides home a bunch of times, and he was nice to her. Although she wondered why he'd never said anything in her defense when Sam got mad at her about that one time in the car. He could have easily cleared the whole thing up, stood up for Angie, explained it was unplanned and just that one time, that one kiss. But he hadn't. Maybe because he also didn't mind if it happened again. Either way, she's not sure if Henry is a friend.

"But you feel bad about this boy being hurt?"

"Yeah, of course. It was horrible. Henry was bleeding everywhere."

"I'm sorry you had to see that. That sounds terrible. But"—her mother pauses before asking again—"why did the girl hurt him?"

"I—I don't know. They were yelling before I got there, and she screamed, maybe. I couldn't hear what she said . . ." Angie thinks about the noises from the football field as she'd approached. She thinks about the sound of a girl shrieking, in between what sounded like sobs. She jerks, feeling her mother pull a knot in her normally glossy, smooth dream-hair. She says, "She sounded upset. Like she was upset about something."

"So the girl was screaming and sounded upset, and one of the boys got hurt?"

Angie nods, but says, "I guess."

"Anjali, why are you doubting yourself?"

Angie gulps. The braid feels almost done. It never feels almost done.

There's always more hair, there's always something to fix, something that needs to be undone and redone. Her breathing feels shallow. She feels unsettled.

"Why are you afraid to say what you think? What are you scared of? And what about that poor girl? The one they're looking for and that your classmates are making fun of?"

"What am I supposed to do?"

"You know what to do, Anjali. I raised you better than that." She pats Angie's hair. "There. All done."

Angie is stunned. She tries to whip her head around and jump onto her feet, to point her finger at this woman and tell her what is what. Only she can't. She can't move. She's stuck. Like she's made of stone, and yet inside her, words are brewing like a coming storm: *You don't get to say that, because you didn't raise me. You weren't around. You left us. You left me!*

She concentrates all her might on moving, turning to see her mother, to look her in the eye. To confirm her face is the face she's been memorizing from the Facebook photo.

And then, the grip of the unknown force that was keeping her glued in place loosens its hold. Her body whips itself around. She sucks in a breath, ready for whatever's next.

But with a flash of white, everything goes blank.

EIGHTEEN

A flash of white ripples through the kitchen, and Babur jolts in surprise. The white is succeeded by a *boom, boom, boom*. Thunder and lightning. Then, *boom* again, followed by a crash. And *zzzap*. The power's out.

Babur has managed not to fall off the kitchen stool he's sitting on, but his balance is shaken. His forearms stiffen as he grips the kitchen counter.

There's rustling from the family room, followed by footsteps.

"Dad. Did you hear that?" Angie appears at the entrance to the kitchen. Her voice is hoarse, thick with sleep, and her face is ghoulishly illuminated in an icy blue by the light from her cell phone screen. Her long hair is astray and her T-shirt crumpled.

Babur shudders.

Angie had been sleeping on the couch when he'd come home this afternoon. He'd considered waking her, to share the news from the McClearys. The good news. But she'd looked so peaceful—stretched out, eyes closed, mouth slightly ajar, an open book resting on her stomach, rising and falling with her breaths—that he left her.

"What was that?" Angie asks, presumably referring to the crash.

Babur pushes aside the document he received from the McClearys and picks up his phone for light. It's not pitch black yet, more like blue-black, low light where you can still make out outlines of objects but where the specifics, like the printed words he's been poring over, are fuzzy—not without more light. Not at his age, anyway.

"I'll go check," he says. Before going, he pulls down a box of tea lights from a kitchen cabinet and sets them on the counter. He'd bought them for Diwali last fall, determined that he and his daughter would light the way for the homecoming of Lord Rama, that he'd teach Angie something about their heritage before she graduated from high school and left home, and it was too late.

Angie sits on the same stool where Babur was seated when he was examining the McClearys' document. She's already so engrossed in her phone, she doesn't appear to notice the papers a few inches away from her on the counter.

In the study, Babur pulls up the window blinds. It's early evening, barely seven o'clock. Yet the heavy rain and dark gray sky have swallowed all rays of daylight that normally linger until at least eight. There are no lights in the windows of neighboring houses, and the streetlights are also out. Straight ahead, beyond his front lawn, he spots the likely culprit: A wooden electricity pole stands crookedly, like it's been tipped over. Broken wires dangle in the wind. Near the pole, he sees a tree that looks like it's been sliced clean in half. He shakes his head; this does not look good. It could be a while before anyone comes to fix the power line in this weather, he thinks. He wonders if the electricity is also out in the McClearys' house, and how they're managing, moving about in the dark in that gigantic home.

This morning was Babur's first time in the McClearys' house beyond their main hallway, where he'd been to fetch or drop off Angie many times. And while he'd normally welcome an audience with Fred and Claire McCleary in their artfully decorated, impeccable home, Babur wished he didn't have to have the meeting on this particular morning, or during this particular month, for that matter. Between Purnima's outrageous email (*that woman!*), Angie's mood swings, an anticipated slowdown in weekend business with the coming tropical storm, and his concerns about missing his monthly financial targets for Move on account of tending to the aforementioned concerns, his usual difficulty sleeping has become full-on insomnia, indigo semicircles under his eyes and a skull-crushing headache the evidence.

Yet Babur couldn't cancel on the McClearys after standing them up on Thursday, despite his very reasonable excuse—a brush with death. Because to go into it, to explain what came to pass, would involve explaining a number of other things that eluded concise and comfortable explanation. It was better to let the McClearys think he'd "lost track of time," even though in truth, Babur tracked time like a bloodhound tracks scent. It was better to let the meeting, during which he planned to affirm a united front in cooperating with the police, go forward. And in retrospect, it was so very, truly, unbelievably fortunate it had.

Another clap of thunder reverberates, and a flash of lightning emblazes the sky. Babur removes his face from the window. As if on cue, his phone screen lights up with an emergency alert, a flash-flood and power-outage warning. He hears the wind whistling through the closed window and shivers.

"Dad . . . ?" he hears Angie call.

"Coming, beta," he replies, remembering Angie has never been too fond of thunderstorms. Babur rushes for the kitchen by the light of his cell phone, stubbing his toe against the edge of his desk (ouch!) and accidentally pushing a pile of papers and the manila envelope from Topeka that had been resting near his keyboard onto the floor. He hastily stacks the fallen items in a sloppy pile back on his desk.

In the kitchen, Angie is hunched over the counter in the same spot as before. She has lit a half dozen of the tea lights. Their flames create a dreamy orange glow.

"Ang, you won't believe this," he begins, getting ready to tell her about the split tree. As he gets closer, he sees she's holding her phone out, angling its glow toward something.

Angie cuts in and holds up the document from the McClearys. "What is this?"

Babur freezes.

He wishes he'd had a chance to explain everything to her. The way she's looking at him, with her eyes pinched together, and her eyebrows arched upward, and the point on the end of her nose looking even more pointed, he can't speak. His throat is caught. *Flashes of Purnima.* Babur feels his face heat up. *What is it about this woman that she won't leave me alone, that she spoils what could have been happy news?* He blinks hard and fast and clears his throat, shaking off the unwelcome apparition superimposing itself onto his precious daughter.

"Oh, good. You found the papers," he says. "I was meaning to tell you when you woke up, beta." He walks toward her, mostly to see her up close, to confirm it's Angie. *Not her.*

She curls her bottom lip into her mouth and her eyes narrow further.

He needs to defuse her reaction, reassure her, he thinks. "I had a meeting, Angie, today with the McClearys, Samantha's mom and dad. It—" He inhales sharply, feeling himself flailing, unprepared. He continues with deliberate cheer, "It was very good, beta! Very, very good!" It worked. He's manifested the cheer. The words spill out from his mouth like water from a breached dam. He can't stop, he can't slow down. "You see, beta, they want to—to sponsor you. They want to fund your swimming and also some of your college. They have a foundation—well, they're starting one—and they will focus on student athletes, and they think"—he pauses to catch his breath—"that you are remarkable." His eyes shine as he recalls how they'd described his Angie, how at one point it seemed that Claire McCleary had been borderline rueful that her own daughter didn't display some of Angie's traits.

"But, Dad," Angie says, "what does that have to do with this?" She picks up the document. It's wrinkled from water damage when Babur had tucked it under his armpit while racing from his car into the house during the torrential rain this afternoon. Angie shakes it dangerously close to one of the tea lights. Babur's grin melts. He holds his breath, fearing the document will catch fire. It doesn't.

"Dad, do you know what this is?" She reads from the document. "This 'Non-Disparagement and Confidentiality Agreement'?"

Babur feels his eyebrows unfurl. He takes a deep breath and exhales carefully, slowly. He'd anticipated she'd have questions. He himself felt some unease about the timing, the broader situation—not that any of that was the Singhs' concern. But if Angie is only worried about the paperwork, he can help her understand. He nods and replies, "Oh, that. It's for their lawyers. Nothing for you to worry about, beta. It's standard. These are the things people do when they conduct business."

He sees her return a skeptical look. She places the document down on the counter and angles her phone light at it. "Have you read this, Dad? 'Wherefore the undersigned beneficiaries, the Singh family, hereby consent and agree that all terms and arrangements concerning their agreement with the McCleary Family Trust and affiliated entities, as defined herein, together the Sponsor, shall be bound to the terms and conditions of this Agreement.'" She stops and turns to Babur. "Dad, did you understand even one word of that?"

Babur shrugs, attempting to conceal his embarrassment with feigned nonchalance. "It's nothing, beta. This is how these people do things. It's business."

"Should we sign something we don't understand? Do we need a lawyer?"

Babur gives Angie's shoulder a light squeeze upon noticing her face tense up. She ignores his hand, and he drops it back to his side. "Don't stress yourself, beta. It's nothing like that. They have lawyers. You only need your own lawyer when you're against someone." He adds for good measure, making a swatting motion, "You watch too much TV."

Angie throws him a sideways glance before she continues reading:
"'The Singh family will not discuss any financial arrangements between itself, any member thereof, and the Sponsor, unless as otherwise
pre-authorized in writing by the Sponsor or required by applicable law
or regulation.'" A pause, and then: "Dad, this limits what we can say.
Like a gag order."

"Gag what? What is there to gag? Angie, beta, you're making too
much of this. Even if they want to gag, what is it to us?" It's his turn
to be annoyed. His American daughter has adopted this country's confounding habit of being obsessed with freedom, even when there are
certain tangible benefits to being tethered.

"What are they giving us?"

"We will discuss that with them. We will finalize," he says more
calmly. No use in becoming agitated, even if Angie is being difficult.
"As a partnership." He repeats the phrase the McClearys used, half
hoping that in doing so he'll sound as self-assured as Fred McCleary,
that he'll be able to further push down some of his own lingering
doubts. "They suggested"—he pauses, attempting to channel Fred
McCleary and his calm, direct gaze—"sponsoring you for a swimming club like you always wanted . . . and we spoke about college."
Angie's unimpressed return gaze sparks a desperation to get her to
see things differently, to consider things. He ignores his own questions about the arrangement and continues with bombast, "This is a
tremendous opportunity, Angie, especially before your sophomore
year, before the college scouts and"—he stops himself from saying
"Olympics"—"other people will take interest. And they want to give
it to you!"

"There are scholarships to colleges, you know. Good colleges, too."

"But, Angie, beta, I don't understand." And he doesn't. "You have
wanted to be part of a swimming club for so long. I have tried to save
away, and I know you also collect some dollars here and there from
that coffee shop, but we have not budgeted for this. And—and college.
Well, college is a massive expense. We don't want—we cannot cut any

corners when it comes to your future. Why not take this generous offer from this family, this family you know so well?"

"Because—because this feels weird."

"What weird, beta?" Babur feels his voice rising and his sentences becoming halted, stilted, with missing verbs and prepositions, as happens when he becomes overly excited.

"Were you going to tell me or were you going to sign this on your own?" He sees the reflection of a tea light flickering in her eyes, and for an instant, it looks like her gaze is on fire.

"I don't understand why you're behaving like this. Of course I was going to tell you. I couldn't wait to. And you need to sign also. And it's nothing. There's nothing to worry about."

"When did you see them?"

"Today. This morning."

"And did they talk about what happened on the football field?"

Babur clicks his mouth lightly. "This is a separate matter, Angie beta," he says, feeling disingenuous for not acknowledging he, too, had assumed the meeting would be about the incident.

Angie shakes her head and starts reading from the document again: "'The Singh family shall under no circumstances directly or indirectly, in public or private, disparage the Sponsor or individual members of the McCleary family with regards to any matter between the parties, whether related or not to or predating this Agreement and—'" She stops short. Her phone light zaps off. "Great. My phone just died." She picks up one of the tea lights, only to set it down quickly, wincing at the temperature of the thin metal holder.

"Careful," he says, leaning in to move the candle away from her.

"I'm fine," she snaps. "Do you have the flashlight?"

He feels in his back jeans pocket. Nothing. He'd meant to get the flashlight when he went to the study but had forgotten. "Sorry, beta, I'll go—"

"No, it's fine. I'll go."

"It's in the—"

"I know where it is."

She stands up more noisily than Babur suspects she needs to, a signal she's annoyed with him. But why? There's no need to get so worked up, to overthink some legal formality.

When the McClearys had explained their reason for wanting to meet with Babur, he'd initially thought he'd misheard them, had too much wax in his ears, perhaps. He'd also been struggling to maintain an appropriate posture on the wicker chair in which he was seated in the McClearys' glass-encased sunroom. The chair was circular like a tilted basin, and every time he shifted his weight the beige-gray cushion on top of the wicker frame slid backward and swallowed him deeper into the seat. When Fred had spoken, Babur had moved and accidentally slipped toward the back of the chair, grasping at the sides to pull himself upright.

"You okay there, Bobby?" Fred McCleary had asked with a light chuckle, offering him a tanned hand, wrist encircled by an elaborate watch.

Fred must be around Babur's age, maybe a few years older, even, but, Babur remembers thinking, the skin on his face is more taut than Babur's. And apart from the laugh lines that appear when he smiles, Fred has none of the crags or sags, or scarred-over evidence of teenage pimples, or blue-purple half-moons under his eyes that Babur finds on his own face.

Babur's cheeks had burned at Fred noticing him fumbling on their seating. They must think he's simple. He'd looked down at his sneakers. Once he'd managed to readjust himself slightly uncomfortably on the edge of his chair, he'd asked, five-star smile back in place, "I didn't get you, Fred. Can you, uh, explain?"

Fred and his wife sat side by side on a love seat with a wicker frame that matched the sink-basin-shaped armchair in which they'd placed Babur. They appeared to have none of the difficulty maintaining their balance that Babur suffered. He'd seen them look at each other, communicating through their eyes. Claire McCleary's face had been in a neutral smile for almost the entire conversation, like a statue, but Babur had caught the husband-and-wife pair exchanging information through glances or light strokes of her hand against his wrist. He'd swallowed and quickly looked away, feeling like an intruder and also wondering what it would be like to have a spouse with whom one could exchange information nonverbally, with whom one could form a unit. He'd had a spouse—and technically, until the divorce is finalized, he still does—but it hadn't been like that.

"We're setting up a foundation, Bobby," Fred had repeated. "We realize how fortunate we are"—he looked over at Claire, who smiled at him and nodded, as if encouraging him to proceed—"and feel it's our duty to give back, bring others up, you know. And Claire and I have always been passionate about helping the next generation . . ."

Babur nodded politely. When he'd asked Fred to start again, he hadn't meant from the very beginning. He'd wanted him to skip ahead to the last part. The part about Angie.

"I was a scholar-athlete in my day." Fred let out a self-deprecating chuckle, and Babur caught Claire playfully drawing her gaze down to Fred McCleary's still-lean midsection. "A long time ago, of course. Anyway, you know we all think the world of Angie. She's a great kid. Remarkable, really. And it's a great story, you know—immigrant kid, tough-as-nails work ethic, overcoming adversity . . ."

Babur had wanted to interrupt him here, to remind Fred that Angie was not an immigrant, she was born here. She was, in fact, American, just like his children. And yes, her work ethic was brilliant, but to describe her home life, her background, as adverse, something to overcome, well, it wasn't exactly how Babur would put it. But of course he hadn't said any of this.

"We'd like to see if there might be interest in her being our, uh, guinea pig. For the foundation, that is. We'd like to support Angie's swimming at a private club through high school and perhaps work out some arrangements to help with college. Through the foundation. If you'd be interested, that is."

So he had heard correctly, but he wondered how this related to the McClearys' request to discuss the incident with him. Before allowing himself to respond to Fred's proposal—and it really was quite a proposal, one that required a thoughtful answer—Babur asked delicately, "You wanted to discuss . . . the accident? Your son, he is doing all right?"

Fred had blinked quickly and shot his wife the briefest of glances, as if this question were unexpected. He then settled into a self-assured smile and said, "Oh, yes, Bobby, Henry is recovering very well. He should be home on Sunday. Thank you for your concern, and thank you again to Angela for acting so quickly." Babur noted that Claire McCleary was patting her husband's hand lightly, as if encouraging him. "The whole thing was unfortunate. Disappointing and unexpected in a town like ours, but the police chief has personally promised me they will do the thoroughest of investigations. In fact, they have over half the police force searching for the girl as we speak. So"—his eyes glinted like new coins—"we'll let them do their jobs." He sat up straighter and continued, "Now, about the foundation, what are you thinking?"

Babur chewed over Fred McCleary's words, deciding whether to dig further into the lawyer's comments that Angie could be in trouble, that the police think she had some questionable involvement; but he decided to drop it, to not dignify this unfounded speculation with a mention. He was, however, puzzled by why the McClearys sought to discuss a philanthropic venture now, with their son still in the hospital. However, to not respond might appear ungrateful or disinterested, and he was neither; the offer, on balance, was incredible, timing notwithstanding. Moreover, what the McClearys wanted to focus on in the wake of their son's stabbing was the McClearys' business. So Babur had cleared his throat and said, more slowly than he normally would, focusing on each word, conscious of not sounding clumsy in his eagerness, "We would be most honored and humbled." He'd looked at

Fred and Claire. Both were smiling, although Claire's smile appeared strained, made her face pucker like she'd tasted something sour. When they didn't immediately jump in, he'd added, "Thank you. I—we—accept this generous offer," with a return smile.

"Excellent, Bobby! We were hoping you'd be interested." Fred's voice was so smooth and commanding, Babur had thought. It was no surprise that he was a big-shot investor. He had the type of voice that made you trust him with important decisions.

"Thank you," he repeated. "This is like a dream." He was blushing and attempting not to lose his balance in his god-awful chair.

Fred had shrugged it off and said, "Well, that's the point. Helping people like you and Angie achieve the American dream."

Babur had felt his jaw tighten. He'd wanted to inform Fred that he'd founded Move on his own, with no help, no partner, barely any savings, and a young child at home. That the two of them were the same. They shared the same work ethic, an American work ethic. But there was something glossy and authoritative about the McClearys that made Babur bashful, reticent.

Fred continued, "We'll need to figure out a few details. Claire's been working with our lawyers to get the foundation set up." To Claire he'd said, "And you've been doing a terrific job, honey."

Claire's face had shifted into a more natural smile and she'd said, in one of the few times she'd spoken during their meeting, "We're so happy we can help. Angie's such a sweet girl. I wish Sam had some of her grit."

At that, Babur had blushed so deeply he could swear his cheeks must have been violet, taken aback by this unexpected comparison between their daughters.

Fred had changed the topic. "It's a bit of paperwork, Bobby," he'd said. "Mostly for us, but there will be a few things we need from Angie and you."

Babur had nodded his head vigorously, stretching his mouth into what he hoped was a confident smile.

"Lawyers." Fred had grinned and looked over again at Claire, who had an open-mouthed smile now. "Claire went to law school, you know."

Both McClearys laughed and Babur felt himself join in, mirroring them, not quite sure how one behaves in front of one's soon-to-be benefactors. Before he knew it, they'd handed him the document that he'd brought home, the waterlogged one that Angie had just waved at him angrily; and by that point, he was loath to do or say anything to shatter the magic of the moment, like re-raise the unfortunate incident on the football field or the ensuing investigation. It had little to do with him or Angie beyond coincidence. So he'd left it.

But as he retreated down the gently sloping driveway, alone in his car, departing the McClearys' majestic home to start an Uber shift, the nagging voice Babur had been shoving to one side reasserted itself. He wondered if he should have pushed to discuss the police's investigation further, if he'd left Angie and himself vulnerable in not doing so, and how this scholarship might appear entwined with the events at the high school, if that could look untoward. But then that catchy pop song about rules for ex-lovers came on the radio, and Babur replayed the McClearys' offer anew, their ringing praise of Angie, their fondness for her. He'd smiled, tapping his fingers in time to the beat, flicked on the windshield wipers—it had started raining—and concluded everything could be explained. Angie and Samantha were dear friends since childhood, after all. Moreover, Angie had practically saved their boy's life.

In the kitchen, Babur holds his head in his hands, resting his elbows on the counter. He's baffled by Angie. Her anger, her accusations, her overconcern about simple things, like a standard contract. It's not healthy for a child her age to worry like this. To be unhappy. Maybe she inherited this malaise—

Before he can assign Purnima culpability for Angie's moods, Angie marches into the kitchen. She holds the flashlight as well as—*oh God*, he gulps—the manila envelope. She points the flashlight away from her face, but he can tell by the cadence of steps, the way her body appears hunched and tight, that her face is strained, pinched in accusation. Her voice confirms this. "Who do you know in Kansas?" she says.

He wasn't ready for this. He isn't ready for this. His throat is itching, and his tongue feels like sandpaper. He could use some water, but if he doesn't answer her, she'll think he's hiding something, and he's not. Not technically. Because he was going to tell her about the divorce papers. It's just that when he thinks about Purnima and gets ready to talk to Angie about her, he gets this tightness in his voice box, in his chest, in his heart, and he can't breathe properly or evenly or think without a fog obscuring his thoughts. But to explain that to her—to try—would be impossible. "I—I was— What's the matter, beta?" He wishes he'd responded more smoothly, like how Fred McCleary speaks.

"Seriously, Dad. What's going on?" She's waving the empty envelope. The one in which the divorce papers had arrived. That he'd meant to shred or file away. He clears his throat, again wishing he could go to the tap and chug a lukewarm glass of water to relieve his insides from the agony overcoming him. He whispers, looking directly at her, "I was going to tell you. Your mother lives in Kansas." A pause. "We're getting a divorce."

NINETEEN

Angela's hands go limp. The envelope and flashlight fall from them. The envelope flutters to the ground, and the flashlight hits the kitchen tiles with a clank and rolls in the direction of where her father is sitting. Angie looks at her dad. They lock eyes. His are wide and large. They appear stricken, fearful, as he searches hers for a reaction she's determined not to give him. Another ripple of lightning radiates through the room, followed by the rumble of thunder. She hears wind screeching through the kitchen windows. It's ghostly. Between the sound and the eerie flicker the tea lights make, she shivers.

Her dad stands up from the stool. It looks like he's heading toward the dropped flashlight.

Angie can't explain why, but that prompts her to scramble for it. Bending down, grasping to pick it up before he can. Like it's a race. She grips the flashlight. She won. She's triumphant but feeling the opposite. She takes a large step back and narrows her eyes at her dad.

He straightens up into standing. "Ang," he says, looking at her, only a foot or so away. His eyes look enormous now. And he's nervous, she can tell, from the way his mouth lightly twitches. Watching her like he's afraid of her.

She shakes her head. "What?" She intentionally snaps at him, as if that will eviscerate the dozens of half-formed questions about things—and people—she doesn't want to care about that frenetically ping-pong through her head. A lump materializing in her throat tugs at her vocal cords like an anchor. No, she will not react.

"Say something." His voice is weak, like he's pleading. It's not how a parent should speak to their child, she thinks, her mouth turning in disdain. He takes a step toward her, and she moves backward, closer to the kitchen entrance. She shines the light at him. Directly into his face. A warning to stay where he is.

"What is there to say? You expect me to care? Because"—she wants to speak as if what she's saying is true, but she can hear her voice wavering, giving her away—"because I don't." She keeps the flashlight shining on her dad. On his face. He squints from its glare, but he doesn't step to the side or look away.

"Are you—do you—do you have questions, beta?"

She audibly exhales and then scoffs loudly. She's ready to launch into it now. "Are you kidding me? Dad, are you joking?" To prevent her voice from quivering, she speaks louder. The anger feels like a salve. "You weren't ever going to tell me, were you—like ever?" She sees him shake and then nod his head furiously in that confusing way of his. *What is it, yes or no?* she wants to yell as he wags his head. "Because you never mention her. I didn't even know you knew how to reach her." Her dad looks at the ground, head still gesturing ambiguously. Angie wishes he'd just say something, spit it out. Her head feels like a volcano smoldering. She can't think; the thoughts come in too fast, too hot, all at once. She speaks louder, but she can't help it. She can't stop. "How could you not tell me about this? I'm not a child! But you never tell me things! And you never listen—you never—I'm sick of it! I am sick of you!"

Thunder claps in the sky like an explosion.

Her dad stands where he is. Arms by his sides. His mouth is open, and his eyes are shining. His face looks twisted, but he doesn't say anything, so she goes on: "I don't care if you get a divorce. Why should I?" She can hear her voice rising. "I don't even know her." She can't stop herself from getting louder, sharper, higher. "I don't even know her!" She's screaming now and her throat aches. It feels raw. "Get your stupid divorce. I don't care!" she shrieks. Her upper body shakes from trying to swallow the lump in her throat. And then more softly, she points a finger at her dad, whose face is strained and furrowed, his eyes glassy, and says, "You never talk to me about her, and I just—I don't understand."

Angie flicks off the flashlight for a second and turns it back on, pointing it away from him, in the direction of the kitchen cabinet, and sniffling as she walks to the cabinet to retrieve a glass. She fills the glass with cold water at the sink and drinks it quickly, feeling a tingle as the water flows through her insides. She refills the glass and drains it a second time before setting it down. Angie turns off the flashlight and rests her hands on the counter in front of the sink.

Her dad clears his throat and says, "Ang, I was going to tell you." His voice sounds strange, hollow, like something's been punched out of it.

She blinks rapidly, continuing to face the sink.

"I promise, beta. I wanted to tell you. I was—I was waiting. Because I thought—" His voice cracks. "I don't know what I thought." He pauses. "I'm sorry," he near whispers.

She doesn't turn to look at him. The inside of her throat feels like it's being wrung out. Whatever's inside of her, she can't suppress it, she can't keep it down. But she doesn't want him to know that. She doesn't want him to see.

"It's difficult for me to . . . talk about your mother." She hears him hesitate before he says that last part, and when he does, his volume drops.

Angie turns toward where he's standing but remains at the sink, leaning with her back against it. In the dim orange glow from the tea lights, one of which has gone out, she sees him. His face looks longer. Wilted and drooping.

"Why, Dad? Why haven't we talked about her?" she asks. Her voice sounds steady once again. She presses her lips together and focuses her eyes on the countertop. Its shiny surface reflects the dancing flicker of the flames. She swallows. Should she say something about the friend request? No, she decides, because there's nothing to say. She hasn't accepted it.

"I didn't mean not to. I suppose I feel confused"—a pause—"about your mother." He exhales loudly enough for her to hear.

Angie inadvertently holds her breath and presses her lips more tightly together until she can feel her skin against the edges of her teeth, waiting for him to say more, pressing harder.

"You may think it's old fashioned, but I never thought we would get divorced. I don't believe in divorce. I—" He stops short and looks at the kitchen floor, his face twisted, as if in pain. He starts slowly, softly then. "She was—she was not feeling well, she said. She was unhappy, you see. Deeply unhappy, so she said, and maybe—maybe I, uh, could have been more patient with her. But at the time, Angie, I—I didn't understand. I still don't." He shakes his head and is looking at the floor, not at her. "But back then, it was hard. It was hard to be around her, and she was—she was difficult, unreliable. She did things that didn't—well, that I couldn't—"

"Like what? What'd she do?"

Her dad stops looking at the ground. He looks at Angie. He seems startled, as if he'd forgotten she's there. "Well, she— There was this one time I came home from work early in the afternoon. You were a baby, maybe one year old. I was in that company job then. And she was sleeping in the bedroom with the blinds down. Just sleeping in daytime, and you were in your crib and you were crying. You'd soiled your diaper. You were crying and crying. And she was sleeping. Just sleeping." Angie feels her jaw tighten. She thinks of the image of the serene-looking woman misaligned against a city skyline. "I woke her, and I was furious. I wanted to know why she was sleeping, why she didn't go check on you when you were crying. And she—she just—she didn't—she said her head hurt so she went to lie down." The bitterness in her dad's voice sounds unfamiliar to Angie.

"That sounds bad, Dad," Angie says slowly, tentatively, "but is it so terrible?"

"What kind of mother doesn't hear her own baby crying?" her dad replies. "And maybe if that was the only time"—she sees he's wringing his hands like he's wrestling with himself—"or if she had been sick, really sick, but she— I can't—"

"But maybe she was sick? Or something was wrong?"

Her dad stiffens and his eyes darken. He says, quickly and more loudly than she's used to, "No. There was nothing wrong with her. She was fine. Absolutely fine. She—she did that type of thing all the time. She said she had a headache, or was feeling too tired, or—I don't know." He's sputtering and his hands are balled up. "Nothing was the matter."

Angie thinks for a minute before she says, "Was she depressed, Dad?"

Lightning flashes through the room, and it's as if it had struck her dad. His face contorts into an expression she doesn't recognize. His mouth is open wide, and his teeth are gritted. His nostrils are flared, and his eyes look like someone lit a fire under his feet. Disgust, she thinks silently. "What, depressed?" He speaks loudly in the broken English he sometimes reverts to when he gets too excited, something that usually only happens on the road, when another driver cuts him off. "What is all this talk of depressed? I don't understand—I—"

Angie's taken aback by his reaction. "Sorry, Dad, I didn't mean to—I just thought—"

He sucks in a long breath. "No, I'm sorry, beta, I didn't mean to get so . . . worked up." His voice is softer, sadder. "I just—I didn't know what to do then, and I—I'm sorry I don't talk about your mother."

His voice cracks again; his eyes glisten. "I don't know how, and for some time, I had told myself since you didn't ask, maybe I didn't need to." He's crying. "Sometimes"—he pauses, as if unsure whether to continue before he does—"it's easier to pretend it's always been just the two of us."

She feels a tear fall down her own cheek. She says, "I didn't ask because I didn't want you to be sad. You were so sad, Dad." She pauses, remembering how it was when she was younger, which she can only recall now in fuzzy vignettes. How lonely he'd seemed in contrast to Neha Aunty and Manan Uncle, who were always ribbing each other or giving each other playful kisses on the cheek, or how nervous he'd been about things like brushing her straight hair properly and helping her dress for school. She continues, "When I was younger—it's stupid, but I thought if I upset you, well, maybe you'd—you'd leave, too." She's never said that out loud before. She barely even says that in her head. She can feel tears sliding down her cheeks. She covers her face in her hands and hunches into herself. In the next instant, her dad is standing by her and hugging her. And this time she doesn't push him away.

"Ang, I'm sorry," he repeats. "None of this is your fault. It was—it is between your mother and me."

Angie stops crying and looks up at her dad, eyebrows raised. His eyes are wide, wider than before. The whites look bluish underneath an orange sheen from the candles. She tries again to swallow the lump in her throat. She wants to ask him so many things: if her mother mentioned her when they decided to get divorced, if she thinks about her, what he knows about her life. But seeing her father so shaken, so vulnerable this evening, it feels wrong; she's afraid he'll misunderstand, that it would feel like a betrayal. She clears her throat, her questions lingering unspoken in her mouth, and asks instead, "Do you want some water?"

He nods, and she reaches into the cabinet for another glass, letting the tap run until the temperature is tepid. She hands him the glass, and when she does, she sees another one of the tea lights go out. The agreement her dad had gotten from the McClearys sits inches from the burnt-out candle, on the counter where she'd left it.

On a stool at the kitchen counter surrounded by a fresh batch of tea lights, Angie reads aloud, flashlight in hand, from the weekend cross-word: "Twenty-one across: Something for something in Ancient Rome. Ten letters, fourth letter's a 'd' and it ends with an 'o.'"

"Say that again," her dad asks, scrunching up his face in concentra-tion. He's at the stove, stirring. He'd insisted on making dinner even though the power hasn't come on. He'd said, "But I've got all the in-gredients, and it's chicken supreme tonight." She'd smiled to be agree-able, their earlier fight still raw and the information about her mother hanging in the air like a series of question marks.

Her dad had taken Angie's feeble smile as a green light to proceed in bumping about in the dimly lit kitchen, using the light of his phone to make his Saturday-night signature dish of stewed chicken in a tomato sauce with whatever vegetables he could find in the fridge or freezer, and Angie had pulled out the weekend crossword.

Angie repeats the clue aloud.

They haven't spoken further about the document from the McClearys. It's still on the counter, where she'd left it, within her reach, but she purposely avoids looking at it. *We can talk about it tomorrow,* she thinks.

"Hmm . . . let's try another one and come back to that," her dad answers, as he's been saying for most of the puzzle clues. Saturday's crosswords are always tough.

"Okay. Twenty-five across is—"

His cell rings and her dad picks up: "Oh, Colleen, what a nice sur-prise." His voice is unnaturally bright, how he gets when he's speaking to customers.

Angie looks down at the crossword and tries not to listen. It's their neighbor Colleen Sullivan, the one Angie tries to avoid. Ever since

Colleen took Angie to buy a training bra a number of years ago, she's developed an annoying habit of greeting Angie with a sympathetic smile, like she's tragic, and commenting on how Angie is "blossoming into a young woman," only to note seconds later, with a pitying tsk, that Angie shouldn't feel bad that some flowers bloom later than others, a not-so-subtle reference to her still-quite-subtle chest. At that point, Angie inevitably covers herself with crossed arms and hunched-over shoulders, wishing she could camouflage into her surroundings. More recently, Angie and her dad had gone to a Fourth of July barbeque Colleen had hosted, and she kept grilling Angie on whether she had a boyfriend. When she'd shaken her head no, Colleen had winked and leaned in so close Angie was eye level with the freckles on the tops of her overexposed breasts and could smell her nauseatingly sweet perfume and margarita breath, and she'd assured Angie she'll be "chasing them away soon enough" with a wink, like they were girlfriends. Rather than neighbors from different generations. That's her dad's fault, though. He's the one who asked Colleen to take Angie bra shopping and talk to her about "female stuff."

"Yes, yes," she hears her dad booming. She shakes her head at his inability to maintain a normal speaking volume on the phone. "We're fine over here. . . . Uh-huh. Yes, the power's been out for an hour or so now."

Angie concentrates on the crossword more intently, determined to block out her dad's conversation with silly Colleen.

". . . Oh?" her dad says. "Are you okay?"

Angie looks up. She tries to make eye contact with him to find out what happened to Colleen, but he's got his phone pressed to his ear and is stirring the chicken supreme, not looking at her.

"Good to hear you didn't get hurt . . . Oh really? . . . Uh-huh . . . Oh, yes, we have a gas cooking range. Just making dinner right now, in fact . . ." He laughs the way he does when nothing is actually funny. She hates his fake laugh. It sounds shallow and tinny.

". . . Oh. Do you— Well, you could come here. If you'd like."

Angie stares at her dad, urgently, with intensity, trying to telepath-ically message to him to turn around. No, she wants to tell him, no, don't invite her over. Please don't invite her over.

"No, no," he says, oblivious to Angie's appeal. "It's no imposition. Please join us." He laughs tinnily. Angie's mouth sours. "See you soon." He hangs up and puts the receiver down.

"What was that?" Angie asks.

Her dad shrugs, opening the spice cabinet. "Colleen, our neighbor." He grinds salt and pepper into the pot. "She had a bit of a fall in the dark. But she's okay. She sounded shaken, and she doesn't have gas cooking so she can't make dinner with the power gone. I invited her over."

"She fell but she's okay to come over?"

"It wasn't serious." He shrugs again and appears to be adding other spices to the pot simmering on the stove. "And it's the nice thing to do."

"She could get takeout."

"Well, she called, beta. I've invited her now."

"I wish you hadn't, though."

He stops stirring and his eyebrows press together. "I thought you liked Colleen. I thought you, uh, confided in her about . . . things."

"I don't know why you don't just ask me what I think," she says more quickly and perhaps harshly than she meant to. Her eyes fall on the document from the McClearys. And then on her dad. He's looking back at her.

"It's just, she always asks me a thousand questions about, like, I don't know, personal stuff, and it's weird," she adds, attempting to soften the blow of her earlier snap. "Can you uninvite her?"

Her dad turns down the heat on the stove and steps away from the pot. He approaches the kitchen counter, across from where Angie's seated. "I don't understand what's going on with you, beta," he says.

"What do you mean?"

"You're so angry these days. So unlike yourself. You've never com-

plained about seeing Colleen before. And earlier today I thought—
well, I thought I'd come home and tell you about this offer from the
McClearys and that maybe you would have some questions but that
you'd be happy. That we'd be happy. And now, well, what is happening with you?"

Angie squints, her irritation insuppressible. She puts down the pen-
cil as well as the flashlight and crosses her arms against her chest. She
hadn't wanted to talk about this right now, but if he's insisting. "I'm
not signing that thing, Dad." She motions with her eyes toward the
document from the McClearys.

"But, Angie, you haven't given me a chance to—"

"I'm not doing it."

"It's actually a quite—"

"No, I said no!"

"Angie, stop it! Stop it. You're—" And then in one quick surge he
says it, spews it: "You're acting like your mother!"

Angie stares at him in dumbfounded silence. His eyes look like they
have flecks of fire in them from the candlelight. He's never looked at
her like that before. He's never said anything like that to her before.
She feels her heart and head pound. It sounds like an insult, but she
isn't sure. She doesn't know what he means.

More softly now, he says, "I—I mean, can we talk about it? I don't
understand why you feel so strongly . . . I am trying to understand. But
you have been so . . . strange the past few days. I know it's been tough
on you, seeing your classmate hurt. But I don't understand."

Angie scrunches her mouth, thinking about what he means, if she
should be insulted, if it's an invitation to ask him more about her
mother. But she doesn't want either of them to start crying again, so
instead, she takes a deep breath and tries to explain her discomfort with
the McClearys' agreement. "Dad, I want to join a swim club. I want
to go to a good college." He nods. "But there's just something not
right about this. The boys—Henry and Chris—they were— Please
don't overreact, Dad, but I think maybe they were buying drugs from

Chiara." She pauses and sees her dad's eyes open wider, but he says nothing. "And when I was walking over, they were arguing or something, and I'm pretty sure Chiara screamed before she ran away, before I showed up. I mean, I didn't see her really afterward, but I saw her for sure when I was walking over to the pool. And—I don't know, Dad. Something's not right."

His forehead looks knitted, the way it gets when he's thinking hard. Her dad takes a minute before he says, "But, beta, what does this have to do with you? The argument, these drugs. Are you— Did you see the drugs?"

"It's not like that, Dad. I'm not involved with drugs or anything." She knew it was a risk to mention that detail. "But it's strange, isn't it, the timing of all this? I heard Henry and Chris arguing with Chiara, then something happened and she screamed and stabbed him. And now the McClearys want to give us money if we sign something that says we can't talk about them. I mean, why? Why would they want to do that? And don't you also wonder why Chiara stabbed Henry? Don't you think the timing is weird? Like, Sam and I have been on-and-off arguing for months. I've barely seen her or her family, and now they want to sponsor me . . ."

"I don't know about any of this drug dealing. But if it doesn't have anything to do with you, why should we make it our business? You saved this boy's life by calling 911, beta. And I—I didn't know you and Samantha were arguing."

"That's not important. What about that contract? Like, all that language? Why is it so strict and complicated?"

"Beta, you are worrying too much. This is standard in business."

"Okay, I guess. I mean, I don't know how this type of stuff works." She pauses. "But the other thing is, Dad, the kids at school, they're saying all these horrible things about Chiara, like, how she's violent and homeless, and I don't know if they even know that or if they're just saying it . . ." She wrings her hands, distraught even describing this.

"I just wonder what if—what if Henry and Chris did something—like, something to make her hurt them? What if she was scared and just accidentally maybe hurt Henry, or thought she needed to? I don't know, Dad. Should we take Henry's parents' money?"

"Angie, you are getting carried away. You don't know what happened, and what is it to us? Who is this girl to you? She's a drug dealer. In the newspaper today they said she's homeless. You said the other day, you don't know this girl. She doesn't sound like a nice girl, beta. Why get involved? The McClearys are good people, and they are setting up a foundation. And yes, we should accept. That is exactly what we should do."

"But what if they're offering us money to help them lie?"

"No one is asking you to lie, Angie."

"But what if—what if they are lying, Henry and Chris? What if they lied about what happened, and then we take Henry's parents' money?"

"Beta, you're getting very worked up. No one is asking you to lie."

"Dad, are you listening to me?"

"Yes, Angie. I'm listening, and I'm hearing you say you don't know what happened. So why interfere? Why assume the worst? You saved a boy's life, and his family wants to help you swim and with college. Let's take their thank-you."

"But what if I don't want it? I don't know if I want help from these people."

"Angie, this is not 'these people.' These are your good friend's parents. Why are you—"

"Dad, I just told you—"

"Okay. I know you are thinking all these things right now. It's caring of you to worry about this girl, this stranger. But you have to think about your future. Affording things like swimming clubs and college, it's hard. I work— Well, you know. I work all the time and save everything I can for us. Even if I stopped sleeping and worked even more, saved even more, I don't think I could afford some of the things you might want, things I want for you. I can't afford things like the McClearys have. This is an opportunity, Angie. This is our chance. Your chance."

"But what about Chiara? Shouldn't we wait to hear her side of things?"

"Again with this girl? Why, Angie? You have to think about what is best for you, for us."

"Wouldn't it be wrong?" Because it would be wrong to take a scholarship if it was hush money. She doesn't understand why he doesn't see things her way.

"Beta." Her dad sighs, then says, "This isn't something people walk away from. This is—"

A woman's voice calls from the front door. "Helloooo!" Footsteps down the hallway and a cell phone light. It's Colleen in the kitchen entryway. Angie points her flashlight toward Colleen. She's wearing a bosomy animal-print top and leggings. She holds a bottle of wine and looks decidedly uninjured. Angie tries her best not to grimace.

Colleen says, "I hope you don't mind I let myself in . . . The door was unlocked, and I tried the bell but—"

Her dad flashes into action and smiles too enthusiastically. "Not at all, neighbor. Welcome. Our casa is your casa, as they say."

Angie offers a tepid smile and weak hi.

Colleen doesn't seem to notice. She continues, "I took off my shoes and left my umbrella in the hall. Boy, it's coming down out there." She looks around the kitchen. "This looks real nice with all the candles. Oh, and it smells great."

Her dad remembers the chicken supreme and goes to the stove to give it a stir. Colleen walks toward him and starts fussing over his shoulder. Angie swears she can see her dad flinch a little when Colleen touches his shoulder, but maybe she's imagining things, since it's dark where they are.

After having been sent by her dad to take a seat with a healthy glass of wine, Colleen walks over to Angie. She smells like an overripe fruit. "What do you have there?" She points at the open newspaper page.

"Just the crossword."

"Oh, well, lemme see if I can help." Colleen pulls up a stool next to Angie and leans in. She adds in her dad's direction, "Unless, Bobby, you need—"

"Oh, no, please, you relax over there," he assures her.

"This is so nice." Colleen grins at Angie. "A father and daughter cooking and doing a crossword together on a Saturday night." She looks at the crossword. "What are you stuck on there, sweetie?" She shines her cell phone light on the puzzle that's mostly unfilled, and after a few seconds she says, "Twenty-one across, Something for something. Quid pro quo." She takes a long sip of her wine.

"This is so nice," she says again.

TWENTY

Chris paces up and down a clearing on Lakewood Drive. He's jittery, the way he gets when he drinks coffee, and hot. Uncomfortably hot. There are beads of sweat on his forehead and his palms are clammy. And the sun is bright. Painfully bright. Like it's making up for not being around over the weekend during the storm. It's making his eyes water. He rubs at them like he's scrubbing out a stain.

He has so much to say but can't work out how to say it. This would be easier if he were speaking to a normal person, someone who doesn't always look like her dog just died. Someone who smiles every once in a while.

On second thought, he thinks for the tenth or eleventh time since he got there, maybe he should go home. He shoves his hands in his pockets, hunching his shoulders up, walking faster, making his turns sharper. But the thing is, he reasons, he's here now. One painfully long forty-five-minute Kitchewan Circulator ride later, and he's here. Besides, it's just Angela.

He stares at the blue-and-white wooden sign for Lakeview Terrace and then at the identical clusters of town houses behind it. The rectangular blocks of connected yellow houses look like puzzle pieces.

They're small, smaller than his and his mom's split-level, but there's something welcoming about them, something cozy about how they fit together.

He mutters to himself, rehearsing the conversation he's been having in his head since last night. It's strange to practice a conversation, to role-play what he imagines the other person will say. Especially when that person is no-fun Angela Singh.

He stops pacing, and his eyes rest on number 37. The Singhs' house. From this distance and in the bright light of the outdoors, everything looks dark inside. The garage door is closed and there's no car in the driveway.

Maybe no one's home. Which is annoying, because he came all this way. Not that it's super far away, but everything takes forever on the bus and he didn't have the energy to argue with his mom about having the car today. If no one's home, maybe he should forget about it. He's not dying to talk to Angela. But wait—he stops himself. He can't just go. At the town hall at Kitchewan High last night, before it unraveled the way it did, Henry's dad had been clear: there's an eyewitness. Which means Angela saw something and said something. Which means, he thinks with a sharp exhale, he needs to talk to Angela.

Going to the town hall yesterday had been Chris's idea. He was surprised his mom agreed. After that newspaper article had come out, she'd made him swear up and down, on his life and her own—so dramatic—that he wouldn't talk to anyone else about what happened on the football field until after she got ahold of his dad and the McClearys, and so far, neither had returned her calls.

All weekend long Chris had stuck to his promise: not answering texts, not posting on Facebook, not responding to direct messages—and God, there were a lot of them—not even answering suspect phone calls. Like earlier today, when the *Westchester Gazette* called, he slammed the receiver down in a panic, his heart racing, before he could even hear what they had to say. It's killing him. Staying quiet is killing him. Especially now that everyone is talking about what happened.

It's like overnight Henry has become a fallen war hero. All these kids from school who barely know him are flooding Facebook and Instagram with #prayforHenry. All sorts of stupid stuff like selfies with pics of their hands over their hearts. As if photos were going to un-stab him. It's dumb, but also a little insulting. Barely anyone is talking about Chris, asking him how he's doing. After all, Chris is a victim, too. He just narrowly escaped. That could've been him bleeding on the football field. That could've been Chris.

The silver lining in all this is that Chiara's past—her being some runaway kid who wasn't supposed to be enrolled in Kitchewan High—reinforces that she must have been the one in the wrong, the bad guy. She must have been the one who started it. Chris didn't know people snuck into nice towns to go to their schools, but apparently they did, and she did, and everyone is riled up about it. Serves her right, though. The way she'd acted when Chris had been joking around.

The town hall had been held in the school gym. Chris and his mom arrived late and had slid into a back bleacher off to the side. An old guy in a suit who Chris had never seen before, someone with the school district or school board, was droning on into a mic about "security protocols" and the school's "commitment to the safety of its students and faculty." He mentioned a student had been injured recently, but the whole description had lasted half a minute and he didn't say anyone's names. Not that he needed to, because by then everyone knew. Chris had felt disappointed at how rushed and sanitized his telling of it was.

The guy kept speaking, but Chris had tuned out, looking around the gymnasium, scanning his classmates, most of whom he hadn't seen since school got out in June, going row by row, searching the backs of heads, looking for the McClearys. No sign of Henry or his sister. Figures, he'd thought, with Henry recovering. Besides, it wasn't like Chris could have cornered Henry, not there, with all these people around.

The old guy with the mic had started talking about new student ID cards when Chris spotted Angela's dad. At least he was pretty sure that was him. He doesn't know Angela like that, but there are only a couple Indian kids in their school, and he's been in the car a few times with Henry and Sam when they dropped Angela off at her house. He could swear he'd seen the same slender guy, clean-shaven face with big, round puppy-dog eyes, watering the lawn. He was sitting a row or two above Chris and his mom, his mouth frozen in a desperate sort of smile. He was alone.

The old guy had opened the floor for questions, and because she couldn't ever let up policing him, Chris's mom had swatted his hand, hissing at him to quit looking around. He'd turned and made a show of slouching and scowling, eyes straight ahead, regretting he'd asked to come.

After a few unmemorable questions—about the new process for student registration and getting a student ID card, if the new, required ID cards would be biometric—right when he was on the verge of sleeping with his eyes open, a trick he'd perfected in math class, things had started to get interesting. First, Abigail Cohen's mom had asked, "I'd like to know exactly what the school knows about the stabbing."

Chris had smirked when he saw the guy with the mic shift uncomfortably; serves him right for spending a whole lot of time saying a whole lot of nothing. He'd also felt his heart beat faster, anticipating the response; but the man, true to his earlier style, mostly avoided the question: "We understand everyone's concern, ma'am, but I will have to refer you to the Kitchewan PD for the latest. We are taking this matter very seriously and doing all we can to assist." Chris exhaled and, when relief had set in, rolled his eyes at how this guy bobbed and weaved his way out of everything.

After that, Lainie Drexler's mom stood up, her dark brown curly hair bouncing indignantly when she asked, "But what is the school doing about the stabber? You must know about that."

There was some murmuring in the crowd, and the old man with

the mic repeated that the school was working closely with the police department to figure out next steps.

Lainie's mom had replied: "We need to know if our children are going to be safe at this school. What are you doing about Chiara Thompkins?"

The murmuring grew louder, and at the mention of Chiara's name, Chris had felt his back and his palms start to drip with sweat. A father with red hair and a large bald spot in the back of his head, a couple of rows in front of Chris and his mom, stood up and asked, "Are you letting Chiara Thompkins back in the high school this fall?," followed by a few scattered calls of "Are you?" and "We deserve to know," from different points in the bleachers.

It took the guy with the mic a few minutes of talking over the noise to get the crowd to quiet down. He began by repeating what he'd said before about working with the police but was quickly met with boos and jeers, at which point, after subjecting everyone to a long screech of mic feedback, in a much louder voice, he said, with his palms raised in a halting motion, "We understand folks are concerned and may have heard there were some"—a pause—"irregularities with Chiara Thompkins's enrollment at the school. Until very recently, the school board was not aware of any of this or her violent tendencies, and we are taking this all seriously. Very seriously. We do not allow a student who uses a weapon on another to remain in the school."

Rather than calm people down, his words seemed to energize people. Some clapped, some called out follow-up questions, some turned to their neighbors to comment on what they'd just heard. And Chris started to feel more at ease, wiping his clammy hands on his jeans, letting out a long breath and rolling his shoulders. Things were turning out okay, he thought. People seemed to accept that Chiara was to blame and were most concerned about keeping her out of the high school.

Maybe the town hall would have been manageable if it had ended there. Something people gossiped about or debated on the drive home

or at the dinner table, but then forgot about. Only then, Principal
Burrowes stood up from one of the front rows. Under normal circumstances, when he wasn't distracted by his own nerves, Chris might have
scowled. He'd had a handful of run-ins with the principal, for cutting
class or allegedly talking back and once or twice for smoking on the
school grounds. She was a no-nonsense, ball-buster type, with a deep
voice and know-it-all eyes, the kind of lady Chris avoids. Chris was
surprised she wasn't on the gym floor with the old guy. She seemed to
like being out front and in charge.

Without a mic, and dressed in a dark-colored pantsuit, looking like
she was ready to meet the president, Principal Burrowes said in a booming voice, "Superintendent, has the school board spoken with Chiara
Thompkins?" Before she could give the old man a chance to respond,
she continued, "Because from what I understand, Chiara is missing. In
fact, there is a police search underway. So, any conclusions about what
did or did not happen between her and another student, or the circumstances of her enrollment, sound premature, don't you agree?"

The hair on the back of Chris's neck stood up.

"Principal Burrowes," the superintendent had replied shortly, "we
know the girl is missing, but it is fair to acknowledge Miss Thompkins
was not properly enrolled at KHS."

"Superintendent, all I'm saying is that we need to give Chiara the
chance to tell us what happened. Hear her side of things, just like we
would with anyone else. Until we do, how will we know whether this
student, *this Black student*, was at fault or in violation of any other
rules?"

Chris's face had gotten hot, and his pulse had sped up. Even though
no one was looking at him, except maybe his mom, he felt like a thousand eyes were burning into him. He didn't do anything wrong, he
reminded himself, like, nothing that actually hurt anyone. His mother
had leaned in toward him and whisper-shouted, "You see, Chris? This
is what always happens. I knew this would happen." He'd gritted his
teeth, refusing to look at her.

The talking in the crowd had risen in volume and frequency to a dull roar, and the superintendent had this pained smile on his face. Chris could swear he could see the guy's forehead shining with sweat even from where he and his mom were seated. Henry's dad, who Chris had missed before, stood up, or rose, really, from the middle of the bleachers, and said, "I'd like to say something, Superintendent." The superintendent looked shocked but nodded vigorously. "I wasn't planning on speaking this evening. It's an emotional time for my family and me. I think it's important to clarify that this isn't about black or white; it's about wrong or right. We know what happened on the football field. My son has provided a full statement." Chris tensed up, wishing he knew what Henry had said. "There's also an eyewitness." He wondered if Mr. McCleary was talking about him. "I hope the school takes swift action to prevent something like this from happening to another student, another family. In the meantime, my wife and I thank everyone in this fine town for their support of Henry and our family." He didn't sound angry, but Chris had noticed his face was flushed when he spoke and there was a vein bulging in his neck and down the center of his forehead.

Principal Burrowes stood again and turned around, directing her comments to Henry's dad, and said, "Mr. McCleary, with all due respect to you and your family, the school needs to wait for the police to complete their investigation, to find Chiara Thompkins and speak with her, before we jump to conclusions about what happened."

To which Henry's dad said, sounding outright angry this time, "But we know what happened, Principal Burrowes. My son was stabbed, and there's an eyewitness who called 911." So not him. "The real question is how a girl not legally resident in this community was allowed unfettered access to our public high school, to our children; how *you*, Principal Burrowes, let this happen?" And from there, the guy with the mic pretty much gave up trying to bring everyone to order because no one seemed interested in what he had to say.

People started leaving their seats and talking in small groups on the gymnasium floor. He'd only heard snatches of conversations, nothing he could make sense of with so many different voices layered over one another. One person yelled, "Pray for Henry. We stand with you!" and there were a few follow-on calls of "Pray for Henry." He thought there were some dissenting calls about Chiara, about being fair to her, getting her side of the story, but by then everything sounded garbled and distant.

Chris's stomach turned, and his head started pounding; his chest, too. The pounding was too loud for him to hear over. Henry's dad had said there was an eyewitness. He glanced over at Angela's dad, also still seated. He looked yellow, sickly, like he'd eaten something that didn't agree with him.

Chris's breaths come in short and shallow, and his hands, shoved in his pockets, are sticky with sweat. He walks up the steps to the front door of Angela's yellow house. He stands on a worn-out beige welcome mat with the silhouette of a house and a heart and "Home is where the heart is" scrawled underneath in cursive. He moves his hand toward the doorbell, expecting to ring it but not get a response. But before he can press it, the door swings open.

It's Angela. He takes a step back before they collide, catching his balance before he teeters off the edge of the step.

She's in a red T-shirt and white shorts with a backpack on her back. She looks smaller than he remembers, shorter. But firm. He can see muscle lines along her forearms and down the sides of her legs. The sunlight makes her skin look like a mix of gold and tennis court clay. For a second, maybe from the heat, he forgets to breathe.

Angela's almond-shaped eyes jerk open when she sees him, then quickly close up into narrower slits. One of the earpieces from the headphones she's wearing slips out of her ear.

His heart's pounding. His head, too. "Hi, Angela," he says louder than he means to.

"Hi . . ." She removes her other earpiece from her ear but keeps her phone in her hand and headphones connected. She looks at him like he's a live wire.

Her T-shirt has BEACH BUM scrawled across it in fun, bubble lettering. Ironic, he thinks, because he doesn't associate Angela with fun. It's a baggy shirt, or at least it looks that way on her. Her shoulders might only be a little broader than the span of his hands, which for some reason—maybe because he hasn't had much social interaction these past few days—makes his heart race. He can see, from how the cotton clings to parts of her, the outline of her mostly flat chest. She's not much to look at, but his eyes feel stuck.

"Are you here to see me?" she says, crossing her arms against her chest and hunching her shoulders forward.

He realizes he's been staring and looks up at her face. "Are you—uh—busy or something?" he asks, noticing her backpack. It reminds him of Chiara's bag, the one he'd dumped open on the football field. His fingers twitch, and he swallows hard.

Her eyes cut to the side, making him feel stupid for asking something so obvious. "Yeah. I'm going for a swim."

"Oh, yeah." He nods quickly. *Figures*, he thinks, *that seems to be the only thing Angela does.* He tries to sound friendly. "At the high school? Yeah, cool."

"Well, no. It's locked, so . . ." She points in the direction of Indian Meadow Road, where he came from, where the bus stop is. "I'm going to the community center. Taking the bus."

He makes a face at the mention of the Circulator, but says, "Can I come with?"

She squints and opens her mouth, but before she can say anything, he adds, "Like, just for the ride over or whatever. I want to talk is all."

He can feel her eyes on him. It makes him fidgety, so he looks down at his hands and then at his shoes. He's wearing a pair of Vans that used to be light gray but are ash-colored with wear.

"If you want, I guess." She locks the door, then tucks her phone and keys into a side pocket in her backpack. She starts walking in the direction Chris came from, not waiting for him. Her strides are faster and longer than he'd expect from someone her height. He follows dumbly, catching up because he's got more than half a foot on her, but not without a little effort.

He's annoyed but catches himself. "In a hurry, huh?" He tries lightening the mood.

She shoots a sideways glance in his direction, and even though it's quick, right when she looks at him, his face gets hot again. She says, looking straight ahead, "You wanted something?"

He pauses and then blurts, "About the other day. I wanted to, uh, make sure we're cool, like, about the whole Chiara thing . . ." He waits for her to say something, and when she doesn't immediately, he adds, "I mean, I heard you're an eyewitness and all, so . . ."

She shakes her head and says, "I don't think we should talk about that." Her eyes face front and she looks focused, robotic. She doesn't break stride.

He stares at her side profile, trying to will her to turn toward him, to slow down, to pay attention to him. But she doesn't. He feels his hands balling up into fists and his heartbeat accelerating. This isn't going how he expected. Although, to be fair, he hadn't actually made it this far along in the conversation he'd been rehearsing in his head. He feels flushed, and there's something buzzing inside his ears. He wishes she wouldn't walk so fast. What's her problem, anyway?

One of his shoelaces comes untied. He wants to stop to fix it, but he doubts Angela will wait, and then he'll have to run to catch up to her, like her lapdog. So he walks with his shoe untied. Ridiculous. She's ridiculous. She doesn't have to be so unfriendly. And rude. He told her from the beginning, he just wants to talk. It's not like he's bothering her. She should slow down and talk, like a normal person. She doesn't need to take herself so damn seriously. Can she just fucking slow down and look at him?

"Hey." He reaches for her wrist. He doesn't mean to grab her, but it comes out that way because her wrist is small in his hand, like it could slip away if he doesn't squeeze it. He's not trying to hurt her or anything. He just wants her to stop for a second, listen to him, look at him, and talk properly is all. "Hey," he repeats more loudly, tightening his grip. He can feel her bones. They're small and delicate, breakable.

She tries to wrest her hand free. "What are you doing?"

"Uh—I—I didn't mean—" He lets go.

"Chris, what do you want?" She's stopped walking and is facing him. She looks directly at him and doesn't raise her voice, but he can see her nostrils are flared and her eyebrows are tipped into points. Her eyes are pools of dark brown, so dark they're almost black, and when he looks into them, he swears he sees flecks of fire. He needs to focus, he knows, and he's annoyed with her, at her, but . . . he's also kind of, a little, turned on.

"Sorry." He holds up his hands in surrender, and smiles to show he was joking, he didn't mean it. "Okay, no big deal. We don't have to talk about that, okay? It's just—I didn't think you were there, like, that day. I didn't know you were there the whole time."

She scoffs and starts walking again. They're approaching the end of Lakewood Drive, where it becomes a T-junction, connecting to Indian Meadow Road, the road with the bus stop. "You should talk to your friend," she says.

"What are you talking about?"

"Talk to Henry. Not me." Her voice is firm.

"Well, yeah. I mean, I would. It's just, well, he's not—Henry's not talking to me." Saying it out loud makes him feel sick. His face gets hot and he wishes he hadn't said it. He sounds so pathetic. Angela Singh must think he's pathetic. Her of all people.

Angela looks at him with raised eyebrows but doesn't say anything. They turn onto Indian Meadow. It's busier than Lakewood, but still quiet this time of day.

"It's—it's not a big deal or anything," he says. "Like, we're cool. Henry and me. It's just—I mean, we were both there, you know. And it was his idea to go in the first place. And the thing is, we didn't buy anything from her. And maybe you got the wrong idea or something because, you know, Chiara was just so damn loud, and we were just joking around . . ." His throat starts to get heavy, like it's weighed down. He's choking up. He doesn't know why he's getting emotional.

She looks at him like he's an alien but doesn't say anything.

"It was Henry's idea to go there," he repeats.

Still nothing from Angela, but he can see her entire chest move up and down as she takes a breath. Her collarbones are jutting out at the base of her neck. They stick out so much they look jagged. He wants to touch them, touch the edges.

"I just thought you should know." To stop the heaviness in his throat, he has to focus on his words, so they come out angry, like he's yelling.

"What do you mean you were joking around?" she finally says.

"I mean we were just having fun. Like, nothing serious. Like, she didn't sell anything to us, so we were giving her a hard time a little." His speech is choppy and she's making his voice sound funny. But once he starts, he needs to keep going. This would be easier if he wasn't talking to Angela. "Chiara's a real fucking lunatic, you know," he says, spitting out his words. "She stabbed Henry. Like a crazy person. I mean, you saw that. She's crazy. And she—and— When did you get there again?"

They've stopped walking, and they're facing each other. He can see she's thinking before she says anything, and each time she blinks, he wants to know what she's thinking, why she's curling her lips like that, what she's going to say. If a car drove by and saw them like this, looking at each other, standing this close, they might think they were about to make out. Because that's how close they're standing. But he shouldn't be thinking about that right now. Because that's not how he thinks of no-fun Angela Singh. He wonders, though, if Angela has the same thought, about how close they're standing. Or if she's grossed out because—because he's not Henry.

He sees her mouth turn, spread out how it might when you look at roadkill or smell something putrid. She's making a face. That can't be for him, though. No way. She wouldn't make that face at him. But she is. That bitch. He hopes she knows he could just wrap his hands around her entire little bird neck and have room left over. He hopes she realizes that. That he could literally, right now, just grab her by her stuck-up neck and press, like, squeeze right where the stupid blue vein line is. Maybe then she'd stop being such a bitch.

"He doesn't give a shit about you, you know," he says, intentionally loud this time. "He doesn't care. I mean, it's pathetic how you stare at him. Pathetic! We all think so. You think you're some hero because you called 911 before I could? And do you think this changes anything? Your meddling? Because it doesn't. You can tell the police whatever you want, you can be this eyewitness hero. But it doesn't mean anything. You don't know shit. You're just an ugly loser Indian kid who"—he pauses, thinking of what to say—"smells like—like a swimming pool," he says in a burst. "If you're going to go around pretending you're better than everyone else, you should know what everyone thinks of you." His face is hot, and he's pretty sure it's bright red. He's been yelling, and somewhere in there, he stepped toward her and put his hands on her shoulders. He can feel her bones, and he's shaking her, feeling his fingers moving toward her neck, like metal to a magnet. He swears he doesn't remember reaching for her, though.

A silver SUV drives by and slows down. It gets closer, and Chris drops his hands. He shoves them in his pockets. He's panting.

Angie looks scared. Her eyes are large, and her lips are trembling. A single tear falls down one of her cheeks and she sniffs. Maybe he should apologize, but he can't. Not in the moment. All he can manage is "I—I didn't mean to—"

"What did you do, Chris? What did you and Henry do that day? Why did she stab him?" She pauses to sniffle. "I didn't get there until after Henry was hurt. I didn't see what happened."

Chris looks down at his Vans, avoiding eye contact, but feeling relieved she hadn't seen anything. He didn't mean to shake her. He didn't mean to raise his voice, either. He didn't know why he said what he did. She actually smells kind of fruity. He also didn't mean to throw in the part about her being Indian. But she's acting like she thinks she's better than him. Like she wants to get a reaction out of him.

"I didn't do anything. This is Chiara's fault. I was—I was just there, and—" He stops because he sees she's full-on crying now. He's not even touching her anymore and she's crying. Her chest is shaking. Jeez. It looks bad, like he hurt her or something. But he didn't.

Angela says more softly, "It doesn't make sense. She wouldn't do this for no reason . . ."

Chris is thinking of what to say when all of a sudden, it's like she zaps off a switch. Angela wipes her eyes and turns back toward the direction in which she was walking and starts moving like nothing happened. "I don't want to talk anymore. I can't—I think you should go."

"Hey, hey. I didn't mean it," he calls after her, walking behind her.

"It's fine." He hears her sniffle. "I'm fine. Can you just leave me alone?"

"Can you slow down for a sec? You're overreacting. I wasn't trying to— It's just that I heard Henry's dad say last night that—"

"Chris. Can you go?" She doesn't turn around when she speaks.

Chris swallows hard. His throat still feels tight, and he feels annoyed again. She's making this so difficult. She could look at him when she speaks at least.

He sees the clunky blue Circulator rumbling up toward the bus stop about a hundred yards ahead, and Angela starts slow-jogging toward it. There's no point, he thinks. He lets her go. He leans against a metal guardrail on the side of the road. Her long hair swishes as she runs to catch the bus. Streaks of amber where the sun hits it.

He watches her disappear onto the bus. The same bus he needs to take to get home.

He'll have to wait for the next one, he thinks as the noisy blue bus rolls by, driving past him. He sees Angela toward the middle of the bus with her face pressed against a window. She looks, as usual, like her dog just died. He wonders if she'll tell her dad or Henry or the police or anyone he came to talk to her.

This was a mistake, he thinks, wringing his hands. *A big mistake.*

TWENTY-ONE

Angie is the last person in a long and noisy line at the community center. She needs an electronic tag to access the swimming pool there—a new rule, she's told. Unfortunately, it's registration period for the fall, so the front desk is chockablock. Parents—mostly mothers dressed in athleisure—queue with their children and strollers, waiting to sign up for vinyasa yoga for themselves and gymnastics or tae kwon do for their little ones. Siblings pull one another's hair and shriek or play some variation of tag, weaving between and under others in line. The sound of shrieking rings in Angie's ears.

She taps her foot to let out some nervous energy. She's still wound up from her encounter with Chris, periodically looking over her shoulder, just in case he'd followed her. A young girl, no more than six or seven, with dark brown hair, freckles, and Coke-bottle glasses, in line with her mom and brother, starts imitating her. The girl stands with arms crossed, light-up sneakers tapping, turning to look behind her and then over at Angie. She giggles. Angie forces a half smile. Her head hurts. It hurts a lot these days.

She can still feel where Chris had put his hands on her, dug into her wrists and shoulders and touched her neck. His hands and hot breath on her neck. She grazes her neck with her own hands and shudders at the creepy-crawly sensation of the memory. This is probably what a few of the girls from school who'd texted her these past few days meant when they called Chris a creep. One had said he could provoke even a Buddhist monk to pull out a knife, hinting at empathy for Chiara, but stopping short of expressing it. By now, Angie isn't replying to her texts. She stopped keeping up, especially after last night. She pieced together from the messages she'd received that Henry's dad had come out in front of the whole school and made it sound like Angie saw everything, that she vouched for everything. She wonders if she should tell anyone about what Chris said to her today, about how he grabbed her. The police had called her dad asking to interview her again. Maybe she should tell them, maybe it could help with the investigation. She stops tapping and bites her lip in concentration, reminded of the eerie dream she had, the advice of her dream-mother.

The little girl has lost interest in Angie. She sticks out her tongue at her brother and rushes to hide behind her mother, yelping as he races after her.

She won't say anything, she decides. She's not hurt, and Chris didn't tell her anything, exactly. He was just agitated. And dream-mothers aren't real.

The little girl squeals; her brother has caught her.

Angie's temples ache.

She steps out of line and walks down the hall, not focused on where she's going, as long as it's quiet, less crowded. She hasn't been to the community center since she was in elementary school. It's bizarre to think she used to come here almost every day after school. It looks the same, mostly—same white-and-gray interior and gleaming linoleum floors—but also different. For instance, flickering fluorescent tubes have been replaced with softer lighting, and they've got electronic combination locks on the valuables lockers now.

She catches a whiff of pool chemicals and feels a flash of shame. She remembers how Chris said she smells like a swimming pool. She wonders how Chris knew about Henry, about her feelings for Henry—former feelings, that is. Maybe Sam said something, or maybe he and Henry laughed about it, laughed about her. Her cheeks heat up at the thought. She wants to shrink and disappear into one of the lockers. She wants—

"Hey, are you okay?" A man probably around her dad's age, with graying light brown hair, is passing her in the hallway, car keys jingling in his hand.

Angie nods quickly, self-conscious, pressing her lips together. Her face must have looked strained, and she'd been whispering to herself.

Her not terribly convincing response seems to satisfy the man that his Good Samaritan duty is done. He continues walking in the direction of the line by the front desk, leaving her with the parting advice, "You should smile! You're getting an extra week of summer vacation."

Angie clenches her jaw and continues walking down the hall, head down, scuffing the fronts of her Converse against the ground. This morning the school announced that Kitchewan will start the school year a week later, to allow for a brand-new student registration and ID card process, as if nothing like what happened on the football field would happen again if they all filled in paperwork. It's strange what adults focus on, Angie thinks. While most of her classmates are gleefully embracing the extra week off, Angie would rather start on time than wait another seven days to use the high school pool.

Near the end of the hallway, by the back entrance, she stops and looks up. She's face-to-face with the Heritage Display.

The Heritage Display is unchanged from how she remembers it, since the days she'd press her cheeks and hands against the glass, passing time, waiting for her dad or Neha Aunty to pick her up from swimming class. To one side of the hallway there's a floor-to-ceiling case of artifacts: fragments of arrowheads and hunting tools made from animal bones and knickknacks that remind Angie of charms on a charm bracelet. Each small artifact is accompanied by a lengthy write-up, courtesy of the Algonquin Historical Society. And on one shelf, just below her eye level, there's a diorama re-creation of a battle scene set against the backdrop of the town's namesake river, figures of people in animal hides with skin the color of burnt sienna. Which reminds her—

She whips around, and there it is. On the other side of the hall, in a parallel case, also behind glass. Angie holds her breath. *It's been a long time,* she thinks as she approaches it, but it's the same as it was: an alabaster bust with a plaque beneath it that reads, CHIEF KINOTEN, SACHEM OF THE KITCHEWAN, A VENERABLE LEADER IN BATTLE AND IN PEACE. ARTIST UNKNOWN.

She stands in front of the chief, and it feels like traveling back in time. She feels a spike of not-quite-nostalgia for her younger days, when she'd gazed at the display cases and the bust with wonder at how her town used to belong to people who'd now be entirely out of place. Seeing it now, it strikes her as odd and even unfair for everything to be named after people who she suspects would no longer be welcome here. She examines the bust's all-too-familiar face: his commanding eyebrows and sloping beaklike nose that reminds her of half a mountain, his searing but pupil-less eyes, his cutting cheekbones that cast shadows upward from the spotlights at the base of the case, and his defiant, close-lipped mouth. She thinks of the whoops of spectators at Kitchewan High football games, their so-called Indian battle cry. She can't imagine this solemn leader doing anything like the goofy cartwheels and jumping jacks of their school mascot to hype up the crowd at sports games.

She was offered the role of the chief's wife back in third grade for the school Thanksgiving play. It was a minor but pivotal role. Chief Kinoten's wife spots a white deer sipping from the banks of the Kitchewan River. The rare sighting is considered a good omen. The wife tells her husband, the chief, and others in the tribe about the deer, and Chief Kinoten prophesizes great fortune. Shortly after, Henry Hudson and his band of Dutch expeditionists "discover" the town, and because of the colorless deer, they're treated to a hero's welcome, now

known as Thanksgiving. Or so it unfolds each year on the stage of
Joseph T. Pliner Elementary.

Angie had declined the part. She'd preferred to draw as little attention to herself as possible, which was already hard, as she was
one of the few students in her entire grade with a complexion more
similar to the chief and his wife than to the expeditionists. It had been
safer to be a chorus-line turkey.

It was all a load of crap, anyway. In fact, last year, during a ninth-
grade social-studies field trip to one of the few reservations left in the
state, the tour guide, a Native, had given them the real Thanksgiving
story. He'd described the "Kitchawang" as progressive and resource-
ful. They'd pioneered new fishing methods, mastered tool and weapon
making, and navigated local bodies of water centuries before the Eu-
ropeans.

According to the guide, the chief had fought Dutch invaders until
his log fort was set on fire, and at that point, he dove headfirst, self-
immolating rather than experiencing defeat. The guide confirmed
that seeing a white deer was considered good luck, but there was no
sighting before the Dutch arrived. And there certainly wasn't a welcome committee or a communal feast. There were, however, deaths
by smallpox, a sketchily brokered resettlement, and the deliberate ab-
sorption of stragglers who remained in white territory into American
oblivion. The guide's telling of how things had really gone down,
particularly the part about the chief setting himself on fire, had made
Angie shiver in awe, but it had upset some of her classmates. They'd
called the guide's stories about the chief "barbaric" and felt their own
heritage was being "attacked." In response, the high school had quietly
replaced visits to the reservation with tours of a maple-syrup-tapping
operation, celebrating the town's less controversial heritage farms.

Angie traces the arc of one of the chief's eyebrows with her finger and
stops when she notices she's smudging the glass. She envies how the

chief acted with such conviction when battling the Dutch, even though it must have been scary; how fearless he must have been in the face of adversity, even though it cost him his life. She doesn't have that kind of courage, she thinks regretfully. She doesn't even feel brave enough to be herself sometimes. From childhood to the present, she often finds herself fixated on fitting in, erasing or muting any difference between herself and everyone around her, being like everyone else, even though she's not, with her momless family and her dad with the funny accent who sometimes Ubers her classmates, with their constant worries about what they can and can't afford, and her skin that's the color of tennis court clay and hair the color of dirt, which allows her to pick herself out of any class photo in less than a second. In fact, when her father suggested changing her name from Anjali to Angela to make it easier for people to understand she was American like them, that she was one of them, he'd explained, she'd quickly agreed, perpetually embarrassed, even as a second grader, when her classmates and teachers would trip over her name.

She stares at the chief, wishing this slab of stone could speak to her, give her advice. She senses something is not right about what happened on the football field, but she doesn't know what to do, whether she should go back to the police and tell them she heard a scream, because she thinks she did, she's almost positive; if she should tell the police and the school that Chiara wouldn't have just done this for no reason, because she wasn't a lunatic; if she should do all that even if it will upset the McClearys and Henry and Sam's friends at school. And also, she's scared. She knows the chief wouldn't be, but she is. A coward.

Angie's phone vibrates in her backpack. She ignores it. It's probably someone messaging her about the town hall last night. Besides, when she does look at her phone, that friend request, the one from the Indian woman with the shoulder holes in her shirt and the too-familiar face, is there. Pending. Waiting for a response. And she doesn't have one yet. She doesn't have a response for her mother.

It's not fair. It's not fair that her dad threw all this stuff at her about her mother that he'd never mentioned before. He told her nothing was wrong with her. But something *was* wrong. Something must have been wrong. No mother abandons her daughter like that.

Angie's fingers have hovered over the accept button half a dozen times in the past twenty-four hours, but the problem is, if she accepts, what then? They couldn't become "friends," and that woman certainly couldn't be her mom. Not now. Not anymore, when she hasn't been around for almost nine years. Angie wouldn't know what to say to her or even know what to call her—she couldn't call her Mom, or Aunty, as she would other Indian women her age. And then, there's her dad. She can't imagine he'd be okay if she spoke to her mother. She's not even sure if he's okay now. The circles under his eyes are so dark these days they look like injuries, and he's been jumpy, distracted, mumbling to himself and obsessively checking the overactive KHS parents' group Facebook page for updates on the stabbing.

Angie had thought that maybe after they'd spoken during the storm, she'd feel a sense of relief, that things would be different between them, more open. But it's like their conversation had never happened. The morning after that awkward candlelit dinner with Colleen, he'd made a point of leaving the McCleary papers, inked with his signature, on the kitchen counter for her next to her milk. He'd commented that he was sure that after a good night's sleep, she'd have "come to her senses" and stopped worrying about "things that didn't concern her." When she'd tried to explain, he'd cut her off and announced that he wasn't going to let her throw her future away. In fact, he'd come back from the town hall yesterday and started up again, calling her downstairs from her room, insisting that "time is running out," that they must "lock this in."

Angie hadn't touched the papers. She avoided looking at them. The more he pushed, the less she wanted to listen.

Her phone vibrates again. Whoever it is is persistent. She shouldn't answer, she's here to swim. She's barely been able to practice since everything happened, and she's not going to let Henry or Chris or the messages on social media stop her from focusing. Because that's what she really cares about. And she's going to have the best season of her life.

Her phone rings again, and this time, Angie angrily unzips her backpack and pulls it out, expecting it to be her dad, because who else would call and call and call.

It's Sam McCleary. She hits decline like a reflex and turns her phone off, slipping it back into her backpack. She acknowledges the chief's bust with a nod, slings her backpack over her shoulder, and marches back to the front desk, resolved, at least, to not let her confusion and fear interfere with her swimming.

The line has thinned out, because there are two women behind the reception desk now rather than one. There are a handful of people in front of her, but it looks like things are moving.

When she gets to the front of the line, she tells the woman she's here to use the pool and needs the electronic tag that lets her in.

"Mm-hmm," the woman behind the counter says, typing a mile a minute, and certainly more words than whatever Angie just said, into a computer. "All right then. We don't have a lifeguard on duty right now."

"Oh, I'm okay without one."

More clacking. "Uh-huh . . ." The woman looks up and asks, "You over fourteen?"

Angie nods.

"Is your mom or dad here? I need an official proof of residence—like a property-tax filing or utility bill. To add you to the new system."

Angie shakes her head. "Can I use the pool for today and get that stuff to you next time?"

The woman shakes her head and the curls in her cropped hair bounce as she does. "I wish you could, sweetie. But things are real strict these days." She adds, "It's that whole mess with the high school. I don't know if you heard about it . . ." She lowers her voice. "There've been some problems. Kids, juvenile delinquent types, sneaking in, selling drugs. What a world . . ." She clicks her tongue.

"But I used to come here all the time."

"Oh, I don't doubt that, but we have a new computer system and new rules. So whatever you used to do won't work anymore."

Angie feels her eyes welling and the lump in her throat reappear. This isn't fair.

The woman must notice. "It's nothing personal, hon. This is to protect us, all of us and our resources. Us legitimate taxpaying people." She looks Angela up and down, taking note of her backpack and the pathetically sad look on her face. She gives her a pitying smile and says, "Okay, tell you what. You look like a nice girl. I'll help you out. Just this one time. Give me one sec . . ." More clacking. She turns to her coworker behind the desk. "Linda—I'm processing a temporary pool tag. Can you take a look real quick?"

Angie starts tapping her foot again while the two ladies huddle in front of the computer and type what sounds like a graduate thesis. She hadn't noticed the others in line before, but she turns briefly and sees a young mother, blond, with two children, directly behind her. The mother's in head-to-toe Lululemon and her eyes are glued to her phone. "Oh my god," she says to no one in particular.

Angie's eyes widen.

Noticing Angie, the blond woman says to her, "I just saw the news about the teenager. The African American one who stabbed the boy."

"What about her?" Angie asks.

"She's dead."

FRIDAY, AUGUST 24, 2018

TWENTY-TWO

Babur drives at exactly the speed limit. Below it, in fact, using each curve as an opportunity to decelerate and taking his passengers on the "scenic route." Nonetheless, they're almost there. He fidgets with his seat belt. Its glossy polyester feels like a knife slicing into his collarbone, and he unbuttons the top button on his polo collar, feeling stifled, sweating, fanning himself with one hand. Perplexingly, the universe appears to have conspired with the township's traffic-control systems to keep all lights green the entire length of this trip, and miraculously, every intersection they approach is empty. Babur asks his conscience for forgiveness and takes a detour down Wappinger Lane. Yet even with this further twist and a potential additional turn, the ETA, like the Prius, continues to creep closer, nearer. They're almost at Kitchewan High.

His eyes flit between the road ahead and the passengers in the back seat, the pale-faced boy with the mushroom cloud of curly hair and his sultry, amber-skinned companion, twirling her wavy hair in her hands, fingers decorated with multiple silver rings. Both appear oblivious to Babur's circuitous routing.

Because he's only bought himself a few extra minutes with his latest turnoff, because it's now or never, Babur clears his throat during a lull in the percussion to the jazzy song playing from the car speakers. He asks the duo in the back seat the question he's been dying to ask, but in clear contravention of his rule against engaging passengers on topics that even border on political, controversial, disputable, offensive, or otherwise murky: "So tell me, why are you protesting?"

He'd picked up the unlikely pair several minutes ago at the Metro North station. The young woman with the wavy hair and nose ring between her nostrils that reminds him of the ring they'd kept on the family buffalo, Choti, back in Hoshiarpur, and the pale thin boy with the hair like the bulbous terra-cotta figurines that sprout unsightly grass. He'd eyed their clothing with disappointment: torn jeans that neither had made any effort to patch up—holes running all the way up the girl's thigh! Nonetheless, he'd plastered on his Move grin, faithfully delivering the customer service on which he so prided himself, only to do a double-take, however, when their destination flashed on the screen of his phone. The high school—they were going to Kitchewan High School! He'd scanned them both once more and gulped so much air that he now felt an irrepressible need to belch.

The girl had leaned toward his seat. She smelled spicy but refreshing, like citrus fruit sprinkled with black pepper. She'd handed Babur an auxiliary wire connected to her phone. "You mind?" she'd asked, her heavily lined eyes blinking at Babur suggestively. Babur had felt himself blush and kept a teeth-baring smile glued on his face, accepting the wire, nodding to indicate it would be his pleasure, only to nearly choke on a gasp as he caught sight of an additional piercing on the girl's bottom lip.

"You okay?" the boy with the big hair had asked, in response to Babur's sputtered coughing.

Once he regained control of his trachea, he'd said, "Yes, yes. Perfectly fine, thank you." And because this was his chance, "Good morning, Ben and friend." It was part of his signature service to greet riders by their name. "How are you both doing today? Off to the high school, I see."

The boy had caught Babur's eyes through the rearview mirror and said, "Uh, fine. Yeah, we're going for the protest."

Babur had gripped the steering wheel until his knuckles turned colorless, nodding vigorously, and in the background, he could hear the girl sing softly to her music. The melodic crooning of a woman's voice layered with the girl's, "Well, it's like cranes in the sky, sometimes I don't wanna feel those metal clouds . . ."

On Monday, the search for Chiara Thompkins had come to an end when police announced news of the girl's passing. According to the paper, her body had been discovered, discolored and caked in mud, along the bank of the Kitchewan River, abdomen bloated but digits shriveled, suggesting death by drowning, time of death likely around the time of the tropical storm last Saturday. Ever since this unexpected news broke, the trickle of mostly local news coverage on the Incident at the high school, as everyone had been calling it, became a waterfall. It even attracted regional attention. With the girl deceased, the already numerous interpretations of the Incident, commentary on who was at fault, how it came to pass, what exactly happened, multiplied and diverged with an invigorated intensity. It seemed as though reading about and discussing the Incident had become a collective timepass, as Babur called it, and for Babur in particular, it had become all-consuming, a borderline obsession.

These evenings, Babur had given up the pretense of even attempting to sleep. These evenings, he didn't head upstairs, he didn't go to bed and toss and turn for a few hours before trudging downstairs in the middle of the night to park himself in front of the blue-white light of his desktop monitor. Rather, after doing the dishes from dinner, he'd go straight to the study. And there he'd be, slurping a mug of warm water with slices of lemon and ginger, reading and rereading all news articles and social media posts on the Incident that he could find. All night.

One could say Babur was entranced by the growing internet chatter about what happened at the high school, who Chiara Thompkins was, how it all came to be. Yet, truth be told, his commitment to reading, studying, immersing himself in each and every article or post that reported more or less the same set of facts or ungrounded opinions, respectively, and the comments to those, and the comments to the comments to those, was an escape. A release. Not quite entertainment—for that would be vulgar—but something that allowed him to ignore the existence of the most recent items in his "Correspondence" folder.

Ever since her callous and flippant note concerning custody, Purnima had been needling him. She had written twice more—both times unanswered—as if now, nearly nine years later, she was ready to prioritize the daughter whom she'd recklessly abandoned. In her first message, she asked if Babur had any thoughts on her earlier email, if he might be able to ask Angie about meeting her, and said that she could fly to New York, perhaps during Angie's swimming season. In her second message, she'd all but threatened him, declared she won't be "bullied" into staying away from her daughter, that "what happened" was a long time ago, that things are different now, that her lawyer told her the courts would see things her way, "if it were to come to that."

It took all the self-control Babur could muster not to smash open the computer monitor. How dare she try to paint him as the villain, to insinuate she will drag courts and lawyers into all of this, into their private lives. And all the while, even when confronted by Angie the other day, Babur has been too magnanimous to expose Purnima's true wretchedness, too much of a caring parent to upset his daughter. *How dare she!* With each rereading (and there have been several) Babur can feel the pressure mounting in his veins like a blocked spigot that could burst at any moment. He needs something that will allow him to forget.

It is for this reason that Babur is well read on the movement of those inflamed by Chiara Thompkins's death and seeking justice—if one could impute coherence to disjointed and pointed remarks, led by a diffuse group of angry young internet users who must live far away from Kitchewan. But justice for what, Babur fails to understand. He is sympathetic about the girl's passing—he has a daughter himself. Beyond that, this was the unfortunate demise of a troubled girl: Chiara Thompkins ran away from home (a problem child), she snuck into Kitchewan High School (a rule breaker), she sold drugs (here, his heartbeat picked up), she carried a knife (dangerous!) and attacked a boy, absconding like a fugitive. And then, she passed. Her passing is sad, but it doesn't symbolize anything larger. Not to Babur. What's more, from his study of the Kitchewan High parents' group on Facebook, it appears the girl's likely motive was desperation for money. It is sad she felt such economic pressure, but it makes sense to Babur. In contrast, twisting the facts into what they clearly are not, using this as a pretense to air grievances about civil rights, does not. It feels opportunistic. And so American. Everyone in this country has a cause, it seems, and waits to pounce into action, under the guise of protecting their freedom, their bloated, overextended freedom.

So why are these two riders in his back seat protesting?

Babur's question catches the girl's attention. She sits upright and stops singing. She says, matter-of-factly and as if it were the most obvious thing in the world, "We're protesting because we've had enough with systemic racism and injustice." She stretches the fabric of her black T-shirt away from her chest so Babur can make out the image and words silk-screened on it from his mirror: JUSTICE FOR CHIARA, he reads, and an African American girl's face with the words CASUALTY OF YOUR IGNORANCE superimposed over it in red lettering fashioned like an ink stamp. Babur recognizes the face from the papers as that of the deceased girl. The female passenger pats the boy on his elbow and says, "Ben's got a different one. Show him, Ben." Babur catches the boy's cheeks flush at the girl's touch. The boy spreads out the front of his white shirt for Babur to read through the mirror: EDUCATE YOUR-SELF. #JUSTICEFORCHIARA, and an image of the same girl's face but with pupil-less eyes and her mouth wide open with a mouthpiece next to it, as if she were broadcasting a message.

Babur intends to nod but finds himself shaking his head.

The boy must notice because he says, "You haven't heard about what happened at Kitchewan High School? 'Cause it's in the news, like, even the *Times*. We live in the city and we've heard about it." He doesn't wait for Babur to say anything before he continues, "There was a Black girl, a high school student, who was run off the football field by some entitled white boys—assaulted, we think—and she ended up dead. Like, dead. She drowned during the recent storm. It's sick. Really sick."

Babur shifts in his seat, adjusting the buttons on his polo again, feeling ill at ease by the boy's blatant reference to race. This should be a warning, Babur tells himself. He should cut this off, abort the discussion, end it immediately. If his nearly two decades in the United States have taught him anything, it is to sprint away from any even tepidly heated conversation linked, even by implication, to race; it is a tinderbox, an unfathomable American rococo he neither understands nor has taken the time to learn how to navigate.

The boy continues, however, "And now this town—Kitchewan—it's going berserk. Like, they're criminalizing this poor girl after she died. All over some legal BS about her address."

Before Babur can end it, the girl in the back seat interjects, her eyes shining and her face pink, "We need an investigation. A real one. Into those boys. Because it doesn't add up. Why would a girl with no history of violence, no criminal record, no mental illness just up and stab someone—assuming she even did?"

Babur is tempted to correct this girl, to tell her about the prevailing theories in the Kitchewan High parents' Facebook group, to remind her the police are investigating. He's tempted to share that the girl was troubled, had aggression and disciplinary issues. For instance, he's read that she'd caused quite a stir, yelling profanities at her physical education teacher over taking the school's mandatory swimming test; a standoff that eventually resolved when the teacher allowed the stubborn girl to doggy-paddle for two full laps, a spectacle that students had apparently spoken about for months. Perhaps these two youths are projecting their big-city problems and big city-crime onto this harmonious town. Perhaps they have too much time on their hands or watch too much television. But before he can say any of this—

"We need to honor Chiara Thompkins's memory with the truth," the girl continues.

"And we need new rules on school districting. It's unbelievable that in 2018 we have economic apartheid like this! A girl is dead, and all these people care about is keeping their prissy school as white as snow," the boy says so forcefully, it is as if he's forgotten his own skin tone.

These teenagers have taken his mildly loaded question and plunged headfirst into a danger zone, using charged language. Babur can't—he shouldn't—engage them. He needs to think fast, put the proverbial clown back in the box. Yet he hears himself asking, unable to help himself, too deeply invested after hours upon hours of internet research, "Did you"—a pause—"know this girl?" Because maybe they did. It would certainly explain their outrage.

"Well, no," the boy says, "but, like, that's not the point. We heard about a few students organizing today and wanted to show our support."

Babur nods silently, albeit surprised that students at Angie's school are behind this misguided protest. They would know as well as Babur does that the unfortunate incident had nothing to do with race, and that the police had found no evidence of wrongdoing by the boys. They would know that if the school were better about detecting non-residents, keeping out violent teenagers who sell drugs, none of this would have happened. After all, this is an outstanding school district, a nice community.

Babur feels his jaw tighten as he recounts in his head the many sac-
rifices he'd made to ensure he and Angie lived in a good school district
even when finances were strained, about how he plays by the rules.
But of course, these two youths would have not the faintest idea. They
wouldn't understand that if Kitchewan schools allow in whoever wants
to go, they'll be overrun, and crimes like the one that took place on the
football field would become an everyday occurrence. These youths
are too caught up in their narrative, in obfuscating the truth. This girl,
the one whose image is on their T-shirts, stabbed someone! But that
doesn't matter to them. They'd rather spend their time and their outrage finding fault with an upstanding town full of civil people on this
bright summer day.

"Excuse me. Hey, driver." The boy taps Babur on the shoulder from
the back seat.

Babur jumps, startled.

"I think the intersection is clear," the boy says.

Babur blinks rapidly, loosening his 10–2 grip on the steering wheel.
The Prius is stopped at a stop sign at the intersection of Schoolside
Way, and Babur seems to have shifted into park without realizing it.
For how long were they like this? How did this happen? He attempts
to shake it off and says, "My apologies. There are many . . . deer, and
I wanted to be certain the coast was clear." From his rearview mirror,
he sees the passengers exchange a look. The girl rolls her eyes, and the
boy mouths something he can't make out. There go his five stars.

He turns onto Schoolside and, reasoning that his rating is ruined
anyway, he decides to ask another question. "The girl on your shirts
stabbed someone. Doesn't that make her a criminal?"

"Allegedly," the girl passenger says. "She allegedly stabbed someone. And it could've been self-defense. Only now we'll never hear
from her." Her voice is sharp.

"Maybe the New York City papers weren't clear," Babur continues, feeling steadier, braver by the syllable, "but you see, this whole

incident, it's not about black and white, this race and that race. No, Kitchewan's not like that. The people here aren't like that."

"Everywhere's like that," the girl says, eyes narrowing, looking to the side.

"No, really," he says, "it's a nice town. My daughter goes to the high school. It's top notch."

"Yeah, because it gets a boatload of property taxes. Nice schools for rich people," the girl responds.

Babur wants to probe further, to ask what is wrong with that. This is the way things work. Of course you pay more taxes in a nice town—Kitchewan's have been hiked in recent years to fund the high school renovations—and of course that means you get a nice school. Maybe as youth, you have an image of everyone living equally, exactly the same, but that's not how things work in America. Maybe it's not fair or equal, but at least things work here. This Babur knows. But these two have likely never lived in another country. They don't understand how good they have it, how things don't work in other parts of the world, how real inequality—protruding ribs and scaled-over bare feet, muddy water, and open-air defecation steps from one's front door in even a nice residential colony back home—looks.

They pull up to the school entrance and Babur looks at them through his mirror. He feels an urge to shake them, wake them from their ignorance. "But why you?" he asks. "Why are you both doing this? Neither of you is . . ." He trails off, stopping himself before completing the thought, uncertain of the terminology to use, but certain the question should be asked.

The girl has already opened her door, even though the car is still moving. She leans forward toward Babur and extends her arm, anticipating the return of her auxiliary wire. He's not sure if she heard him or is choosing to ignore his question, but either way, he's lost her. He inhales the scent of orange and black pepper once more and unplugs the wire. Her music, which had been strangely soothing, abruptly cuts out, and an ad for used tires blares from the radio, pummeling Babur's ears.

There are a few dozen people in fragmented groups gathered near the front doors to the high school. Mostly young, majority white, some seated on the ground, some standing, some with plastic cups of what looks like Gatorade or pretzels. A small group is performing skateboarding tricks off to the side, seemingly oblivious to the systemic ills they are fighting. Others are clustered on the grass—several barefoot—around a sound system blasting an angry-sounding rap song about losing oneself in music (of all things). Curiously, a handful have duct tape over their mouths. Babur wonders if that's safe, if they can breathe. He also wonders if this is it. Apart from some signs with Chiara Thompkins's image and handwritten demands for justice that a few hold up every so often, this doesn't look like a protest. There's no yelling or chanting or even marching. No organizer with a loudspeaker. Just teenagers milling about in front of the school, as if this were a mela from Babur's youth in Hoshiarpur, minus the stand-wallahs hawking animal-shaped balloons and sweet and savory *behel* and *chaat* (his mouth waters). Perhaps he should confirm with the boy that they're in the right place.

"Here's fine," the boy says before Babur can say anything else. He seems in a rush to follow the girl, who's embracing another boy, a tall, brown-skinned boy with thick glasses and a white T-shirt like his passenger's. Before walking away from the car, the pale boy with the big hair stops and turns. He taps on Babur's window, which Babur rolls down, feeling a certain pity for his passenger, so hurriedly forgotten by his companion. The boy says, "Because I believe in radical honesty, I feel like I owe you this feedback. You seem like a safe driver, and a, uh, nice guy, but your sense of direction is messed up. You took, like, four wrong turns." He holds up his phone screen and Babur can see the boy has selected two stars.

"Anyway, no hard feelings. We're in this together." He pumps a fist and hits send on the abysmal review of Babur's service, walking off to join the girl.

Babur forces a broad smile to hide his embarrassment and confusion at the boy's last statement. He shakes his head in bewilderment, then sighs and reaches for his phone, ready to swipe for his next trip, when a text appears across the ribbon of his phone screen: a text from Fred McCleary.

Babur inhales a gulp and shifts into park. He wishes he could unsee the text and not be tempted to read it, but it's too late for that. It says: "Hey, Bobby, just checking in." ". . ." Fred is typing. An additional text appears: "Do you want our lawyer Tom to come by to pick up the signed paperwork from you today?"

Babur's head gets hot. No, he certainly doesn't want that. Especially since the paperwork is not signed. He types, "Hello, Fred! I will bring them to you. Today or tomorrow."

Fred replies, "It's no bother to Tom. Really."

Babur grits his teeth. Of course it's no bother to their irritating lawyer. The same lawyer has been calling Babur multiple times a day—he's certain of it—from his private number, no less, and Babur has, of course, been letting each of these calls go to voice mail. Babur types, "No. I'll bring them. I want to."

Fred says, "👍 You and Angela take care."

Babur sighs and types, "👍 😊" He sets his phone back in its holder next to his dashboard. His hands are damp, and his stomach is churning. He'd told the McClearys he and Angie were "all set" a few days ago, and ever since then, they keep checking in. It makes sense, he supposes. They suggested having everything finalized in time to help Angie with a swimming club as soon as this school year, and they don't know that Angie still hasn't signed, that she won't even look at the document, much less talk to him about it. He has been trying to rationalize Angie's behavior. She could be sad about the runaway girl (she knew her, after all), or perhaps this is an extension of her argument with Samantha (which he'd had no idea about until recently, he's ashamed to admit). Or maybe Angie is feeling emotional about finding the McCleary boy bleeding on the ground (a frightening sight) or, like

Babur, wary of associating herself with a family whose son is a drug user (he shakes his head in disapproval). Yet none of that should stop her from seizing this opportunity.

He wrests his hands through his wavy, wiry hair, his head feeling heavier than usual. Angie is being inconceivably stubborn. Even if Babur hit it big in his investment account, which currently hovers at a pitiful few hundred dollars. Even if Babur worked twenty-four hours a day for the next half decade, without a single holiday, break, or nap. Even if Purnima with her fantastical threats of claims for maintenance disappeared off the face of the earth. Even then, the odds of ever finding financial resources equivalent to what the McClearys' offer will provide are . . . inconceivable.

Babur is about to shift into drive and accelerate out of the high school parking lot when he is overcome by an urge to speak to Angie, to settle the question of the McClearys' offer once and for all. They will accept the offer. They must.

Babur turns off his Uber application and parks in the school lot. He tries Angie's cell. She doesn't answer. He hangs up and immediately redials. It goes to voice mail again. Babur massages his temples, which are throbbing. He calls once more, but still to voice mail. (Where is she?!) He wrings his hands, thinking in desperation of the papers from the McClearys.

Outside, the protest appears to have officially begun; the youths have gathered in a semicircle formation on the grass next to the main entrance of the school. A slender Caucasian girl no older than Angie, with turquoise-streaked hair and circular glasses that remind Babur of Gandhi-ji, is standing in front of the others on the grass. She's dressed in a black T-shirt like the one his former passenger had shown him. She gesticulates grandly and even holds up a closed fist. From this distance Babur cannot hear what the girl is saying, but he sees the boy from the Uber ride leaping to his feet to give the girl a standing ovation. Others join him and mirror the girl's revolutionary-style fist or raise their signs with images of Chiara Thompkins on them.

Babur stares until his eyes water, but he cannot make sense of this motley crowd and their picniclike gathering. If they cared for Chiara Thompkins, she wouldn't have been homeless, or friendless, as it's reported she was in Facebook posts, during her life. If they cared for Chiara Thompkins, then she could have called one of them when she was in trouble, but then some of them, like the two youths he drove, didn't even know her.

Babur's head feels heavy, so he cradles it between his hands, massaging his temples again. The motion triggers a prickly feeling across his face, which in turn leads him to scratch vigorously at his stubble, as if trying to reach an itch underneath his skin, inside his face. But it's no use.

He is agitated. Agitated by his daughter, who can't bother to pick up her phone, who won't agree to advancing her future; by the arbitrary passions of the ill-informed youths he'd driven and their mishmash of companions who can't even wait for a coherent reason to trumpet their cause; by the absurd asks of his soon-to-be ex-wife; by his shirt collar that feels like it's cutting into his neck and that he's now airing out; by his skin, and his eyes, which feel inexplicably dry and sticky, and are stinging . . . He rubs his eyes aggressively and looks out his windshield, unsettled, miserable.

His phone rings. Babur flinches before answering it.

"This is Bobby." His voice is hoarse.

"Hey, Bobby." It's a man's voice, a smooth voice, but not one he recognizes.

He looks down at his dashboard, too irritated to continue observing the protest. "Hello . . ."

"It's Tom, Bobby—Tom Ghirardelli, the McClearys' lawyer."

"Oh—yes." He clears his throat. "Hello—hello, Tom."

"You sound . . . busy. Is this a bad time?"

Babur exhales and with forced cheer says, "No, nothing like that." As soon as he speaks, he regrets his words; his face feels scratchy again and his neck hot. It is a terrible time. He wishes this man would leave him alone. "About the papers, Tom—"

"It turns out, Bobby, I'm in the neighborhood. Are you near home? I thought I could swing by and pick them up. Save you the trip."

"No—uh, no need. I told Fred. I'll go drop them."

"You sure? 'Cause if it's easier for you, I'm real close by. Lakeview Terrace, right?"

Babur wants to know why Tom is close by, what business he could possibly have driving by Babur's road, but instead he says, "That's okay. I'm working and won't be home for a while."

"Ah, right. Well, you just say the word."

Babur feels his mouth stretch into a forced smile. "Will do, Tom."

He's ready to end the call when Tom says, "Say, Bobby, you see the news?"

"News? What news?" Babur racks his brain. "Did the principal resign?" Babur had read that Principal Mabel Burrowes was expected to step down. He'd had mixed feelings about this, felt a bit sorry for her even, as he'd found the woman to be impressive and fastidious during their encounter at the high school. However, following her remarks at the town hall and after reading pages upon pages of views about her on the KHS parents' group on Facebook, it was difficult to defend her. As a parent in the Facebook group succinctly summed up, nothing like the Incident had ever occurred at Kitchewan High under principals prior. It was difficult to argue with that fact.

"Not yet, believe it or not. Quite gutsy of her not to accept responsibility. Especially after what she said to Fred at the town hall. But, uh, I actually meant news about the cousin. The police brought in the cousin of the Thompkins girl for questioning this morning. It looks like she was in on the fraud."

Babur sits up in his seat. "Fraud?"

"Yep. Fraud. Being enrolled in a public school under false pretenses can get you in jail, you know."

Babur didn't know. He puts his phone on speaker and attempts to refresh his phone's internet browser to search for the latest news on the Incident. *Come on*, he thinks, as the website fails to load. He clicks and reclicks on the latest link from the *Gazette*, and finally, he sees it: a short, three-paragraph update noting, as Tom said, that the adult cousin of the late Chiara Thompkins is being questioned for her involvement in Thompkins's enrollment in Kitchewan High. He says slowly, while skimming, "This is a crime?"

"Well, that part's complicated, Bobby. Strictly speaking, maybe, maybe not. But it's good for us that they're asking these questions."

"Good . . . for us?" He's confused by what Tom means. Surely now that the Thompkins girl has passed, this is moot. There is no reason to protest in her name, but similarly, no reason to trouble her grieving family.

"Oh, you've probably seen." The lawyer sighs like he's balancing a boulder and says, "There's a whole lot of agitators out there—today, in fact, at the school—trying to turn this whole thing into a referendum on race." Babur contemplates telling Tom he's in the school parking lot, but decides it might look like he sympathizes with the cause, and besides, Tom doesn't pause long enough to let him chime in. "Ridiculous, really. Every time one of them is involved, people are quick to escalate." Babur nods, wondering if Tom can hear his heart thumping as he looks out ahead of him and sees said agitators now standing in a large circle, holding hands and swaying. "If we can keep the focus, so to speak, on the girl"—Babur cannot help but note how calm the agitators look, rocking back and forth—"the Black girl, who was a troubled youth, believe you me, well, all the better."

"I see . . ." Babur says, even though he doesn't. Not quite. He doesn't support the protest, but he also doesn't like the idea of agreeing with Tom. Also, what did Tom mean by "one of them," exactly? "But, Tom," he decides to ask, "now that the girl has . . . passed . . . why get into . . ." His eyes retrace the article on his phone screen, reading with more care the words his eyes danced over the first time. He nears the end and then—there—right there—*How could I have missed this?*—directly beneath the brief text is a black-and-white thumbnail image of a woman. She has neatly groomed shoulder-length dark hair, familiar brown skin, with soft eyes, a gently curving nose, and full, youthful cheeks . . . It couldn't be. It can't be. "The nurse?" he murmurs.

Tom must have been speaking, although Babur hadn't been listening. There's an abrupt "What was that, Bobby?" from him into the phone.

"Nothing—it was nothing. You—you were saying?" The caption reads: "Cousin of the late Thompkins, Desiree Matthews, nurse at local hospital." It is. It's her!

Tom continues, "Now you ask a good question. The thing is, these elements, let's call them, are trying to turn this into a race thing, make the Black girl into the victim. And on what grounds? For what? It's ridiculous, really. A boy—our boy—was stabbed!"

Babur looks back at the image, stuck on it, unable to close a synapse, to forge a connection between the woman who saved his life and this stabber, this . . . fraud. Was it fraud?

". . . the agitators have the police poking around now. And you know that the McClearys are longtime supporters of the police force—big contributors to their annual fund—but it's about the optics now, Bobby. The police have to make it seem fair, PC, you know. So they're questioning the McClearys' kid again and again—the same kid who was stabbed and blacked out. To prove what point?" He pauses here before continuing. Babur can hear Tom breathing into the phone. "And—well, never mind, because does it matter? The girl's gone and she shouldn't have been there. Although, with all these agitators, we can't say that and neither can the police. We have to be *sensitive*." He scoffs as if choking on that last word and says, "You know there's nothing more these people love than taking down a successful all-American family."

Babur's puzzled. He didn't realize this was a takedown. Maybe Tom should drive by this so-called protest and see for himself that it's just a few children socializing in silk-screened shirts on a summer day. Hardly cause for alarm. Moreover, Babur has noticed there isn't mention in any public reports that the McCleary boy had gone to the school to buy drugs. Now *that* would be a takedown.

"You understand," says Tom with a sudden urgency in his voice. Babur can feel his words like a Chinese finger trap around his throat, tightening its grip the more he resists it. "You work hard. Your kid works hard. You're not—well, you're immigrants, but the good kind— and this is why we need to work together. So . . . anyway. I'll let you get to it. To the work."

Babur's chest constricts. He wishes he could teleport his hand through the phone line and push Tom Ghirardelli away. He doesn't want this man with a greasy voice and pumpkin-colored skin giving him and Angie his approval; even if it is on behalf of the McClearys. Yes, Babur and Angie work hard, but not for the approval of people like Tom. He also wonders what Tom means exactly. About police and optics and shifting the focus. Surely he's speaking out of turn, express- ing the ill-formed personal opinions of the help gone rogue. Surely the McClearys don't know he speaks so crudely.

"All right, buddy, good chat. You have a good one!"

Babur nods and swallows. He hangs up without saying good- bye and stares at the image of the nurse on his phone screen. He asks himself if in critiquing the protesters, he is aligning himself with Tom Ghirardelli, if he is condemning the attractive young nurse— the cousin—with the chestnut-colored eyes and comforting voice. A coin-sized lump metastasizes in his throat, and he feels himself sinking into the driver seat, dipping lower and lower, being swallowed, faster now, as if in quicksand. He grips the handle of his car door until his knuckles turn white. The same feeling he'd had in the hospital parking lot, of the sky falling in on itself, only this time, of the corners of his Prius also collapsing toward him, the same shortness of breath, shallow breath, shallow breaths, out of breath, of the world moving, spinning, falling, of losing his balance, it all comes back. It's coming back! *Who will come save me this time?*

TWENTY-THREE

Angela's wet ponytail hits the nape of her neck when she turns around at the sound of her name.

"Ang! Hey, Ang!" calls the familiar voice.

She knows who it is before she sees. Yet she says with surprise, "Sam?"

Angie had been racing in the opposite direction, toward the front of the community center, after a military-speed shower, rushing to catch the Circulator home. Her hair is hastily tied back in a way that she knows will tangle if she doesn't brush and blow-dry it, and her still-damp body is blanketed underneath a baggy white T-shirt with the Kitchewan Indians logo emblazoned on it. There are wet patches around her shoulders and the top of her back. Her skin steams off vapors of chlorine, of all the chemicals used to disinfect the pool from the children's pee.

Sam McCleary is at the opposite end of the hallway, by the Heritage display. She flags her down like they're in the middle of a parade rather than the only ones in an empty, well-lit hallway. Sam's standing near the bust of the chief, oversized sunglasses on her head, in a petal-pink tank top and white shorts, twirling a set of car keys around her pointer finger.

Not used to having her name called out so loudly in a public place, Angie blushes, and without thinking, she walks toward Sam.

When she approaches, however, she wishes she hadn't. She shoves her hands in her pockets and her shoulders ride up. "Hi . . ." Angie says, letting her voice trail off. She stares at Sam's manicured pink toes peeking out from her silver Birkenstocks.

"I've been trying to call you." Sam continues twirling the keys.

She looks different, Angie thinks. Something about her face looks more knowing, more mature—maybe it's makeup, but her cheeks look firmer, less soft. Also, her eyebrows are different. They look neatly arced, like Mrs. McCleary's. This makes Angie feel both jealous and sad that her friend is changing without her. Angie swallows and looks down at her feet before replying, "Yeah, I know." Because it's true. She's been declining Sam's calls and everyone else's, too.

"I went to Willoughby's to look for you. They said you don't work there anymore?"

Angie makes a face. That was probably her annoying coworker. She still works there, only she's not on the schedule for a few months. To focus on swimming. Although these days, she's been having trouble focusing on anything. She keeps having these dreams—both sleeping and awake—with images she isn't sure are flashbacks or her imagination. About the football field, being at the football field. Henry and Chris are there with Chiara, holding her down. They're laughing and she's crying and scared. Only everything sounds far away, distorted in jagged bursts, and when Angie moves closer, it's only Henry. He's bleeding, calling for help, and she takes his hand.

Angie wishes there was someone she could talk to. Only she can't talk to Sam. So she shrugs and wrings her hands, which are clammy from cold sweat. She lets Sam think she doesn't work at the coffee shop anymore.

"Well, I hope you didn't get fired or anything," Sam says in a way that Angie can tell she's trying to lighten the mood, teasing. But it's not funny and reminds Angie of how out of sync they are. "I figured I'd find you here," Sam continues, still jingling her key ring. The sound of metal on metal is grating. Angie wants to clasp her hands around Sam's to stop it. As if she reads Angie's mind, Sam stops twirling and leans her head forward in Angie's direction. Her blue-gray eyes glint like she's suggesting something mischievous, and she says with a smile, "I've got the car. I'll give you a ride?"

"But you don't have your license yet."

Sam shrugs and says with a sly grin, "It's not a big deal. I've practiced enough and the speed limit in this town is, like, twenty miles per hour, so it's not like we'll be going fast. Come on."

Angie hesitates and looks back over her shoulder at the main entrance to the community center. She must have missed the Circulator by now.

"Seriously, come on. We've barely hung out all summer."

Angie nods, mouth closed, nostrils flared, piqued by Sam's words, which sound like an accusation. But they're true.

They walk past one of the entrances to the pool and Sam says, "God, it's been ages since I've been here. I must have peed in that pool like a hundred times when we were younger."

"Relax," Sam says, with a sideways glance at Angie, who has just triple-checked that her seat belt is fastened. "I've been driving all over by myself. Like, on the highway, too."

Angie gulps and nods, looking straight ahead, unconvinced by the choppy way Sam's reversing the silver Acura without checking her rearview mirror, by her sunglasses that swallow up half her face and make her look like a fly, and by the way she's nodding her head along to some overplayed pop song about being in a Range Rover.

"Seriously, you're making me nervous, Ang. Can you, like, chill out?"

Angie drops her right hand, which had been clenched around the roof handle.

Sam laughs and says, "Ever since Henry got hurt, my parents have been totally cool with me taking the car."

That's weird, Angie thinks. Mrs. McCleary doesn't seem like the type of parent to not care when it comes to things like driving without a license.

Sam pauses before changing into drive and looks at Angie. "It's true. They've been so distracted with Henry's stuff that no one cares what I do." She drives toward the parking lot exit. "It's awesome."

But Angie can tell by the way Sam says it, it's not.

They pull out of the community center and turn in the opposite direction on Route 18 from Angela's house.

"Sam, you went the wrong—"

"Yeah, I know. Let's get a Frappuccino or something first." Sam turns to look at Angie, making Angie want to ask her to keep her eyes on the road. "We haven't done anything together in forever. My treat."

Angie bites her lip, wishing she hadn't agreed to this ride home with Sam, and wishing Sam would stop reminding her they haven't spent time together. Because with everything that's happened, between the passage of the summer, the stuff with her family, and Sam going away to Jacksonville for the swimming program Angie had been dying to go to, that can't be a surprise. Besides, now that they are together, Angie feels on edge. She can't remember what before felt like; she doesn't know what to say or how to act or how to pretend things are normal and fun around this person who looks like someone who was once her friend but who flips her shiny yellow hair when she talks and drives without a license. But Angie can't say any of this and she's in the car already, so instead she says, "Okay." And then, realizing how ungrateful that must sound, she adds, "Thanks."

An ad for an online university comes on, and Sam starts playing with the radio dial.

"I'll change it. What do you want?" Angie says quickly.

"I don't know—just something good."

Angela starts clicking through Sam's presets.

Sam's eyes are back on the road, to Angie's relief, when she says, "We were all kind of surprised, you know, when you and your dad just, like, shot my parents down. For the foundation." Angie feels her ears prickle and her cheeks get hot. She pauses on a station playing a Selena Gomez song, figuring this will meet with Sam's approval.

"Well, it wasn't—"

"Nah, it's cool." Sam shrugs. "It was free money, like a gift, so it's kinda weird, like super weird. Like, we were trying to be nice, because, well, you're always complaining about how you can't afford stuff." Angie didn't know Sam thought that. "It wasn't like anyone was forcing you to take it. And I guess everyone was upset because there were all these protesters with the black power shirts making noise and, like, demanding things. Like Henry's the criminal. Like he did something wrong. And we thought—well, my parents thought—maybe you'd said something."

Before she can censor herself, Angie blurts, "You thought I said something—like what?"

Sam responds, "I don't know—I mean, I didn't think so. Like, not for sure, but you and Chiara were kinda friendly, and I dunno, maybe—"

Angie angles the AC vent away from her and rubs her arms. She's got goose bumps and her breathing feels heavy. "But if Henry didn't do anything, what could I say?"

Sam turns to look at her and the car veers closer to the right side of the road. "I don't know, Ang. I haven't really thought about it." Her eyes shift back on the road, and the car jerks to the left.

Angie cringes. When the car is back in its lane, she asks slowly, "Sam, did something happen with Henry that—"

The car jolts to a stop at a red light and Sam turns back to Angie. "This is what I mean, Ang. You've been acting so weird. I get that it's sad that Chiara died and everything, but it's not my brother's fault." Angie shifts uncomfortably at the mention of Chiara's death. Sam presses the accelerator abruptly when the light turns green. "Besides, the police finished their investigation, the one they had to do because of those protesters, and officially cleared my brother. So if you're stressed about it, it's all good, you know."

Angie's face gets hot. It's news to her about the police investigation. She bites her lip and wonders if her most recent interview with the police, the one this past Saturday, the day after the protest at the high school, was part of this investigation. It would be strange if it was, because the police had barely asked about Henry and Chris. Instead, they'd called Angie and her dad into this tiny room with no windows and wobbly chairs and a flickering overhead light that would give any sane person a headache and asked her dozens of questions about Chiara. What was she like, where did she live, who did she live with, how did they become friends? (Angie had wanted to correct them on this last question—they were acquaintances more than friends—but thought it might sound harsh, like she was trying to distance herself from someone who was dead.) Only to breathe out sort of heavily, as if annoyed, when she responded, sharing what she knew, which wasn't much.

They'd also asked a thousand questions about swimming. Like they were either amateur sports enthusiasts or thinking about joining the KHS girls' swim team themselves. Her dad had eaten it up. He happily filled them in on Angie's practice schedule, usual strokes, best times, and so on. She'd tried to motion with her eyes that he should stop talking, they should go home, the police couldn't possibly need this level of detail about swim team. But he was on a roll, in his element, and not ready to leave until the officers knew beyond a reasonable doubt that Angela was the fastest freshman on the Kitchewan High team last year. The only freshman girl who's been on varsity.

Henry and Chris, on the other hand, came up maybe twice, and even then, the police didn't let Angie clarify that she wasn't positive she'd seen Chiara running away or let her explain she'd heard arguing and a scream beforehand. She also didn't know how to describe what happened when Chris showed up at her house the other week, even if she'd tried.

"So what did the police say about what happened when they finished their investigation?" Angie finally asks.

She sees Sam glance in her direction. It's annoying how her eyes are hidden by her sunglasses. Looking back at the road, Sam shrugs and says, "Just a bunch of stuff, like, that Chiara attacked my brother for money, you know, and ran."

Angie nods, although *she doesn't know*. She thinks of how skittish Chris had been when he'd shown up at her doorstep and notices Sam hasn't mentioned him. "And Chris?" she asks.

"What about him?" Sam says. She keeps her eyes on the road, thankfully, but Angie notices her knuckles whiten around the steering wheel.

"Is he also, um, cleared?"

"Oh, well, yeah." Sam shrugs and lifts her eyebrows so they peek out from the massive sunglasses, in a way that Angie knows means Sam is impatient, irritated, or both. "I mean, he totally owes my parents and Henry, because, well, they figured everything out for him. Like, we didn't want to, but it was better to clear stuff up for Henry, and jeez, he was a total mess—" She cuts herself off and says, "You know what, though—I didn't mean to bring any of this up. I shouldn't talk about it, really, because we're probably suing the school district, so . . ."

"You're suing the school district?" Angie can hear her heartbeat now. "Like, your family? But I thought Henry's okay?"

"My parents are thinking about it. Nothing's official yet. I mean, yeah, Henry's going to be all right, like no permanent damage except for this nasty scar and that he can't run cross-country this fall. But there's medical bills and trauma and . . . and my dad says it's the school's negligence—like, letting in some kid who doesn't live here, not knowing she was living in the high school over the summer. I don't know." She stops and, as if she just remembered something, she looks at Angie, her face tensing up. In an urgent voice, she says, "I really shouldn't be talking about this. Forget I said anything." A pause before she adds quickly, "Oh, and don't say anything to Chris. He doesn't know, and he's kind of spastic so we're trying to— Well, just don't say anything to him."

Angie raises her eyebrows, curious about what's going on between the McClearys and Chris, and also why Sam thinks she voluntarily discusses anything with Chris.

Sam continues, oblivious, "If it were up to me, I kind of wish this was over. Every day my parents are on the phone with their lawyer and the school people for hours. They put the foundation on hold, too, because they're so busy. And Henry's just playing video games while Audrey watches him like it's the most interesting thing in the world." Sam rolls her eyes. "I wish things were back to normal."

Angie looks straight ahead, her eyes glued on the road, as if she's the one who's driving. She can hear her heart thumping, not able to drown it out even with the Ed Sheeran ballad on the radio. Henry's back with Audrey, which she shouldn't care about, and she doesn't, but it nags at her nonetheless. And the police have finished their investigation, without, as far as Angie can tell, really investigating. And there's also this controversy about Chiara's death—how it was racist and how public schools are unfair—but it would make more sense to Angie to figure out what happened. And no one's thinking about the foundation that her dad was so excited about. Angie wishes something in her life was even half-perfect. She feels her throat get heavy but tells herself to stay calm, to think about something else. They're stopped at a traffic light. Angie says, to change the topic, "You're a decent driver, Sam," even though she's a little erratic.

Sam smiles brightly and, as if taking a cue, asks in an overly playful voice, "So . . . I haven't even asked. What ya been up to all summer?"

Angie wants to remind Sam that she knows what Angie's been up to: training, summer school, working at Willoughby's, training, sleep. And if she actually cared she would have called Angie, like when she got back from swimming camp in Florida, or maybe messaged her from camp. "Nothing much. Same old," Angie says, trying her best to sound unaffected.

As if she can read her mind, Sam says, "You know, Jacksonville was intense. Like barely any downtime. I don't know if I liked it that much. Plus it's so humid there. It rains, like, every day."

"Why are you telling me this?" Angie's voice is sharper than she means for it to be. She feels her eyebrows, two caterpillars in comparison to Sam's perfectly arched pair, squeeze together.

Sam sounds taken aback. "I—I figured I should let you know because I know you want to go there next summer, and also . . . I've been thinking. I think I'm not going to do swim team this year." She hesitates, like she's waiting for Angie to say something, then continues. "I guess I was never that good at it, and it's so much time and makes my hair super dry. Besides, I'm always so exhausted after practice and then I have to do homework at night. It was fun before because you did it, but you're way better than me, so whatever."

At odds with herself, Angie sniffles, suppressing a tear. She doesn't know why she's sad over what Sam said. She shouldn't care if Sam doesn't swim anymore. Good riddance, is what she should think. But instead, all she can think is how this feels like the end. The end of their friendship. If Sam doesn't swim, they're barely going to see each other, and things will never be like how they were. It hits her like a blow, and she feels indescribably sad.

"What do you think, Ang?" Sam presses. "Have you ever thought about it . . . like, not swimming for a season or taking a break?"

Angie looks at Sam's profile and says as calmly as she can, feeling anything but, "If you feel that way, then it's probably the right decision."

They approach the strip mall. "Ang, I wanted to say something. Like tell you something." Sam slows the car, preparing to turn. "I'm sorry for getting so mad at you in the spring about Henry. My brother can be dumb. I know. Like, he doesn't think with his head, and he probably, like, made a move because you were there and maybe it was to get back at me or something, because he always needs to be the center of everything, or maybe he was in a fight with Audrey. Anyway, I know I blew up about it, and I shouldn't have . . . It's just—well—I guess it kinda always feels like people are only nice to me because they want to hang out with Henry or with adults, because they're friends with my parents. And it gets old, you know?"

Angie can feel Sam turn to look at her, but she refuses to meet Sam's eyes. They're in the parking lot.

Sam continues, "I know you're not like that. I shouldn't have assumed—"

"Sam, I—" She wants to tell her to stop speaking. Because the more Sam says, the tighter Angie's throat feels, the hotter her cheeks burn. She wants to sink into herself out of embarrassment at the memory of Sam confronting her.

But Sam cuts her off. She pulls up to the Starbucks and says, "Want to just go to the drive-thru? I should probably get home soon."

Angie nods quickly, relieved.

Angie slowly sips on her strawberry Frappuccino and watches the whipped cream melt in Sam's neglected mocha frap. They're driving in tense silence, broken only by the radio, which is playing that same song about the Range Rover. For once, it's Angie who feels uncomfortable with quiet. She wants to say something to Sam. She feels a surge of nostalgia for their friendship, their jokes, swimming together, hanging out at Sam's house, walking in the halls in between classes. She misses having someone who breaks up the monotony of her life and who makes her feel like she fits in. Maybe after Sam's apology there's hope. Maybe things can go back to how they were. Because Sam said sorry, and she sounded like she meant it. Maybe if Angie tries, they can still be friends. So it pops into her head, and she speaks before she can stop herself: "I heard from my mom."

Sam turns to her for an instant, lifting up her sunglasses, eyes wide, and says, "You did? I can't believe this. How? When? Where is she?" Before Angie can answer, she continues, "Remember when we made up all these stories about her being, like, an international spy or an astronaut called away on a secret mission?"

Angie pauses, struck by how silly that sounds, and unsure how to describe the reality of a middle-aged woman with a vaguely familiar face and shoulder cutouts against an underwhelming background. She wonders if she should tell Sam about any of the things her dad said about her mom being unreliable and moody and falling asleep in the middle of the day. But that feels too personal, private. She decides on, "She added me on Facebook. Out of the blue. She looks . . . normal. She lives in Kansas. I haven't spoken to her."

"What do you mean you haven't spoken to her? Why not? Aren't you dying to? What's she doing in Kansas? Why'd she leave?"

"Well, I just—I haven't figured out what to say yet. And—I don't know—I think she and my dad didn't get along too well." Her breath is heavy. This is the closest she can get to sharing what her dad said. "And if I do talk to her, like, what's the point?"

"The point is to know her." Angie can see Sam's face scrunching up the way it does when she thinks something's ridiculous. "Like, she's your mom. She's fifty percent of your DNA. Don't you want to ask her why she left, hear her side of it? Or like, know how she talks and what she's like, who she is?"

"I'm not sure if I want to talk to her. Or know her. I think"—she pauses—"I'm mad at her for leaving."

"Well, yeah. Obviously. But don't you want to tell her that?" Angie doesn't respond, so Sam says, "You have to talk to her, Ang. Should I pull over? Should we write to her on Facebook together?" She slows down the car.

This was a mistake. "No." Angie shakes her head quickly. "It's fine, Sam. Let's keep going. Please."

"Because, Ang, you were so sad about her leaving. Like, torn up. You used to cry about it all the time. We were kids. But it was, like, one of the first things I knew about you when we met in swim class . . ."

"Thanks, Sam. But I'm not sure if I want to speak to her. And if she wants to speak to me, she can come see me, or write to me, or call me. It's not like anyone's stopping her. And she's the one who left."

Sam's silent for a moment. They're almost at Angie's house. They drive by the bus stop on Indian Meadow, where Chris had followed Angie last week.

Angie shudders.

All of a sudden Sam says, "I miss you, Ang. I miss us being friends."

"Me, too."

"But with all this stuff that happened, everything feels really weird . . ."

Angie feels relieved that Sam said that. She agrees, "Yeah, things feel different. Especially after the stabbing and the stuff with your family."

Angie notes a change in Sam's posture. She sees her jaw tighten, and Sam says, "What's that supposed to mean? My brother almost died. You know that, right? And he didn't do anything wrong—we didn't do anything wrong. You know, you're not so easy to be around some-times. Like, whenever I ask you to hang out with other people you never come unless it's a swim team thing. And even then, you never try. You always hang back and don't say anything, like you're upset or something. You never even try to be friends with people, like, I have to do it all for you, and even then, you're just not—I don't know. Like, Emily Hobbs is convinced you hate her. I can't only be friends with you, you know." Angie can hear Sam breathe out loudly, like she's unburdening herself.

Angela's throat catches. She's not sure what to say. She never knew Sam felt like this, like she's a burden or a charity case. And she does try. It's just that it takes her a while sometimes, to warm up to people, to find her groove. It's easier when she's in water. When she's in control and aware of the plane of her body, her limbs, her breath, her weight, and when sound is filtered so she can only hear the important stuff—or nothing at all. *I want to be normal, too*, she wants to tell Sam, but all she can manage is "I don't hate Emily."

"I've told her that. I think—I think it wouldn't be the end of the world if you tried a little harder, because we're in high school now, and you should lighten up a little. Have fun. Make friends, maybe even a boyfriend. You're always . . . swimming."

Angie's voice box has closed up on her. All she can muster is to swallow.

They turn into Lakeview Terrace, and Sam says, in an unusually bright voice, "Anyways, here we are! Was I a good driver or what? Tell your dad—or wait, don't tell him, he'll flip out." She laughs at the thought.

Angie allows herself a small smile, agreeing that her dad would not react well if he knew she'd gotten into a car with an unlicensed driver.

"It was good to talk and stuff," Sam adds. "And, Ang?"

Angie's hand is on the door handle. "Yeah?"

"Do you ever get bored of it? Swimming, I mean. Like you never answered when I asked if you'd want to take a break."

Angie opens the door and says before stepping out, "Not really. I like it. And—and this year's really important for me."

Sam is chewing on her bottom lip, and her lip is trembling. She looks like she might cry, although Angie can't be sure since Sam's eyes are hidden behind her sunglasses again.

"Are you okay?" Angie asks.

"Yeah, I'm good." Sam sniffs, giving herself away, and she nods a little too furiously to be believable. "Say hi to your dad from me."

Angie gets out of the car, and Sam, after a jerky reverse, speeds away.

When Angie opens the front door, she hears her dad's voice booming into the kitchen phone: "But you're all right?" he says. "Do you need me to meet you? Okay . . . Which hospital?"

Her lingering questions about Sam's strange parting behavior are quickly forgotten. She rushes into the kitchen with her backpack and shoes still on. "Dad, is everything okay? Dad?"

He looks up at her and nods quickly. He holds up one hand, as if to say one minute. He has a pen in his other hand, the phone receiver cradled against his ear, and he's scribbling furiously on a notepad on the counter. His face is strained in concentration. He crosses out what he's just written and says, "But where exactly are you? What street? . . . Tell me a landmark if you aren't sure . . . Did you take the other driver's information—his insurance? . . . Good, take a photo of the license plate . . . No, no, there's no use in arguing with the driver. Just wait. Wait until the police get there." After a pause, "The important thing is you're okay." He continues nodding into the phone and saying "uh-huh" and "okay" a few times. "I'll call you in a little while then," and he hangs up.

Angie's eyes are wide. "What happened? Who were you talking to?"

Her dad lets out a long breath and starts rubbing his temples as if in anguish. His eyes are bloodshot and the whites, rather than their usual milky white, are off-color, eggshell. Like spoiled milk. His skin sags in places she'd never previously noticed.

"That was Igor," he says.

Angie nods. She knows Igor, one of the Move drivers. A youngish guy with a thick accent and bold aftershave.

"He had a road accident. But he's okay."

"What happened?"

"He says someone sideswiped him at an intersection. But it sounds like he sideswiped them, since it's his front and their side." He runs his hands through his hair and says, "I don't know . . . I'm sure he was on the phone when it happened. How else could he have been so distracted? No one else was in the car, no customers, thank God. Igor has a stiff neck. He says he's not hurt. But the car is totaled."

"Was it . . . your car?"

"It was Move's car, yes. I was paying the lease on it."

"I'm sorry, Dad."

"It's okay, beta. It's not your fault."

"Are you going to go over there?"

"No . . . they're going to tow the car. I'll call the insurance company, and we'll figure out how much they'll pay and how much we owe . . ." He sighs. "And somehow we will make it through."

"Are you concerned, Dad?"

"I—uh—you don't worry, beta."

"Dad, do you wish we'd taken that offer from the McClearys?"

They hadn't actually spoken about it. Well, she supposed they had, as far as her dad was concerned, but not so bluntly. He'd removed the papers that had sat with his lone signature, untouched by her, gathering dust like a passive-aggressive reminder, last week, the day of the first protest. He hadn't said anything, so she didn't, either, when she'd noticed the free space on the kitchen counter. It was only when she'd gone to throw away a yogurt carton and saw them torn up and crumpled in the trash that she'd said, "You're okay with this?" without further explanation, to which he'd responded, without missing a beat, as he'd stirred sugar into a mug of milky tea, "I didn't realize there would be so much . . . controversy. It's better not to step into other people's problems." And they'd left it at that. She didn't even ask him how he'd told the McClearys, or if he'd told them. They'd received the message, though, based on what Sam said.

Her dad's eyes float to the side of the room and then to the ceiling, as if he's searching for an answer with his pupils, before he says, "No use in thinking about what's already done." And then, with an adjustment in his posture to straighten his neck and stand taller, he says, "I'm going to the study. I need to call the insurance company." He picks up the pad on which he'd written his crossed-out notes and starts walking out of the kitchen. Before he leaves, he turns and says absently, "Angie, Coach Ford called. He said he tried your cell, too."

Angie takes her cell phone out of her backpack. She sees a few missed calls from Coach. He must have called when she was with Sam. There's a text from him, too: "I'm so sorry. I told them you're a good kid. Our star. It's not so bad. Call me."

Her heartbeat picks up, and her breaths get shallow and fast. Whatever he means doesn't sound good. She dials Coach Ford. He answers on the second ring. "Coach?"

"I'm sorry, Angela. I—"

"What's going on?"

"I— The— Has the school called you?"

"Coach, what are you talking about?"

"Oh, jeez. Angie, I . . . I thought you knew. I thought they called."

"No one's called. What—"

"Angie, they've asked you to not swim for a little while"—a pause—"not as a punishment exactly, but as a consequence . . . for sneaking onto school property."

"What are you talking about, Coach? I didn't sneak in anywhere." She thinks about all the questions the police officers had asked her and her father about her swimming routine, encouraging him as he explained how Angie used the pool to train on her own during vacation.

"They aren't happy you were using the school facilities over summer vacation, and—"

"But I wasn't breaking in. It was open! That's not my fault. And I wasn't hiding it or anything. Like, you knew I was swimming there, and you never said—"

"Angela, I know you're upset, but let's not overreact."

His words set off a small fire within her. *Let's not overreact.* He knows how much this means to her, how hard she's worked, and that she hasn't done anything wrong. In a higher pitch than she intends, she says, "Can they do this? Who's they? For how long?"

She can hear Coach breathing into the phone before he replies. "It's only a few weeks, a month or so max. The school was supposed to call you directly. There's a lawsuit the school district is worried about."

"This isn't fair! I've been waiting all summer, Coach. Like, for months. I've been working so hard. And there's no way I'll qualify for . . . anything."

He's silent.

From the other room, Angie hears her dad in his overly loud phone voice: "No, that can't be right. I cannot owe that much. I'm looking at my policy right now. I must insist I speak to the manager."

She closes her eyes and sighs heavily into the phone, trying not to cry, when it hits her: It all makes sense. Sam and her questions about Angie not swimming, her comments about her family's lawsuit, and the strangely regretful look on her face before she drove off.

"Angie, it's not so—"

"Coach, I need to go." She hangs up, teeth gritted.

THURSDAY, SEPTEMBER 13, 2018

TWENTY-FOUR

Babur moves with a start and bangs his elbow against the cash register. His eyes shift from the muted image of an angry television judge to the face of a teenage boy standing in front of him.

"Can I pay?" the boy repeats.

The boy is a few inches taller than Babur, with a box-shaped head and small mouth. Babur wonders how long he has been there and looks down at the bag of sour-cream-and-onion Lay's and can of root beer on the counter in front of him. He sees the kid tap a crumpled five-dollar bill against the counter.

The boy had startled him. Babur had been staring at the muted TV mounted against one corner of the convenience store, but in fact, he'd been lost in thought. Or, more accurately, lost in the absence of thought, a condition once foreign to him but these days growingly familiar. Particularly when he nears the tail end of a shift at his not-job—because, to be clear, this isn't a job, only a temporary engagement to help with finances.

Two days after Igor's accident, when he'd been filling up his tank, Babur noticed a Help Wanted sign at E-Z Pump Petroleum, the gas station off Route 18. He'd been tentative about expressing interest to the apathetic clerk behind the register—the same register behind which he now stands. He'd been hesitant to even entertain the thought of a second (not-)job, lest it forbode the end of Move rather than a short-term income supplement. In fact, he'd driven off without asking about the sign, only to drive back hours later, drawn by a nagging pull to at least find out more. Besides, his transportation expertise would make him an attractive candidate.

Babur met the owner, Sushant Patel, the next day. Sushant had driven in from Queens in a decades-old Mercedes that more closely resembled a boat than a car, dressed in open-toed *chappals*, dirt-colored trousers, and a short-sleeved beige button-down shirt that exposed the contours of a generous stomach and tufts of salt-and-pepper chest hair cushioning a thick gold Om chain. The "interview" was more of an advance admonishment and lasted less than fifteen minutes. Sushant had grunted acknowledgment of their shared Indian heritage and moved to quickly confirm Babur had a Social Security number and no criminal record. He then recounted his improbable rags-to-riches story (that he'd landed in this country with only twenty-two dollars in his pocket and now owned four filling stations in the greater New York area), and sped through the laundry list of responsibilities, emphasizing what he expected Babur not to do. He closed with a warning that he maintained good security cameras and did routine, unannounced spot checks to detect any "hanky-panky." There had been little time for Babur's planned chitchat regarding his passion for transportation and top-notch customer service. Babur accepted on the spot, in the tone of a child confessing to commission of mischief.

He started the following day.

Babur lightly rubs the elbow he just jammed against the cash register and nods to acknowledge the boy. He rings up the chips and soda and holds out his hand for payment, only to notice the boy has stopped tap-

ping the bunched-up five-dollar note against the counter. He is gripping it and looking at Babur squinty-eyed. His mouth hangs open.

"It's four dollars and twenty-seven cents," Babur prompts. The
young man would fare better financially to make this same purchase
at Stop & Shop, hardly half a mile down the road, but of course Babur
doesn't say this. He doesn't even smile or maintain eye contact. Instead, he allows his gaze to lazily drift back to the image of Judge Judy
on the tiny TV.

Something about being at E-Z Pump has morphed Babur into someone quite unlike his usual gabby, cheerful self. More reticent, more impassive. Perhaps it's the dehumanizing machine mounted on the wall
next to the supply closet that he uses to "punch in" and "punch out,"
or his closing-time routine of mopping the floors of the small convenience store, which always manage to get sticky and grimy, especially
in the corners, and of the murky restroom connected to the station. The
smell of the bleach solution makes him queasy and kills his appetite
for dinner. Even with the best of intentions to keep his brain active,
engaged, to use this time for deep thinking and strategizing, perhaps
even to listen to the audio version of a book on self-advancement, the
work is mind numbing. Besides, it's difficult to concentrate on anything meaningful with constant interruptions from rushed commuters
in a hurry to swipe for a tank of gas, or pack of cigarettes, or unnaturally colored sports drink.

The boy blinks a few times, mouth still open, bill still in hand, before
he says, "Are you Angela Singh's dad?"

Babur's cheeks and ears warm at the mention of Angie.

She'd begged him not to work at E-Z Pump. "Can you please not
work there? Please. Everyone at school goes there, Dad. They'll
see you," she'd said with uncharacteristic desperation. It had been the
most she'd uttered to him in one single stretch in a while. Ever since
she'd been asked not to swim for an undetermined period of time,

she'd retreated into sullen and discomfiting silence. Spending long hours in her room with the door closed, or watching television, but not watching so much as sitting zombielike in front of a television set. Sleeping in on weekdays to the point where he had to pound on her bedroom door to ensure she wouldn't be late for school. He'd tried to gently ask about homework; maybe while on hiatus from the team, she could get a head start on academics for the semester. But she'd mumble a response about how she'd finished it already.

He worried Angie might shatter if he pushed too hard. She seemed fragile, breakable, so Babur held back. He was scared to say more, to do more. He didn't know how to bring her back to him, nor how to banish one particularly self-destructive, self-pitying thought from his mind: that he was the victim of a cruel trick by history. *Like mother, like daughter.* The specter of the unfit un-spouse and un-mother and her recent desperate emails to him elicits a spike in his blood pressure and palpitations in his heart. He's been trying to push Purnima and her messages out of his mind, to assure himself his Angie is nothing like *that woman.* And yet the feeling of having lived this before is palpable, like an anchor hurtling deeper into a dark sea.

So when Angie had objected to his un-job, he'd taken her fervor as a sign that he could tease out a longer conversation, yearning for the sound of his daughter's voice. He'd reminded her that his name tag would say "Bobby," and not "Angela's dad," with an overdone smile, hoping it would catch on. Nothing. He could have said it didn't matter if people saw him working at E-Z Pump. Only he didn't, because for starters, he didn't work at E-Z Pump. It was a temporary arrangement. Igor's accident made an unprovisioned and substantial dent in the Singhs' income, so Babur needs the money. And Sushant needs some temporary assistance while his nephew returns to Gujarat for a few months to find a bride. In truth, Babur also doesn't want to be recognized by Kitchewan residents at E-Z Pump Petroleum. But there is no use in admitting that to Angie.

So instead Babur had said, "You're being silly. Money is money.

Work is work," while in fact, he could not help but feel there was something incredibly wrong with going from being a master of his own destiny, the owner of a once-growing business, ascending the ladder of the American dream, to someone who cleaned the toilet at a gas station.

Before he answers the boy behind the counter, it's Babur's turn to squint. He shifts his eyes from the television screen and examines the young man. He must be about five ten, five eleven. He's thin and his head is small for his frame, reminding Babur of a stegosaurus. His mouth appears curled in an indecipherable expression—a smirk, maybe.

"You know my daughter?" Babur says at last.

The boy blinks. "Yeah, from school."

Babur nods quickly. This is exactly what Angie (and Babur) didn't want.

The boy looks down at his hand and gives Babur the bill he's been clenching, as if just remembering the reason he's at the register.

Babur accepts the note, breaking eye contact to concentrate on uncreasing it.

Without warning, the boy says in a spurt, "I'm Chris Collins. I was on the football field when Angela . . ."

Babur looks up, and he feels his body freeze. He can taste something metallic on his tongue. Christopher Collins. Companion to the McCleary boy. Senior at KHS. Purchaser of drugs. Too incompetent to call 911, dragging Angie into everything instead. He grinds his teeth.

"I haven't seen Angela around as much. How is she?" Chris asks.

Babur nods, careful not to betray his inner voice that shouts, Of course you haven't, *lafander*. My Angie would not have anything to do with you. He instead counts out Chris's change with absolute concentration.

"Hope she's all right. She always looks so sad and alone. Like someone just died or something." Babur stiffens. This is too much.

Babur looks up and reexamines the boy. Despite his broad shoulders and height, his face is one of a child, unshaven. His eyes are large and unstable. They move back and forth quickly, anxiously, like someone being pursued. Normally Babur would pity someone who looks so helpless and young. But this child, this silly child caused pain to his own, his Angie. Needless pain.

Babur reaches his hands across the counter toward Chris to hand him his change, but when Chris reaches for his coins, something overtakes Babur. He grabs the boy's hand in both of his. Grips it. Clutches it. And he leans in. The sound that comes out of his mouth is unrecognizable, a growl. "Do you know what you have done?"

The boy's hand is sweating, or maybe it's Babur who is perspiring. Chris's eyes are glassy and dart from right to left, left to right.

"Do you?" Babur demands.

"I—I didn't . . ."

Babur tightens his grip. He's in no mood for nonsense or lies. The boy must admit his role in Angie's unnecessary removal from the swim team; he must confess his culpability in the distressing police interviews involving his daughter; he must acknowledge it's his fault Angie was dragged into this in the first place, that she's so unlike herself now.

Chris sputters, "I mean— I didn't— We didn't do anything. We didn't mean to . . ."

Babur maintains a steely clasp. He imagines pulverizing the boy's hand into a fine powder with his grip.

The boy continues, shakily, averting eye contact but not attempting to dislodge himself, "I—I just— We never— We didn't mean to scare . . . anyone. I tried to tell her that, but she wouldn't— I never knew anyone was going to get hurt. I didn't know stuff would be like how it is . . ."

"You know exactly what you did." Babur spits out each word like it's venom.

The boy looks stricken. "Did—did Angie say something?"

"What, say? I'm her father. I know!" Babur feels a fire smoldering within him. He shakes with rage, shaking the boy's hand in the process. "It is your fault my Angie is not on the swimming team! It is your fault she had to be questioned by the police! It is your fault that she was punished, that she is not the same! *It is your fault!*"

Chris looks confused. "I don't know anything about Angela being punished. I—I swear."

Babur stares the boy down, trying to read the lies on his face.

"You could talk to the McClearys," Chris says slowly. He pauses and then adds, "They can be a little stuck-up, but they took care of stuff with the police, so maybe they can do something . . ."

The mention of the McClearys makes Babur feel short of breath, short of air. He lets go of the boy's hand. Panting, perspiring.

Chris shoots backward, off balance. His eyes look like they might bulge from their sockets. He says in an alarmed voice, "Why are you looking at me like that? Can you stop looking at me like that?" He shields his face with his hands. "Why does everyone think everything is my fault? Even my mom. The McClearys act like they did me this huge favor, but it was Henry's—"

A car horn honks outside.

The boy jerks at the sound, as if freed from a spell. He stumbles in the direction of the door, staggering out of the store, leaving his potato chips, soda, and change on the counter.

In his wake, Babur blinks rapidly, heart pounding. His pupils are dilated with excitement such that his surroundings appear in Technicolor. His mind is alert, having been violently shaken from the usual foggy grayness of his shift.

He is puzzled by what Chris said about Angie. Could it be true? Babur wonders. Is his daughter lonely and sad? He swallows, attempting to suppress the suffocating shadow of a particular, dreaded someone. Had he not noticed, missed it?

His neurons are animated, alive. He can feel them zipping around in his head, frenetic, supercharged, until they converge in a single piercing thought: *Does the girl need her mother?*

MONDAY, SEPTEMBER 24, 2018

TWENTY-FIVE

Angie doesn't hear the front door open, so when her dad peeks his head into the living room and says, with concern in his voice, "Beta, you're home? Don't you have a swimming meet?," her heart rate spikes. She freezes like a criminal being caught in the act.

She's slumped on the couch twirling and untwirling the same strand of her brittle dark hair around her finger, staring blankly at a yet-to-be-completed take-home biology quiz on the coffee table in front of her. In the background, a *Big Bang Theory* rerun plays at a barely audible level. Every time the laugh track on the sitcom goes off, her eyes gravitate to the television. The quiz remains untouched, blank, but she's chewed through a handful of pen caps.

Her dad's right. She shouldn't be here right now. At home this evening. She should be at the away meet in Scarsdale. More specifically, getting on the bus back from the meet for a postrace Subway dinner, having competed in the 200- and 400-yard freestyle, the 100 breaststroke, and maybe also the 100 butterfly and a relay, just as she and Coach Ford had strategized over the summer. A combination of strokes, sprints and middle distance, individual and team. Because as of last Friday, after a three-week suspension, she's officially back on the swim team.

There had been no welcome committee or fanfare to let her know— just a short call with Coach: "Angela, great news. The school has looked into your situation and decided that your use of the pool was a harmless error in judgment, one they might speak to you about some more. But you're back on the team!"

She'd paused before speaking. On one hand, she'd wanted to be happy, ecstatic even, to jump up and down jubilantly, excitement gushing like a fountain from her voice, because this was what she wanted. Exactly what she wanted. On the other, the sting of being excluded from the team and that no one, not even Coach Ford, cared enough to do anything to help her, was acute. Still there. This wasn't something she could wipe clean from her memory, blot out, like a robot. It was all unfair. Grossly unfair. And apparently, no one was going to say anything.

"Angela, you there?" Coach had said.

"Yeah, that's great, Coach," she'd said in what she hoped would be a bright tone but in a voice that sounded lukewarm.

"So we'll see you over the weekend for practice?"

"Yeah, see you."

"Great, kiddo," and then he'd added, "I know this was a pain, but you're back now. See you tomorrow." And that was that. As quickly as the school had taken the team away from her, they gave it back.

Angie sits up straighter on the couch and says to her dad, "I don't feel good." She cups her hands around her stomach, as if to indicate she has stomach pains, but apart from the gesture, she feels half-committal.

Her dad tightens his mouth and nods his head. She can see his large eyes glistening. He marches into the living room and touches his palm to her forehead, confirming she doesn't have a fever. Even though he's been working there for a month now, she still can't help but grimace at the sight of his navy-blue shirt with E-Z PUMP PETROLEUM in white stitching on the sleeve and his oversized name tag, as if it were a matter of urgency that everyone knows his name is Bobby.

If her dad notices her reaction, he doesn't let on, which makes her feel a twinge of guilt.

"How was work?" she asks, an attempt to ease her conscience.

He breaks eye contact but pastes a broad smile on his face. "Fine," he says, uncharacteristically briefly. That doesn't sound fine to her. But she'd begged him not to work there, so if he doesn't want to tell her about it, she won't re-ask. "Should we— Do you need a doctor?"

"I'm fine. It's just, uh, my stomach. It's hurting." She wishes she'd thought this through.

Her dad nods, but she can't tell if he believes her.

Maybe she should tell him the truth. She's home because she didn't feel like going. She doesn't feel like swimming anymore.

Angie had gone to practice on Saturday as she'd promised Coach. Even though she'd only missed a little over two weeks plus preseason, it felt like an eternity.

There was a whole new class of freshmen, all on JV, none of whom she knew, but who seemed to have heard enough about her to give her curious stares and tentative smiles. And of the others, the ones from her grade and above—Sam no longer on the team—they'd smiled close-mouthed when she'd walked into the locker room over the weekend and a few high-fived her to welcome her back, good sportsmanship being something Coach took extremely seriously. She sensed the welcomes were shallow, though; they were devoid of the energy and authenticity she was used to when she was racing, swimming races one of the few blips in her life when she felt popular, well liked. She could see how their eyes floated to the side of the room or to one another, when they thought she'd looked away, and she could hear how the normally vibrant, overlapping threads of locker room conversation hushed, became more orderly, less giggly. Only Coach Ford, after giving her a brief hug, seemed happy to see her. Normal.

She hadn't swum at all since the day she found out she was suspended from the team. There hadn't been a point. If she couldn't swim during the season she'd been training for, there wasn't a reason to practice.

Back in the pool, her head and body felt weighted down, slower, clumsier, uncoordinated. She couldn't knife through water with her hands like she usually would, her flip turns felt choppy like her ankles were on the verge of knocking into each other, her legs were drained after only a short spurt of kicking, her arms felt stiff, and her breathing was labored, shallow, off rhythm. Then, when they were doing timed drills, a strange thing had happened: a ringing that she'd sometimes hear when she changed elevation too quickly or felt out of breath had started without warning. A high-pitched tone, like a radio frequency but without any static. And it wouldn't go away. She'd thought maybe her ears were waterlogged and batted at her ears with her hands and shook her head, even wiggling her fingers in her ear canals, but it persisted. And when it was time to dive in as part of the drill, she'd remained at the starting block whacking at her head, likely looking insane, while her teammates had dived in.

"Angela, you okay?" Coach had asked gently, walking toward her so he was only a few feet away and could speak in a hushed voice.

"Yes," she'd said, surprised to feel her body shaking, trembling with anger as she spoke, and inelegantly dived in to catch up with her teammates. Waterlogging her ears for certain that time.

"Is it a particular side of your stomach, beta? I had to get my appendix out when I was around your age and it hurt dreadfully on my right side. No wait, my left side. In fact, let me check." He's hovering by the couch, his face buried in his phone screen, trying to diagnose her. If he's not convinced she's telling the truth, he's doing a good job of hiding it.

"Dad, can you give me some space, please?"

He steps back abruptly, as if he'd broken a fragile object. His eyes shine. "Sorry, beta," he mumbles.

Not what she expected. She wishes he'd be normal. She wishes everyone, everything, would just be normal.

The school year so far has been anything but. It's been lonely, even for Angie, who is used to being alone. Sam passes her in the hallway at school like she's transparent, and without Sam, her other so-called friends have fallen away, too, some not even glancing in her direction, others less discreet, giving her sideways glances, or if their eyes meet, artificial if not pitying smiles, provided Sam's not around, Angie's noticed. Against her better judgment, Angie tried talking to Sam a few times, like a test to confirm things have changed and she's not just imagining it; each time, Sam mumbled something about being late to class, or the dentist, and rushed off without looking at her. For his part, Henry seems oblivious to Angie. He's back at school, in regrettably good-looking form—she tries not to notice—not yet back to running cross-country, but back to walking the halls like a giant among mortals, Supreme logo stamped across his chest and Audrey Ryan's arm tucked in the crook of his elbow, dimples and hero face on prominent display, flanked by hangers-on like Chris Collins, who she notices remains in Henry's orbit but no longer right behind him or next to him like he used to be.

Unlike Henry and Sam, Chris seems hyperaware of Angie. He persistently volleys for her eye contact whenever he sees her at school, like he doesn't understand or doesn't care that she's not interested in having anything to do with him. She mostly looks away, determined not to acknowledge him, only one day a couple weeks ago, piqued by how he wouldn't relent, she'd made the mistake of staring back. Only then, he'd started ambling toward her, like she was inviting him to talk, and she was forced to duck into the girls' bathroom, heart sprinting and upper lip perspiring at the uncomfortable memory of the last time they spoke.

The school year might be tolerable if it were only the McClearys and their friends who snubbed Angie, but even students upset by Chiara's death and critical of Henry and Chris—a small but vocal minority—disdain her. A junior named Thalia Sussman with blue hair and circle-shaped hipster glasses, the ringleader of #JusticeforChiara, had let her know as much earlier that day. Angie had been on her way home—rather than at her swim meet—and cutting through the school parking lot; Thalia was leaning against the door of a beat-up Honda sedan, vaping. "Hey, Angela Singh," she'd called out, startling Angie. When Angie didn't respond right away, she'd continued, "I didn't see you at the Justice for Chiara vigil last week." Angie had looked at her, bewildered; she hadn't told Thalia she'd be there, and she hadn't gone to any of the other events for Chiara, like the protest at the high school or the silent swim at the nature reserve. "You should have been there," Thalia continued. "You should have been there for Chiara." Angie had thought about how to explain how she felt about everything, how it haunted her—Chiara's scream, the blood pouring out of Henry, how she didn't speak up when the police first interviewed her, how she'd gotten confused, and how she now lives with the guilt of not saying anything, and also not knowing what to say, the guilt of being the one who gave Chiara inadequate swimming lessons that didn't save her from drowning, and knowing her more than many, but never actually knowing her. She must have been silent for too long, because with a surprising amount of venom in her voice, Thalia had said, "But yeah, like you care. It was stupid of me to think someone *like you* might care about what's fair and right and not just what's convenient for the head-up-their-ass limousine liberals who run this fucking place." With a scoff, Thalia had said, "Shame on you," then got in the Honda and slammed the door shut, leaving Angie speechless, confused, and trembling.

She'd thought by staying silent, staying out of it, she was doing what was fair and right—she didn't take the foundation money; she didn't go along with Henry's request that she not tell the police about how she heard arguing and Chris chasing someone, but she didn't criticize him or Chris, either, because she didn't know exactly what happened. She didn't join the gatherings being held in Chiara's name; even though some of the texts about Chiara and things people said about her sounded mean and unfair, she wasn't sure if they were racist or what this had to do with the public school system. It turns out, by not choosing a side, no one's happy with her. She wants to not care what people think. But she does.

The thing about being alone and universally disliked, Angie's discovered, is that her days feel hollow, empty, pointless. Especially since she stopped swimming. Like, for example, waking up in the morning feels pointless. Brushing her teeth, changing her clothes, eating breakfast, doing homework, going to school, pretending she feels fine. Pointless. It's all pointless. All she does all day is sit in classes about subjects she doesn't need to know in real life. She wonders how everyone else does it—how they fake not being absolutely miserably bored out of their minds from the lack of a point of it all. Maybe this is how it always was, but she never noticed since she had something to look forward to—swimming, seeing her teammates, who she thought were her friends, even doing her homework in anticipation of it setting her up to go to a good college. But now, nothing.

She's started walking between classes with her head down and earphones on loud, playing Lana Del Rey, drowning out her surroundings, flooding her head with the singer's dreamy, ghostly voice. It helps, kind of. But not really.

Angela and her dad hunch over the kitchen counter on neighboring stools. Cereal for dinner. Again. Not that she's hungry. Her dad slurps the milk in his bowl of granola. She picks at an oat cluster with a spoon and ladles and redistributes spoonfuls of milky cereal mixture back into the bowl, not taking a bite.

Her dad turns to look at her. "Angie, you have to eat."

She continues trickling cereal milk from her spoon back into her bowl, not looking at him. It's not worth it telling him she's not hungry. She can't remember the last time she was hungry. And when she does eat, she chews and swallows quickly, furiously, not tasting anything, determined not to enjoy anything, getting it over and done with. Like medicine.

"Angie," her dad repeats gently but sternly.

She stares into her bowl and starts shoveling large spoonfuls into her mouth, barely stopping to chew the soggy chunks that scratch her throat as she swallows. Her spoon clinks noisily against her bowl, but she doesn't stop. She eats like it's a competition, milk dribbling down her chin. When done, she wipes her mouth with the back of her hand, stands up, and says, "I'm tired. I'm going upstairs," even though it's only a little past eight.

She doesn't wait for her dad to say anything, and he doesn't call after her.

Upstairs, she plunks onto her bed, her body like an anvil. It's early, but she's tired. Exhausted. Ironically, the less she swims, the less physically active she is, the more drained she feels. Angie blinks rapidly, fighting the heaviness on her eyelids, fearing it. She doesn't want to fall asleep. Because when she does, she'll be back there. On the football field. Only Chiara will be pinned on the ground this time, she'll be in pain, crying, and Henry and Chris will be standing over her with clown grins and laughter. Chiara will spot Angie. She'll lock eyes with her and mouth unsteadily for help, but when Angie approaches, runs toward her, screaming, shouting, she'll be gone. In her place, only Henry. Covered in gushing blood.

Angie sits up and crosses her legs. She reaches for her phone and puts on her headset, turning on "13 Beaches." Lana's mesmerizing, ombré voice fills her ears while she checks Facebook. A photo posted by one of the girls on the swim team pops up on her news feed. It's a group selfie from the bus on the way back from the meet, four or five girls from the team with their faces overexposed by the camera flash, cheeks pressed together. They're smiling and look happy-tired. She swallows. She should've gone. She should've been there.

She shoves the thought from her mind and navigates to Purnima C. Her friend request still looms under "pending." Angie's breath is heavy. It's always weighted when she does this, and her heartbeat is audible. Once again, she examines the profile photo. The half smile, in front of the bland cityscape. She checks for a new photo, a new post, new activity. But nothing. She wonders if her mother has even noticed Angie hasn't yet accepted the request. If it bothers her, if it keeps her up at night. She wants to know why her mother hasn't tried harder to reach her. Her head pounds and she feels her eyes droop. She blinks rapidly again and clenches her fists. She wants to scream.

Angie turns off the music and sits up straighter. She holds her breath and dials the number she's saved in her cell phone as "P," followed by a four-digit extension.

The phone rings until it goes to the voice mail message: "This is Purnima in the Spencer Library Archives Department. I am not at my desk. Please leave a message."

In the weeks since Angie had stopped swimming, she'd researched the woman fanatically, looking for anything she could learn about her. There was next to nothing apart from the bare Facebook profile, but she had found that her mother, who goes by her maiden name (which feels like a jab at Angie), works as a research librarian at the University of Kansas. Maybe that means she likes books, which led Angie to wonder if her mother would have liked the reading assignments she did over the summer for English class, if, for example, she could have helped Angie with *Jane Eyre*, if she would have been proud of her for making it into advanced English, if they would have regularly talked about books and gone to the library together. Through some more digging she'd found the university telephone directory online and a work extension for Purnima Chauhan. Angie had called the number thrice before now. Always after work hours to ensure it would go to voice mail, silently taking in the recorded message, as if it were a clue, an entry point to something greater, before hanging up.

Angie breathes heavily into the phone. She has a piercing longing for something she can't identify. The sound of the gentle, faintly accented voice, unfamiliar but at once familiar, sends a throbbing ache pulsing through her. It's so strong she can hardly stay seated through the spinning, the dizziness, the turbulence, the noise. Her throat burns with words she can't form. She blinks furiously, fighting a weight that feels like it's strangling her. It's no use.

She exhales heavily and hangs up.

TUESDAY, SEPTEMBER 25, 2018

TWENTY-SIX

The first thing Angie thinks when she looks up to see Desiree Matthews looking back at her is that she appears nicer—and prettier—than she did in the unsmiling photo of her printed in the newspaper. The contours of her face are softer and heart-shaped, and her dark brown eyes are deep, calming. She thinks this even though when Desiree comes out to the waiting area on the fourth floor of the hospital, her lips press tightly together like she is trying not to have an expression.

Angie gets to her feet and steps toward Desiree. "Hi"—a pause—"Miss Matthews." She realizes she hadn't decided what to call her. "I'm—"

"I know who you are," Desiree says in an even voice that's not warm, exactly, but that to Angie's hopeful ears isn't entirely clipped.

Angie watches Desiree studying her, her mouth slightly ajar and her eyes taking Angie in. Angie's stomach somersaults with anxious energy.

"They told me you've been waiting for me." Desiree squints before adding, "Shouldn't you be in school?"

Angie swallows and averts her eyes to Desiree's sea-green scrubs. "I wasn't feeling well," she says, "so my dad let me stay home." Angie looks up for a reaction, but Desiree is good at being hard to read. Worried she may be rebuffed, Angie adds quickly, "He doesn't know I'm here," which is true. She'd waited until her dad had left for the gas station that morning before slipping out of the house and taking the bus to the hospital.

Angie can hear Desiree breathe out and can tell from the way her eyes are scanning Angie that she's thinking: deciding her next move.

Angie holds her breath, trying not to let her desperation, her sense of urgency to speak with Desiree, overwhelm the moment. *Please*, she thinks, *please talk to me.*

Desiree appears to have made up her mind. She motions with one hand for Angie to follow and says, "All right. Come on."

Without asking where they're going, Angie races to catch up. Her heart, too, is racing with anticipation and her head swims with fragments of thoughts of all the things she can say to Desiree Matthews. She can tell her about the dreams, about that day, how there was arguing, maybe about how she and Chiara spent some time together in the high school pool, about how the police didn't really ask her any of the right questions or wait for her answers. She doesn't know why, but as she follows Desiree down the hall, to the elevator, down another hall, and through the hospital cafeteria, she has an increasing wish for Desiree to like her, approve of her.

Desiree leads Angie to a small open-air area adjacent to the cafeteria. Empty chairs hug the tables that fill the space. They are alone. Desiree motions for Angie to sit at a small circular table for two, the farthest from the cafeteria door.

"Okay," she says, seated across from Angie. Angie notices that her previously impassive expression has settled into something else. Desiree's eyes have narrowed, and her mouth is curled slightly into a frown.

Angie tries not to show the panic that's coursing through her. She wasn't expecting Desiree to look at her like this. She needs to say something to change Desiree's expression, to draw her in, get her to see they're on the same side. She settles on "I'm sorry about Chiara." It sounds strange to say that out loud. She avoids eye contact, self-conscious of disapproval.

"What exactly are you sorry about?" Desiree's dark brown eyes are fixed on Angie's like magnets, drawing Angie's directly to hers.

Angie's face becomes warm. She doesn't know how to answer.

"That she's dead?" Desiree raises her eyebrows as if daring Angie to speak.

Angie feels Desiree putting up a barrier between them from the way her mouth curves with distrust, from the way she sits, arms not crossed, but hanging at her sides, rigidly, at attention, so they might as well be in the shape of an X. Angie's not a touchy person, but she has an impulse to reach across the wobbly table, to reach for Desiree's hand. Instead, she picks at a stray thread along the seams of her jeans, tugging at it furiously. She can't explain in words how desperately she wants to speak to this woman, how there's a volcanic pressure building up inside her. How it's been slowly gnawing away at her ever since she saw Desiree's photo in the paper and started thinking about her, wondering about her, how she's feeling, what she'd say if she knew what Angie did about that day. How this morning when Angie woke from a turbulent sleep, the urge to talk to someone was so strong, so consuming that she could hardly breathe. How this morning it was too much to bear, not to come, not to speak to someone, someone who understands. She needs her.

"Well, the thing is"—Angie hesitates—"I'm . . . um, I mean I've been having these dreams, or maybe flashbacks." She pauses, waiting for her voice to stop shaking. "And . . . and I thought I should tell someone—tell you. Because, well, when I was there that day, I think maybe they argued—" She stops to look at Desiree, check for a reaction. Desiree appears to be concentrating, listening carefully, betraying no emotion. Angie continues, "Those boys and Chiara—I think they argued. And maybe they did something, to hurt her. I'm not sure, but I think—"

"Did you tell the police?"

Angie hangs her head. "I wasn't— It was all really blurry that day, and then after, I—I couldn't. I wasn't sure." Angie can feel her throat clogging up. She hopes Desiree won't be angry with her, won't think it was stupid of Angie not to tell the police. Angie swallows and adds, "And then Henry said there were drugs, and I didn't want anyone to get in trouble . . ."

Desiree's eyes pinch together. She asks in a calm but deliberate voice, "Why are you telling me this?"

Angie spots faint crescents under Desiree's eyes, lighter than those on her father's face but there nonetheless. She tucks a stray strand of hair that's fallen across her face behind her ear and looks away, unsure of what to say, and self-conscious for noticing Desiree's fatigue.

"Angela, why are you here?" Desiree's voice is lower, and her eyebrows appear as two dark lines.

"I—" Angie pauses, considering what to say. She doesn't know where to begin, how to explain that she's been thinking about Chiara, she can't stop thinking about her, she can't stop thinking about that day. "I want to help," she finally says, looking directly at Desiree in as steady a voice as she can manage.

Desiree blinks back and replies coolly, "It's a little too late for that. My cousin is dead."

Angie's shoulders inch upward as she takes a long breath. She's sitting, but she feels like she's falling backward. Her hands grip underneath the sides of her chair to steady herself, and she blurts, "I saw her that day. I saw her earlier. On the bleachers by herself. And then I heard her later"—her voice trembles—"I heard her cry out. But—but then I got there, and she wasn't there. I didn't know where she went. But I just— I keep thinking about it. I needed to tell you. Because I think something must have happened. Something bad. Only I don't know what, and everyone's saying she hurt Henry for—for money. And I don't know if she would, if she did. I needed you to know." A pause, and then in a whisper, she repeats, "I keep thinking about it."

The pressure that had been building in Angie's shoulders slowly releases.

Desiree's eyes are wide. It's like her pupils are reaching toward Angie, grabbing her, shaking her. "What am I supposed to do? Because you"—she says this last part with unsuppressed disdain—"keep thinking about it?"

She'd assumed that telling Desiree would be enough. She hadn't thought through what Desiree would do. Angie wrings her hands. "I thought—" But she doesn't know what she thought. Only that she feels foolish.

"Maybe if you'd said something that day." Desiree's volume rises as she speaks, and Angie feels her hands trembling. "Maybe then, we could have done something. But now, there's nothing to do. Those boys got away with . . . something, something so bad that now"—Desiree pauses—"Kiki's gone."

Kiki. Angie turns it over in her head. She feels her lips creep into a small smile, thinking about how familiar it sounds to call Chiara Kiki.

Desiree notices her expression and snaps at Angela. "Chiara wasn't a hobby or cause for you and your silly friends to plaster on T-shirts or use to rant about inequality from your mansions along the river." The bitterness in her voice cuts like a knife. "She was a person, and she trusted me. And"—her voice cracks and reduces to a whisper—"now she's gone."

Angie stares at the stray thread on her jeans. She doesn't dare correct Desiree's assumptions about her, nor look at her.

"If you really wanted to help," she says more loudly, more confidently, "you should have said something. I'm tired of you people pretending to care now that she's dead because it makes you feel good about yourselves." She glares at Angie, her eyes like lasers, and asks, "Did you even know her?"

Angie opens her mouth to try to explain she knew Chiara, but she doesn't know how to describe what they were, so she closes it.

Desiree scoffs and crosses her arms against her chest. "Yeah, I thought so. You're the worst of them, you know. You could have said something. And you didn't.'"

Angie's mouth feels dry. The fantasy meeting she imagined between herself and Desiree where they hugged, where they understood each other, slips further and further away from the realm of possibility, but she wants Desiree to know that she's not *them*. Angie's desperation overcomes her and words spill out in one breath. "I knew her. And I never wore those T-shirts. I didn't say anything because I don't know what happened. I didn't want to make things up."

Desiree leans forward in her chair as if she's examining Angie. In a low but eerily calm voice, staring into Angie's widened eyes with such intensity they sting, she says, "Bullshit. You know enough, or you wouldn't be here."

Angie's breath stops. Her shoulders stiffen and pressure builds inside her. "I'm sorry," she says, blinking fast and looking down at the thread she'd been picking at. "I wish I did something. That day. I wish I said something. I didn't know people would talk about her like they are. I didn't think the police would end their investigation without asking more questions. I should have said something, to everyone . . ."

She holds her breath and shuts her eyes, the way she used to as a child before cannonballing into the pool. She thinks about what she could have done, if she'd gotten there sooner, before Chiara ran off, or if she'd insisted on telling the police, confused or not, that Chiara may have been in trouble, if she could have forced them to look into what happened before Henry got hurt. But they never really gave her a chance to say those things in the follow-up interviews. The high-pitched sound that had attacked her when she was at practice the other day is ringing in her ears, like a taunt that she'll never be as good a swimmer as she wants to be. She thinks of the sideways looks from the girls on the swim team and kids at school and feels a creepy-crawly sensation across her skin. She's reminded of the hushed whispers in the halls that her headphones don't fully drown out. She thinks of her dad. Of his sleepless nights and bruised eyes, of his thwarted dreams, and how they can't—they don't—talk to each other. The noise stops, but rather than silence she hears her mother's answering-machine message. The lilt in the accented voice elicits a swelling in her throat, a longing for everything she wants but can't have, for everything she wants but can't admit to wanting. It's choking her.

When she opens her eyes, they brim with tears and she says all at once, "I messed everything up, and now I feel really alone. I am alone. And I think—I think about Chiara. I think about her all the time. She was alone, too."

Desiree continues looking at her, but this time, her face is less strained, her eyes less searing. She examines Angie but doesn't say anything for what feels like many minutes. They sit across from each other at the two-person table outside the hospital cafeteria. Leaves on the crab apple trees planted along the outside of the cafeteria rustle in the light breeze. Angie, through self-conscious glances, sees Desiree blinking the way someone blinks when their eyes are filling up; she hears Desiree swallow and can sense the familiar lump in Desiree's throat.

When Desiree begins speaking, she sounds distant, like she's talking to herself. "I'm the one who identified her. Her mom's been sick, and she"—a pause—"she wasn't able to take care of her like I know she wanted. Chiara came to me, and I—" Her voice cracks. "I let her go. They showed me her body in the basement of the hospital, all bruised and dirty. There was mud in her hair, and a bump on one of her temples. It looked like she'd run into something, or"—she swallows—"or someone had hit her. Her skin was swollen and splotchy, like she'd been tie-dyed." A pause as she lets out an ironic chuckle. "I wanted to touch her. I wanted to hug her so badly. She looked cold, so cold." She stops and wipes her nose with the back of her hand. Angie's too scared to look at her, and instead wrings her hands on her lap, as if by applying more pressure she can make her discomfort go away.

"She was my favorite," Desiree continues. "I know you're not supposed to say that, but she was. She was the youngest among the cousins, and she was— She used to just light up the room with her dimples. Only when she got older"—she swallows—"they disappeared, or maybe she stopped smiling like that." The words prick Angie's ears, reminding her of when Chiara had burst into an all-body smile the first time she'd done a lap in the pool, only to quickly erase any sign of happiness when she'd noticed Angie looking. "And she was tough, you know, so tough, but not in that rough-and-tumble criminal way like people around here are saying. As in she had grit. She did things for herself; she wanted to do for herself." Desiree's face twists into a bittersweet almost-smile. "Even when sometimes she should've asked for help. She wanted to do well, better than what was in front of her. But"—her voice becomes heavy and vibrates—"no one around here understood that. Those police officers stared at me the whole time like I was an alien, like Kiki was . . . God, I really wanted to hug her! I wanted nothing to hurt her anymore, but then I remembered." She turns suddenly and stares at Angie, small tears rolling slowly down her face. "Nothing can. She's dead." Desiree covers her face with her hands and inhales loudly.

When she removes her hands from her face, there are marks along her cheeks from where she pressed her hands into them. She sniffs and looks at Angie anew, only this time she appears solemn and worn down. "You know," she begins, "I don't know if it would have made a difference if you said something." She shakes her head as she speaks. "The police care more about why she went to the high school than about what happened—like going to school is the crime. I told them Chiara wouldn't have hurt someone for no reason. She wasn't violent." She sighs. "But they made up their minds. They even brought me to the station and told me I committed some crime by letting her use my address. It doesn't make sense, but I guess that's how it goes when your daddy is friendly with the police department." She scoffs. "A rich white kid does something stupid, and they have to go and make it about one of us. It's not enough that she's dead. They want *everything*."

Angie sits motionless. Desiree's words pummel her like bricks. Her

face gets hot as she thinks about how unfair things are. How she re-
lates. If she weren't intimidated by Desiree and if she were more
confident in being affectionate, she'd reach across the table and hug
her, but she is and she isn't.

Desiree's chair scrapes against the ground, startling Angie as she
pushes back from the table. She stares at her in a way that makes
Angie feel translucent. In a firm voice, Desiree says, "I hope you didn't
come here and expect me to make you feel better."

Angie bites her lip, ashamed that Desiree saw her intentions more
clearly than she did.

"I'm sorry." Angie's cheeks are on fire. Her head is spinning. "I'm
sorry," she repeats. The ringing in her ears is back, forcing her to raise
her voice to hear herself speak. "I've been feeling messed up"—but she
still sounds faint—"and I don't know who to talk to." So she speaks
louder still. "I don't have anyone." She stands up from her chair. "I
shouldn't have come here. I shouldn't have bothered you. I'm—I'm
sorry."

The ringing crescendos, and she's ready to make a run for it, to cut
through the parking lot to the bus stop, when she hears Desiree say,
"Wait."

Angie turns around.

Desiree is standing and reaching into her pocket. She pulls a small
piece of paper out of her scrubs. She holds it up, waving it.

Angie steps back toward her, moves closer to take a look.

"Is he . . . ?" Desiree points to the paper.

Angie's eyes pinch into focus. It's a familiar card that reads MOVE
WITH BOBBY and has her dad's contact details. Her mouth opens as
she wonders why Desiree has her dad's business card in her hand.

Desiree looks at her, expectantly.

Mouth still ajar, Angie nods.

Desiree nods back. She presses her lips together but this time in a
slight pout. In the way people look at someone they pity. "Then you're
not alone," Desiree says. "Go home to your father, Angela Singh."

SATURDAY, AUGUST 18, 2018

THE DAY OF THE STORM

On the third day, with no end in sight, Chiara's only option is to get out of there.

She has been lying on the ground, stomach down, in the same spot in the thick of the woods in Kitchewan Nature Reserve, mostly hidden by the overhang of a large rock, far from any hiking trail. She's scared to change locations in daylight, alternating between freezing up at every sound—the rustles of insects and forest critters, the warbles of birds, and the hum of traffic in the distance—and falling asleep from the monotony of it all, only to wake up in a frenzied, dirt-caked sweat. She's ventured out when it was absolute dark these past three nights, but it's been stressful. She feels jumpy, constantly looking over her shoulder and diving to the ground at every unfamiliar noise. She's tripped more than once, gashing herself and her clothes without the benefit of a flashlight. Last night, when she thought she couldn't take the hunger pains any longer, she'd spotted a group of teenagers smoking up around a bonfire. She'd kept her distance, watching them casually eating pizza, laughing, smoking. Seeing their food made her mouth water with such intensity she caught herself chewing on the inside of her own cheek. The group had thrown away about half the pie, still in its box. Once they'd left, with only the embers of the fire remaining, Chiara had picked the box from the trash, ashamed but also ravenous, and she'd wolfed down what remained of the pizza so quickly, skipping over chewing, inhaling it, that her stomach hurt for the rest of the night. Maybe her own body was disgusted with her, too, she'd thought.

But she can't do this anymore. Not even for another day. She has to leave. She has to get out of here. Her stomach rumbles as if in agreement. The problem is how.

When Chiara came to Kitchewan, she'd taken a bus from Philly and called her cousin Didi on the way. It was different then. She'd had her phone and some money she'd swiped from an empty shoebox hidden in the back of her mom's closet. She'd felt bad about stealing from her mom, even after what happened, but she'd needed to get out of there. She'd needed to get far away from him.

This time, however, Chiara doesn't have money or anything else. She'd lost all her stuff when she fled from the high school, after those boys had dumped her belongings on the football field, after—she gulps—she'd done that horrible thing. Miraculously, when she'd run, she still had her phone on her, but it died a few hours later and since then it's been an uncharged weight in her pocket. And the thing is, even if she did have money, her clothes are torn and streaked with enough dirt and sweat to raise eyebrows in plain sight. And even if she did have a phone that worked, she doesn't know who she'd call, or where she'd go. There's Didi, of course, but she shakes her head. She can't drag her cousin into this. *She killed someone.*

Chiara's face bunches up and she gets goose bumps. She tries not to tear up at the last part, but her eyes brim. She still can't believe it, what happened, what she did. How quickly it happened, before she could think.

Chiara had been crashing at the high school for a couple of weeks, sleeping in different parts of the building—on the guidance counselor's couch, or the bed in the nurse's office, or one of the beanbags in the library. It was surprisingly comfortable and easy to stay at the school. There were showers; she'd stowed her clothes, thrown in a black garbage bag, in one corner of the library; and since summer school was over, hardly anyone was around except for maintenance staff a couple of times a week. Chiara knew she couldn't stay there once the school year started, but she still had a few weeks, and she hadn't quite figured out what to do next. If she went back to Didi, she'd have to apologize, and beg her to get her own place, something separate from Lucinda; she'd have to explain that it was Lucinda's idea that she sell her dope at school in the first place; and in typical Lucinda fashion, she wanted to keep basically all the money for herself, which was unfair, so Chiara had evened things out. Didi would disapprove, lecture her, but she'd come around. Looking back, Chiara wishes to God she'd gone back to her cousin sooner. But at the time, she was still hurt that Didi hadn't done more to stop Lucinda from going crazy on her. Also, even though she hadn't brought it up in a while, she was worried Didi would start to nudge her about Philly again, try to get her to tell her what happened, why she left. But Chiara wasn't ready to talk about it; she wasn't sure if she could yet without crying, or at least without her voice turning into pudding.

Chiara didn't have much to do during the day, so she'd started borrowing books from the library. She'd never been much of a reader, but if you don't have TV, it's an okay second choice. On that particular day, the day it all happened, she'd been outside on the bleachers reading a surprisingly engaging book called *Sula* about a girl with the same name who lived in some funny part of Ohio called the Bottom. (She'd chosen it for the inviting smile of the older Black woman on the book jacket.) She'd seen this Indian girl who'd helped her learn how to swim cut across the football field. Chiara toyed with waving. But she didn't want Angela Singh taking that as an invitation to walk over, asking her why she was on the bleachers. It was better to pretend she didn't see her.

It was the middle of the day. The sun had been beating down on her, but there was a breeze, so Chiara didn't feel overheated. She'd been reading the part of the story where Sula's grandmother jumps out a window to save her daughter, Sula's mother, whose dress catches on fire. Chiara remembers holding her breath, stunned by the grandmother's actions, frozen in place like Sula when she watched flames engulf her mother. The grandmother hadn't appeared to love Sula's mother that fiercely, and yet she jumped out of a house for her. The scene made Chiara think of her own mother, and how she'd begged her to do something before she'd left Philly. She'd been so absorbed in her thoughts she hadn't noticed the two boys approaching. Not at first.

She'd never spoken to either of them in person before, but she recognized them. Popular kids. One of them was Henry McCleary, a popular jock with blond hair, and the other was Chris something, a tall boy with darker hair, pale skin, and a head that seemed too small for his shoulders.

Chris had texted her earlier that day. They'd never exchanged messages before, but she'd been unsurprised to hear from classmates; word had gotten around that she had good product, potent product. He wanted to buy weed and promised whatever price she asked for. She'd been tempted because the extra money wouldn't hurt, but she'd already sold the last of what she had taken from Lucinda to settle what should have been hers. When she'd told Chris that if he brought her money, she'd try to get some, he'd gone silent. She figured he'd changed his mind when he showed up with his friend on the field.

Chris had stalked up to her and repeated his request to buy weed. She reminded him she didn't have anything. Before she could repeat her offer to try to figure something out, he'd acted surprised, like they hadn't texted earlier that day. Maybe he was putting on a show because his friend Henry seemed pretty annoyed. He said something to Chris about how he thought Chris had spoken with her—meaning Chiara—before they came to the high school. Chris had gotten defensive and said he didn't know why she was playing games. He'd then sat down next to Chiara, really close so their legs were touching. She pressed her knees together to make herself narrower. She could feel his breath on her neck like pinpricks. Chiara had tried to ignore him. She tried to ignore both of them, even though her body stiffened, and her heart was beating extra loud. She tried to pretend her hands weren't getting sweaty and kept her eyes on her book. Even though she didn't know Henry or Chris, she knew how white boys could get when something didn't go their way.

Chris sat next to her for what felt like a long time. She could feel his stare burning into her face. It made her stomach turn in a familiar way. She heard Henry ask him what he was doing. She continued trying to ignore them, clutching her book, trying to read, but she was getting stuck on the same sentence.

Chris leaned in closer and snatched the book out of her hands, tearing one of the pages as he did. "What ya reading?" he'd said. "Looks exotic." He scanned the face of the kindly older woman on the book jacket and said, "Written by some old lady." He asked again if Chiara was sure she didn't have anything. She looked at him and shook her head. She pushed her backpack aside and reached for her book, trying to put on a tough, firm expression, trying not to look as weak as she felt. Chris grinned. It was like her discomfort gave him energy. He shook his head with a smile across his face and held the book in his far hand above his head. He pointed with his chin to Henry, who was a few feet away, on a lower row of the bleachers. He said, "He's got money, if that's what this is about. He'll pay you what you want." Chiara didn't say anything. She stood up to try to reach for the book. Chris laughed.

She'd wanted to ask him to let up already, to leave her alone. She wasn't bothering anyone, but when she looked into his eyes, she felt angry. Why was he bothering her? What was his problem? She told him she didn't have anything. She could feel her throat closing, but she swallowed, took a deep breath, squinted, and clenched her jaw. As fiercely as she could, she said, "Give me my book back, you piece of white trash." She'd never called someone that before. She remembered thinking those words sounded funny out of her mouth.

Chris looked taken aback. His eyes widened. In the next instant, he threw her book, flung it under the bleachers forcefully, and said, "Who's trash now? Fetch, bitch." He watched Chiara looking at the book and snickered. Henry was watching silently, like he was interested in seeing what Chiara would do next. Chiara's lip had started trembling and she could feel her body getting hot in patches. She stared under the bleachers and gritted her teeth. She begged her eyes to stop filling up. She wanted them to leave. Why couldn't they leave her alone? Even as she thinks of it now, she feels a tear falling down her cheek.

Chris had then snatched her backpack. He'd tossed it to Henry with a playful "Think fast." Henry had caught it with a self-assured laugh. Chiara could feel her breaths coming in quick, short, like she couldn't get enough air. Her head was throbbing. She didn't know what to do. She didn't know how to get them to listen. She tried asking them nicely, pleading with them, her voice cracking. "Please. Can you give me my bag back? Please." But they didn't. Instead they thought it was the funniest thing in the world. Chris started imitating her, and the two boys tossed her bag back and forth between them what felt like a hundred times, like they were playing a game of keep-away. She remembers them laughing at her panic, at her unsuccessful attempts to intercept the bag, laughing as she became dizzy, disoriented, nearly losing her balance.

One of them, she can't remember who, had run onto the football field with her bag. She'd been yelling by then, crying out, maybe even crying. She had everything in there. Her money, her favorite photographs, her toothbrush, even spare underwear. She'd run onto the field after her stuff, but she'd tripped on some uneven grass and fallen, face-planted. She remembers pressing her eyes shut from the sharp pain shooting into the center of her head, smelling grass and dirt, brushing off grass and dirt from her cheek, from inside her nose, feeling open skin, wet skin, but ignoring it when she saw Chris. He'd unzipped her bag and was throwing everything out, tossing it with carefree flicks of his wrist. He looked over at her and asked Henry to hold her down, that he was going to check she was telling the truth.

Henry had hovered over her and stopped her from getting up. He tussled with her a bit, grunting like he was exerting himself. The sound made her anxious. She'd resisted, but his grip was strong, cold, commanding. She could feel her body caving, collapsing, giving in. He turned her so that her back was to the ground, she was pinned by her wrists. The feeling of his cool hands holding down her wrists sent spikes of familiar panic coursing through her. She didn't mean to, but she held her breath and began seeing orange spots; started feeling sweat patches in every corner of her body, from her upper lip to under her arms to her neck. She felt herself being pressed into the ground. "Please let me go. Please stop." But he gripped her harder and said, "Easy there. Shhhh," like she was the one acting crazy, wild, like everything was normal. His breath smelled of beer. She turned her face to one side. She didn't want to smell him, to smell that sickeningly sweet, overripe smell, to be pulled back in, dragged back there, knocked under. She felt the dirt, the grass opening to swallow her up, eat her alive. *Please. No. Not there. Please, I can't go back there!*

Back home.

The slaps stung, and the shoves sometimes left bruises. But she could tolerate the pain. She'd trained herself not to whimper or cry out, to instead concentrate on being still, not flinching, keeping her eyes open without blinking for as long as she could, even when they filled with water, even when his palm across her face made her bite the inside of her cheek so fiercely she could taste blood. Because to give him the satisfaction of a reaction was more unbearable than the act.

He'd demand that she acknowledge him and that she apologize for whatever she'd done, goddammit, and instead, despite the pain, despite her fear and discomfort, she'd force her mouth into a smirk and look away. It was around then that he'd pounce, pinning her to a wall or backing her into a corner, his calloused, scratchy hands pressing into the pressure points on her wrists, his self-righteous face inches from hers, swatting at her chin to force eye contact. He'd tell her he was helping her, training her, didn't she see, taking the devil out of her, his declarations punctuated by sprays of saliva. It made her sick. His preachifying. That and the smell of him. He told her mother he only drank two beers a week—both on Sunday, ironically—but his breath told her otherwise. She needed him away from her. She needed his hands off her. *She needed her stepfather off her.*

"Get off me!" she screamed at Henry, flailing her legs. Her breaths were short and fast, but shallow. She couldn't get in any air. She couldn't breathe. "Get off me!" she repeated. She must have been loud that time, because Chris, who had turned her backpack inside out and was shaking it to make sure he didn't miss anything, had stopped what he was doing to look at her. "Leave my stuff alone!" she screamed again. Henry was still holding her down tightly, but he said to his friend, "If she doesn't have anything, can we hurry up and get out of here? Her face is starting to look funny."

The first time he'd laid a hand on her, he'd been living with them for nearly a month and a half and had married her mother three weeks previous. She'd argued with her mother earlier that day. It was nothing particularly heavy. She wanted money for new sneakers. Hers were worn down at the soles and browned along the sides; they made her look poor, she'd said. In front of her mother, all he'd said was "There's a rag and some shoe polish under the sink," and gone back to heckling *The Price Is Right* as if he were in the studio audience. He'd waited until her mother was napping, something she did on account of her pain meds, and ambushed Chiara like a sniper, pinning her against the yellowing, oil-stained kitchen wall, using his cracked, barklike fingers to squeeze her wrists with unsettling force. She'd tried to free herself from him, writhing under his grip, knees buckling. But he held her like that until the blood had drained from her hands and they tingled. He'd hunched toward her face, close enough for her to smell his fetid breath—it was like spoiled fruit mixed with vinegar. He'd told her that when he was younger, if he'd demanded anything for free from his old man, he'd have gotten a beating, and that he had to work for everything he had, the clothes on his back and the shoes on his feet, else he'd have been naked and barefoot.

She'd been terrified, perspiring profusely, but didn't want to give him the satisfaction of seeing that, so she'd said as coolly and steadily as she could manage, "Mind your own damn business." Maybe because it was the first time, he'd rattled her a bit and then released her, shifting back into a relaxed posture as if nothing had happened. She'd escaped to her bedroom, trying her best to walk nonchalantly, aware of his seething glare. Only to crumble into full-body silent sobs when she closed the door.

She told her mother about it afterward. She'd said Chiara was exaggerating, that he wasn't like that. But he was, she'd said, pointing to where he'd grabbed her wrists, certain there would be bruises by the next day. Her mother had shaken her head and launched into how he was a God-fearing man who did honest work, and sure, he was a little strict, but he was a former army man so it was part of his upbringing; besides, he was so much better than the alcoholics and drug addicts and hoodlums with a criminal record that other women she knew messed with. Yes, his values were old fashioned, maybe, but if you asked her, it was better having a man who had rules and limits and provided for their household than a deadbeat. Chiara reminded her mother that her monthly disability checks were more than what he brought in from his occasional home-repair and plumbing jobs, but her mother told her to stop trying to steal her happiness, and that Chiara didn't understand how hard things were without a man around, that she wasn't going to drive him away over one disagreement.

Within a month, his commands and demands, premised under the guise of caring, establishing order in the house, escalated.

She'd bought the pocketknife off a kid who also sold counterfeit Jordans at her old high school in Philly. She'd gotten it not to use it, exactly, but to flash it, maybe, in front of her stepfather, startle him, warn him he couldn't set rules for her like he was actually her dad; that he had to stop ordering her to do housework; that he needed to stop grumbling about how she was spending too much of his hard-earned money (what money?); that he better not dare lay his scratched-up hands on her ever again. But that weekend, when he started up about how she broke curfew and switched off her phone, she'd felt the knife in the pocket of her jeans and couldn't will her fingers to reach for it, flash it, do it. It was like they'd gotten stuck. And she was left, taking it.

After that, she'd made a final appeal to her mother, who by then knew what was going on, witnessed it, even, but hadn't intervened. "It's him or me," Chiara had said.

"Kiki, baby, you know I—I can't. I can't be on my own again," she'd said back.

"But you won't be," Chiara had replied. "You have me."

"It's not the same," she'd told her, and as Chiara's heart dipped, free-fell, in fact, her mother had added, "It'd be better if you didn't fight back. I don't understand why you give him lip like you do and why you have to look so proud of yourself. He may not be perfect, but he's a good man. He really does try to be."

Chiara felt sick. She wanted to scream so loud she'd burst her lungs open. How could she choose *him*? She thought of the knife still in her pocket, burning a hole in her pocket, igniting her, and told herself, *If I don't get the hell out of here, the next time I see him, I won't hesitate. I'll do it.*

"Chris! Fuck. Chris, get over here," Henry yelled. "She wet herself." Chris had rushed over to Chiara and Henry. He looked at them with disgust and intrigue. Her sweatpants were wet. There was urine running down her legs. *When did that happen?* Her face was hot with fear and shame. Perfectly calm, Chris crouched down and leaned toward her. His face was only inches from hers, and he was dangling her cash in his free hand. She felt herself suffocating, sinking, drowning, and she couldn't stop it. Her vision went cloudy. Sound was distant; it echoed. Her head felt like it had split open, like her brains were spilling out.

She closed her eyes and couldn't tell if she was on the football field or in Philly. Hands reaching for her, that putrid smell. When she opened them again, she couldn't see. *She couldn't see!* Everything was spots and her heart was beating so fast she thought she might drop dead. Her breath was coming in quick like she'd been sprinting. But the thing was, her hands were free.

Before she could pause, process, focus, slow down, she reached for her pocket, for the knife. She clicked it open, clutched it, and jerked it as hard as she could. It made contact, tore, stuck into something.

She let go of the knife. Henry staggered backward. It was protruding out of him. How could—how did—did she—but she couldn't finish a thought. Her face was drenched in sweat. Her legs were clammy, cold. The hands were gone. The bodies above her were gone. She scrambled onto her feet and ran.

She ran so fast nothing was in focus, just colors, spots, and more colors. A blur of green grass, a streak of blue sky, of road, of the gray-and-brown Philly streets—*where am I, anyway?*—of neon mixing into itself from the bus station that smelled like piss. She ran like she was being chased. She ran until her throat burned from her forceful, desperate breaths. Her heart beat faster than she thought possible. She heard hollers behind her; they struck her eardrums like dog barks. Her entire spine shuddered and propelled her forward. She was getting the hell out of there. Running from those boys. Running from *him*.

She'd run to the nature reserve and collapsed on her knees in the woods. She was dizzy, wet from sweat, and her pants were damp, her legs itchy from her accident. She panted for an eternity to catch up with her breath, to refocus her vision. As the trees, moss, fallen leaves, and dirt grew sharper around her, a single thought impaled her: *I killed someone today.*

Chiara stands at the bank of the Kitchewan River. She examines the water and the gray sky, shivering at both in turn. She'd left her hiding spot in the woods, her body stiff from lying motionless all day, her head aching with hunger and thirst, and had walked until she got to the river. She'd been to the reserve before, and she knew the woods bordered the water.

The water looks choppier than the swimming pool where Chiara learned to swim, but it doesn't look so bad. At least that's what she tells herself.

Chiara hasn't swum since she had to take the swim test, but when she did, she easily made it, doggy-paddling the length of the pool and back. The river is wider than two lengths of the pool. She also can't tell how deep it is. But if she pushes herself, she can make it.

She hopes the water isn't too cold. Today of all days it's overcast and windy. She'll have to cross with her clothes on and it'll take forever for them to dry in weather like this. She's not sure what exactly is on the other side, but she knows it's in another town, possibly another county. She can buy herself some time before they find her; maybe they won't find her. She needs to get moving, far away from here, out of here. In Kitchewan, she doesn't stand a chance. Not after what she did.

She dares herself and jumps in. The water is frigid and like an electric shock to her system. She starts to doggy-paddle, surprised her body remembers how. For an instant she thinks of Angela Singh, how she'd taught Chiara calmly, patiently, without making fun of her or asking a thousand nosy questions. She could have been nicer to Angela, but she didn't want anyone getting in her business. She didn't want anyone pitying her.

The current is stronger than it appeared from the shore, and Chiara overestimates her ability to paddle through it. She gets about forty, maybe fifty yards out when her arms start cramping, tiring, her legs, too. She can't reach the bottom of the river with her toes, and she panics a little. She's out of breath and the choppy water is slapping her across the face, making it hard to see, to breathe, to focus on which direction she's going. It starts raining and the raindrops blow sideways. She's cold, shivering. Between the rain and tumult of the water, she feels dizzy, light-headed, feverish. She pumps her legs and arms more quickly, desperately, but she's only inching forward due to the current. This is going to take forever, she thinks as she gets tossed backward.

She looks back, considering if she should turn around, wait things out in the reserve until the water calms down, but the shore looks farther away than she remembers. She lifts her face to the darkening sky. Everything around her looks angry. If she stays in one spot, it feels like the river will swallow her up. She has no choice but to keep going, keep moving.

I'm sorry, she thinks, apologizing to the universe or Henry or God, if there is one. *I'm so sorry. It was an accident, I swear . . .* A small wave slaps across her head and her face. Water gushes into her mouth. She tries not to gulp the river water, but she tastes it, mixed with the raindrops that fall with increasing intensity.

She coughs, sputters, and loses her balance. Water refloods her eyes, making them burn; they sting. When she goes to rub them, she flails and gasps for air. A heaving wave submerges her.

She thinks of her mother and what she'd said about not fighting back. With all her strength, she kicks, wheezing, gasping, grabbing, clawing feverishly, but not reaching the surface.

WEDNESDAY, SEPTEMBER 26, 2018

EPILOGUE

Babur's eyes tear from the glare of the midday sun reflecting off the surface of the Kitchewan River. He tries again to maneuver his body into the elegant float demonstrated by Angie when she'd lain on her back on top of the river like a divine being only moments earlier.

He takes a deep breath, telling himself he can do this, even though if you asked him a mere half an hour earlier, he would have insisted he cannot. He lowers the back side of his body toward the water. His face basks in the unseasonable warmth of this late-September day, in the thrill of this impromptu outing with his daughter in the quiet of the middle of the week.

He lifts up his feet from the riverbed and exhales. When he opens his eyes, he finds himself not quite above the water, since his midsection and ribs are sunken a few inches beneath, but with the help of the tangerine-colored floaties around his arms, close enough. Close to the surface. Floating, or something like it.

"Angie," he calls out, eager for her praise. "Angie," he says again, lifting his head ever so slightly, tucking his chin into his neck. "Angie, look! I'm . . ." Before he can say any more, he loses his balance and water floods into his ears and up his nose. He swallows what feels like a bucketful of river water, coughing, sputtering. His legs splay and slap against the water. His feet stab in every direction, frantic for terra firma. "Angie!" he cries, fully vertical now, tussling against the restless river.

Angie emerges from the water with the stealth of a sea serpent. She's next to him, smiling.

He grips her thin forearms, panting, reeling. "Angie, I—I— Where did you go?"

"Dad, it's okay." She touches his shoulder. "I'm here. I let go of you for a few seconds so you could try floating on your own. But I'm here."

He nods, still catching his breath.

"When you're ready, straighten your legs and try to stand. It's not that deep, but those things on your arms"—Angie points to his floaties—"are pushing you up."

Babur nods his head more, taken aback by her calm, in-control tone, how confident she is in water, how she's been diligently coaching him through this swimming lesson like he's the child and she the adult. He holds her arms more tightly and feels his breaths normalizing, his pulse slowing, water spilling out from his ears and nose. He extends one leg to test the river depth, his toes quickly grazing the river bottom. Angie is right. He can stand. The water is at about shoulder level, deeper than his comfort zone but not above his head. He smiles at Angie.

In response, Angie breaks out into a full-body laugh, the kind that makes her shoulders shake. It's the first time he's heard her laugh for weeks.

The swimming lesson was Babur's idea. He'd normally be against calling Angie in sick when she's perfectly healthy, but today is one of two days a week when Babur doesn't work at E-Z Pump. And he was getting desperate. He was losing Angie, he felt sure of it. She was slipping further away from him, disengaging, detaching, missing swim meets, and bunking off school. Also—he shivers—there were the words of the boy, Chris Collins. He's tried to ignore them, the musings of an immature, graceless teenager. But he can't shake what he'd said. Had Babur missed, overlooked, or worse, been too scared to see this truth about his daughter?

It had taken Babur resolve and courage to suggest a swimming tutorial in the Kitchewan River, given his lifelong fear of water—an affliction he blames on his overly cautious parents. But it seemed the unexpectedness of his request worked in his favor. He'd momentarily stunned Angie out of her resolute solemnity, eliciting a brief widening of her eyes, followed by a mumbled "I guess . . . if you really want."

"Terrific!" Babur said with an open-mouthed grin. "After all, how can the father of a swimming champion not know how to float?," only to wince after he spoke, recalling the similarity between his words and a line from one of Purnima's emails.

Angie didn't appear to notice. Instead she said flatly, "I'm not a swimming champion."

But it didn't matter. She had agreed, and that was all the encouragement Babur needed to whistle gustily all the way to Kitchewan Nature Reserve.

Babur is still gripping Angie when her laughter subsides. He eyes with suspicion how the river water constantly dips and rises, and makes a mental note that a swimming pool might be a calmer option for the future. Nonetheless, he asks, "What next, beta?"

"I think this is good for your first day, Dad," Angie says. "You did better than I thought."

Babur delights in this tepid praise and how Angie's voice is returning to a tone he recognizes. He's also surprisingly disappointed that the lesson is over, already nostalgic for moments that had just passed: when Angie coaxed him to get in the water beyond hip depth and just as she promised, he's still alive; when he mastered treading water; when he submerged his face and his entire head, in fact, in the river;

how Angie shone as a patient, intuitive instructor; and when he'd con-
quered floating—lying on top of the water (on top of it!), like magic,
his temporal hindsight already recasting his recollection of the past
few minutes as a sublime, serene experience. Most important, over the
course of the lesson, his Angie came back; she's coming back. If they
stop now, he worries she'll slip away again. Besides, Babur still hasn't
done what he'd promised himself he would because he hasn't yet decided what exactly to say, about *her*—Purnima—how to make things
right for Angie.

Thinking fast, Babur blurts, "I'm not tired, beta. Let's do more river
swimming."

He catches Angie biting her lip to suppress an upturn in the corners of her mouth. "It's not river swimming, Dad, just swimming. And
we'll do more another day."

Babur stares at his pruned-up fingers on one hand, as he continues
to hold on to Angie with the other. He searches for words to bring up
Purnima, to ask Angie, to recommend, that she see her mother. But
they don't come. Instead, he says, "I'm proud of you, beta."

Angie shrugs. "It's not a big deal. You still have a lot to learn."

"No, I mean, I was not happy before"—he pauses and looks at the
light reflecting in small ripples in the water—"about rejecting the
scholarship offer, but I think—I think we did the right thing. You did
the right thing. And I'm proud of you for that."

He feels Angie's shoulders tense in surprise, and he readjusts his
firm grip on her, ever conscious that he's in the river.

Her eyes open wider, and she says slowly, "Thanks, Dad. I guess I
thought you wouldn't understand."

"I didn't, beta, not in the beginning, but you were right." He studies
her expression to see how she reacts. Her eyes look glassy. He blinks,
and in that instant, he feels her leap toward him and embrace him so
tightly it's as if she's the one holding on for her life and not the other
way around. She hasn't held on to him like this since she was an infant
and he'd rock her to sleep in the middle of the night. He feels her

breaths coming in quickly, and her slender frame clinging to him. For a moment, he forgets to be afraid of the water.

When she releases him, he reattaches his arm to her shoulder (safety first) and the courage he'd been searching for presents itself. "Beta," he begins slowly, tentatively, "your mother would also be proud of you."

She doesn't respond right away, so he takes her silence as an invitation to continue, albeit gingerly. "You know, beta, you don't have to be like me. You don't"—he rakes his free hand through the water, observing how it creates ripples on the surface as he wills himself to continue—"have to divorce your mother." He swallows, concentrating on his hand, still raking, too nervous to look at her. "She and I had some problems, some disagreements—and I suppose I should have told you this a long time ago, but those were our problems."

Angie chews on her lip and blinks fast.

"What I mean is, she's your mother. And you can see her and get to know her a little bit. You should. If you want, that is." He exhales deeply, as if he's set down a heavy load, only to feel his daughter's shoulders tense up again and her upper body trembling. He worries he's upset her, gone too far, perhaps. He waits for her to say something, only she doesn't, so in an artificially bright voice, after what feels like a long silence, he changes the subject. "Can we do one more thing before we go back to the shore? Maybe you show me something, beta. Like a demonstration. I will watch you to study for next time, next lesson." He smiles broadly, hoping she sees, hoping it catches on.

"You've seen me swim a thousand times, Dad." She sounds diminished, deflated.

"But I will really watch this time," he says so enthusiastically his cheeks hurt. "And," he adds, "I can practice treading the water."

Angie presses her lips together in consideration. He notices the bottom one is quivering. He holds his breath, and for a few seconds, he thinks she'll bring up her mother. But instead she says, "All right, fine," and guides Babur closer to land, at a depth where his feet can comfortably rest on the riverbed if he gets tired, and asks, "You'll be okay here, Dad?" Her eyes search his face, and while he's not quite sure, he nods firmly, and as an afterthought, forces a grin. Angie wrinkles her eyebrows, but says, "All right, I'll show you the first stroke you'll learn. The crawl. Watch how I move my arms . . ."

She starts her demonstration. Babur squints from the sunlight reflecting on the water's surface. He strains to examine her movements. He'd never before paid attention to how Angie almost pulls the water with her hands and turns her head to one side to inhale, how the kick comes from her hips rather than her ankles, how she moves swiftly and with purpose even when swimming against the current. He recalls Purnima's request to see her swim and wonders what Angie thinks of what he's just said; if he didn't say enough, changed the subject too quickly; if she'll see her; when she'll see her; how it will be; if, it strikes him, in meeting her she'll feel differently about him. Angie continues farther from him, farther than he expected. She must be twenty yards away, twenty-five now . . . He can't make out much more than the movement of her arms. She'll turn around soon, he thinks. Yet she continues.

Babur tires of making scissor movements to tread water. He rests his feet against the sandy deposit on the floor of the river. Angie is still swimming away from him, only she appears to have changed direction to a diagonal from the path she was taking before. Odd, he thinks, but she'll turn around any second now. The smaller she gets, the more he starts to regret that he mentioned seeing Purnima. After all, Purnima might turn Angie against him. The sole of his foot senses a slight jab, like the edge of a jagged pebble. He wobbles and his pulse quickens, but he's able to regain his balance. Angie continues swimming farther.

Babur puts one hand against his forehead to block out the sun. He makes out a group of animals on the opposite side of the river, deer, perhaps. They're near the riverbank, sipping water. Four of them.

"Beta!" Babur calls, asking himself why she hasn't turned around.

Angie stops and points to the deer. She smiles at him, beams, in fact. Babur exhales in relief at the sight of her happiness. He is, however, confused by why she's pointing with such exuberance. They see deer all the time in Kitchewan. And yet she looks excited, as if there's something extraordinary. He squints harder.

And there. There it is: a fifth deer. It had been hidden behind the others, and this one is—he gasps—colorless. Snow white. It cranes its neck toward the river, taking a long sip. How unusual, he thinks, unsure whether he's ever seen a white deer before. It's beautiful. He's reminded of a song Angie danced to in her elementary school Thanksgiving play. She'd been dressed as a turkey and she and her classmates had held hands and encircled a white deer. He wonders if Angie remembers.

"Dad! All okay?" Angie calls out.

Babur thinks for a moment, and rather than stand on the uneven ground, he starts cycling his legs, slowly at first, but then with zeal. He feels himself maintaining his balance in the water, treading water. All by himself. He looks at Angie and contemplates calling her back, but in hearing her voice and seeing her face, he realizes he's okay. In fact, he feels confident. Free. Like a real swimmer. Between his rhythmic treading, the memories of his first swimming lesson, and the grin on Angie's face, Babur settles on "I'm great, beta!," because he is. He gives Angie a vigorous thumbs-up. When she returns, he thinks, he'll tell her again that she should see Purnima. He'll do it properly this time: he'll tell her he thinks it's a good idea, and he'll say this with a smile on his face, a real smile, because he knows she needs him to be okay, and he knows she needs this. And he knows, he thinks with an effortless cycle of his legs, that she'll come back to him.

"Are you having fun, Dad?" Angie asks.

Before he can answer, a mass of clouds shifts in the sky, giving way to a beam of light. The rays drench Babur and Angie. He squints to see, but the light whitens everything in his vision until it's all the color of the deer.

Babur tilts his head back. He feels the warmth of the universe smiling upon him. Upon them. And he smiles back.

A NOTE FROM THE AUTHOR

A few years ago, in an Uber from JFK on my way to my parents' house in Stamford, I began chatting with the driver, a fellow Indian American, about the latest news in the New York suburbs. We were speaking about his high-school age children, and he started telling me about several recent assaults involving students who attended the public high school of his town, an affluent Northeast suburb, and where at least one of the alleged perpetrators was a student of color and rumored to be homeless. He described the sentiment from families in the town, which included debating school safety and school enrollment policies and questioning whether their children might be better off in a private school. He then added that many parents were questioning whether the minority students were contributing to a perceived decline in school quality. In fact, he confessed, he shared the concerns about an increase in less-educated and less–financially stable families in the town and was also thinking about enrolling his children in a private school.

The more I listened, the more intrigued I became. I hadn't expected there to be such judgment toward minority students, nor flight to private schools—not in the supposed progressive town in which these incidents took place. I was also simultaneously surprised and unsurprised by the reaction of the Indian American driver. On one hand, there are stereotypes about Indian Americans consciously separating themselves from other minorities and embracing model minority archetypes. On the other hand, Indian Americans themselves are often excluded from being treated as "mainstream" Americans, so one might expect more empathy from those of Indian origin.

As I turned over what had happened in this town, I started imagining how the families of the victims felt; I wanted to know more about the alleged perpetrators and the police investigations. I began thinking about the school administration and whether they were at fault, remembering a comment the driver had made about how the principal should be fired. I became fascinated by the assumptions even an open-minded community could be willing to make.

Little by little, I found myself creating plots and subplots in my mind: inventing dinner table conversations among families in the town, rumors among the students, and tensions as people tried to make sense of the situation. I also kept coming back to the driver and the questions I've grappled with while growing up in a fairly homogenous Northeast town—questions about how and if people like me fit in, both in our community and also in discussions about race, being neither black nor white. Should we feel solidarity toward other minorities, or is it understandable to want to "blend in"? What are the defining characteristics of our group identity? How would I feel if I were a student or parent in this town?

From these thoughts, the plot of *Our Best Intentions* started to emerge. I created a fictional suburb in New York and invented a single assault that takes place on public school grounds involving some high school students; I started filling in different characters' backstories, motivations, and conversations. I kept returning to my discussion with the Uber driver, and as I did, two Indian American characters, Babur and Angie Singh, took vivid shape in my mind: Babur, a slightly obsessive-compulsive, protective parent with eternal optimist tendencies but who also prefers to avoid ambiguous topics—like race and belonging—until he's forced to confront them; and Angie, an introverted and self-conscious teen who struggles to define her opinion and herself, but who desperately wants to identify, if not do, the right thing.

As I began writing their story, it was important to me to show how society responds to traumatic events like the stabbing depicted in the book: how we make sense of them, the assumptions we're willing to accept, the judgments we make, the fingers we point, and the lengths we go to protect ourselves and our loved ones. By putting the Singh family at the core of *Our Best Intentions*, I offer a portrayal of being Indian American: what it's like to kind of fit in, but not quite, and what it's like to navigate America as a hyphenated American. Through writing this novel, I reflected on my own feelings about identity, race, and privilege in America. I hope readers will be similarly inspired to look within themselves and talk with each other about these issues. Moreover, I hope Babur and Angie's relationship journey inspires us to learn how to grow with and better understand one another.

ACKNOWLEDGMENTS

My deepest thanks to my village:

First and foremost, my husband, Sumeet, for challenging me, never sugarcoating the truth, being my thought partner and best friend, and for helping me rediscover writing. Every day with you and Sahana is a blessing.

My dear friend Jamie Karnes for your guidance, your patience, and your care for this novel and me. I never could have written this without you.

My agent, Alexa Stark, for being my champion and for making my dream a reality; and to Ellen Levine for putting this in motion.

Liz Stein, Eliza Rosenberry, Francie Crawford, Ariana Sinclair, and the entire publishing team at Morrow for bringing this novel to life. It has been an absolute joy to collaborate with you.

The best beta readers and friends a gal could wish for: Peter Friedman, Mitali Nagrecha, Jen Strauss, Christine Chang, Dorothy Jean Chang, and Phoebe Boardman.

And finally, to my mother and father, for your love and support and a childhood full of books.

ABOUT THE AUTHOR

Vibhuti ("Vib") Jain lives with her husband and daughter in Johannesburg, South Africa, where she works in international development. She began her career as a corporate lawyer in New York City. She holds degrees from Yale University and Harvard Law School. She grew up in Guilford, Connecticut. *Our Best Intentions* is her first novel.